The light wasn't working, so Paul undressed in the dark.

He sat on the edge of the bed and lost himself in delicious fantasies about the two girls from Texas. Which one first? They were both so beautiful . . . and so rich. And some of the others weren't half bad. He sighed happily. What an art school!

Suddenly two warm arms clasped him around the waist. He tried to spring away, but insistent arms hauled him back and an aroma of spice, perfume, onion and woman enveloped him. "*Pobrecito*," whispered a soft voice. "*Mi Pablito. No tenga miedo, pajarito.*" A chill went through him.

Margarita! The chambermaid—that impudent, voluptuous creature must have been hiding in his bed for hours!

A low, throaty chuckle met his gasp of surprise. But it was not until later that his swimming brain picked out from the cooings, giggles and murmurings the whispered words: "Geef me ten dollars."

Fawcett Books
by John D. MacDonald:

PLEASE WRITE FOR DETAILS

JOHN D. MacDONALD

FAWCETT GOLD MEDAL • NEW YORK

PLEASE WRITE FOR DETAILS

Published by Fawcett Gold Medal Books, a unit of CBS Publications, the Consumer Publishing Division of CBS Inc.

ISBN: 0-449-14080-6

PRINTED IN THE UNITED STATES OF AMERICA

18   17   16   15   14   13   12   11   10   9

**PLEASE
WRITE
FOR
DETAILS**

BOOK ONE

IN WHICH *a small Institution of Art is devised in an Exotic Clime for the purpose of Immediate Profit; a Staff, Faculty and Student Body are acquired by Random Methods; these Assorted Persons arrive at a Curious Edifice and acquaint themselves with One Another; Certain Tensions become Apparent; the Courses of Instruction begin.*

Chapter One

ANNOUNCING THE CUERNAVACA SUMMER WORKSHOP: A limited number of painting students will be accepted for the Workshop for the months of July and August. Instruction in painting by renowned artists Gambel Torrigan and Agnes Partridge Keeley. Fee of $500 includes de luxe housing in beautiful small hotel, gourmet food, expert instruction, and a chance to summer in the beautiful city of eternal springtime. Write Miles Drummond, Apartado #300, Cuernavaca, Morelos, Mexico, for details and application blank.

On a bright morning on the twenty-second day of June, Miles Drummond walked five brisk blocks from his tiny bachelor house to the Cuernavaca Post Office. He was a spry, small-boned man in his fifties, wearing sandals, weathered khaki trousers freshly pressed, a green rayon sports shirt. He carried a leather zipper case fat with documents. He had too much iron-gray hair, curly and carefully tended. Behind the bright glint of the Mexican sun on octagonal rimless glasses, his was a clerical face, rather pinched, myopic, with a look of chronic apprehension.

He stepped from the sunlight into the dusty confusion of the small post office, reaching for his box keys as he nimbly skirted the outstretched hand of the elderly beggarwoman who partially blocked the doorway. He was tempted to continue at his headlong pace toward the boxes, but he was conscious of a feeling of breathlessness and an impression that his heart sat too high in his chest, tapping impatiently against his collarbone. He made himself saunter to Box 300. Through the dirty glass, beyond the peeling gilt of the number, he could see that he had mail. At his third stab the key went in and he opened the door and took out three letters. He took a deep breath, exhaled slowly, and took the mail over to a vacant place at one of the high, slanting counters by the windows.

The top letter was from his sister. He set Martha's letter aside. She was ten years older than he, lived meagerly in a co-operative rest home outside Philadelphia, and wrote him once a week. He wrote her once a month. He had not seen her since he had moved to Mexico on a *rentista* status fifteen years ago.

The second letter was on heavy bond paper, letterhead paper, and apparently typed on an electric machine. Jennington and Kemp, Architects. Mr. John Kemp wrote that he was enclosing his check for four hundred and fifty dollars to cover the balance of the fee for the Summer Workshop, and that he would fly from New Orleans to Mexico City on Eastern Airlines, arriving at noon on June thirtieth.

The check was on salmon-colored paper and had been written on a check-writer. Miles Drummond folded it and put it in his wallet. The last letter was from an Agnes Archibald in Denver. She had sent her fifty-dollar registration fee back in February, the first money to come in. She had carried on an exhausting correspondence with Drummond demanding all manner of nonpertinent information, and had at last decided not to attend the Workshop. The current letter was in answer to Miles Drummond's letter explaining that it had been clearly stated in the literature that the registration fee could not be returned. In the current letter she again demanded her fifty dollars, and made dark threats about people who used the mails to defraud.

Drummond unzipped the case and looked for his master list. He thumbed through all the papers and could not find it. He emptied the case completely, thoroughly alarmed as

8

he thought of the confusion that would ensue had he lost the master list. He had mislaid just enough of the correspondence so that it would be difficult if not impossible to construct a new master list. When he was close to despair he found it, folded twice and hidden inside the list of food requirements.

He unfolded the master list of the fifty-three persons who had responded to the advertisement for the Cuernavaca Summer Workshop. He took out his pen, ran it down the list until he came to Kemp, John A. After the name he wrote, "Pd. Arr June 30, noon, Eastern, Mexico."

He put all the papers back into the case, along with the three letters he had received, and headed for the Banco Nacional de Mexico, Cuernavaca Branch, on the corner of Calle Dwight Morrow. He walked by the new government building and through the small north *zócalo* and past the Bella Vista. Once he was in the bank he had to take everything out of the zipper case again in order to find his deposit book.

One of the pretty little girls behind the counter entered the check in Drummond's peso account. Five thousand six hundred and twenty-five more pesos. It made him feel pleasantly flushed and slightly dizzy to look at the new grand total. Nearly seventy-five thousand pesos. It seemed unreal to him that he could have acquired this much money merely through the writing of various letters. It seemed unfair, somehow, that in ten days the Workshop would begin and he would have to run it, and a lot of this money would have to be paid out. He could not begin to visualize what the summer would be like. He knew only that he dreaded it. And dreaded it more now that Gloria seemed to be losing interest so rapidly.

He walked four blocks from the bank to the establishment of the mechanic who was trying to restore to a state of relative health the Volkswagen bus which Drummond had acquired for the summer through a very complicated deal. The first owner was not known. The second owner had been a man who dreamed of establishing a great new bus business. He had begun with the Volkswagen, building a huge luggage rack on top, and driving it himself on a punishing run between Cuernavaca and Cuautla. It had been *Número Uno* of the Consolidated New World Transport Company. After untold miles and great endurance of goats, rockslides, and passengers saturated with pulque, the embittered owner-driver had lettered a name on it. *Estoy*

9

Perdido. I am lost. And soon after that he went out of business. When it was known that Miles Drummond wanted the use of such a vehicle without actually owning it, his cook-houseman, Felipe Cedro, came up with a deal involving *Estoy Perdido.* The new proprietor of the broken bus was willing to rent it to Miles Drummond for *x* pesos for the summer, provided Drummond had the bus completely repaired in the shop of Antonio Vasques, a cousin of the new owner's wife. One half the cost of repairs would be deducted from the rental. Furthermore, Señor Drummond would agree to employ, as driver of said vehicle, one Fidelio Melocotonero, the *novio* of the new owner's daughter, at a salary of two hundred pesos a month, or sixteen dollars American. As Drummond did not own and could not drive a car, and because the home of the Cuernavaca Summer Workshop would be in the structure four miles north of town, the old building known as the Hotel Hutchinson, Drummond agreed to the arrangement, knowing, from past experience, that Felipe Cedro was somehow making some money from the arrangement.

Estoy Perdido was wedged into a corner of the small shop, resplendent in a coat of new, very red paint. On the side was painted The Cuernavaca Summer Workshop under a representation of a brush and palette, spotted liberally with raw pigment.

Antonio came bustling up to Drummond to say proudly that the very good used tires had arrived and had been installed. He patted the big VW emblem on the front of the bus and said that it had indeed been a very weary creature, but it was now responding to the understanding care that only Antonio Vasques could give to such a defeated object. Miles inquired as to what remained to be done. After fifteen years in Mexico his Spanish was very fast, very fluent, and almost entirely devoid of verbs. He managed to make the present tense do for all situations, and tried to overlook the confusions that were sometimes caused by this linguistic hiatus. Antonio advised him that after some woeful deficiency in the *electricidad* had been corrected, it would remain only to reweld a torsion bar and it would be ready to fly.

That particular word made Drummond uneasy. He looked into the bus. Fidelio Melocotonero was, as usual, asleep on the floor of the bus on a grubby serape. Ever since the arrangement had been made, Fidelio did not permit himself to get far from the bus. He was a heavy-faced, sleepy-looking

10

young man who wore the ducktail hairdo, jeans and T-shirt of the American cinema. On two previous visits to the garage Drummond had found Fidelio hunched over the wheel wearing a snarling expression and making roaring noises. Yet he had been assured that Fidelio was of the very top excellence as a driver.

"The day after tomorrow then it is ready?" Drummond asked.

Antonio shrugged. "It is entirely possible."

"One of my professors, a very important man, arrives by air on Sunday in Mexico and it is important the bus goes and gets him. On Sunday."

Antonio patted the bus. "Without fail, Señor Drummond, this bus will go and get this important man and return him here in speed and great comfort."

After he left the repair garage, Miles Drummond went looking for Gloria Garvey. He found her seated alone at one of the sidewalk tables outside the Hotel Marik. It was noon and she sat reading the Mexico City *News,* a half bottle of Dos Equis beer beside her, waving a casual hand at flies, beggars and vendors when they became too annoying. Miles put his zipper case on the table and sat down across from her.

"Good morning, Gloria," he said most affably.

She glanced at him and returned her attention to the paper. She was a handsome and vital-looking blond woman in her middle thirties, a big, cool-eyed, Viking type with classic features and an ample and stunning figure. She was always slightly soiled—and partially and almost undetectably drunk. Gloria wore a rumpled peasant skirt, sandals with thongs that tied around perfect and grubby ankles, a red blouse with a ripped seam and several spots. Most of her nail polish had flaked off and she had made her mouth up lavishly and carelessly.

Gloria Garvey had lived in Cuernavaca for four years, ever since her third and avowedly final divorce. Her full name, which she could always remember after a pause for thought, was Gloria Jean Bennison McGuerdon Van Hoestling Garvey. She had that unfortunate blend of characteristics which combines a capacity for intense enthusiasm with a curiously short attention span. She had taken a big house when she had first come to Cuernavaca, but the responsibility of it had irked her. For the past three years she had lived in a small hotel on a side street near the *zócalo.* The hotel was called Las Rosas. Gloria had a second-floor suite

11

where she lived alone in a welter of knotted straps, stains, empty bottles and French fiction. The hotel provided maid service, served cheap and adequate meals and tolerated the eccentricities of Señora Garvey who, from time to time, when the urge was upon her, would take unto herself a suitably robust male tourist for a night, a week or a month, depending on how soon she became bored.

Possibly she was tolerated by the management of Las Rosas for much the same reason that she was acceptable in the peripheral areas of American society in Cuernavaca and Mexico City. Her physical unkemptness, which sometimes approached the squalid, and her amoral deviations, which were often startlingly direct, could be classed as eccentricities because Gloria Garvey was very rich. And very, very stingy.

The Misters McGuerdon, Van Hoestling and Garvey had each been in a financial position to make a solid settlement on her. And in an emotional position to sue for peace at any price. It mattered not to Gloria that aged members of her clan were frequently dying and leaving her a little here and a little there. Her lawyers extracted from her ex-husbands the maximum attainable.

She received the *Wall Street Journal* by mail. She spent two consecutive days in every month in absolute sobriety going over the issues that had accumulated, and making marginal notations in red crayon. Then she would review a complete list of her holdings and send to her broker in New York precise instructions as to what she wanted done.

Gloria was addicted to short periods of intense enthusiasm about one project or another. They rarely cost her anything. In between projects she existed in a state of petulant and irritable boredom. Miles Drummond had been caught up in one of Gloria's fits of enthusiasm and that was how the Cuernavaca Summer Workshop came about.

It had started at a pre-Christmas party at Tammy Grandon's house, a huge party that included most of the American residents of Cuernavaca. Miles knew who Gloria was and had a nodding acquaintance with her, and was certain she had not the slightest idea of what his name was. Undone by eggnogs, Miles found himself by the Grandon pool during the second day of the party, telling Gloria Garvey his troubles while he applied sun lotion, in a most gingerly way, to her strong brown back.

His problem was very simple. Money. He had worked for six years for a Philadelphia banking house, from the time he was nineteen until he was twenty-five. It was a family firm. He had been given very little to do. When he came into his inheritance at twenty-five, he had gone to France to live and to become a great painter. In 1942 he had moved to Mexico. What had previously been an adequate income had been slowly eroded by the rising cost of living. Under more normal circumstances he would never have thought of confiding in Gloria Garvey. She frightened him. But he had heard of her financial shrewdness. And there was, of course, the eggnog.

He explained that he could continue to exist, but there was no longer any money for the nice things, the little things that spelled the difference between living and existing. And he did not dare dip into his capital. It was suitably and safely invested, and if hereditary factors could be trusted, he might well live beyond ninety.

Gloria had rolled over on the pool apron and stretched with an indolent feline litheness and had said, "By Christ, Drummy, we'll cook you up a project."

And Miles Drummond soon began to feel like a Kansas chicken which, with the aid of a tornado, finds itself flapping frantically at two thousand feet. The Cuernavaca Summer Workshop idea was born in Gloria's quick and capable mind. She lined up the lease option on the defunct Hotel Hutchinson. She wrote the advertising, and told him where it should be inserted. He paid for the advertising. She had the impressive stationery and application blanks printed in Mexico City. He paid for them. They had many strategic conferences in her untidy suite, and when the first fifty-dollar fee had come in, from Agnes Archibald, she had grabbed Miles Drummond and hugged him until he had felt his rib cage creak alarmingly.

But for the past month and a half he had been aware of the ebbing of her interest. She was increasingly reluctant to hear anything about the CSW. And Miles Drummond was alarmed. He had pictured Gloria Garvey at his side, helping him run it. Without her, he did not see how he could cope. He wished himself back in the quiet times, the morning paper along with egg so carefully poached by Felipe, a spot of sketching in the morning, some chess with Walter Breidbeck after his siesta.

People had paid their money and were actually going to arrive, and Miles wished he could quietly and inconspicuously drop dead.

"Gloria?" he said plaintively.

13

"What is it now?" she asked impatiently, continuing to read.

"Gloria, I don't think the Volkswagen is going to be ready in time to go up and get Mr. Torrigan. Antonio says it is, but I don't believe him."

She pushed her paper aside, drained the glass of beer. "Is that a calamity, for God's sake? Gam Torrigan will get here all right. No doubt of that. He knows he's getting a free ride, and that big bastard is too cheap to take any chance of missing out on it. Let him take a *turismo*."

"I want it to start off right, Gloria. He's the first one arriving. Do you think he'll be any good? I mean as a teacher?"

She shrugged her big strong shoulders. "He knows all the yak. He's done a lot of teaching. I haven't seen him in . . . six years anyway. In Maine."

"Gloria, if the bus isn't ready . . . would you drive up and get him Sunday? You'll know him by sight. We could go up together. It would be easier for me to meet him that way. With somebody who knows him."

"What time does he get in?"

It took Miles Drummond a good five minutes to answer the question. He found that he had left Gambel Torrigan off his master list, and so he had to locate the last letter from him.

"Four-thirty in the afternoon."

Gloria sighed. "All right, all right. We'll go get him. But you pay the toll and buy the gas, understand?"

Miles smiled his relief. Then his nervous frown returned. "I don't think there's enough coming, Gloria. I don't think it's going to work."

"How many are coming for sure?"

"Well, as you know, we got fifty-three answers to the ads and . . ."

"Don't give me the whole picture, Drummy. You've got the money from how many? The total fee from how many?"

He got out his master list again and, biting his lip, counted those who had *Pd*. "Eleven," he said at last.

"So what's wrong? You've taken in fifty-five hundred dollars. I can remember the expense figures we worked out. Twenty-six hundred dollars. So you'll have a net of twenty-nine hundred anyway. I'll tell you where to put the money so you'll be able to count on another two hundred dollars a year income, Drummy. Call it twenty-five hundred pesos. That'll put you over the hump, won't it? Have you arranged how to meet the students you have to meet, and when?"

"I certainly wish I could figure things out so quickly. Eleven isn't really too bad, is it? It really isn't bad at all."

"Where's your list of the ones coming?" She started to paw through his papers. "Good Christ, Drummy, you are hopeless. Got any clean paper in there? Fine. Now give me your pen. Let's see who we have coming. When I call off the name, you find me the application form."

It took fifteen minutes to get a new list of the eleven students, along with date and method of arrival, and the separated application blanks.

Mrs. Hildabeth McCaffrey, 64, widow, was driving from Elmira, Ohio, with her friend Mrs. Dorothy Winkler, 65, also of Elmira, and would arrive on Friday, June 30, in Cuernavaca and would go directly to the Hotel Hutchinson.

Mr. Parker Barnum, age 33, of New York, would arrive by air but did not have to be met as he had friends in Mexico City who would drive him to Cuernavaca.

Miss Mary Jane Elmore, age 20, and Miss Bitsy Babcock, age 19, both of Fort Worth, were driving down.

Mr. and Mrs. Gilbert Wahl, both aged twenty-two, were driving down. From Syracuse.

Miss Monica Killdeering was flying down from Kansas, arriving at six-twenty in Mexico City on the evening of the thirtieth, and expected to be met.

Mr. John Kemp expected to be met at noon at the airport that same day.

Mrs. Barbara Kilmer, of Akron, would apparently be on the same flight.

And Colonel Thomas C. Hildebrandt, U. S. A., Ret., would drive down.

Gloria rechecked the list and said, "How about the other teacher, that bag from California?"

"Oh! Agnes Partridge Keeley. Let me get her letter. I think she's driving. Yes, I know she is. I suggested she arrive early to . . . uh . . . familiarize herself with the setup."

"Okay, Drummy. Now pay attention. We get Torrigan on Sunday. Then your bus has to make two trips on the following Friday, or else you can keep Kemp and Kilmer amused until . . . what's her name? . . . Killdeering gets in."

"But I should be out at the hotel to . . . welcome those arriving by car."

"Hmm. So send Gam Torrigan up with your driver to meet them. They'll be his students anyway. How are things coming out at the hotel?"

15

"Well, they're supposed to have the water fixed by now. And there's twenty rooms ready. I'm going out right after lunch to check up on everything."

"That old crock of a hotel is going to scare hell out of this arty-farty bunch of happy students."

"Gloria . . . do you think you could come out for a few days when they start to arrive . . . to help me get things going?"

"Drummy, I will come out and take a look at them because I want to get a look at the types who fell for the pitch we made, but I am not going to hang around."

Billy Delgarian came trudging up to the table and sat down. "Hello, Miles. Hello, Gloria. Excuse me. Miles, I've been hunting all over for you. I've got a rental for your house. A pair of old creeps from Nebraska. They don't look as if they're strong enough to bust up the furniture. The trouble is, they want a place right away. Today. And they want it through September. How about it?"

Miles felt slightly nauseated whenever he thought of strangers in his little house, sleeping in his bed, sitting in his chairs, eating out of his dishes. "I don't see how I possibly could move out today, Billy. I really couldn't. And just as soon as the Workshop ends, I want to move back into . . ."

"Will they pay his price?" Gloria asked.

"They didn't even try to haggle. I got their check right here and their signatures on the lease, but they understand that the owner might not be agreeable . . ."

"He's agreeable," Gloria said.

"Now, Gloria, really. How about September?"

"So rent a room for September. Drummy, you just don't *want* to rent that house. Get off the dime. Billy will be happy to cart you and your duffle out to the Hutchinson, won't you, Billy?"

Billy looked at his watch. "Be ready about three, Miles."

Miles looked at Gloria and then at Billy and gave a helpless nod of agreement.

"Those clowns we hired will get the place in shape faster if you're living there, Drummy."

Miles stood up. "Well . . . I guess I better go pack."

They watched him head for the *zócalo* and nearly get run down by a battered Land Rover.

"Poor little guy," Billy said. "He's going to have a hell of a summer. How did you ever talk him into this deal, Gloria?"

16

"He needs some money."

"So why didn't you just give him some? You're loaded."

"Hah! This is good for Drummy. It'll stir him up. He's been in a rut all his life. Anyhow, Billy, you damn bandit, think of the fun we'll have watching his mixed-up school operate."

"Even to three it doesn't last through July."

"I'm not about to give you any money either. Buy me a beer, Billy."

Chapter Two

THE HOTEL HUTCHINSON was located four miles north of the center of Cuernavaca, on the east side of a deep barranca which successfully isolated it from the main highway and all transient tourist traffic. It had been built in 1921 by a Texan named Homer Hutchinson, with moneys acquired by selling the same oil leases to many different persons. Their reaction to his ingenuity made it advisable for him to leave the country.

The hotel was designed by Hutchinson. It was a grandiose, putty-colored building, two stories high, with twenty-foot ceilings, built in the form of a hollow square and surrounded by a high wall into the top of which had been set a great deal of broken glass. It looked somewhat like an abandoned prison. It had forty guest rooms, an owner's apartment, a building in the rear for storage and staff quarters, ten primitive bathrooms in the main building, a ballroom-dining room that could seat two hundred, and a metropolitan cockroach population.

The ceilings were high and the windows narrow, so it was a place of gloom and hollow echoes. The kitchen facilities were barbaric; the lighting was early Edison; hot water was generated by devices in each bathroom called *rápidos*. They were not misnamed. Once kindling had been shoved into the firebox and a good fire started, they were rapid indeed. The long corridors, floored with an odd khaki shade of tile, were haunted by the long-ago screams of paying guests who had not expected boiling water to jet from the lean and deadly faucets.

It was not long after his grand opening that Homer Hutchinson discovered that he was attracting very few guests. To remedy this situation he had monstrous and sturdy letters placed on the roof spelling out HOTEL HUTCHINSON, letters so large they could easily be read from the main highway. And still the hotel did not prosper.

In 1927 Homer Hutchinson passed away suddenly of a heart attack while being entertained in the owner's apartment by one of the hotel maids. After that sudden demise, local residents lost track of the number of times the hotel changed hands. In every case the new owner, intent on renaming the place, would clamber to the roof and take a long look at the monolithic letters and decide to retain the old name. At one point in the forties a new owner, more ingenious than the others, and desirous, perhaps, of giving the establishment a more Latin flavor, employed a work crew who, with sledges and crowbars, managed to remove the HOT, leaving EL HUTCHINSON.

The hotel had been empty for two years when Miles Drummond leased it for six hundred dollars for the two-month Workshop. The current owner estimated that it would take about half the rental to get the utilities functioning.

Miles hoped to operate the hotel with a staff of six. He was explaining this to Billy Delgarian when they arrived at the hotel in Billy's sedan at three-thirty. The big iron gates were wide open, and Billy drove in and parked on the baked earth near the front door. He leaned on the horn for a long five seconds.

"We ought to get one of the six," he said.

"I don't understand this at all," Miles said. "Oh, here comes Alberto."

"We woke him up," Billy said. Alberto was a stringy and weathered man who did not pick his feet up when he walked. He was employed as gardener and janitor and handy man. He approached the car slowly as Miles got out, and on his sleepy face was a look of utter idiocy.

"Alberto, you are not taking the broken tiles out of the yard here as I am telling you five or six times," Miles said.

"First I will put beautiful flowers in the patio," Alberto said.

"No. First you will remove the tiles."

"What will I do with them, Señor Droomond?"

"I don't know. Throw them in the barranca."

"How will I carry them to the barranca?"

"On the wheelbarrow."

"It is now broken."

Miles stared at him in helpless exasperation. "Now carry all these things to the room where I will live."

Alberto went to the car, picked up one small suitcase and shuffled sadly off with it. When he was fifteen feet away Miles called to him. "Where is Rosalinda?"

"She has gone someplace to purchase a hen."

"And the maids?"

"The rooms were clean so they both went home."

"And Pepe?"

"He has gone to the city."

"Mind if I look around?" Billy said.

"Not at all. Not at all."

Billy wandered off. Miles picked his largest suitcase out of the car and struggled into the hotel with it. The central patio, through the doors that opened off the shadowy lobby, looked scurfy and beaten. It contained a flagstone walk in the shape of an X, three cement benches, one sundial with the end broken off the blade, one cement birdbath and one small defunct fountain. And fifty kinds of weeds.

After he was unpacked and settled in, and after Billy had left, without comment, Miles went into the patio and began pulling weeds.

Gloria Garvey picked Miles up at the Hutchinson at two-thirty on Sunday afternoon in her powder-blue Jaguar sedan. Cars were Gloria's single expensive vice. She kept her car garaged near Las Rosas, but gave it no other care. When it ceased running properly, she would order another one.

Gloria wore her Mexico City costume, a black suit, white blouse, white gloves. But the skirt of the black suit was shiny in the seat, and the lapels of the jacket were tinged gray with cigarette ash, and the finger seams of the white gloves were split. Her careless hair had the look and texture of lion mane in thorn country.

As Miles got in beside her, she said, "For Chrissake, Drummy, stop jittering. Gam Torrigan is absolutely nobody. What happened to your hand?"

Miles looked down at the bandage, "I cut my fingers on some broken tile I was throwing into the barranca."

"You know darn well that if you potter around doing manual labor, they'll let you do it all."

She yanked the Jaguar around and plunged through the gate, making it skitter sideways on the road before it leveled away and roared by the military barracks where a lone Sunday soldier, lounging on guard, caught a glimpse of long fair hair and responded with the expected whistle, a mechanical and customary courtesy.

She pulled the Jaguar to a shivering halt at the toll gate of the *autopisto,* took the five-peso note from Miles and gave it to the man. She accelerated smoothly, keeping the tach just under the red until the car was climbing toward Tres Cumbres at a hundred and thirty kilometers an hour and the wind roar made conversation impossible. She saw that Miles was firmly holding his own frail knees and staring dead ahead in hypnoid alarm, and it amused her. She took pleasure in driving. She had always had a knack for it, an instinctive ability to judge distances, a sense of timing. But the finishing touches had been added one summer in Italy. It took a few seconds to reach deep into memory and pull the name out. Rufino Cellero. A very wiry, arrogant little guy. And that great beast of a competition Mercedes that made a noise like a runaway sawmill, and when you had it up there, really up there, you lived on the dirty edge of disaster, and it was very fine. She remembered the misty morning, fighting the gear box, sliding into curves, booming down across the mountain bridges, while Rufi, beside her, yelled with joy and banged the side of the door with his brown fist. Rufi had told his manager how good she was and the manager had taken a trial ride with her and then had gotten all heated up about the idea of having her enter some of the road races coming up. And that had seemed good too. But one day she had looked at Rufi in the morning light at that inn and knew that it was finished. Rufi had wept in rage and disappointment and the look of him with his face all twisted up had made it even more finished for her. But she had kept the driving skills he had taught her.

Far ahead on the divided toll road she saw two trucks about two hundred feet apart, grinding up the slope. An American tourist car was starting the process of passing both trucks. Gloria's eyes narrowed as she judged speed and distances. She tramped the gas pedal down and rocketed toward the group of vehicles. She came up on the tourist car just as it had passed the first truck. She swung right between the rear of the tourist car and the front of the second truck, then cut back to the left lane, passing narrowly between the rear of the lead truck and the front of the tourist car. She glanced at Miles. He still clutched his knees. His eyes were closed and his lips were moving. She chuckled against the sound of the wind.

It would be fun to give Gambel Torrigan a gutsy ride back

across the mountains. He would probably respond by pretending to go to sleep.

It was odd how when the idea of Drummy running a summer art school had occurred to her, she had immediately thought of Gam Torrigan. She knew other artists, and better ones. And some of the better ones would probably have jumped at the idea of two months in Mexico on a free ride. But she wrote to somebody in New York who kept track of such things and found out that Gam was teaching at something called the Peninsular Art School and Foundation in Englewood, Florida, and wrote him there, suspecting that, as in Posketnob, Maine, Gam would be close to wearing out his Englewood welcome.

That had been a crazy month in Maine. Which one had it been? Garvey, of course. And near the beginning of the end. Gussy Garvey, with a forlorn idea of mending marital rifts already well past repair, had leased that sullen dog of a schooner with its tiresome crew of three and they had gone a-journeying up the New England coast, stopping off to party here and there with friends, and with friends of friends.

They tied up for the longest stay in the Posketnob Yacht Basin. Gussy had dear old friends there, a limp old pal from Choate days who had a hell of a big house and a neurotic pretentious wife. It was the wife, Coralee something, who brought her art teacher, Gam Torrigan, down for cocktails on the schooner. After the first fifteen minutes of idle yak Gloria had acquired all the tactical information she needed. Gam was having a thing with Coralee. He was bored with the whole deal. He was being pointedly charming toward Gloria. And, quite obviously, he was a big, arrogant, selfish, ignorant, picturesque phony. Who suited her completely. During their affair they got carelessly drunk one afternoon and Coralee made an unfortunate entrance. After an attack of screaming hysterics, Coralee went home and cut her wrists with great care, cut them just enough to get about ten drops of blood from each one, and then made a tragic confession to the item from Choate, including what she had interrupted. The shaken Choate type passed it along to Gussy, as a sort of friendly gesture. And so that was the end of the marriage, right there, and the schooner was sent on home without passengers. And Gam's teaching contract was terminated without notice—a sort of local substitute for tar and feathers.

Gloria realized that her recent correspondence with Gam might be open to misinterpretation on his part. He might think she wanted a continuance of the so abruptly severed relationship back in Posketnob. She did not think she did. When she thought of him, there was no answering visceral tremor. But if it occurred once she saw him in person, then let him believe what he wished. But if it was still dead, he would have to be abruptly educated. Perhaps he preened himself on being the cause of divorce. If so, he would have to have the word on that.

The flight came in at four-forty, just ten minutes late. At the international section of the Mexico City airport, those meeting passengers stand in an open-air area behind a fence and watch the incoming passengers walk along a long shed arrangement that leads to the glass-walled customs room.

"Which one?" Miles asked nervously.

"That one. Right there," Gloria said, pointing.

"That one!" Miles said, staring at a very big man who strolled along with the manner of a man who owns the airline and is making a check flight to study passenger service. But in that manner there was an undercurrent of the con man, hunting a victim to whom he can sell the airline. He was big—thick through the chest, heavy in the arms and legs. He combined a bristling black brush cut with a bushy beard, tinged with gray. Nestling in the beard was a wide and petulant red-lipped mouth, a nose pink with tiny broken veins. His cheekbones were high and brown and solid, the pale eyes set in Mongol tilt. He wore an obviously ancient, rust-colored corduroy shirt, the collar open, a yellow silk ascot at his throat, faded baggy khaki pants, and the kind of black pseudo-cowboy boots that A.T.C. personnel used to buy in Brazil in the early forties. He wore a bulging and ratty musette bag slung over his shoulder, and carried a large painter's portfolio.

When he was opposite them, ten feet away, Gloria said, "Gam!"

He stopped and turned, and a big slow smile spread the red lips wide, and he said, in a rich and resonant bass-baritone, "Gloria, love! You look edible, darling. Ravishing. What a foul thing this air age is. I'll be with you as soon. as I permit a horde of officious little men to paw over my poor belongings." And he strolled on.

"Good heavens!" Miles Drummond said.

They went inside and watched him through the glass as he went through customs. He had one enormous black metal suitcase which he apparently kept closed with a complicated arrangement of khaki straps and buckles. When he came out of the terminal building, carrying his suitcase, they met him. Gloria made the introduction. Miles felt his hand give slightly under the hard engulfing pressure. Torrigan had put the big suitcase down. Miles decided it would be polite to carry it out to the parking lot. He picked it up. His eyes bulged. He raised it several inches off the floor before it clunked back down.

Torrigan picked it up without effort, and they went out to the car. Miles and the suitcase and the portfolio and the musette bag shared the back seat. Torrigan seemed to talk constantly in that rich black voice of his. Miles, in a rare flight of imagery, thought it sounded like hot tar being poured out of a golden jug. He wished Gloria had told him more about what Gambel Torrigan was like. He had imagined many things, but not this.

Gloria, for her part, had detected no visceral quiver. Gam was merely ludicrous, mannered, and slightly boring.

Miles Drummond was the only witness to the first meeting between Gambel Torrigan and Agnes Partridge Keeley. He had stayed up late on Sunday night after they got back to the Hutchinson, stayed up with Gam and Gloria, listening to a bewildering conversation. Gam had showed him the paintings in the portfolio. They did not look like anything Miles had ever seen before. There were blobs and whorls and swoops of pure color. They had such titles as "Illusionary Number Eleven" and "Transcendant in Ochre" and "Majorcan Melody."

He said to Gloria, "You can see from this recent stuff, darling, that I've gone beyond my Dynamic Impressionism period. I was in stasis. There was no longer enough there to satisfy me. But the mood was germinating, even when I was most discouraged. Now I'm into what I like to call my period of Reversive Romanticism. I'm dealing entirely in the balance of tensions through luminosity and focal levels. Some of my critics seem to think I'm betraying my purposes with a retrogressive step, but I say that sometimes it is time to go back to your beginnings to find the source of your strength. I feel that these have a lot of verity and I find them enormously exciting. Don't you, Gloria?"

"Oh, sure," said Gloria. "Can you scrounge up any more ice, Drummy."

Miles went off and made certain there was no more ice. Though Torrigan awed him and the paintings confused him, he was grateful that Torrigan had not complained about the hotel or the accommodations. In fact, Torrigan seemed almost oblivious of his surroundings.

As he came back toward his apartment he heard Gloria's voice, sharp with irritation, and then he heard Gambel Torrigan give an explosive yap of anguish. When Miles went in they were standing six feet apart. Gloria was lighting a cigarette. Torrigan stood in peculiar fashion, bent forward at the waist. He straightened himself with effort, grimaced and said, "That was a hell of a thing to do!"

"You weren't getting my message, doll."

"I've got it now," he said with dignity, and picked up his portfolio and said, "Good night, Gloria. Good night, Mr. Drummond. I am going to bed." He marched out.

"What happened?"

Gloria gave him an odd smile. "I applied a little Reversive Romanticism, Drummy. No ice? Hell. Fix me a warm one then."

After her drink, he walked her out to her car where it sat pale in the moonlight. "Gloria, those paintings. I don't know. I mean I want to preserve an open mind. But . . . are they any good?"

"My God, I wouldn't know. They may be nothing. They may be art for the ages. How can you tell? When he was in his early twenties, a couple of critics got onto him and made a big deal out of him. He had a show in a New York gallery and damn near sold it out for pretty good prices. And that's the last good thing that happened to him. He teaches around in little schools nobody ever heard of. He sells a painting once in a while. Don't worry about it, Drummy. He'll do a snow job on your little people. Good night now."

The Jaguar plunged down toward the sleeping city, rumbling through the night. She rang the night bell on the garage until a sleepy attendant appeared to take her car. The lobby of Las Rosas was empty. When she was in her small suite she unhooked, unbuttoned, unzipped, unsnapped and let her clothes lie where they fell. She read for about fifteen minutes and then turned out the bed light. She lay in darkness on the edge of sleep and thought of Gam Torrigan, of his sudden look of shock and outrage after he had tried forcibly to embrace her. She grinned a dirty grin and scratched the mound of a soft warm hip, and rolled over into sleep.

Agnes Partridge Keeley arrived at nine o'clock on Monday morning in a sea-gray air-conditioned Cadillac with California plates. She was a billowing, pillowy woman of fifty, all pastels and jangle of junk jewelry, full of soft cooings and velvety little cries and exclamations. She had a face like a pudding, small, bitter blue eyes, and coarse, tightly curled hair bleached a poisonous yellow-green. She had her studio in Pasadena, and her little group of disciples. When she had been a miserably shy and thoroughly unattractive child, it was thought she had a pretty talent for drawing. In the past thirty years Agnes Partridge Keeley, hefty virgin, had painted and sold some 8,000 seascapes, landscapes and portraits of children and animals in the $15 to $60 price range. A shrewd and avid businesswoman, she saw to it that there were Agnes Partridge Keeleys in every retail outlet in the Pasadena area where an Indiana tourist might be tempted to buy a genuine original painting by a California artist.

After Miles had greeted her and made arrangements to have her staggering amount of luggage transported to the room he had set aside for her, he took her on a quick tour of the hotel. "How deliciously quaint!" she kept exclaiming, but at certain areas of the tour she was seen to swallow with difficulty.

Miles felt more at ease with her than with Torrigan. "For years and years, Mr. Drummond," she said, "I have wanted to paint the Mexican scene. These quaint and delightful people. The grandeur of the mountains. I must confess that I could not possibly tell you how many times I stopped by the roadside to dash off a few sketches. I sketch wherever I go, you know. It is the indispensable tool of the working artist. I will insist that my students this summer carry their sketch books everywhere. Absolutely *everywhere!*"

Miles sometimes sketched with a very nice old lady named Mildred Means, a Cuernavaca resident who, when she had lived in Pasadena, had studied for seven years with Agnes Partridge Keeley. It was Mrs. Means who had recommended her and had given Miles a letter to enclose in his first contact with her.

"Now I really must get settled, Mr. Drummond. You're being so kind. And then I must paint this charming patio the very first thing."

It did not take Agnes Partridge Keeley very long to get settled. She reappeared in dusty pink slacks and a pale green blouse, carrying paintbox, easel, and folding canvas stool. She set herself up in one corner of the patio and went diligently to work. It was Miles's curiosity about her methods that caused him to be present when his two instructors met at about ten-thirty that morning. He had asked her if she knew Gambel Torrigan, and she had apologized for her ignorance in a way that somehow conveyed the idea that nobody knew Gambel Torrigan, and why should they?

Miles was looking rather timidly over Agnes Partridge Keeley's plump shoulder when he was startled by a loud noise directly in back of him, rather like the snorting of an irritated horse. He turned sharply and saw Gambel Torrigan standing there looking with acute revulsion at the half-completed water color on the Keeley easel. Miles had not been entirely satisfied with the way the water color was progressing. She seemed to make the patio too pretty, putting in flowers where none had yet grown. But it certainly could not be as bad as the expression on Torrigan's face indicated.

"Bah!" said Gambel Torrigan and reached out a long heavy arm and took the water color and tore it in half, and tore the halves in half and scattered them on the ground and spat in their general direction. Agnes leaped up, cheeks and chins shaking in shock and anger, spluttering incoherently.

Gambel Torrigan overrode her with that rich voice of his, smiling confidently at her, saying, "My good woman, you have come down here to learn what painting is. You must forget all you think you know. I will not have one of my students turning out sickly, insipid little daubs. Leave the pretty flowers, my dear, for tourists going clickety-click with their Kodaks. Under me you will learn that painting is fire and iron and blood. Not sugar cookies. You are down here to work. To learn. I will start you from the beginning. I will teach you to use your eyes and your hands and your soul. And first you must throw away all those stinking tiresome water colors in that precious paintbox of yours."

Agnes Partridge Keeley's screech finally cut through the velvety unctuousness.

"Just who the hell do you think you are!"

Slight bow. "I am Gambel Torrigan, your painting instructor."

"In a pig's ass you're my painting instructor!" She thumped her chest with a pink fist and yelled, "I am the instructor! I am Agnes Partridge Keeley."

Torrigan stared at her in comprehension and consternation and then turned with majestic regret toward Miles Drummond. "Mr. Drummond, I was not advised that I would have to try to conduct a school with the dubious assistance of an illustrator of post cards."

Agnes advanced on him, brush held like a dirk. "Oh, I know your type. Hah! I've seen a thousand of you. You couldn't draw a horse without making it look like a chow dog."

"I have no intention of . . . excuse the expression . . . drawing a horse."

"All of you look like bums. I have made over three hundred thousand dollars from my paintings!"

"A monstrous tribute, madam, to the cultural level of our society."

She whirled toward Miles. "I will not have my students confused and misled by this . . . this . . . Communist."

"And I," said Torrigan, "will not be a party to any conspiracy that pours over the inquiring souls of my students this . . . vast heritage of molasses." Torrigan stalked off. Agnes Partridge Keeley snatched up the tools of her trade and trotted off in the opposite direction.

By three in the afternoon, Miles felt as though he had covered endless miles between Torrigan's room and Agnes' room. But he had effected a compromise. Agnes would take all the students all morning. Torrigan would take them all during the afternoon. At the end of the first full week of instruction, each individual student would elect which group he would belong to for the rest of the Workshop period.

On Tuesday, the red VW bus was released by the *mechánico*. Fidelio Melocotonero, sitting proudly behind the wheel, drove Miles Drummond around town on his errands. Because Miles could not drive, he could not properly appraise Fidelio's skill. But it seemed to him that Fidelio stalled the bus rather often, that he excited more than the customary number of horn sounds from other vehicles, and that several times he bumped up over a curb unnecessarily when rounding a corner. And, when parked and waiting for Miles, he liked to make the motor roar.

When Fidelio drove him to the post office, Miles found two more acceptances. Two new students, both men. Paul Klauss of Philadelphia, and Harvey Ardos, also from Philadelphia. Thirteen students in all. And close to four thousand dollars for Miles. Seven female and six male. He wished one more male would sign up. It would make it so . . . neat.

After depositing money, Miles drew out some cash and, accompanied by Felipe Cedro, who had been his houseman for many years, and Alberto Buceada, the stringy and ineffectual hotel janitor he had hired, Miles took the red bus to the public market to acquire the first large block of supplies as indicated on the list Gloria had helped him prepare.

He had expected the job to take an hour or so, but it was late afternoon before he had finished. He was certain he had gotten the wrong quantities of many items and had overlooked others. Yet even the luggage rack on the roof was full of supplies. The red bus complained sullenly about climbing the long hill to the Hutchinson with such a load, and it went very slowly indeed, to the disgust of Fidelio who, from time to time, indicated his irritation by banging the horn button with his fist until Miles ordered him to stop. Felipe Cedro rode with them in remote dignity, isolating himself with a perfect indifference. Felipe was a strikingly handsome man . . . from the waist up. But he had been cursed with small, knotty, bandy legs that reduced him from the height that should have been his to an inconsequential stature.

He was the son of a gardener, and in his childhood had aspired to be a *torero*. But when he had acquired sufficient skill and knowledge of the animals to appear, at fifteen, in his first *novillero* fights at small village festivals, he found that not only did his physical construction make him an object of derision, but he was not sufficiently fleet of foot to avoid horrible buffetings from the horns. He had sense enough to quit before he was seriously gored. And, with reluctance, he had given up his dream. He told himself that had he been able to be a great bullfighter, he would have been rich, and noble and honest. The most suitable revenge on the world was to become rich, through ignobility and dishonesty.

He thought his employer a fool. He knew that during the six years of his employment by Miles Drummond, the servant had surpassed the master in worldly goods. On the back streets of Cuernavaca, Felipe Cedro was known as a shrewd and greedy and dangerous man. He owned fragments of many small business enterprises, some of which were almost entirely legitimate. Through his excellent contacts with police officials and politicians, he had become a valuable man to know, whether your problem was that of disposing of stolen goods or finding a young woman suitable for a certain German tourist.

Felipe had about decided to terminate his association with Miles Drummond and had, in fact, made a mental list of the small objects he would take with him upon his departure

28

when this Workshop venture had taken form. Felipe decided at once that it might present sufficient chance for gain to warrant remaining with Miles until September. And on this day his hunch had been partially justified. He had steered Miles to those vendors who could be depended upon for a kickback. And the quantities purchased had been large enough to make for a profitable afternoon. He was certain that rich and foolish American women would come to study painting. And there, if you kept your eyes open and your wits about you, was a chance for much greater profit.

He nodded and dreamed in the red bus on the way back to the Hutchinson. Don Felipe Cedro would one day own a vast house with a pool for the swimming, and three mistresses, all of whom had been in the cinema or appeared upon the television. He would ride in a great, long golden car with a top that went up and down, and they would bow to Don Felipe when the car passed them.

And then they arrived and he had to unload the supplies and help carry them into the kitchen area. Work for a burro.

Chapter Three

ON WEDNESDAY MORNING at ten o'clock Miles Drummond held a meeting of his service staff in the big gloomy kitchen. Though it heartened him to have them all in one place and to be able to look at them, when he examined them individually he had a feeling of misgiving, a dread knowledge of the inevitability of disaster.

He could find no reassurance in the familiar face of Felipe Cedro. Felipe had seemed moody lately, and his work had not been entirely satisfactory. Rosalinda Gomez would be in charge of the kitchen. She was a very fat Mexican woman with a generous mixture of Indio blood. She wore a broad smile upon her dark face. She had a small black mustache and eyes like wet anthracite. Miles had found it extraordinarily difficult to establish communication with her. No matter what he said to her, she giggled as though he had made some delicious joke. And, from the few meals she had served the small group thus far, he was certain that she was a startlingly bad cook. When he had overheard her talking to Alberto Buceada, the stringy janitor, her speech had been bristly with the clickings and glottal stops of

29

Indian words. And from her manner toward Alberto he had come to suspect that, out in the building that served as storage space and staff quarters, Rosalinda and Alberto had come to some intimate arrangement satisfactory to both parties. He had no intention of investigating this arrangement further.

The least consequential member of the staff was named Pepe. Miles assumed he was about twelve years old, a raggedy child with black hair that grew down from the top of his head like a conical thatched roof. His function was to serve as kitchen help to Rosalinda, to run errands and perform other duties that might present themselves from time to time.

Pepe, Rosalinda, Alberto, Felipe and Fidelio Melocotonero would live at the Hutchinson, though it might be assumed that Fidelio would retain his habit of sleeping in the red VW bus.

The two maids, who would double as waitresses, both lived nearby in humble family dwellings perched on the slope of the barranca. The prettier of the two, Margarita Esponjar, made him particularly uneasy. She was smoking a cigarette and leaning her pert and jaunty haunches against one of the kitchen tables and looking directly at Miles with a telling and sensual vacuity. She wore a rather sleazy red dress and red shoes. The shoes were apparently too large for her, and it gave her a perculiar gait when she walked in them. There seemed to Miles to be too much extraneous movement in her walk.

The other one, Esperanza Clueca, was more reassuring. She was neatly dressed and stood at attention. Her eyes were set rather closely together, and she had a long, severe upper lip. She had obtained permission from Miles to be away from her job from four in the afternoon to eight in the evening five days a week. She was attending school and would one day become a schoolteacher. Esperanza spoke politely and quietly, but with an ominous firmness, whereas Margarita had a peculiarly gay and piercing voice.

When he looked at the seven of them as a group, he could almost believe that the services might run smoothly.

He cleared his throat and said, "There is coming thirteen students. I am going in the bus tomorrow, picking up the first two students. El Señor Torrigan is going to Mexico City Friday to meet others. The rest are coming in their own cars. The food, each meal, is sufficient to feed the two teachers, the thirteen students, and the eight of us who now

30

stand here, and sometimes there is guests. I am clear?"

There were nods and little murmurs of agreement.

"Breakfast is from eight to nine. Lunch is from noon to one-thirty. Dinner is from eight-thirty until ten. Felipe is doing the necessary buying in the market. Rosalinda is telling Felipe what is needed. Fidelio is driving Felipe to the market, and to get the mail each day. But the bus is not going anywhere until it is with my permission. And at all times everything is made very clean here. I am clear?"

Rosalinda giggled and said, "I will buy what is needed, señor. You will give me the money and I will go in the red bus and buy the things we need."

"She will stay in the kitchen where she belongs," Felipe said.

"Then I will not use what he buys," Rosalinda said and giggled some more.

"Then you are both going together," Miles directed. Rosalinda and Felipe looked at each other with hostility.

"And we will take Pepe and Alberto to carry the purchases, señor," Felipe said.

"Uh . . . it is well," Miles said. He had the feeling he had been outmaneuvered.

Margarita dropped her cigarette on the floor and stepped on it with a tall red shoe. Miles looked at the cigarette and swallowed and said, "It is important all things are clean. It is important our students are . . . happy. We are working hard this summer making them clean and happy, no?"

"Si, señor," they said in smiling chorus. He smiled back and squared his shoulders and marched out of the kitchen. He heard them all start chattering at once, Margarita's voice more clear than all the others, proclaiming, "I too shall ride in the red bus, Fidelio!"

On Thursday morning the red bus gasped, choked and died. Fidelio blew the horn angrily for a few moments after he found that he could not start it again. He got out and kicked the door on the driver's side and stalked away. Miles got out and examined the new dent. Miles went in and phoned Las Rosas, but Gloria was not in her room. He phoned Antonio Vasques, the mechanic, and made a report on the symptoms the bus had shown just before expiring. Antonio sounded most distressed and said that he would most certainly try to come and visit the bus as soon as possible.

When, by eleven-thirty, he had not been able to reach Gloria, he looked for Agnes Partridge Keeley, and found her outside the wall being solemnly watched by four small children and a large brown cow as she was finishing one of her nimble water colors of the shacks on the lip of the barranca. She sat in the sun, flushed and humid, biting her lips as she worked.

Miles explained about the bus and she said she would be delighted to drive him to Mexico City to pick up the two gentlemen, the first students to arrive.

As, a half-hour later, they drifted almost silently up the mountain highway in the big gray Cadillac, Miles leaned back into the softness of the upholstery and was pleased that he had not been able to get in touch with Gloria. Agnes seemed a very careful driver. Almost too cautious. The interior of the car was scented with her flower perfume. And she talked and talked and talked.

And, at the same time, in the DC-7B droning south toward the high spine of the Sierra Madres, Paul Klauss was being inundated by a relentless flood of conversation, directed at him moistly and forcibly by a young man named Harvey Ardos. Klauss had been bored into a state of helpless and irritable stupor. When he had sent in his late registration for the Cuernavaca Summer Workshop, along with his payment in full of five hundred dollars, Paul Klauss had hoped that, this summer, he was not making a mistake as grave as the one he had made last summer. Harvey Ardos had very nearly convinced him that this might be an even worse summer.

Had Paul Klauss not been almost half asleep when Harvey Ardos approached him, he might have avoided these endless words. But he had looked blearily up into the eager and pimpled face, into the young spaniel eyes behind the thick lenses in their black frames, and said, "Wha?"

"I said are you going to the Cuernavaca Summer Workshop?"

"Uh . . . yes."

And Harvey Ardos had dropped into the seat beside him, grinning with a sort of oily and ecstatic warmth, and clasped Paul's hand in a long, cold-fingered, damp hand and said, "How about that! How about that! I'm going there too. How about that!"

During the intervening hundreds of miles Paul Klauss had learned more about Harvey Ardos than he wished to know. Harvey was twenty-four. His formal education was limited. "No real good artists ever went for that college crap," is the way he put it. He was an orphan. He was not married. He had worked as a stock clerk in a Philadelphia department store that winter. "I figure a man has to keep on the move. See the world." He said that he lived very simply, and whenever he got money ahead he would takes courses, study under someone. And this was his big adventure. He carried black-and-white prints of what seemed to be to Klauss several hundred of his paintings. Most of them seemed to be of back alleys illuminated with a scrawl of neon.

"I figure I'm maybe of the James Penney school. Anyway, somebody told me that once. I haven't just got the right breaks yet, Mr. Klauss. As soon as I start getting the breaks, I'm going to have it made. The way I figure it, I've got something to say. That's the main thing, you got to have something to say, and then you got to work like hell to say it the way you want to say it. And when you can do that and you've got the breaks, you've got it made. You know, I've never been out of the country before. The army didn't want me on account of my eyes. But let me tell you, I know how to use my eyes. I don't look at anything without thinking of painting it. That's the way I look around me all the time. You know. The colors and shadows and stuff. Shadows aren't ever black. They're lousy with colors. Isn't it the funniest damn thing in the world, you being from Philadelphia and us never running into each other?"

"It's a big place," Klauss said weakly.

"I know, but when you've got the same kind of interests, you run into people with the same kind of interests, you know what I mean. What kind of painting do you do?"

"I'm . . . a beginner."

"Oh! Well, you've wasted a hell of a lot of time, Mr. Klauss, but I don't guess it's too much time. I mean a lot of the good boys got a late start. I figure what makes a painter is being sensitive. I'm real sensitive. You wouldn't think it, but my feelings get hurt easy. And I think a painter has to work, too. He has to be working every minute. Everything he looks at is part of his work. Just looking at it is part of what he has to do. The guys I work with, they think I'm nuts, but they'll find out some day. Nobody wants to give you a chance. They all the time want to laugh at you instead. I don't let them bother me too much. They can go on out and bowl and drink beer and pick up girls, but let me tell you, I go on back to the room and get the stuff all laid out and I start in painting. You know, I even forget what time it is or whether I had dinner or not. The painting is the main thing with me. Mr. Klauss!"

"Uh?"

"Hey, I thought you were going to sleep or something. Honest to God, this is going to be a great thing. Mexico! And nothing to do all day every day but paint. It's the greatest thing that ever happened to me. I'm so damn excited right now I feel like running up and down the aisle. You know, this is the second time in my life I ever been on an airplane?"

And on and on and on. Paul Klauss could imagine, dismally, that the Cuernavaca Summer Workshop would be peopled with dozens of dull, intense, and pimpled young men named Harvey Ardos, all of whom have the same long, black, dank hair and the same stained line around the collar of their cheap white shirts. And so it would be another wasted summer. Two of them in a row. And time was going by too fast to risk the ruin of two summers in succession.

Paul Klauss was thirty-four. In the right light he could pass for twenty-six or seven. He was a trim-bodied man, five feet eight inches in height, who, by the way he carried himself and through the assistance of his constant use of elevator shoes, gave the impression of being five ten or perhaps a little more. His hair was dark blond and carefully tended. Feature by feature he somewhat resembled a blond Gregory Peck, but the pale eyelashes were longer than they needed to be, and there was a look of weakness around the mouth.

His life was orderly, exceedingly well organized. He was a bachelor, and owned and operated a small men's clothing store near the University of Pennsylvania. He lived in a small and tasteful apartment ten blocks from the store. He did not drink or smoke. He took splendid care of himself, and purchased many medicines and devices which promised to prolong the appearance of youth indefinitely. He had no close friends. All other potential interests in his life were subordinated to his single, intense, almost psychotic compulsion—the hunting of women.

He operated his shop diligently and successfully because it provided the funds necessary to his compulsion. He had made his apartment most attractive, not because he particularly cared about his own surroundings, but because he saw a direct relationship between the frame and the eventual picture. Though not a particularly vain man, he tried to look as well as possible at all times because it enhanced his average. He had foregone the luxury of having any specific and positive personality of his own because it was so much more effective to guess what sort of person the woman would be most vulnerable to, and then assume that personality.

He had both the cold gray eye and the unthinking cruelty of the professional hunter of any sort of game. Some men climbed mountains because they were there. Other men spent frozen hours in duck blinds, or sweaty hours on a high platform over a staked goat. Paul Klauss had equivalent patience and equivalent skills. And he paid just as much attention to the efficacy of his weapons and their condition.

When he was twenty he had begun his first journal. He had used his specialized but prodigious memory to look back across the last five years of his existence and recall each name, each face, each figure, each circumstance, each perfumed nuance and set them down in perfect order of accomplishment, in prose as cold and functional as his eyes. Ever after that he kept his journal up to date, making the entries as they occurred. When he was twenty-five he purchased several soft and expensive loose-leaf binders and a quantity of heavy, creamy bond paper. He transcribed all his previous records into the new journals, using a portable typewriter equipped with green ribbon. He worked evenings for many weeks, changing many awkwardnesses of phrase and expression as he transcribed the records of his success. They were kept in a locked case in his living room, except for the three most recent ones which he had brought with him. They were his trophy room. His fishing log. His hunting journal.

As other men might recall the look of the brown bear on the mountain slope, or the crashing fall of a moose on the shore of a Canadian lake, Paul Klauss would remember the precise configuration of a dimpled buttock, or the approximate decibel count of a wordless cry of completion. On those evenings between expeditions, Paul would leaf through his journals. The name of the female person involved was used as a heading for each entry. Directly underneath appeared the dates, showing the duration of the affair. They did not endure long. And they never, never overlapped. After the date appeared certain statistics: her age, and whether it was verified or estimated, approximate height and weight and so on. After this appeared two numerical ratings based on a scale of ten. The first rating was that of the woman, appearance, energy, co-operativeness. The second rating was that of his own estimate of his own effectiveness in inaugurating, completing and removing himself from the affair. It had been a long time since, out of desperation, Klauss had spent time on any woman who rated less than five on his scale, and equally long since he himself had blundered to an extent where he could rate himself lower than six.

After the factual data began the text of his entry. "Ruth (Mrs. John Williams) entered my shop at three o'clock on the rainy afternoon of April 3rd. She was attractively but not expensively dressed in a green wool suit, a transparent raincape and hood over her dark-red hair. She said that she was interested in buying a present for her husband, and said that she had been thinking of a sport shirt. I told her it would help me if she were to tell me what sort of a man her husband was, thus putting me in a better position to advise her . . ."

He thought of his journals as having some special value. It was an account of over six hundred trophies pursued, tamed and released. He thought himself unique in the world, and would have been most distressed to know not only how many others enjoyed the same cold game, but also the rather obvious psychological reason for their enjoyment.

Each winter he made the best of the rather limited opportunities on the Philadelphia scene, and for the past nine years, he had been able to leave the shop each summer in the charge of a trusted subordinate and go forth to where the game was more abundant, the handicaps fewer.

For several years he operated on the cruise circuit, but there came to be a disheartening sameness about the shipboard conquest of the adventuresome secretary, schoolteacher or nurse. When, even with the help of his journal, he found it difficult to remember their faces and their mannerisms, he decided to seek other hunting grounds.

Three years ago he had spent the summer at a music camp and conference in New Hampshire. It had provided nine unique episodes for the journal, and had made him feel as exhilarated as a spear fisherman at Marine Studios. Two years ago he had attended a summer writing conference, and it had been a splendid equivalent. But last summer he had erred dreadfully by signing up for a sculpture course in Florida. The selection had been grossly meager. Of the three entires in the journal, he suspected that he had been overly generous in awarding them all fives. Two could have been considered fours. And one might possibly have been adjudged a three.

When he had come across the announcement of the Cuernavaca Summer Workshop in the February copy of *Diary of the Arts,* he had clipped it and set it aside. He had been dubious about it, but finally, unable to find anything that sounded better, he had sent his money at the last moment and made his air reservations.

He had embarked with anticipatory visions of a workshop galaxy of delectable trophies, bold and perfumed and vulnerable, and of himself strolling among them, in slow and thoughtful selection of the perfect blooms for a perfect bouquet. The chase itself was, to Paul Klauss, the heady and delicious aspect of conquest. The culmination, though pleasant enough, was, he sometimes confessed to himself, rather mechanical.

Now Harvey Ardos had faded anticipation to a kind of sour pessimism. Possibly the ad had attracted a damp swarm of Harveys, and their female equivalents. Abused and disheartened by the intensity of the repetition of banalities, Klauss was pleased when there was a subtle change in the engine noises and the NO SMOKING sign began to flash. Harvey Ardos terminated his conversation abruptly and began to adjust himself to the imminent task of absorbing all the color of an early afternoon landing in Mexico City.

After they had gone through customs and emerged into the station proper, Klauss heard a tremulous male voice saying nervously, "Mr. Klauss. Mr. Ardos. Mr. Klauss. Mr. Ardos."

Paul turned and saw a clerky-looking little gray-haired man in a chamois jacket standing next to a vast middle-aged woman with metallic yellow hair who stood babbling and billowing beside the little man, peering around with quick movements of her head.

With sinking heart Paul Klauss went over and introduced himself to Miles Drummond and Agnes Partridge Keeley. Harvey Ardos acted overwhelmed with the distinction of being met in such a huge and glamorous terminal building, and there was a nervous squeak in his voice.

After a certain amount of bumbling, passengers and luggage were settled into a great gray Cadillac across from the terminal building. Paul managed to maneuver himself into the front seat beside Agnes. He did not feel that he could endure another moment seated beside Harvey. He thought that Miles Drummond was certainly a bold and resounding name for the nervous and apologetic little man who was running the school. In his anticipations of the school he had placed Agnes Partridge Keeley on his list of possibles. He removed her in a tenth of a second. Agnes Partridge Keeley talked volubly about delightful old Mexico as she eased the car through traffic with such an excess of caution that they were trailed at all times by a file of taxicabs hooting in frustrated anger and derision. Miss Keeley did not appear to notice them. They sought opportunities to cut around the Cadillac, glaring as they passed, inches away.

It was a new city to Paul Klauss, but he looked at it with that limited interest born of specialization, in much the same way that an experienced hunter might survey new terrain from the air. There is a water hole. There is heavy brush country. There is a game trail through the hills. Paul noted that there seemed to be a great many bars and a great many hotels. And it was heartening to see the high percentage of trim young females, particularly on one street they traversed. At a corner he found the name of the street and filed it away carefully in his mind. Juarez.

As Agnes Partridge Keeley talked, Paul extracted pertinent information. They were the first two students to arrive. The rest were coming tomorrow by air, or arriving by car. As Agnes paused for a moment to inch her way around the circle in front of the Continental Hilton and turn south on Insurgentes, Paul said, "How many students will there be?"

"Thirteen," Miles Drummond said from the back seat.

Paul was appalled. Thirteen was far too small a group to provide not only adequate choice, but sufficient room for maneuver.

"I suppose there are several married couples?" he said with forced cheer.

"Really, I expected more than we are getting," Miles Drummond said. "Just one married couple. Their name is Wahl. Doubleyou aye aitch el. Mr. Klauss, tell us about your painting."

Paul hesitated long enough for Harvey Ardos to pounce. And pounce he did. From then on whenever Agnes would try to break in, Harvey would run right over her by increasing his decibel count. She gave up and drove up the mountains in silence, a pinched look of exasperation on her mouth.

Soon after they left the toll road at the Cuernavaca end, they turned through an open iron gate in a high wall and parked directly in front of a building that was not only

38

an exceptionally ugly structure, but seemed to be in a state of utter disrepair. A motley collection of servants came out after the baggage. One of them was one of the dirtiest small boys Paul had ever seen.

Drummond, with his continual air of apology, took Paul to the ground-floor room that had been assigned to him, and handed over the key and said, "Ha ha, Mr. Klauss. You may find it a bit primitive, but it's clean and after all, we're here to paint, aren't we?"

"Mmmm," he said.

"I'll let you get settled while I go show Mr. Ardos his room. Dinner at eight-thirty, Mr. Klauss. Until then, ha ha, you are on your own. The town is four miles away. If you feel you need transportation, see me and I'll see if anything can be arranged. Cuernavaca is very . . . picturesque."

It did not take Paul long to unpack. He changed to a pale-gray wool shirt and dark-blue slacks. He sat on the narrow bed. It was made up with clean gray sheets, a blanket with two holes in it. The narrow window was open. He looked through the patched screening and between the bars and saw a stretch of baked earth between his window and the high stone wall. Broken glass of many colors topped the wall, gleaming in the sun. He turned and looked at the cane chair with a broken seat, the huge bureau that looked as if at one time it had rolled down a rocky mountain. He looked at the single bulb that stuck out of the wall, a big bulb made of clear glass so that he could see the filaments inside. He went over and turned it on by pulling the chain. He could look directly at the light without blinking. He could imagine how dismal the high-ceilinged room would be at night. The center of the narrow bed was a good five inches lower than the corners. And the mattress was stuffed with discarded truck springs and milk bottles. A cockroach strolled out from under the bed, paused and looked at Klauss with insolent appraisal, and went back under the bed. For the first time since childhood Paul Klauss felt like breaking into tears.

At ten o'clock on Friday morning, the little red bus toiled slowly up the mountains, from the fifty-five hundred feet at Cuernavaca toward the ten-thousand-foot pass a little beyond Tres Cumbres. Fidelio Melocotonero sat gloomily grasping the wheel, sometimes urging the vehicle forward by bobbing back and forth.

Beside him sat Gambel Torrigan, equally depressed. When,

at the Peninsular Art School and Foundation of Englewood, Florida, he had received the letter from Gloria Garvey, he had lunged at the opportunity. Englewood had been a fine place for a time. When they had hired him as instructor in painting, they had turned over to him a rickety but extremely private beach cottage on lower Manasota Key. Classes had started the first of October. He taught in the morning and worked hard on his own stuff in the afternoon. He'd bought an elderly vehicle that got him back and forth from the school to the Key, and into town for groceries. He had decided that this was the time to turn over a new leaf. Get a lot of work done. Big paintings. Swim and sleep and work. Get in shape. Lay off the bottle, and don't fool around with the students.

But by the time Gloria's letter came, it had all changed, the way it always did. He would look at the paintings he had thought were so good when he was doing them, and they would be meaningless to him. By the time Gloria's letter came he was spending the good working hours in a beer joint on the Key, with or without Arabella Boycie, the spoiled, rich, drunken, domineering bitch who had bitched up his plans and bitched up the job so that he was certain that when the school closed on the last day of April, he would not be invited back for the following fall.

It was a timely invitation and, in addition, he remembered Gloria Garvey with pleasure, remembered her untidy magnificence, and was quite certain that she sought a renewal of an all too brief affair. He had been Arabella's house guest on Casey Key during May and June. After he had purchased his one-way airline ticket, he had nearly five hundred dollars left, some of which was from the sale of the old car, and most of which was a pseudo-loan from Arabella Boycie.

He had thought it would be a pleasant summer. But Gloria had made her lack of co-operation in some of his plans most painfully evident. The hotel was grim. The food was barely edible. Drummond was a tiresome little man. And fat Agnes and her work were equally unbearable. Also, the two students who had arrived, Klauss and Ardos, were unpromising.

The red bus came to the highest point and began to descend to the plateau of Mexico, twenty-five hundred feet below. Fidelio sat tautly, brown hands grasping the wheel, the speedometer climbing as he pressed the gas pedal flat against the floor. Gam Torrigan had learned that Fidelio had no English. In a very short time the speed began to make Gam feel uncomfortable. He glanced over at Fidelio's wide grin. The tires yelped on a corner and Gam had the feeling they had come close to turning over. The speedometer went only to sixty, and the needle was lying firm against the pin.

"Hey, you!" Gam yelled over the roar of the wind. "Take it easy!"

Fidelio gave a great roar of laughter. The wind had disrupted his ducktail and long strands of glossy black hair dangled in front of his face. He laughed again. Gam saw at once that there was very little choice. They were going too fast to risk jumping out. It was too dangerous to risk grabbing the wheel. The little red bus rocketed down the mountain, dancing and squealing on the curves, passing everything on the road. At one point there was a stone wall, a low wall, close to Gam's elbow, and beyond the wall was a dropoff of hundreds of feet. Gam tried to wrench his fascinated gaze away from the drop, but he kept turning to look back at it.

Fidelio kept yelping, and his face was wet with sweat, his eyes wide and shiny, his knuckles squeezed white. From time to time he gave the horn button a quick bang with his fist. He was in a frenzy of ecstasy. Finally they whipped around a corner and ahead of them was a long straightaway with the toll booths at the end of it. Fidelio stamped on the brake. The bus slewed and rocked and yelled. They bounced wildly over the concrete ripples near the booths designed to slow traffic down, and after a final screaming skid, came to a grandiose stop directly opposite the window. Fidelio gave the man the toll ticket. He drove on, very slowly. He pulled over and parked. They both got out. Fidelio went over and sat on the grass, chuckling weakly. Gam leaned against the side of the bus and stared at Fidelio glumly. Gam felt as though his knees would bend either way.

When Fidelio at last stood up, Gam took three steps toward him, doubled his fists, and knocked him down. Fidelio lay flat on his back on the grass. He looked up at Torrigan and suddenly began to giggle again. Torrigan went to the bus and got behind the wheel. No key.

It took a considerable amount of sign language to establish the status. If the señor did not get out from behind the wheel, Fidelio would walk away with the key and never come back. Fidelio would drive. But he would drive slowly. If he did not drive slowly he would get one more big thump in the mouth when they finally stopped, if they were alive.

And they proceeded to the airport.

Chapter Four

AT ELEVEN O'CLOCK on the morning of Friday, the thirtieth day of June, while Barbara Kilmer and John Kemp were sharing the same airliner over the barren lands some four hundred miles north of Mexico City, and while Fidelio was lying on the grass, giggling, and while Felipe Cedro and Rosalinda Gomez were having a deadly quarrel in the kitchen over the split of the morning kickback, and while Miles Drummond was sitting at the table in his apartment, adding up figures, and while Agnes Partridge Keeley was doing an opaque water color of Popocatepetl, managing to make it look like a huge oversweet vanilla cookie, and while Gloria Garvey was drinking beer at her table in front of the Marik, and while Esperanza Clueca sat in the sun behind the staff quarters studying and while Alberto Buceada was asleep in the shade, and while Pepe was abusing a stray puppy, and while Harvey Ardos was buying a straw sombrero in the public market, and while Paul Klauss was lounging grimly on his bed . . . Margarita Esponjar came into Klauss's room without knocking, carrying a pile of folded sleazy towels.

Paul Klauss stared at her for a frozen moment and then came lithely to his feet.

"*Buenos días, señor,*" Margarita said in her joyous and piercing voice. "*Dispénsame, pero quiere dos de estas limpias? Dónde están las sucias?*"

Paul gave her expert inspection. Young, possibly too young. Gay and confident. Something pathetic about the unsuitable, slutty red dress and those too-large shoes. At her throat was a cross on a chain that could mean trouble. And, of course, there was a language barrier. The figure was pert and exquisite. The youthful joy of living made her very enticing. She would respond most quickly to a gay approach. So he smiled broadly and shrugged with a charming helplessness, and with his eyes squinched up, he said, "I'm sorry. I speak no Spanish. I haven't seen you before."

She returned his smile and clomped over to the bureau

42

and put two towels on top of it. She took his two dirty towels from the back of his chair and started toward the door. He moved over and blocked her way and made himself tall and smiled down at her. He pointed at his chest and said, "Paul."

"Ball," she repeated, smilingly, dutifully. He pointed at her chest. "Margarita," she said in her loud, clear, penetrating voice. He winced inwardly. Drop the rating from nine to eight.

"You are very pretty, Margarita," he said softly.

She moistened heavy lips and looked at him with a smile of empty good will, of almost idiotic pleasure.

"Qué quiere?" she said.

"I do not understand," he said, and he was so encouraged by her smile that he reached out a wary hand and clasped her waist, narrow and supple under the sleazy red rayon, warm to his touch.

She looked quite startled for a moment, and then a broader smile of complete comprehension lit up her rather heavy face. She turned and put the towels on the chair and stepped out of her red shoes and, in front of Paul's horrified eyes, made a series of gestures so unmistakably specific, so unbelievably crude, that Paul felt his cheeks grow hot with the first blush since childhood. Despite the range and diversity of his amatory conquests, Paul Klauss was, in his heart of hearts, a prude. During her gestures and gyrations, Margarita had not lost her broad delighted smile of inquiry.

"Sí?" she said. *"Sí? 'Stá bien, horita, Señor Ball."*

And she reached down and grabbed the bottom of the red dress and started to yank it up off over her head. Paul lunged toward her and pawed the dress back down and said, "No! No!"

She tilted her head onto the side and looked at him in confusion, *"No?"*

"No."

"Ah! Más tarde, creo?"

"I don't know what you mean. But no."

"Esta noche? Después de la comida? A las once horas?"

"No."

"Qué falta, Señor Ball? No le gusta amor? Entonces, por qué la mano aquí?" She touched her waist where his hand had rested, her dark brows knotted in bafflement. Her voice was so clear and loud he was certain it could be heard all over the hotel. By gestures he told her to leave. She left

43

with the pile of towels and a look of hurt, red heels clumping.

Paul shut the door and went over and sat on his bed. He felt abused and cheated. Damned little slut. Probably a half-wit. No sense of decency. Didn't mean a damned thing more to her than if I'd asked for two extra towels. Or wanted to shake hands.

After Margarita had delivered the rest of the towels, she wandered thoughtfully out into the back of the hotel looking for Felipe. Because he had worked for so long for Señor Drummond, Felipe, of all of them, would be the one most likely to be able to explain to her the odd behavior of the *Americano*.

She found Felipe Cedro sitting on the stone step in front of the doorway of the room he had appropriated in the staff quarters behind the hotel. He was languidly shining Miles Drummond's black dress shoes. She leaned against the side of the building patiently until he was ready to take notice of her.

"*Qué tal, Margarita?*"

"Felipe, a most curious thing has happened. I took the towels to the room of Señor Ball."

"There is no Señor Ball. I have seen the list. What room?"

"Number eight."

"Ah, that is Señor Ball Klauss. In English Ball is the same as Pablo in Spanish. What of this Señor Klauss?"

"When I started toward the door he stepped in front of me. He told me his name. I told me mine. He looked at me in that certain way. You know that way. And he put his hand here, on the waist. So . . . I knew what it was he wanted. And I was not very busy. And you know I am a loving person. And he is a pretty little man with yellow hair. And I suppose I am curious. In a sense. So with motions I make certain it is what he wants and I can see from his face I am right, so I begin to take off the dress, and he stops me, and his face is red and he says no, no, no. From that moment, whatever I say, he says no, no, no, and he makes signs to me to go and I do so. I do not understand such a man, Felipe."

Felipe mustered his thoughts while he scratched at a daub of black polish on the side of his thumb. "It is not an easy thing to have an understanding of them, *chica*. Their blood is cold. I swear by all the saints that in all the years I have worked for Señor Drummond, I have not known him to be with a woman. Yet he is not one of the others."

44

"Incredible!" Margarita gasped.

"It is the truth of God. Here is what I believe about this Señor Klauss. I believe that he is shy and timid. I believe he is frightened of you. They are like that. He made a little gesture and he believed you would be ashamed, and with them it is a game without meaning. He could not know that you are a woman of warm blood and honesty. Maybe he has never been with a woman. There are thousands of them who have never attempted it, not even as a child."

"Incredible. The poor frightened little man with yellow hair. What can I do to help Señor Ball?"

"They grow more bold at night, but still not bold enough for such a one as you. Let me make a plan." She waited patiently, squatting on her heels, as Felipe thought. He reached into his pocket and took out a key, looked warily around and handed it to her. "Hide it away. Do not tell anyone you have it. And you must give it back to me. It will open every door in the hotel."

"A valuable thing to have."

"What you must do is go to the room of this Señor Klauss and let yourself in. Hide naked in the darkness in his bed. Before you do so, unscrew the bulb a little bit so that the light will not function. Then when he comes to bed he will be unable to help himself."

She laughed softly. "Ah, then he will not say no, no, no. I will make him say yes, yes, yes."

"One more thing you must do, in return for my courtesy in loaning the key to you. Once it is finished, you must say one thing in English. Now say this after me and remember it perfectly."

A few minutes later Margarita was able to say, "Geef me ten dollar."

"Felipe, what does it mean?"

"It means give me one hundred and twenty-five pesos."

Margarita sprang indignantly to her feet and glared down at him, arms akimbo. "Margarita Esponjar is not *puta*, Señor Cedro. Yes, I do things which must be confessed but it is because I have the warm blood and a loving nature. But not for money. No. There are the miserable old dried-up ones that call me *puta* out of jealously because at home with my mother I have the two babies without a father. But I spit on their wrinkles. I am not a *puta*. I will not do such a thing."

Felipe made her sit down and spoke to her calmly. "This is not the same class of thing, Margarita. A *puta* is a

45

woman in a room behind the cantina who is available to all men, serving them for money and without love. You feel a desire for this yellow-headed man. Good. They all have hundreds of thousands of pesos. So it is a thing you will do from your loving nature. But afterwards you will say what you have learned. And you have a beautiful, clear, loud voice, Margarita. Say it softly in the beginning, and if he does not give it to you, say it more loudly until he does. Should he not pay for the favor you are doing him, for warming up, for a little while, that cold blood of the North?"

She looked dubious, but she nodded. "Perhaps you are right. And it is a lot of money, Felipe."

"And half of the money you will bring to me."

"Why?"

"Because I found this job for you, and I told you this way to make money and you will make money for all of the summer, more than you have ever seen before, if you will listen to what I tell you to do. How else could such a one as you earn sixty-two pesos, fifty centavos in such a short time with such pleasure—and pride in knowing that you are doing a good thing for Señor Klauss?"

"It is truth," she said, and nodded and smiled and stood up and walked toward the door of the kitchen. He squinted into the sunlight and watched the swing of sprightly hips under red rayon, watched the red shoes kick up little puffs of dust. When she was gone he began to rub a higher gloss onto the black shoes and began to hum a ranchero tune.

Barbara Kilmer sat in the rear of the aircraft at a starboard window during the flight from New Orleans to Mexico City. She had had a two-hour wait in New Orleans after the flight down from Youngstown. A heavy Mexican businessman sat beside her on the Eastern flight to Mexico City. He breathed in an asthmatic way and spent the entire trip going over sheet after sheet of figures and tabulations, writing very small marginal notes with a very large gold pen.

Barbara was twenty-five. There was a sadness in her face, a residue of grief. She had silver-blond hair, black unplucked brows, dark blue eyes. In the coffee shop in New Orleans, a half hour before flight time, a man had come in and sat on the far side of the horseshoe counter, facing her. He had glanced over at her and thought her a rather pleasant-looking but quite plain girl. As he waited for his coffee to cool he found himself looking at her often. Nice

46

bone structure of brow and cheek. Nice line of jaw. Nose tilted just enough. And when she used her hands he saw they were long and slim and very pretty. After fifteen minutes of discreet appraisal, he found himself wondering how he could have thought her plain. She was actually exceptionally lovely. He decided perhaps his first impression had been wrong because there was so little animation in her face. When he had noticed the engagement and wedding rings he had felt a curiously sharp regret, but he was still curious enough about her to time his departure so that he followed her out. She was tall, and her legs were good, and she moved with grace.

He saw her again just entering the airplane as he started up the stair platform, and wondered if he felt sufficiently venturesome to sit beside her, but by the time he entered the plane, a heavy man had sat beside her and was opening his briefcase.

For the first part of the flight he wondered about her, and wondered why she was going to Mexico. There was a certain aura of lifelessness about her that seemed to him to be unnatural. Perhaps the result of grief or shock. It seemed a reasonable supposition that she might be going to Mexico to acquire a divorce. A very messy divorce situation could turn out all the lights behind a beautiful woman's eyes.

As Barbara Kilmer looked down at the brown burned land of northern Mexico she felt the first weak tremor of anticipation. After having felt nothing for so long, it both surprised her and annoyed her. This stupid Cuernavaca Summer Workshop was her father's idea, her father's big surprise birthday present. She had tried her best to look pleased, but she knew from the expression on his face that she had failed. The least she could do, she thought, was attend the thing. But it could do no good. Nothing in the world could do any good. She would never respond to anything again. Thus she despised herself for feeling any inward flutter of butterfly wings, no matter how feeble. It seemed a monstrous disloyalty to Rob. To his memory.

It had happened last summer. On the third day of July, a hot still day in central Michigan. Rob came home for a quick lunch. He was tense and preoccupied. They were paving, and the segment of big divided highway was behind schedule. Yet, before he left, he had swung her up at the doorway of the farmhouse they had rented for the duration of the road job, kissed her soundly, set her down and, grinning, whacked the seat of her shorts with the flat of his hand. She had waved at the dusty car as he headed back for the job.

Much later she had learned how it had happened that hot afternoon. A wind had come up. Rob Kilmer, the young superintendent, had been standing near the big paver, talking to an engineer and a state inspector. A paper had blown off his clipboard. Rob had lunged to get it before it blew under the paver, reaching under the guard rail to snatch it. And in that instant the operator had dropped the scoop.

By the time they got him to the nearest hospital he was dead.

It had been all nightmare and confusion from then on. Two of Rob's brothers and one of his sisters had flown to Michigan to do what they could, and take the body home to Tulsa for burial. They were big people, as Rob had been. Big and brown and giving that curious impression of being a little larger than life. They were stunned and bitter with grief. It was a big close family, and Rob had been the youngest of them, and, as nearly every one of them found a chance to tell her, the best.

They had sorted his possessions and disposed of his things, giving Barbara the intimate and personal things she would want to have, and arranging to ship her belongings back to her family's house in Youngstown. Then there was the unreality of funeral, where she felt like an outsider. She had known him for only two years, and had been married to him for most of that time. But these people had known him for all of his life, and their grief was honest and obvious. She could feel nothing. Only a numbness and an emptiness.

When it was over she went back to Youngstown and she moved into her old room, the room full of memories of high-school intrigues, college vacations, so that sometimes, awake in the night, she could almost believe that the marriage had never happened, that it had no more reality than some of the other dreams and visions she had had during the mystic years of adolescence.

But in morning light it was real, and it had happened to her. It had happened to Rob, and nothing in her life had prepared her for this shocking knowledge that life could be so utterly cruel, could present you with the insoluble, incurable problem of complete loneliness.

Financially she was not too badly off. There had been compensation and accident insurance and life insurance. She had put a little over three thousand in a savings account, and, right after the first of each month the two checks arrived, one for eighty-two fifty and one for thirty-one dollars. So long as she lived with her parents it was more than enough. And there was the car, Rob's car, that she seldom used. Once, during the third month of her grief, she had taken the car out and driven it at high speed through the clarity of an autumn morning, knowing how simple it would be to wrench the wheel and die in violence as Rob had died, but could not bring herself to make that final fatal gesture.

She was an only child and she knew that it saddened her parents to see her so withdrawn from life. But she could not help resenting the many ways, some subtle, some all too obvious, that they used to try to draw her back into involvement in life.

She knew that so much brooding was not good for her, but she did not want to find a job that would involve her emotions in any way. She wanted something mechanical and tiring, so she could sleep. Her father was a dentist. Much to the consternation of her parents, in spite of their gladness that she was doing something, she found a job in an electronics plant where she sat each day at a long table and stapled printed circuits to amplifier chassis. The other women, a bawdy and talkative crew, spent the first few weeks riding her, calling her Princess and Lady Barbara, doing their work with little fingers crooked. But when she did not respond, they tired of the game and left her alone.

On her twenty-fifth birthday, early in May, she could think only of her twenty-fourth birthday, with Rob. It had come on a Sunday and they had taken a huge picnic lunch and two bottles of chilled champagne into a remote Michigan meadow and he had toasted her as "this elderly party to whom I am married" and later on they had made love in the tall, fragrant spring grasses, and napped there, and stayed to watch a moon come up, and driven slowly home, his arm around her.

But this birthday was stiff and strained, the three of them around the dinner table, the cake brought proudly from the kitchen. Forced laughter at forced jokes. And the presents to unwrap. A cashmere sweater, a scarf, a small bottle of good perfume. And, finally, the envelope from her father containing the round-trip airline ticket, and the letter of acceptance from a Miles Drummond, stating that he was pleased to welcome her to the Cuernavaca Summer Workshop.

In high school Barbara had shown some small talent for

drawing and painting and design. She had been the art editor of the yearbook. In college she had taken a fine arts course, and she had dreamed of being a career woman, possibly in the art department of one of the large advertising agencies, or on one of the big magazines. But Rob had changed all that. A month after they had met she knew that all she wanted in her life was to be married to him, to be totally involved with him, emotionally and physically, and bear his children and raise them and love him all the days of her life.

She knew what her father was trying to do, and she knew it could not work, but she was deeply touched. She left the table and went to her room and wept, and then came back and said that she would go, and did not tell them that it was of no use at all. Her mother had gone into the attic and found her old paintbox and the palette and the brushes.

And now as the plane banked she fastened her seat belt and looked ahead to the southwest and saw the high buildings of the city, and once again she felt that queasy tremor of excitement.

When John Kemp came out of the customs room he heard himself paged by a great bearded brute of a man, a powerful and unkempt type who looked as though he could have ridden to the wars with Genghis Khan.

After what seemed to be to John Kemp an utterly childish exchange of powerful handshakes, the man said resonantly, "I am Gambel Torrigan, Mr. Kemp. Usually called Gam. Mr. Drummond sent me up to meet this plane. I am the head instructor for the session this summer. A Mrs. Kilmer is supposed to be on the same flight. Did you meet her?"

"No, I didn't."

As three more people emerged from the customs room, Torrigan said, "Mrs. Kilmer. Mrs. Kilmer."

John Kemp felt his heart give a little joyous leap as the tall ash-blonde with the black brows and the dark-blue eyes turned and came toward them. It was the girl he had watched at the counter in New Orleans. He moved quickly forward to help her with her two heavy suitcases, one step ahead of the porters who suddenly appeared.

John Kemp felt that Torrigan held onto the girl's hand too long as he made the same speech he had made to John, and he sensed that the girl was not pleased by it. He was glad to know she would be one of the group. He had had numerous misgivings about what he might be getting into. For a time he had been tempted to give it up, write off the five hundred as a bad and impulsive gesture. Torrigan had made a bad impression on him. The rest of the group might be impossible. But at least 'there was one other student to whom he would be able to talk. But he guessed from her manner that it would be unwise to try to move too quickly.

They all got into a red VW bus that, in spite of a fresh coat of paint, looked as though it had seen better times. The driver was a cretinous-looking young man who, when introduced as Fidelio, responded with a remote and surly nod. Torrigan sat in front beside the driver. John Kemp sat behind the driver, with Barbara Kilmer beside him.

When Fidelio started the motor, Torrigan reached over and turned the key off. Fidelio gave him an enraged look which Torrigan ignored. He turned in the seat and said, "Friends, we have a small problem. This so-called driver is a madman. He very nearly finished both of us off on the way down the mountains into Mexico City. He has no English and I have no Spanish."

"I have a little Spanish," John Kemp said.

"Good. The trip back takes an hour and a half. There is another student arriving by air today." He took a piece of paper out of the pocket of his corduroy shirt. "Name is Monica Killdeering from, honest to God, Kilo, Kansas. But she gets in at six-twenty this evening. So I can leave it up to you people as to whether we go back right now or kill time in Mexico City and meet her plane. I will tell you one very certain thing. If I get back across the mountains alive with this party, I am not going to be the one who comes back after Miss Monica."

"Can't you drive us back?" John asked.

"I can't do anything with this Fidelio. He wants to drive. It's obsessional with him."

"If we wait, we'll be going over the mountains at night?"

"Yes."

"Then by all means let's go now. Do you agree, Mrs. Kilmer?"

"It really doesn't matter to me," she said in a subdued voice.

"*Ya vámonos a Cuernavaca, por favor, Fidelio,*" John said, "*Y, por favor, despacio en las montañas.*"

"*Si, señor,*" Fidelio said with a quick glance over his shoulder.

"That certainly sounded fluent, John," Torrigan said.

"It isn't fluent, Mr. Torrigan. It isn't even grammatical. But it's serviceable. I'm an architect. I've worked in Peru and Cuba. I've picked up a little."

There was little opportunity for conversation as Fidelio fought the Mexico City traffic. They were too busy helping him watch the other cars. But once they were through the toll gate and grinding up the mountain with a slowness that obviously depressed Fidelio, Torrigan turned around again and hooked a big hairy arm over the back of the seat and said, "I'd like to give you nice people a briefing on the situation you'll find at the Hutchinson. We'll have thirteen students. The first two arrived yesterday, and there are probably more there by now. This Miles Drummond is a nice enough little old fellow, but this is his first venture in this sort of thing. I was going to spend the summer on my own work, but I got a cry for help from a friend of Drummond's and an old friend of mine, Gloria Garvey, to come down and keep it from turning into a complete farce. The only other instructor is a horrible, tiresome old biddy named Agnes Partridge Keeley. She turns out sickening little post-card scenes by the hundreds. She even paints sunsets, by God. The way it is arranged, all students will spend a half day with Agnes and a half day with me for the first week. And then the group will split. This satisfies me completely. I'll get those students who have the capacity and imagination to look upon painting as emotional and artistic expression rather than trying to make a cow look like a cow. And Miss Agnes will get those dull little people who want to paint burros and Mexicans leaning against a wall."

"Maybe I'm one of those people who want to paint burros," John Kemp said gently.

Torrigan swallowed and said, "I took a chance talking so frankly because I sized both of you up as intelligent, imaginative people. This Keeley woman should be painting pansies on the sides of teapots."

"How is the housing?" John Kemp asked.

Torrigan seemed glad to be off the hook. "Grim," he said. "Utterly grim. And the food is foul so far. But don't you think that the important aspect of the environment is the intellectual one?"

John nodded and began to look out the window at the scenery. Torrigan tried to talk to Barbara Kilmer and, after receiving nothing but monosyllables, gave up and turned around.

"Are you a painter, Mrs. Kilmer?" John asked in a tone low enough to discourage Torrigan from turning around again and rejoining the group.

"Oh, no. I haven't tried to do anything in years. I took a Fine Arts degree at the University of Ohio, but I never did anything with it." And she turned away from him with the same finality that she had used on Torrigan.

John Kemp wondered why she had signed up for the Workshop. And he wondered what he would say to her if and when she should ever inquire why he had done so.

Perhaps, he thought, he could say, It is because I am a very slow-witted, slow-moving man. Had I the ability to make snap decisions about important things, I would not be here.

At thirty-three John Kemp was half owner of the New Orleans architectural firm of Jenningson and Kemp. A very young and childless marriage had ended in divorce, and he had been wary of marrying again. Six years ago, he and Kurt Jenningson had resigned their positions with two large architectural firms and started their own firm. They had expected lean times, but to their mutual surprise and pleasure, it had been a success from the very beginning. They complemented each other perfectly. Lean, balding, high-keyed Kurt Jenningson was very sound at structure, and adept at achieving and maintaining splendid relations with the contractors who bid their jobs. John Kemp, a bigger, slower, milder man, had a genius for design, and a comfortable knack of keeping the customer happy during construction. Both men were personable and likable, and brought in new business on that basis alone, aside from their high order of competence.

Mary Jenningson was the perfect wife for an architect. She was a redhead with almost frightening energies, and great managerial ability. She ran their showplace home on the lake with taste and style and an apparent minimum of effort. She dressed like a model, entertained graciously, was raising two well-mannered children, and yet had time for a lot of civic and charitable activity.

The three of them made a good team. Mary and Kurt often kidded John about it being time for him to marry. And Mary did not seem to tire of trying to make a match. John assumed he would marry. He did not know when, or to whom, but the years were beginning to add up. Kurt's kids were beginning to get tall.

And quite suddenly, quite without intent, three months ago, Mary Jenningson had fallen deeply and helplessly in love with John Kemp. She was a decent and not a devious woman. She tried to conceal what had happened. She knew that it meant pain and heartbreak. She wanted desperately not to be in love with John Kemp. But somehow, over the years, over the hundreds of hours the three of them had spent together, the little accretions had taken place, and had that spring reached their critical mass, and blown up three lives. One rationalization as to how it could have happened was that Mary had married Kurt on the rebound from an earlier romance. She knew that she had never felt toward Kurt as she now felt toward John Kemp. She knew what it could do to her children, to the firm, to Kurt. She told herself that she was a grownup. But at last she told them, told both of them.

Both men were stunned and bewildered. John Kemp knew that he loved Mary Jenningson, but not in that way. He loved her as a friend, as a loyal and amusing and generous woman. He found her physically attractive, but not any more so than a dozen other women of his acquaintance. But his regard for her was not of that order which would enable him to consider a divorce and remarriage.

He said to Kurt, "I swear by everything that means anything to me, that I've never consciously done anything to bring this about. I've kissed her on New Year's Eve, yes, but I haven't . . ."

"I *know* that! I *know* that, God damn it. Neither of you are sneaks. You don't have to . . . tell me that. It's like a sudden sickness with her. I thought everything was fine. I thought she was happy. I know I was happy. And then . . . this."

After John Kemp had made it desolately clear to Mary that he could not and would not marry her, she still persisted in talk of divorce. She said she could not live a lie. She said she could no longer live with Kurt as his wife, and Kurt was not certain he wanted her to try to do so. It was arranged that she would go to San Francisco with the kids and put them in school there and stay there through the summer, and when autumn came, they would discuss it again.

By the time that arrangement had been made, it had become clear to the two men that the partnership could not endure. Even though Kurt held John blameless, there was the constant tension of knowing that John, all unknowingly, had been the factor which had broken his marriage. And there was the blow to his pride of having his woman prefer this other man. John, in turn, could not avoid a constant feeling of guilt.

The partnership agreement was so written that should they desire to split it up, either man could have the option of buying the other person out. There was no subsidiary clause, because at the time the papers were drawn up, they knew they could always reach an agreement amicably. The sale price was to be one-half of current net worth, with the allowance for good will to be determined by an impartial committee.

Kurt and John spent a long time talking it over. Kurt felt that if Mary came back to him, which did not seem likely, he would want to continue with the business, but without John as a partner in the firm. If she did not come back to him, he was not particularly interested in continuing with it, or even staying in the same city. John, for his part, felt that the wise thing to do economically was to buy out Kurt's share. He could get bank credit to do so. Yet he did not feel that he wanted the heavy responsibility.

They decided to wait, and John knew that he wanted time to gain that perspective that would enable him to make the best decision. But it was obvious to both of them that they could no longer work together. So John agreed to go away for the summer. Two weeks later he saw the advertisement for the Cuernavaca Summer Workshop and sent in his fee. He had been a hobby painter for many years. During the last few years he had been sending his work to local shows at the Isaac Delgado Museum and had had them accepted and hung. One was sold out of a show and another won an honorable mention in a juried show.

Now he glanced over at the quiet woman beside him, looking at the line of her cheek and brow as she looked out the window, looking at the slim hands which lay clasped and quiet in her lap.

Yes, Mrs. Kilmer, the reason I am here is because a woman fell in love with me. I rather suppose I should feel flattered, feel a bloat of the male ego. But, Mrs. Kilmer, I remember Mary and the look of shame and bafflement in her eyes, and I feel a little ill. And who fell in love with you, Mrs. Kilmer? Who slipped those rings on that delicate finger? And where is he now, by the way?

The red bus passed the small white sign that proclaimed they were three thousand and forty meters above the level of the sea, and started down the slope.

Two minutes later John Kemp spoke sharply to the

driver. The youth made no sign that he had heard. So John Kemp clasped the brown nape of the neck in his big right hand and bit down hard with thumb and fingers and repeated his instructions in Fidelio's ear.

After the gasp of pain, they proceeded safely and sedately down the road, around the hairpin turns, with Fidelio pouting and looking very close to tears.

Chapter Five

COLONEL THOMAS C. HILDEBRANDT rattled into the front courtyard of the Hutchinson at exactly eleven-thirty on Friday morning in a ten-year-old Dodge station wagon containing all his worldly possessions. He was a tall, spare man in his seventy-second year, erect, with deep folds in his cheeks and fierce bright eyes and a white brush cut. He had a hawk nose, a hearing aid, khaki walking shorts and lean, exceptionally hairy knees. He took out his compass and observed that the hotel was set a few points off a true north-south line. He wished it was perfectly in line.

A fussy little man, a sort of elderly company clerk, checked the colonel's name off on a roster and showed him to his ground-floor room. The colonel inspected it carefully, and then went out to the station wagon and laid out a great pile of suitable articles. Fifteen minutes after they had been carried into his room, Colonel Hildebrandt had made himself entirely comfortable. He had blocked the bed level and spread his pneumatic mattress and sleeping bag there. The water with which he would soon shave was bubbling on his primus stove. His folding camp chair was in place. His easel was assembled.

A fat woman with hair the color of a shell casing came in and shook his hand and said, "I'm Agnes Partridge Keeley, and I'm delighted to welcome you as one of my students, Colonel."

"Thank you," he roared, with a stiff bow.

She looked at the easel and said, "I see you paint."

He stared at her. "By Gad, woman, of course I paint! What in the bloody hell would I be doing here if I didn't?"

"Well . . . what sort of work do you do?"

"Terrain."

"What?"

"Terrain, woman, Configuration of the earth. Cover and concealment. Most essential part of all tactical considerations. I've painted every major battlefield in the United States. Oh, other artists have painted them too, but they get the landscape all crapped up with soldiers in period costumes. I just paint the terrain, the way it is. I look at it from the military eye. Why the hell would anybody send a platoon up that defile? Where would you place your artillery? Where would you mass your cavalry for an assault? By Gad, I've read up on this Zapata that operated around here and by Gad I'm going to paint the places where he operated." He had slowly backed Agnes to the door, roaring at her in that great hollow voice that echoed much more faintly in the deafened corridors of his mind. "You understand me?"

"Y-yes," said Agnes Partridge Keeley, hand at her plump throat, and fled.

The Wahls, Gil and Jeanie, arrived shortly after lunch in a black, three-year-old Chevrolet. They were both twenty-two, they had both just been graduated from Syracuse University. In September they would both join the faculty of a small private school up the Hudson from New York, he to teach English and art, she to teach Spanish and art appreciation. They had been married now for nineteen days and nights. The Cuernavaca Summer Workshop was the result of their having decided to do something "practical" with their wedding checks.

There was something unformed about them. Hand in hand, they looked like one of those posters that extol the benefits of an international youth conference with some religious motif. They were both of medium height, both blond with rather round faces, and they looked rather like brother and sister. As Drummond checked them off the list they stood looking at each other with such a tender intensity, such a humid, blinding sexuality that Miles Drummond felt slightly breathless himself.

After Alberto and Pepe had been roused out of their early-afternoon stupor to carry in the Wahl luggage, Jeanie Wahl directed them in clear Spanish so perfectly grammatical and spoken with such a nasal Indiana accent that neither Pepe nor Alberto understood a word of it. But, because she pointed as she spoke, the task was made possible.

Their room was like the single rooms except for the additional narrow bed, the mismatched extra bureau. Once they were in the room with their luggage, and the door to the corridor closed, Gil said, "Gosh, this isn't much of a room."

But Jeanie was holding him tightly around the waist, her mouth an inch below and an inch away from his, and she looked up into his eyes and breathed, "It's a gorgeous room, darling."

"Uh . . . yeah, it's a fine room, Jeanie."

"Just gorgeous, darling," she whispered.

"Sure, darling," he said, and fastened his mouth on hers and they shuffled sideways, locked together, with perfect instinct, toward the nearest bed.

"Darling, darling, darling, darling, darling, darling, darling," whispered Jeanie Wahl, the happiest girl in the world.

Parker Barnum drove down to Cuernavaca in a new green-and-white Ford station wagon. He drove too fast and he drove too slow, and sometimes he frowned at the road ahead and sometimes he smiled, and in the mirrors of the motel bathrooms he would make faces at himself, a smirk, a sneer, a look of compounded lechery, or an open, honest grin that looked as if it had been tattooed in place.

It was difficult for him to believe there was such a thing as a Parker Barnum. A Barker Parnum. A Barkum Parner. A Parkum Barner. They gave you a designation, like a code. And this little Barnum we will name Parker after his mother's folks, and all his thirty years they will call him Park Barnum which has an odd ring, like a memorial to a circus.

And it believes with all its heart it is good ole Park Barnum, and then all of a sudden it doesn't know what the hell it is.

Slow and clinical voice of Dr. Gottrell offstage: "You must recover your identity, Parker. This has been a great shock to you."

So in the motels he looked at all the faces in the mirrors trying to find the one that really belonged to him. But the basic face seemed to belong to Larchmont-Madison Avenue-Spectorsky-Abercrombie's-split level-CBS-Shor's-Cherio. Man, he thought, in the gray-flannel face. He could march twenty abreast and pass for three long hours down Madison Avenue, fifty thousand dark brush cuts, and fifty thousand pair of glasses with heavy black frames, with 263,779 holes punched in the commuter tickets, and fifty thousand briefcases, politely battered, with initials stamped in gold—lower case. One hundred thousand wary and slightly nervous eyes, myopic.

58

Of course, being logical and so on, you could say there were a hell of a lot of Parker Barnums.

Take the real ones first:

A twelve-year-old in Columbus, who could get the pivot on the double play and was sure as hell going to the Yankees, who broke his arm jumping off the Millers' porch roof, who could do a lot of trick stuff on his bike.

A sixteen-year-old in a phase of calling himself P. Lewis Barnum, who painted, with a minor but obvious talent, pictures of wind-torn trees, who worried about his pimples and felt a sinking, horrible sense of guilt whenever he thought of the theory common among his contemporaries about what caused the pimples—the white, red and purple significations of secret evil.

A twenty-two-year-old Park Barnum in one of the ten thousand dingy studio apartments of Gotham, who worked days doing the backgrounds for those early animated advertising cartoons for that querulous and demanding infant called television, who worked diligently on his own painting at night, who lived with and was married to Suzie Sanders from Indianapolis—that hoyden balletomane with all her leotards and boundings and improvised bar—Barnard graduate—pixie-headed—full of rumpus moods—daytime clerk at Saks (gloves)—bedmate *a crescendo*—casserole cook—cruel mimic. They knew beyond a doubt that with the ardor of her lessons, and his devotion to his painting, their life would change. She would come to the galleries when his shows opened. He would attend the first performances of her ballets. After success, they would think of babies. But after one of those floor-sitting parties and too too much muscatel, the leotards had to be put in a box in the closet, and the thought of a baby had them both equally terrified.

And the thirty-year-old Parker Barnum, who owned an equity of one seventh in the split level in Larchmont, who was art director, at twenty-one thousand five hundred dollars at Sessions and March, one of the smaller agencies, who had fathered Kim and Nancy, the seven-year-old twins, who was held in esteem by employers and clients, who told good jokes at the too-long lunches and went back to afternoons blurred by vodka, who broiled a fair steak in a Larchmont back yard, who had programed his insurance, who was unable to save a dime, who managed to stay over in the city one night a week to enjoy the somewhat theatrical embracings of a nineteen-year-old television actress named Meg Allis.

59

Who didn't know he had lost his wife.

Until she was gone.

It was so damn fast.

He came home and nobody was there. There was a note from Suzie, a number to call. He called her. She told him the address, where to come. It was a twenty-mile drive, a hell of a big house with a circular gravel drive. Suzie had sounded odd over the phone. He had thought it was some kind of a party. But the big house was quiet. A servant let him in. Suzie and a man in a big room where a fire had burned down to embers. Suzie introduced him. Douglas Bench. Park Barnum knew the name. It was connected with shipping and railroads and oil and that sort of thing. A name with a Big Rich clang to it.

Sort of a nice guy. Quiet and broad and forceful. Maybe forty-three, forty-four. Suzie had been crying. He could see that.

"Park, I want out. Now."

"What do you mean, out?"

"I'm going to marry Doug."

"What the hell are you talking about? You come home!"

"This is home. The kids are asleep here."

She started to cry and Bench told her gently to leave the room, that he would handle it. She left. Park tried to raise hell with Bench, but his voice sounded squeaky. Bench smiled indulgently. Park went over with a vague intention of hitting him, but Bench handed him a Scotch-and-soda. And gave him the word. He was a widower. He loved Suzie and he loved the kids. She loved him. They had met in an innocent way. There had been nothing intimate between them. Suzie had been unhappy, knowing that her husband was having an affair. So he had gotten some people to get the facts for her. It can all be done quietly. You will be able to visit your children by arrangement, of course. Naturally she will want and need nothing, no alimony, no settlement. Tomorrow she can move what she wants out of the house. Certainly a young man like you can be more relaxed without the responsibility of a family. You can be assured the children will have the best of everything.

And he found himself driving home alone. It was all so damn fast. Douglas Bench arranged to have Suzie, the kids and a personal maid fly to the Virgin Islands. In six weeks she was divorced. A week after her return, she was Mrs. Douglas Bench. By then Parker Barnum had sold the house and moved into town, into a small apartment. As soon as the

60

affair with Meg was no longer clandestine, he was able to see her for what she was, a shallow and mannered nympho, with as much sense of humor as a bush rabbit.

It had happened too damn fast.

He would be working hard, and then he would stop working and for a few minutes everything would be back in place —Suzie and the kids at home, and a train to take, and she would bring his drink to the bathroom while he was showering and . . . Somebody else lived in the house and she was Mrs. Douglas Bench, and to see your own kids you had to make an appointment and say please.

So he told himself Suzie had never loved him. She'd been looking for the Big Dollar. But he knew that wasn't true. She had loved him. And he hadn't measured up to it. And he had the sick suspicion that Bench did, that he was a kind and good man. A better man. May the best man win. He did.

On a tender April morning he saw himself. He had come up out of the subway and when he reached the sidewalk level he saw a man who had just fallen. It was one of the fifty thousand Parker Barnums. He lay prone, his cheek against the sidewalk, glasses shattered, narrow-brimmed hat a foot and a half from the brush-cut head. He lay helpless in his gray flannel suit, his face the color of a wet phone book, his right hand still clutching the leather handle of the dispatch case, the morning people skirting him deftly, each giving one backward glance. A cop was approaching with authoritative stride. Heart, Parker thought, and went on his way. But he had the strange feeling that even as he walked on toward the office, he was also back there on the sidewalk. He felt that if he walked lightly it would be all right, but if he stamped his foot hard he could punch it right down through the dirty cement of the New York sidewalk, and the things you would see down there would be so horrible you wouldn't dare squat and peer down through the hole you had made.

At eleven that morning he was looking over some layouts for an outdoor advertising series. He took his wood-clinched Ebony pencil, jet-black, extra-smooth, and with deftness and great calm, began to turn each layout into an obscenity, rubbing in the shadowing with his thumb.

When Herbie March came to see him in the rest home, he was damn decent about it. Herbie had gotten the pitch from Dr. Gottrell. He came out onto the sun porch and pulled a chair over and said, "Park, I've talked it over with

John Sessions, and frankly, this is what we want to do, and we hope you'll think it's fair. Rather than go into the market and bid for a new AD, we'll move Becky up into your slot with the understanding that it's temporary. We'll farm out anything that's over her head. Dr. Gottrell says he'd feel better if you plan to take a full six months. So, doing some thinking overheadwise, we'll cut you to a grand a month, Park, and when you come back you come back on the old figure, naturally. And John Sessions and I certainly want you back. We need you, boy."

"It's . . . more than fair, Herbie. Honest to God, I feel all choked up."

Herbie clasped his shoulder and shook him gently. "It's the least we can do for a friend and a nice guy. Let us know if there's anything you need. Anything at all."

It was Dr. Gottrell who suggested a complete change of scene, after many hours on the couch, and Park who had run across the ad for the Cuernavaca Summer Workshop.

He had been going to fly down, but he became restless and traded the car for a new Ford wagon and set out, giving himself a generous ten days to make the drive.

But once he was south of Jersey he had the feeling that he had lost track of who he was. There didn't seem to be any connection between this joker in the wagon and all the other Parker Barnums. The real Parker Barnums. This joker seemed more involved with all the imaginary ones; the one who did make the Yankees, and the one who could put up such a hell of a sword fight on the stone steps of the castle leading to the private quarters of the princess, and the one who could make himself invisible at will, and the one who could dance like Astaire, and the one who was a jet pilot, and the one who was a spy.

So he looked at this one in the motel mirrors, and when he drove through the small towns there would always be a girl who, from the back, looked like Suzie. The Italian hairdo. And . . . not chunky . . . but . . . well . . . solid.

He arrived at the Hutchinson at one-thirty on Friday afternoon. It was a sad-looking operation. There were some sad-ball people wandering around. If it turned out to be as bad as it looked at this stage, there was nothing to keep him here. He could kiss the five hundred goodbye and drive on down to Acapulco. After he had unpacked in the drab room, he changed and went out to see what was going on.

Two women had just arrived in a pink-and-blue Buick hardtop convertible, with Ohio plates. Both were on the shady side of sixty and both wore cotton print dresses, and both wore straw sun hats shaped exactly like baseball caps. The driver, the larger of the two, bore a striking facial resemblance to Casey Stengel, and when she walked toward the hotel doorway, it was ole Case again, trudging out to the mound. Her companion was a smaller woman, timid-looking, and her hat was too big for her. She trotted along after the big one.

About twenty minutes after they arrived, Park Barnum was in the central patio talking to a nice guy, a New Orleans architect named John Kemp, when the two women who had arrived in the Buick came bearing down on them, the big one in the lead. They had changed to fresh cotton print dresses, but they still wore the hats.

The big one stuck her hand out and said, "I'm Mrs. Mc-Caffrey, Hildabeth McCaffrey from Elmira, Ohio. And this here is my good friend, Mrs. Winkler, Dotsy Winkler, from the same place."

"John Kemp."

"Parker Barnum."

"Pleased to know you," she said. Dotsy bobbed her shy head in smiling agreement. "Dotsy thinks this was a real nutty thing for us to do, coming down here like this, but like I told her, we could sit up there in Elmira all summer and rot and fan ourselves and drink a couple of barrels of iced tea, and who would care. I've been widowed four years now. Mr. McCaffrey was in the building supply business. I try to take a different kind of vacation every summer. This is new to Dotsy, though. She's only been widowed a year and a half. Her Bert had three hardware stores in the county and a feed mill. We got enough to do with, and the children are grown and all, so I found the ad and told her this was what we were going to do. She said it was crazy and I said why and she said because we couldn't paint a lick and I said how did we know if we didn't try. She shoulda seen me get talked into those hula lessons out to Hawaii last summer. Seems like the older I get the more foolish I get. But, like I say, if it's a second childhood, you might as well just settle down and enjoy it. To tell the truth, I didn't get half so much enjoyment out of the first one. Sooner or later Dotsy will get in the spirit of the thing." She turned and beamed proudly at Dotsy, who bobbed her head and blushed.

"Now," said Mrs. McCaffrey, "we're taking a little tour of this place." She scowled. "It certainly is a ratty old place, isn't it? We were talking to a man named Torrigan. He

63

seems to be one of the teachers. I don't think he's all right in the head. Let me see now, you're John Kemp and you're Parker Barnum. There's Barnums over in Buffalo, New York. Distant kin of my husband. You from around there? No? Well, I guess it's a common enough name. From New York, you say. Well, I suppose we'll see you boys in school." She winked and chuckled and strode on, Dotsy trotting along behind her.

"Hmm. Casey Stengel?" John Kemp said.

"Definitely. But how about the other one?"

"Snow White on Social Security."

"I'll buy that."

"But nice," John Kemp said. "Definitely nice."

"Hildabeth and Dotsy."

"Foregoing a summer of iced tea on the screened porch in Elmira. And providing for themselves, you may be sure, a full, round winter of conversation and anecdote."

"They won't be alone," Parker said. "Want to ride in with me and look the town over?"

"Thanks, yes. I didn't drive down. I'm beginning to think it would have been smart."

When they got back a little after four, Mr. Miles Drummond came trotting out as they got out of the car and said, "I'm terribly sorry to impose on you, Mr. Barnum. This is the car you came down in, isn't it? Well, here is what has happened. After talking to Mr. Torrigan, I don't dare send my driver over the mountains to return after dark, and Mr. Torrigan refuses to ride with him again, and I'd ask Miss Agnes Partridge Keeley to do this, but she's having an . . . uh . . . a digestive upset, and I thought you might be willing to run up to Mexico City to the airport and meet a Miss Monica Killdeering. She'll be in on a six-twenty flight. There are ten students here now. There's just Miss Killdeering, and the two young ladies who are motoring down from Texas. I hesitate to impose on you, Mr. Barnum, but . . ."

"But I don't know where to find the airport."

"I could go along and be a guide," John Kemp said. "Between us we ought to be able to find it."

"Would you really!" Drummond said. "That would be so good of you. I'm at my wits' end trying to . . . keep everything running smoothly." He pulled bills out of his pocket and handed one to Park Barnum. "This will pay the toll both ways on the *autopisto*. Thank you so very, very much, both of you. It's a great help, indeed." He scurried off.

John Kemp and Park Barnum got back into the car. "Great little organizer," John said.

"Reminds me of something I read in a book one time: 'He had all the administrative ability of a kitten with diarrhea.'"

"Wonder what kind of a name Killdeering is?"

"Indian?"

"I am under the impression there are damn few Indians named Monica."

Park said, "I give odds she will be creepy. But there is one item present, I think. I glimpsed it from afar. A sort of toothsome blond item. Who is she?"

John Kemp suddenly decided that maybe he wouldn't like Parker Barnum as well as he thought he would. "She's a Mrs. Kilmer. Barbara Kilmer. Very reticent sort. We were on the same flight from New Orleans down, but I didn't know she'd be a classmate until they met us at the airport."

"Too bad. Where did she come from?"

"Youngstown, Ohio."

"Do you know where this pseudo-Indian is from?"

"I heard, but I do not believe, that she comes from Kilo, Kansas."

The flight was late. Monica Killdeering, in a starboard seat next to the window, saw, beyond the wing, the golden tones of sunset. She was filled with such an enormous, tremulous sense of anticipation she thought she would burst. Her moist breath fogged the window and she rubbed it away with the sleeve of her suit coat.

Yes, this would be the summer, she thought. And she tried not to remember the other summers when she had felt precisely this same excitement that she never knew precisely what she meant by *this*.

Miss Monica Killdeering was twenty-nine years old. She had a graduate degree in Physical Education. She had been born on a prosperous Kansas farm, orphaned in a train-auto collision when she was seven, raised in Cottonwood Falls by a maiden aunt who had died during Monica's last year of school. Upon graduation she obtained a position as gym teacher and dancing teacher at the George D. Insley High School in Kilo, Kansas. During the six full years she had taught at the high school she had lived in a rented room in a small house on the edge of town owned by Miss Hipper, who had taught Home Ec at the high school for twenty-seven years.

The gods had endowed Miss Monica with one body in ten

million. At twenty-nine she was five foot seven inches tall and weighed one hundred and twenty-eight pounds. Her measurements were a barely credible 38-24-35. The texture of her body was flawless, creamy, incredibly smooth, without sag or wrinkle or unaesthetic bulge. It was a goddess body, pure as marble from the high proud globe of breast to arched and dainty instep. Her digestive system could have handled scrap iron without pause or pang. The interlocking network of glands, secretions, hormones, worked in a perfect and rhythmic harmony. Underneath the rounded softnesses of arm and thigh there were muscles of such splendid elasticity kept in such perfect tone that she could work out with the senior girls' basketball team until all the children were exhausted—but Miss Monica would experience only a slightly accelerated heartbeat, a minor increase in the rate of respiration, and a little moisture on her brow and upper lip. She was physically uncommonly strong, stronger than most men, and this knowledge shamed her. She thought it unladylike.

The body moved in seeming awareness of its own perfections, in grace and provocativeness of which Miss Monica was largely unaware. Her hair was glorious, inky-black with bluish highlights, glossy as the pelt of a healthy animal.

But having progressed this far toward perfection, the gods, in sudden irony, had given Miss Monica the startling and unmistakable face of a sheep. Slope of brow, wide and fleshy nose, long and convex upper lip, square heavy teeth of the ruminant, brown nervous eyes—all were in deadly pattern.

It would be unfair and inaccurate to say that Monica Killdeering's personality and pattern of existence were in any way molded by hereditary factors. Her personality and her habits were the result of the horrid conflict between face and body.

She was an intense, explosive, almost hysterical bore. It was well known in Kilo that if you were putting on a carnival or a drive or a church affair, you should get Monica working on it. Her energies were inexhaustible. But if you wanted to turn a dinner party into pure horror, just invite Monica. Whoever she botton-holed would end up in a curious condition—nerves frayed from the shrill and nervous tumult of her intensity, lapels damp from the fine explosive spray of her conversation, and quite ready to scream with such an excess of ennui that, afterward, it was difficult to understand just what she had done to you. Analysis would disclose that she had bored you by talking about you, a feat almost unparalleled in its rarity.

Childhood had been the best time for Monica. She had been skinny and ugly but in great demand because she could hit the long ball, climb the highest tree, and catch any kid her age in the county.

Adolescence had been the black time. The body bloomed, warm and ripe, full of an independent arrogance, aware of its own obvious destiny. But for a time Monica was too shy to speak to anyone. She acquired hopeless, helpless, bitter crushes, and wept them into her pillow. And there were the constant cruelties. The phrase overheard, or meant to be heard. And then to lie in the tumid night, and sense, but not understand, all the strengths of the body's yearnings, and touch then the flowering breasts and feel such an aching emptiness that she wanted to die.

But the adjustments came in time. The painful shyness was obscured by a highly nervous imitation of an outgoing personality. And it was inevitable that she would choose a career that would chronically exhaust the unfecundated body. In her adjustment she taught herself to believe that a career involving the young was a more valid and satisfying destiny than the obvious triviality of home, husband and children. She became militant about the rights of women. And, with more difficulty, she taught herself to believe that the physical act of love with a man would be degrading and repulsive, a nastiness that she was highly fortunate not to have to endure. She believed all rapists should be gelded.

As her expenses were small—she ate with Mrs. Hipper and spent little on clothing and practically nothing on cosmetics —and her salary was adequate, she saved her money during her first year of teaching and, that first summer, attended a Festival of the Dance in Biddleton, New Hampshire. She remembered the joyous sense of anticipation that grew stronger and stronger throughout the last weeks of the high school term. Surely, in Biddleton, she would meet people far more interesting and receptive and cultured than could exist in Kilo, Kansas. They would be able to appreciate Monica Killdeering. It would be a warm and wonderful and stimulating three weeks.

But after the first five days of the Festival, she felt that she had made a mistake. All the others seemed to be in cabins for two and three and four, and somehow she had been stuck in a shed in the middle of an apple orchard. Close little groups had formed, and she did not belong to one of them. She attended the lectures and the demonstrations and the recitals and the group participation experiments with dedication and energy, but she had the feeling that somewhere there was some other Festival, and she had attended the wrong one.

One night, toward the end of the second week, she had been awakened at about two in the morning in her orchard shed by hoarse cries outside. She sat up and heard a man nearby, calling, "Ruthie! Ruthie! Where the hell'd ya go, Ruthie?"

She felt indignation rather than fear and put on her robe and went out onto the shallow porch into the cool white moonlight.

"What do you want?" she demanded, and saw a man come wavering toward the porch, holding a bottle by the neck. She recognized him as a man from New York, one of the staff of the Festival, a big round-faced man with a small neat mustache.

"Wha'd'ya do with Ruthie?" he demanded.

"I haven't seen Ruthie, whoever she is. You better go home, Mr. Rudnik."

He planted his feet, uptilted the bottle, lost his balance and caught it again, and said, "Hah!" and wiped his mouth on the back of his hand. A disgusting spectacle, Monica thought. He came closer to her and said, "Ruthie run out on me."

"That's too bad. You better go home."

He lost his balance again and swayed toward her and clasped her in an effort to save himself. She half turned and caught his weight easily but she was off balance and they both sat down heavily, side by side, on the edge of the porch.

"Li'l drink?" he said. "Din't spill a drop."

"No, thank you," she said and started to get up. He caught her by the waist immediately and kept his arm around her.

"You stay right here, honey," he said.

Monica was outraged. She had no intention of being pawed by a drunk. It was degrading. She tried to pull away from him. He set the bottle aside and got both arms around her, one hand sliding further around her so as to be able to reach her breast.

Monica wanted absolutely no part of such a messy situation. But, quite suddenly, she could no longer resist. It was as though she had to stand aside, in a revolting and helpless dream, stricken by horror as she had to watch herself get up and help Mr. Rudnik up and then lead him into the black of the shed toward her narrow bed.

The unused body had suddenly taken over. It had been

like a retired fire-wagon horse cropping grass in a pasture and suddenly hearing the sound of the siren down in the village. It lifted its head and its eyes went wide and its ears went flat. And quite suddenly it was off in a cumbersome, rocking gallop, panting, whinnying and blowing, pounding toward the pasture gate and the sound of the siren, aware of its essential function, tousled mane flapping in the wind.

When she woke up in first daylight, Mr. Rudnik was putting on his shoes. She looked at him in fear and yearning and a horrid shyness. His face was gray. He looked at her and looked away. Neither of them said a word. He went out and she heard him walking heavily away.

She was certain she was pregnant. She could not stand the thought of looking at him again, of looking at anyone who could know how she had been, like a crazy person. She had no way of knowing that Rudnik had suffered a complete blackout, with no awareness of anything that had happened from about ten the previous night until he had awakened at six so entangled with a woman on a narrow bed that he had to extricate himself gingerly to get far enough away from her to see who it was. Nor could she have imagined the appalled horror with which he had stared at the sleeping countenance of the young woman he had privately termed the Venus Sheep.

Monica packed and left that day, in emotional confusion and a sentimental agony. She existed in a special nightmare until she learned that she was not with child. Only then could she permit her memory to range timidly back to the episode with Rudnik, and feel a delicious disgust at the unexpected abandon of the traitorous body. It was said a virgin should expect, should be prepared to endure, intense pain. But the eager, reveling body had felt no pain. She could no longer entertain the conviction that such union was entirely degrading and disgusting. It was degrading and disgusting, she thought, to the sensitivities of a lady, but now a new factor had to be admitted—and guarded against in the future. She had learned there was a terrible weakness of the body, a veritably bestial need, which should never be given the opportunity of displaying itself again.

She rigidly suppressed the sleazy and shameful little twinge of pride she felt in the body's co-operative competence, and resolved that from then on she would spend her summers in Kilo where she belonged, and where there would be no opportunity for evil temptation.

But, by April of the following year, she had signed up for The Horse Mesa Writers' Conference in Atcheson, Nevada, telling herself that Rudnik was an unfortunate episode in the remote past of Monica Killdeering.

There, in the penultimate week of the conference, she was enthusiastically and repeatedly undone by a squatty, hairy, fiftyish man from San Diego named Vincent Hurlberth who operated a florist shop and composed unsalable science fiction on the side. Hurlberth, unlike Rudnik, was not in his cups. He was merely an eminently practical and hot-blooded little man who, having ascertained the unavailability of other possible targets, had decided to ignore the face and the personality as being factors having no bearing on his immediate needs, and found no cause to regret his decision.

So Monica Killdeering had crept back to Kilo, feeling soiled and betrayed and degraded. She had gone with such high anticipation that *this* would be the time. Certainly, from now on, a twice-burned child would shun the fire.

But the next summer was the Rocksport Music Festival. Where nothing happened. And she told herself she should feel proud and staunch that nothing happened. But as she had been given no opportunity to test the strength of the will power she had determined in advance to exert, it reminded her of those childhood days when she had swung mightily at a fat pitch . . . and missed. She had wanted a chance to prove her own ability to say *no*, to exert the dominance of the mind over the body's insidious frailty, to prove that it had not really been the real Monica Killdeering who, at the first blunt, quizzical and knowing glance from Vincent Hurlberth's small blue eyes, would go all swarmy and humid and buttery. That couldn't be the real Monica.

Came next the Caribbean Camera Cruise, a rather squalid venture that took off from Miami in an elderly ship and made a twenty-day circuit of Caribbean ports of call, during which circuit she spent a humiliating number of days locked in her cabin with a lean, balding, very brown and thoroughly tattooed eccentric named Vasquez Mooney. She saw him in one of two conditions, either naked, or clothed and festooned with a dangle and jangle and clatter of light meters, lens cases, cameras, reflectors and flash bulbs.

During the winter that followed, while enduring the double curse of a Kansas winter with gym classes, she came to realize that she was the victim of a dreadful disease, an unwilling victim of her own unselective lust. Once the epidemic form of the disease was in progress, the mind and

70

spirit of Monica Killdeering could do nought but stand aside, wringing its hands and moaning, like an embarrassed, idealistic and sorely troubled lady-in-waiting who is forced to watch her beloved queen in orgy and debauch. She had to admit to herself that she rationalized the pre-cruise trip to Miami shops where the body purchased for itself shipboard clothing designed to prevent a recurrence of the barrenness of Rocksport. And, in cruel honesty, she could not permit herself to forget that she had enticed Vasquez Mooney to her cabin to repair her camera on the second day out.

Yet the vagrant body had to be punished, and so she spent the following summer in Kilo, doing good works. And, in February, found the advertisement for the Cuernavaca Summer Workshop. And, after signing up, began to feel that first tingle of hope that *this* would be the time. Hope and anticipation had reached a crescendo as the big aircraft turned into the landing pattern over Mexico City.

She did not know what she meant by *this*. This time, this place, this summer. If she had been forced to put it into words, she might have said that somewhere, somehow, she could find a situation which would combine the bright bursting delights of the body with a lack of consciousness of evil and shame. She wanted to be involved and used without being soiled and afraid and alone. She wanted a joy that would involve both the body and the soul, combining them in good purpose.

The lights were on when she came out of customs. She heard her name called. She turned and saw two men, both of them so attractive that, as she hurried toward them, her nervousness was like a recurrent spasm. They introduced themselves. She shook their hands with fevered strength. She made sharp jolting sounds of delight and showed a wide expanse of the square, powerful teeth and adored both of them with her brown and helpless eyes.

Chapter Six

THE GIRLS CAME OVER the mountain just before dusk in the cream-colored convertible Mercedes SL 190 that Mary Jane Elmore's father had given her for her twentieth birthday two months before. Bitsy Babcock sat beside her with a half bottle of José Cuervo tequila pinched safely between her

71

bare brown thighs. The girls came whizzing down the mountain and, in voices made husky by cigarettes and raw liquor and a conscious effort to pitch their voices lower, they sang "Jailhouse Rock."

They were the girls of Texas, Mary Jane—twenty, Bitsy—nineteen, leggy and brown and arrogant and derisive of everything in the world including themselves. They wore very short shorts and very narrow halters and, at stops during the trip down, had come dangerously close to causing civil riot and insurrection.

They were the girls from Fort Worth, and from the moment they had learned to talk they had begun to ask for things, and they had gotten everything they had asked for, and it had been paid for out of the almost limitless funds that came from fat herds and deep wells. They were slim and they were beautifully constructed, and they had sun wrinkles and laugh wrinkles at the corners of their eyes. And they had been asked to leave two schools simultaneously, not for academic reasons. Mary Jane was the blond one, and slightly taller one, her hair cut like a boy's—a style which was not at all likely to lead to any confusion. Bitsy was just a little more solidly built, but equally slim of waist and long and sleek of leg—a coppery, curly redhead, the tight cropped curls like old coins in the late sun as they came down the mountain.

At twenty, Mary Jane Elmore had seen and done and knew well a great many things that, in a more orderly world, she would have neither seen nor done nor known. Daddy was a big man. He had the ranch and the duplex in the apartment hotel in town, and he had lawyers and tax accountants and a slew of corporations—little ones that sort of traded stuff back and forth, and he had his cars and his plane and his pilot, and when he wasn't busy with business, or with the hunting crowd or the poker crowd, he was terribly busy with Prissy, who was wife three, a pretty little horse bum who wouldn't hardly ever leave the ranch unless it was to go to a horse show with all that picnic off the tailgate stuff, and everybody half blind before it was over. Mommy had gone off on the religion bit, and she was in some kind of retreat in California, and those long letters came from her, all full of God and Suffering and Inner Vision. There was a wife in the middle between Mommy and Prissy, and her name was Caroline, and she was sure a drain on Daddy because in addition to the alimony thing he was all the time supporting her in one of those happy houses for the bottle babies. Soon as they let her out, pow, she was back in. Mary Jane hadn't felt so alone in the whole mess while Brud was still around, but Brud had been queer on the road rally bit, and two years ago he had racked up the Porsche so bad you couldn't even tell what it had been, and like they always said, he didn't feel a thing. Mary Jane had been just stoned for months and months, crying at nothing and everything because Brud had been a really darling guy and when you thought about it it seemed like such a waste.

There wasn't quite as much money behind Bitsy Babcock, almost twenty, but you'd never know it from the way ole Bits flang it around. Bitsy had been born in a tarpaper shack, first child of Pops and Maggie Babcock. Pops was one of the last of the shoestring wildcatters, a dry-hole specialist, a con man at getting his backing. When Bitsy was three Pops had spudded in right over the Chisholm dome, and for once his leases were in shape. When Bitsy was nine, and the little kids were two and three, Pops had a perfectly timed coronary that hit him while he was standing in the men's bar at the Waldorf in his big rich hat and his seven-stitch boots with a beaker of Jack Daniels in his big hard hand, while Maggie was on a looting expedition up and down Fifth Avenue. Pops was dead before he hit the floor. Had it happened six months earlier, the estate would have been all tangled up, and had it happened six months later, he would have been all committed on the Cuban deal. It happened when he was liquid, between deals, and it happened just thirty-two days after he'd made a will, made it because Doc Schmidt had scared him a little.

It set up a trust for Maggie and one for each of the kids, and it minimized the tax bite, and it made damn well certain that nobody was ever going back to a tarpaper shack. Maggie was a big-boned, vital, handsome, redheaded, forthright woman, and you would have thought she could endure anything without falling off at the curves. But losing Pops cut the living heart out of her. Maggie spent a couple of months in black depression, then stuck the kids in private schools and took off for postwar Europe. When she came back she had gaunted herself by dieting off twenty pounds. She wore high-fashion clothes and a weird hairdo. She stuck French and Italian words here and there in her conversation. She was on a nickname basis with minor members of defunct royal houses. And she brought back a husband, a big, sleepy, twenty-five-year-old Swede named Lars, who had an accent, perfect manners, solid-gold accessories and a bottle-a-day habit. Maggie opened up the house, got the kids back, staffed the house, and embarked on a lot of entertaining.

Lars lasted until Bitsy was twelve, and then the kids were plunked back into private schools until Maggie was ready to try again, this time with a hell of a big man named Pete Kitts she met in San Francisco. He was bigger than Lars. He was even bigger than Pops had been. Among other things he had been a wrestler, pro football player, carnival strong man, sports reporter, and bodyguard to a gangster.

He had lasted until Bitsy was nearly sixteen. The current one was Captain Walker-Smith, a man of such insignificant stature that Maggie had given up high heels entirely, and, when she walked beside him, tried to keep her knees slightly and inconspicuously bent. Captain Walker-Smith, one-time hero of the RAF, had a cold gray eye, an arrogant mustache and a manner of speech so incomprehensible that one was led to wonder whether perhaps the mustache grew on the inside as well as the outside. Maggie had dominated Lars and Pete. And was now dominated by the Captain, as thoroughly as she had been by Pops. So Bitsy had a hunch this one might last.

These were the girls from Fort Worth, the leggedy young ones, with the hoarse voices and the wise and weary young eyes. They had learned precisely how to handle their own family situations, to appear before their elders with the right combination of sauciness and deference. They had learned that only casual conversations are possible. They had learned how to deal with a drunken adult of either sex, when to quietly disappear as a family scene began to shape up. When any organism is subjected to strain over a period of time, it forms adjustments. Mere survival is the primary motive. When there is no secondary drive, or conviction or involvement, the organism becomes a specialist in survival.

Both girls knew how to stay in school without work or strain, how to handle liquor, how to extract maximum pleasure with minimum risk. Each felt that one day she would be married, but it was a far-off thing. Neither girl considered herself amoral or immoral. They had agreed that they were not promiscuous. Mary Jane had gone steady four times, and Bitsy three. Each association on the going-steady basis had been an intense physical affair, with assignations occurring in automobiles, motels, horse barns, parents' houses and the homes and apartments of friends. That was not promiscuous.

74

It was all right if you were going steady. Everybody knew that. Only one time had a scary thing happened, and that was when Mary Jane had become pregnant at sixteen. She was in school in the East at the time and, after she got over her initial panic, she found out where she could get something done about it. She could have gotten the money from her very own checking account, but it was the code that Chuck should pay for it, and when he had scraped the money together he drove her to Philadelphia and it was done, and now sometimes she would think of how old the kid would be and how he might look and it would make her feel grim and odd, and like crying.

But the lesson was valuable, because after that you made dang well sure it wouldn't happen again, and maybe the lesson saved Bits from having the same trouble.

Bitsy had been going steady with a boy for nearly a year, and it had broken up in April. Mary Jane's affair, of slightly longer duration, had broken up at about the same time, and so they had decided that they would spend the summer together and cheer each other up. They talked about taking a bicycle trip in Europe, or maybe getting waitress jobs at a resort just for kicks. Then they heard about the ball you could have at the summer session for American students at the University of Mexico. There was no trouble getting permission, but then they found out they had registered too late. It was a shame, because Scooter, who'd gone last summer, said the place was full of darling boys. Bitsy found the ad for the Cuernavaca Summer Workshop, and, through verbal sleight of hand, they had given their parents the impression that this was a part of the University program.

So the girls came down the mountain. Mary Jane slowed the car and reached again for the tequila bottle. Bitsy leaned over and steadied the wheel as Mary Jane unscrewed the cap and took two dainty swallows. They had come down through Mexico in a pleasant haze of tequila. There were a thousand things to talk about and laugh about, and it was a ball. It was going to be one of those summers.

To the obvious and sullen annoyance of the staff, Miles Drummond ordered that dinner should be delayed until Mr. Kemp and Mr. Barnum returned from Mexico City with Miss Killdeering. Seven tables for four had been pushed together in one corner of the huge and gloomy dining room so as to provide a makeshift banquet table for the thirteen students, the two faculty members, and the director.

Miles trotted out to the dining room many times after it

75

was dark to look at the table and worry about the seating. Between each narrow tall window and the next, one of the big, dim, naked bulbs stood upright in a wall fixture, each with a small brown parchment clip-on shade. The light filled the room with eerie shadows and left the high ceiling in darkness. He got a chair and removed the shades and then stepped back to look it all over. It was worse without the shades. He replaced them. The place settings distressed him. He liked things to be very nice. He hoped that the light was so dim that they would not notice the dozen breeds and brands of glasses, silver and china, or the dim stains and mends and worn spots in the tablecloths. He took the place cards out of his shirt pocket and, with much thought, distributed them around the table. And then he went out into the kitchen. The gloom there was much like the dining-room lighting, but there was also a stifling heat that came from the big wood range. Rosalinda and Felipe assured him that the food would have been of the most excellent quality had it been served on time. But now, of course, with each passing moment, it became less palatable. If one is to cook to a schedule, then, señor, it is obviously necessary to . . .

Miles fled from the kitchen and went to the lobby where the battered furniture had been pushed around to form two distinct groups. Agnes Partridge Keeley was holding court with the two elderly widows, Hildabeth McCaffrey and Dotsy Winkler, and Colonel Hildebrandt in attendance. Every few minutes the commingled chatter of feminine voices would be overridden and silenced by a great hollow braying sentence from the Colonel. After an awed pause the female voices would start again, tentatively at first, and then rising to full chorus.

In the opposite corner Gambel Torrigan consorted with Paul Klauss, Harvey Ardos, and the two young girls from Texas. Miles was pleased to see that the cool of the night had driven the two young girls into slacks and sweaters. They had arrived in an astonishing state of undress and, if he was not entirely mistaken, a little bit drunk. And they were still drinking. Torrigan and the girls and Harvey Ardos. There were two bottles and a bowl of ice on the wicker table. Miles noted that they all seemed to be talking at once. Torrigan was talking to the blond girl with the haircut like a boy. Elmore. Mary Jane Elmore. Paul Klauss was not drinking and he was talking to the other girl from Texas. What was her name? Babcock. Elizabeth Babcock. Bitsy, she said she was called. They ignored Harvey Ardos who seemed to be talking to all of them in a very excited way. At least Mr. Klauss was not drinking. Miles wished Gloria Garvey was there to help him handle this first meeting of the entire group.

Who was missing? He counted heads. Mrs. Barbara Kilmer, the nice, quiet, pretty blond woman. And the young couple. The Wahls. He realized he had not seen the Wahls since they arrived. He hoped they weren't under the weather. And Kemp, Barnum and Killdeering made thirteen. Just as he was wondering if he should start without them, he heard a car drive in.

As Alberto and Pepe carried Monica Killdeering's luggage toward the lighted doorway of the hotel, John Kemp and Parker Barnum paused beside the station wagon, and John Kemp gave Park a cigarette. They felt very close. They felt close in the same way as do two people who have ducked out the side door of a community theater after the house lights go down for the second act of some very bad amateur theatricals.

Park exhaled a plume of smoke and said with tired fervor, "Jesus H. Jumping Christ!"

"How many words a minute, Park? All the way back. Captive audience. She sat right between us. I feel as if I had been beaten to death with a tape recorder."

"But did you get a good look at how she's stacked, John?"

"That I did. It's incredible. It's beyond all reason. As if somebody took a big rich wonderful steak, and then smothered it in butterscotch sauce."

They sighed in unison and trudged toward the door. As they went into the lobby, Parker Barnum looked across the room and saw a shoulder, a curve of cheek. His heart gave that familiar, sickening lurch, and sweat broke out on his body. Then he saw that it was not Suzie, and knew it could not be Suzie, and in fact the resemblance was very slight. She was younger and slimmer, with coppery hair.

The first meal of the assembled group consisted of a clear soup with a heavy sheen of fat floating atop it and, under the fat, a faint and elusive flavor of meat. It was served with flexible soda crackers. After the soup came boiled chicken, chicken so thoroughly boiled that all chicken taste had gone from it. But the boiling had not appreciably softened the sinews and muscles the fowl had acquired through a lifetime of running up and down the slopes of the barranca. There was a chopped leafy vegetable, unidentifiable, of a curiously vivid and sinister green. And mashed potatoes at room temperature, in an ominous shade of gray. The salad was guacamole, and could have been excellent had not Rosalinda become overly fascinated by a large bottle of green hot sauce made of small, crushed, green Mexican chili peppers. The universal reaction was a forkful of salad, a pause, a sudden bulging of the eyes accompanied by moisture, and a hasty heaping forkful of gray mashed potato. A black and gritty coffee was served and, for dessert, that breed of Mexican papaya which has the permeating and unmistakable taste of kerosene.

Conversation was general and somewhat confusing. Miles Drummond sat at the head of the long table facing Miss Agnes Partridge Keeley at the other end. Drummond had Monica Killdeering at his right and Harvey Ardos at his left. Beyond Harvey was Dotsy Winkler, then Paul Klauss, then Hildabeth McCaffrey, then Gil and Jeanie Wahl and, at Agnes' right hand, the colonel.

At Agnes' left was Bitsy Babcock, then Park Barnum, then Mary Jane Elmore, then John Kemp, then Barbara Kilmer, then Gam Torrigan, and thus back to Monica Killdeering at Miles's right.

John Kemp felt unduly pleased that the luck of the draw had put him beside Barbara Kilmer, but that advantage was canceled out by Gam Torrigan being seated on her left, a Gam Torrigan who, after twenty stricken seconds of exposure to Monica Killdeering, thrust his left shoulder forward and ducked behind it. Gam had brought a new bottle to the table. He hopped up frequently to replenish the drinks of Mary Jane, Bitsy, Kemp, Barnum, Ardos and the colonel.

Agnes Partridge Keeley felt curiously isolated from the group. At her left was the redheaded young girl who seemed to give all her attention to Mr. Parker Barnum. On her right was the colonel who, for the solemn purpose of eating, seemed to have turned off his hearing aid. And beyond the colonel were the young Wahls. They had pulled their chairs close together. They held hands as they ate, and they fed each other tiny little pieces of white meat. Further up the table Mrs. Hildabeth McCaffrey carried on a long conversation with Dotsy Winkler, talking right across that Mr. Klauss who sat wearing such an expression you might have thought he'd been served boiled rat. He glared across at the people on the other side of the table, quite as if they had betrayed him.

Miles thought the food tasted a bit strange, and he looked up and down the table. Only the colonel, Monica and Harvey

Ardos seemed to be eating everything. He made a mental note to talk to Margarita and Esperanza about serving. It was unnecessary to bang things down so briskly.

After Margarita had made a round with a second pot of coffee, Miles braced himself and, with the feeling that some-one had him by the throat, stood up and rapped on the side of his glass with a spoon. They all stopped talking and looked at him.

"Ah . . . I want to welcome all of you to . . . ah . . . the Cuernavaca Summer Workshop. I have . . . ah . . . met all of you. My name, as you know, is Miles Drummond. I am sure we will have . . . ah . . . a productive summer. A . . . ah . . . worthwhile summer together . . . here in . . . ah . . . beautiful Cuernavaca, the city of perpetual springtime. Many of you have . . . ah . . . already gotten acquainted . . . but I think the best thing for us all to do is . . . ah . . . introduce ourselves. We will start with the faculty. First Miss Keeley and then Mr. Torrigan and then, starting on my left, go around the table. Just . . . ah . . . stand up and say . . . who you are . . . and maybe . . . ah . . . a word about your painting. First, Miss Agnes Partridge Keeley, renowned California painter and teacher." He sat down and began to clap and all joined in.

Miss Agnes Partridge Keeley stood up and simpered until the clapping stopped. Then she looked most severe. "The first thing I am going to tell you all is that you are going to work. You are going to sketch, sketch, sketch. You will do hundreds of sketches, to train your fingers and your eye. This is a marvelous opportunity. We will go on little field trips together. I will give everyone individual criticism. Remember the name of this organization. The *Work*shop. Mr. Drummond has informed me that he has acquired a stock of materials for the artist, and can sell them to you at what I must say are *very* reasonable prices. I will expect to see every one of you at nine-thirty promptly tomorrow morning in the patio. Please bring sketching equipment. Thank you."

As she sat down, Gambel Torrigan rose slowly to his feet. He went behind his chair and leaned big brown hands on the back of it and gave everyone a long meaningful glower.

After ten seconds of silence he said, "I am an artist. Do you have any conception of the word? What it means? What it involves? It involves dedication. Dedication, not to a routine of silly little finger exercises and lessons in perspective. Dedication to a way of thinking, a way of living. You can't be a painter unless you are first of all a person. An organism of guts and blood and passion and fear and love and hate. A person who isn't afraid to live, completely, fully, even recklessly." He straightened up and thumped his chest. "I am going to make you cut your hearts out and spread them across canvas in raw, strong, powerful color." He stood for several seconds with his eyes closed, and then in a much lower tone, in a weary voice, he said, "I will give a demonstration of painting tomorrow at two-thirty in the patio," and sat down. Agnes Partridge Keeley stared at him with murder in her eyes. The students clapped.

Miles nodded at the rather alarming young woman on his right. He saw her throat work as she swallowed. She jumped up convulsively, and took a breath so deep that every male at the table found himself staring with awe and disbelief at the front of her blue sweater.

"My name is Monica Killdeering. I teach in a high school in Kansas. I'm not really a painter. I've had art courses. I think it is everybody's *duty* to bring out the ar*tistic* side of himself. I do interpretive *dancing*. And music and photography, and *creative* writing. And I spend every summer trying to *better* myself." She halted the torrent to suck in a deep breath. "I think this is going to be a *wonder*ful summer for *all* of us, and everybody I have talked to is so *stim*ulating, and I am so terribly *excited* about what Miss Keeley said about work and what Mr. Torrigan said about spreading my *heart* on the canvas, and I think this is a terribly *quaint* place and I can't wait to see it in the daylight."

She sat down abruptly, perspiring and pale. Barbara Kilmer stood up quietly. "My name is Barbara Kilmer and I am from Youngstown, Ohio. I took a Fine Arts course in college, but I haven't done anything with it for several years."

"I am John Kemp, an architect from New Orleans. I'm more or less a hobby painter, but I have had the good fortune to have my work hung in several national shows."

"My name is Mary Jane Elmore and I'm from Fort Worth. I had some silly little old art courses in school, but I think this will be very different."

"My name is Parker Barnum, from New York. A long time ago I was going to be a painter, but I ended up as the art director of an advertising agency—Sessions and March. I'm on a leave of absence."

"I'm Bitsy Babcock and I'm full up to here on tequila and Mary Jane said what goes for me too."

"I am Colonel Thomas C. Hildebrandt, United States

Army, Retired. Since I retired in 1946, I have painted over two thousand oil paintings of battlefield terrain." His large voice made metallic echoes in the big room. "My picture show why bottles were won or lost. When I die, my paintings will be willed to The Point."

"What? Me? Oh, I'm sorry. I'm Gil and Jeanie Wahl. I mean this is my Jeanie. I suppose she'll half kill me for letting the cat out of the bag but, well, this is a sort of honeymoon for us."

"I'm Mrs. Hildabeth McCaffrey and I'm a widow and so is my friend Dotsy Winkler sitting right there. I can't draw a straight line and neither can Dotsy, but we're willing to make a stab at it. It might make a nice hobby, and it's better than sitting up there in Elmira, Ohio, where we both come from, all summer, rocking on the porch."

"My name is Paul Klauss. I am a businessman from Philadelphia. I am here to learn how to paint. I feel that it would be good relaxation for me. Thank you."

"H-Hildabeth said it for both of us."

"My turn now? A long time ago there was an orphan kid with no advantages and all that kid wanted to do was draw stuff. He got whopped plenty for drawing on the schoolbooks and the walls. Well, that orphan kid was me, Harvey Ardos. All I've ever wanted to do was be a great artist. And I'm gonna be. I know it takes a long time. I got a lot of time. They don't discourage me. I know I got what it takes. You got to be sensitive. You got to use your eyes. You got to work. For me, the tough thing is supporting myself. I've had a list of jobs as long as your arms. Dishwasher, waiter, short-order cook, store clerk, bus driver. Someday they'll put in a book all the things I did so I could keep painting. I've took all kinds of courses all over the place. All in painting. I brought along a lot of pics of my work. I got a lot of stuff in storage and believe you me keeping up the storage payments on that stuff is enough to break your a— back. I remember one time . . ."

Gam Torrigan stood up and said, "Nobody can doubt that we have a wonderful group here, sensitive, intelligent, perceptive. May I say that I feel proud of this opportunity to work with you. Miles, I guess our pretty little waitresses will want to clear all this up now, so I suggest we adjourn. Every man to his own devices until we begin to work tomorrow afternoon."

"Tomorrow morning at nine-thirty sharp!" Agnes said shrilly.

81

Park Barnum followed Mary Jane and Bitsy into the lobby. It was nearly eleven-thirty. During dinner as he had talked to Bitsy he kept noticing the little ways in which she resembled Suzie. An immature Suzie, but with many of her same small tricks and mannerisms.

He caught up with them and said, "Think this town has any night life?"

"We could go check it out, hey, Mary Jane?"

"Okay."

Bitsy linked her arm in Park's. "This here one is mine. Who do you want?"

Mary Jane stood hipshot, frowning. "Not that big messy Torrigan type, and certainly not that oily little Klauss. Can you line up the architect, Park? He's a doll thing, but he looks smote with the sad blondie."

"Stick around and I'll give it a try."

He found John Kemp talking to Barbara just inside the door to the dining room. She was saying that she was tired and thank you anyway, but good night. After she left he told John the plan.

"Aren't they a little young, Park?"

"Remember, you're in the tropics. And I just heard you get a brushoff. So let's go."

They found the girls in the lobby being talked to by Torrigan and Klauss. Park joined them, looked obviously at his watch, took Bitsy by the hand and said, "Well, let's be off. See you around, Mr. Torrigan. See you tomorrow, Mr. Klauss."

And they walked off with the girls and got into the station wagon and headed down toward the center of the city. Klauss and Torrigan stared at each other with mutual dislike.

Gil and Jeanie Wahl had gone to bed.

Paul Klauss made a quick and alert tour of the area and found to his disgust that Barbara Kilmer had disappeared. This was a damn bad beginning. The two Texas girls and the Kilmer woman were all prospects, and good ones. And he hadn't managed to establish a decent contact with any one of them. The Killdeering woman was definitely off any list. From the neck down she was ten plus. But add the other factors and she came very close to being a minus quantity. He noted as he went through the lobby for the last time that Monica and Harvey Ardos seemed to be hitting it off splendidly. They sat in chairs facing each other, knees almost touching, while Ardos continued the speech that Torrigan had so fortunately interrupted. Monica was following every word, lips parted, head bobbing in agreement.

". . . so I said to him look is there any law against a guy painting pictures? Show me in the constitution, wise guy, I said to him and what I do on my time off is my own business and if you don't like it you can take your crummy job and you can . . ."

Harvey's eyes glittered fiercely behind the thick glasses, and a strand of dark hair had fallen across his earnestly corrugated forehead.

Paul Klauss went disconsolately off to bed, yet with a certain anticipation regarding the way he would occupy his mind while going to sleep. There were considerations of tactics and strategy. Which one to work upon first. How to split the Texas girls.

He pulled the chain but the room light did not go on. He undressed in the dark, put on robe and slippers and, carrying his toilet case, went thirty feet down the corridor to the bathroom. When he came back he shut the room door, took off his robe and sat on the edge of the bed, stretched and yawned.

Just when his stretch was at its greatest extension, fists high and wide, two warm arms suddenly clasped him around the waist from behind. He let out an explosive yelp and tried to spring to his feet, but the insistent arms hauled him back. And a woman was chuckling behind him, chuckling low in her throat. He turned around toward her, turned into an aroma of spice and cheap perfume and onion and woman, and was pulled protestingly, inevitably down into a Margarita labyrinth of humid warmth, and cooings and reassuring chuckling sounds, and questing, stroking, insinuating hands.

"*Pobrecito,*" she murmured. "*Mi Pablito. No tenga miedo, pajarito.*"

Paul was affronted, indignant, repelled by her. He struggled, but even for a man of his austere sexual patterns, there was a physiological limitation to protest, soon arrived at. In short, he was raped. And he knew it. And then, having been flung down to rest on the rubbled beach of one of the back islands of his mind, he lifted dazed head to hear the horrid, clarion, piercingly sweet, grotesquely gay: "Geef me ten dollar!"

He tried to cup the telltale mouth with debilitated hand, but the dark head was turned strongly away, and it came again, with laughter bubbling up through it, dark bubbles in molten silver: "Geef me ten dollar!"

With a sob, Paul Klauss got up and blundered to the bureau and carried his wallet to the chill moonlight of the narrow window and found the ten and took it to her.

He lay on the narrow bed with his eyes closed, heard the snap of elastic, the slur of rayon. Tiny pat of finger tips on his cheek. *"Conejito mío,"* she crooned. And went *clump-clop* to the door. It closed firmly behind her. And, more softly, *clop-clump-clop* down the khaki tiles.

And thus was the hunter betrayed. A man poised in a blind, turning incredulously when he feels the tweak of the beak of the angry mallard. Or, in a grassy field, feeling the teeth of the rabbit meet in the flesh of his leg.

It was a reversal of values. It negated the labored pages of the journals. He had the tortured feeling that he had become a page in her journal, a quarry bagged so readily the incident would not merit more than two lines—with a ruled column on the right for gross profit.

Chapter Seven

GLORIA GARVEY awoke at ten-thirty on Saturday morning, the first day of July. Her mouth felt grimy and her heart knocked with a brittle, alcoholic insistence, and a strand of her hair lay under her nose, smelling like an ash tray. When she felt able, she slid her long husky legs out of the bed and planted her bare feet on the cool tiles and sat up slowly. She groaned and bent forward, elbows on her knees, fingers deep in the raw tangled mane of hair, scratching her scalp gingerly, her eyes tightly shut.

This, she knew, was a bad start. One of those Abner Dean, what-the-hell-am-I-doing-here mornings. The morbid aspects of hang-over. You were better off when you did not wonder what you were doing, or why. With no consciousness of thirty-seven years strapped on your back like stones.

Damn Tommy Grandon and his pool and his drinks and his yak and his parties and fairy friends. Bits of the previous evening and awful fragments of her dreams were spattered and clotted against the black walls of her mind, unidentifiable, like the aftermath of a bomb in a crowded station.

She straightened and scratched her belly and looked with dulled interest at the four red lines her nails made. She plodded to the bureau and uncapped the pitcher and poured a glass of tepid water, spilling some of it over her hand and wrist, and gulped it down. She poured another glass and stood, holding it, leaning against the bureau, a cut-glass drawer pull biting into her left buttock, and looked at the strew of her clothing from bedroom door to bed. Skirt just outside the door, sweater just inside, then bra there, pants over there, shoes beside the bed.

With a dull burn of anger she said, "Sloppy damn drunken bitch."

Anger became more vivid, and she took a step and kicked violently at the sweater. But she took the step into the pool of water she had spilled when pouring the first glass. And both feet went up, and she sat on the damp tiles with a spine-jarring finality that clacked her teeth, set off black-and-silver pinwheels behind her eyes, and propelled the full contents of the second glass of water directly into her face.

She gasped and spluttered and was filled with an enormous helpless rage. And then, for a divine moment, she was privileged to stand aside and look at herself, and the laughter came. It hurt her head, but it felt good. She got up and drank some more water and, while the tub was filling, put water on the hot plate for coffee.

An hour later she felt much much better. She had wallowed like an albino seal and scrubbed herself pink and washed her hair and put on clean clothes. The peasant blouse was rather carelessly mended under the right arm where a seam had burst, and the bra was threadbare, and the elastic in the panties was without resilience, and, over the years she had owned it, the colors in the Seminole skirt had faded and run together, but she was clean and the morning thump had ceased, and she was permitting herself a liberal dollop of cheap local brandy in her third cup of coffee, a reward for industry. She checked the contents of her straw purse, bellowed for Gigliermina, the room maid, to come clean up the place, and walked to the garage and had them bring her car out. It would be interesting to see how Drummy was making out.

She drove through the gates and parked and looked with interest at the six cars lined up there. A cream-colored convertible Mercedes with Texas plates, a new Ford wagon from New York, a big beast of a gray Cad from California, an Ohio Buick with a sickening color scheme, an old junker of a Dodge wagon, and a drab black Chevy. Alberto was listlessly polishing the Buick.

There was no one in the lobby. She looked into the

dining room and saw one of the maids setting up a big long table for lunch. She decided that if they all ate together it must be very grim.

When she went back into the lobby Drummy came bustling across the room toward her, wearing a wide nervous smile.

"Good morning, Gloria! Good morning!"

"Hi, Drummy. How is it going?"

He held a trembling match to her cigarette and shook it out and said, "It's so terribly confusing, Gloria. I mean there's so many things every minute. There was too much drinking last night. Those Texas girls, they arrived practically naked. Alberto was trying to carry their bags in and look at them at the same time and he walked right into the side of the hotel. It was embarrassing. Mr. Torrigan passed out in the lobby, and the Colonel and I had to get him to bed. He was too big to carry, but he slid rather easily on the tiles. Mr. Ardos and Miss Killdeering stayed up for hours, talking to each other and I couldn't sleep. I could hear their voices. And then when Mr. Kemp and Mr. Barnum came in practically at dawn with the Texas girls, they were all laughing and singing. The food is really very bad, you know, and I don't know what to do about it. And Fidelio is such a bad driver, nobody wants to ride with him. Felipe is being absolutely no help at all. And that Margarita served breakfast this morning with a cigarette stuck in the corner of her mouth. She is a very strange-acting girl. When she served Mr. Klauss she patted his face and he turned such a terrible color I thought he was going to be ill. Only seven of them showed up for Miss Keeley's nine-thirty class, and she is most terribly upset about it. She blames it all on Mr. Torrigan. And Mr. and Mrs. Wahl haven't had breakfast yet. And . . ."

"Whoa! Down, boy. Take it easy."

"Gloria, could you please have lunch with us and then stay around a little while and just sort of . . . let me talk to you and advise me about things? I don't know if I'm doing anything right."

"Absolutely no, Drummy. I'm sorry. I've got a lot of things to do today. But I would like to get a look at them. Where are they?"

"Oh, they're right out there in the patio with Miss Keeley. They're sketching the fountain, I think."

Gloria went out the side door of the lobby onto the loggia that encircled the open patio. Most of the ground-floor rooms opened onto the loggia. She stood in the shadow and looked out through the nearest stone arch at the group in the scrubby patio. Agnes Partridge Keeley had placed them in a semicircle on chairs taken from the rooms and the lobby, facing the fountain. Some used easels and others drew on their laps. Some of them glanced curiously at Gloria and then continued with their work.

"Good Lord!" Gloria said.

Miles, standing beside her, said, "What's the matter?"

"That one, the one getting the instruction."

"Oh, that's Miss Killdeering."

Agnes, looking over Monica's shoulder, was saying, "Oh no, dear. You have the proportions all wrong. You have the base twice as tall as the little boy on top. You can see they're about the same size. Measure with your eye, dear."

Miss Killdeering was wearing an exceptionally snug dark-red leotard, and, quite apparently, nothing else. Her glossy black hair was tied back into a high pony tail. There in the sunlight she represented all of the anatomical distortions prevalent in girlie calendar art, from gun-turret breasts to superpneumatic thighs.

"The schoolteacher from Kilo, Kansas?" Gloria whispered.

"That's right."

"She must lead a very repressed winter season."

She tore her astonished eyes away from Monica and looked at the others. A gaunt old man in khakis, who wore a hearing aid and a look of utter boredom with the task at hand. A rather pimply citizen with unkempt black hair and thick glasses and a look of avid intensity. Cast that one as the boy Communist, she thought. And two elderly ladies in floral prints, biting their lips, as they peered from fountain to sketch block, charcoal sticks clutched with a certain desperation. And, beyond them, a very pretty man with dark-blond hair and regular, quite sensitive features. He wore a Basque shirt in gray and white, and copper-colored walking shorts. Gloria, out of her thousand years of instinct and experience, sensed that the pretty man was quite thoroughly aware of her presence there in the shadows. Hers was the instant response of the game creature sensing the presence of the hunter. But there was within her no flutter of fear or interest. She looked at him and felt a dark amusement. It was as though she were the wise cow elephant standing in the brush and the heat of the day, trunk raised, ears tilted, wondering in a mild way whether to drift silently back into heavier bush country, or go and kneel on him and twist off his head.

Agnes went to give instruction to someone Gloria could not see because the fountain was in the way. She heard Agnes say in a teasing voice, "You came to class very late, Mr. Kemp, but I must say that you have a very nice technique. Yes, that is a very nice sketch indeed, and you did it very quickly."

"Thank you," a deep voice said.

Gloria moved along the loggia and looked out through the next arch. This Mr. Kemp was a big man. Early thirties. Dark hair and good heavy bones in his face, and knowledgeable eyes. There was a mildness and an amiability in his face that Gloria sensed was only part of the story. There were other things there, less obvious. Dignity and pride. Irony and strength. Passion and conviction. Here, then, was a man. There were so damn few of them around. Not a rooster, prancing and flapping its comb. Not a goat, stamping and reeking. He wore a white sports shirt, pale-gray slacks, a light-blue fabric belt. He looked solid and contained within himself. She ran her eyes again over the thick slant of the shoulders, and the strong column of the throat. And she felt that visceral tremor, that weakness of knee, that faint clogging at the base of the throat which customarily informed her of the awakening of her own desire for a specific male person.

It had always come to her with very little advance warning. And seldom had it been this strong. But, as with all the other times that it had happened to her, she was immediately aware of the basic reason for the past few weeks of irritable ennui, of gray and petulant depression. She felt perfectly capable of dropping to her hands and knees and galloping out there to him, howling like a dog, to lay her head on his knee and beam up at him, panting. Here was the standard cure for the grismals, a Band-aid to cover the place where the soul leaked ancient sawdust. Here was a tidy and energetic way of becoming renewed.

"Well," Drummond was saying, "at least there are only five missing now, and . . . "

"Drummy!"

"Yes, Gloria? Yes?"

"I have decided to stay to lunch after all. I have decided I'm not being fair to you. I helped you make all the plans, and then I back out on you. I'm ashamed of myself, Drummy. I should be taking more interest. I intend to take more interest. I intend to help you."

"Gloria . . . that's wonderful!"

When Mary Jane Elmore came out of room thirteen at noon on Saturday, she left Bitsy Babcock sitting on the edge of her bed making low moaning sounds. Mary Jane had a whiff of hang-over, a faint cranial thud, a sprinkle of sand behind the eyeballs—but she was superbly confident that the symptoms would soon disappear. She was young and in splendid health, well able to throw off the after-effects of a quantity of tequila that would have felled a bison. She wore candy-striped pants in red and white, with a big red cuff button that came just below the knee, a red canvas halter and white sandals. As she walked down the loggia she passed from shadow to sunlight as she walked by each arch, and the sunlight struck the cropped blond hair, giving it a metallic luminousness.

Parker Barnum came out of room six a dozen feet ahead of her, closed the room door and gave her a rueful smile.

"Well, hi!" she said.

"You look revoltingly brisk, Mary Jane. How's Bitsy?"

"She got herself some miseries. You just now getting up?"

"I've been up a whole half hour. I came back to the room to get some cigarettes. I'll give you the word. We've got a black name with Agnes Partridge Keeley. You and me and Bitsy."

"What about John?"

"He's a foul traitor. He got up and went to class."

She looked at the empty patio. "I thought class was right here."

"It was. They dispersed a little while ago, showing each other their sketches of that fountain, giggling and prancing."

He gave her a cigarette and they went into the patio and sat on one of the stone benches.

"Is there any good reason," he asked, "why we had to try to drink up all the tequila in Morelos?"

"Well, it was fun, and it was a nice little bar, and anyway I think the altitude has something to do with it."

"It was fun going out with a couple of middle-aged types?"

"Now you're fishing for me to say something nice, Park."

"So say something nice."

"Well . . . you and Bitsy seemed to get along just fine."

"She reminds me of . . . somebody I used to know. What about her?"

"What do you mean, what about her?"

"Well . . . tell me about her."

"She's my very best friend. I mean we've known each other for a thousand years."

"How old is she?"

"Nineteen."

"Wow!"

"Now you listen, she's no baby. She just broke up with a wonderful boy. They went steady a long time. She wants to have fun. That's why we came down. You know, Park, it was funny about last night. I mean that John Kemp seemed to be . . . well, sort of amused at the three of us, at you and me and Bitsy, as if he were a lot older than all of us, but he can't be much older than you, can he?"

"Not much older. Thirty-three or four, I'd guess. I'm thirty-one."

"What's he doing down here, anyway?"

"He hasn't said."

"What are you doing down here, Park?"

"I told you last night. I'm on a leave of absence from my job." He tried to change the subject. "So you didn't have a good time with John?"

"I didn't say that, did I? It's just hard to . . . get close to him. I mean he says funny things and all that, but all the time he seemed to be watching us. Like he was taking notes. Oh, here comes the tequila kid."

Bitsy came across the patio toward them, scowling in the sunlight. She wore an aqua sunsuit, and her coppery hair came alive in the sun.

"Hi, kids," she said and sat beside Mary Jane. She looked at Park. "Did you or did you not get us lost on the way back here, darling?"

"Guilty. Finally John asked that soldier."

"And he wanted to come along with us. Brother, if every night is like last night, I'm not going to last. I wonder how much they love us around here for coming in hooting and stamping at three in the morning?"

Park looked fondly at her. "Bitsy, you look horrible. Maybe you remember that I bought a bottle of José Cuervo's best when we left that joint."

She came to attention and ran a tongue tip across her lips. "It couldn't make me feel worse, could it?"

"Come on," he said.

When they had all assembled for lunch, Miles Drummond made an announcement. "I suppose that everyone is . . . uh . . . delighted that we have finally gotten under way. Miss Keeley's class was . . . ah . . . particularly . . . rewarding this morning and she has asked me to express her disappoint-

90

ment that . . . uh . . . several of you did not attend. But I am certain that . . . on Monday morning she will see all of your . . . ah . . . bright and shining faces. This afternoon at two-thirty in the patio, Mr. Torrigan will give a lecture and do a demonstration painting and I am sure that . . . uh . . . none of us will want to miss it. We have a guest with us today, and I sincerely hope that she will be . . . uh . . . with us often. She should be with us because the Cuernavaca Summer Workshop is . . . her brain child. May I introduce, for those of you who have not met her, Mrs. Gloria . . . ah . . . Garvey, sitting there between Mr. Kemp and Miss Mary Jane Elmore."

Miles Drummond sat down and picked up his soup spoon, beaming nervously, bobbing his head.

Mary Jane had been curious about the Junoesque and unkempt blond stranger. She had seen the unmistakable directness with which Gloria Garvey had moved in to sit beside John Kemp, and she sensed in Gloria the flavor and arrogance of money.

Gloria turned to her and frowned and said, "Did he say Elmore?"

"That's right. Mary Jane Elmore."

"Fort Worth?"

"Yes ma'am."

"I'll be damned! Rix Elmore's kid, you must be. Look a little like him around the eyes. Key-rist, you make me feel like an antique. You know, the last time I saw Rix and Caroline was one hell of a long time ago. My second husband, Mike Van Hoestling, was in the ranch racket."

"I've heard Daddy mention him."

"Oh, Lordy, I remember one time we all got loaded in Houston and Rix phoned the ranch and had his pilot bring the old DC-3 down and take us all to Palm Springs. There must have been seven couples along. Rix had just won some kind of a tax thing, something about oil wells. Good old Caroline. After the sixth drink she'd always start to take off her clothes. How is she?"

"Not very well, Mrs. Garvey. She and Daddy are divorced and Daddy is married again. She spends a lot of time in . . . institutions."

Gloria pursed her lips and nodded. "She never could handle it. She could get pretty messy. Rix used to get disgusted with her. Well, kid, I'll see you around."

And Mary Jane suddeny found herself looking at the back of Gloria's large, strong and shapely right shoulder, and heard her say, in a voice pitched a full octave lower, "Hello, John Kemp." She had turned around toward him with, Mary Jane thought, the same forthright manner with which a woodsman might spit on his palms, pick up the ax and square off in front of the big tree. By leaning forward a little way, not conspicuously, Mary Jane could see John Kemp's expression. She could not see the expression on Gloria's face. But she could guess at it from the way John reacted. His throat worked as he swallowed, and he responded with a small, sickly and apprehensive smile. It reminded Mary Jane of the time out at the ranch when the big white goose had decided that Bugsy, the brown dachshund, was its friend for life, and had taken to following him wherever he went. For weeks, until the goose had backed under the front wheel of one of the jeeps while intently admiring Bugsy, the dog had gone about wearing the same look of apprehension, apology and half-concealed alarm.

Park Barnum said, his mouth close to Mary Jane's right ear, "And he was such a nice guy."

Mary Jane suddenly felt quite irritated and annoyed. She turned toward Park and hissed, "You men are so dang *stupid*. She's so obvious. And messy."

"But real eager."

"Oh, shut up."

Barbara Kilmer sat quietly at John Kemp's left, eating her tasteless lunch and trying not to listen to the conversation between John Kemp and Gloria Garvey. She felt grimly amused at the predicament in which she found herself. She knew her parents would be appalled were they to learn the living conditions to which they had so innocently and fondly subjected her. But she knew she could not be truthful in letters to them. Her father had paid the money. It was most unlikely that anyone could get any part of it back. Better to write them and make it sound like what she imagined they believed it to be.

Such a very strange group. And I, she thought, am as odd as the oddest. I want to keep myself to myself. I don't want to be drawn back into life by these people. I should have known from the ad Daddy showed me that it might be a curious collection of students. The old widows are sweet. Mr. Drummond is sort of nice and helpless. Every time I look at those newlyweds I feel all lost and unused. That Killdeering woman is a real grotesque. Mr. Klauss is a strange one. I don't understand him at all. He seems shy and lonely . . . too. And quite nice-looking. The colonel is very fierce. The girls from Texas are certainly not down here to study painting. I've never liked the Park Barnum sort of man. All poised and glossy and full of sharp little remarks. And right now, I know just what I am doing. I'm trying not to hear a word that Garvey female is saying to Mr. John Kemp. He seems nice. And the sketches he did were truly handsome. I have to train my hand and my eye all over again. I was clumsy. Please, John Kemp, don't let her move in on you. I shouldn't care. I really don't care. But just don't be gullible. She's a harpy . . . It's none of my business. Why shouldn't you have your fun and games, Mr. Kemp? The fact that there is something about you that reminds me just a little bit of Rob should have nothing to do with it. Do as you please. Every one in the wide world can do just as he or she pleases. Just so long as I am left alone.

Paul Klauss sat across the table from Barbara, and as he ate he studied her subdued and delicate and lovely face, the slender line of her throat, the structure of her shoulders. As he ate he tenderly, deftly undressed her. This mental game is, with most men, a rather inexact procedure. They visualize the unveiling of an idealized version of the female form or, out of the fuzziness of an untrained memory, endow the dream object with a figure once seen, perhaps on a calendar. But with Paul Klauss it was a precision operation. He had seen Barbara Kilmer walk. He had accurately estimated her measurements. He had selected her as his first venture of the Workshop summer. Out of his past experience he had learned the more intimate physical characteristics to be expected of the fair, Nordic, slim-boned, long-legged, short-waisted female in the middle twenties. So, given that knowledge, and a look at the clothed dimensions, and the other small clues, such as the skin texture of her throat and the curl and shape of her mouth, the shape and size of her hands, he could reconstruct the nude figure with such a marvelous accuracy of detail that he might err only in the size and placement of an appendectomy scar.

This was, of course, no more remarkable than the skill of the white hunter who, given a few pad marks in the moist earth, can tell not only the variety of the beast, but the size, weight, sex, whether it has recently fed, how fast it was moving, and how long since it has crossed the game trail. It is a compound of experience, intuition and natural talent.

Klauss could achieve an almost equivalent degree of accuracy in estimating which approach would be most likely to succeed, and, after success had been obtained, just how the victim would react during ultimate conquest. But this was not of the same high degree of accuracy as the construction of physical detail, because it had been conditioned by invisible factors, such as a mother's tales of marital horror, or a husbands' impatience, or too impressionable a reading of the works of Henry Miller.

Just as, by candle light, he had removed the final wisp of dainty garment, Margarita Esponjar reached around him and refilled his coffee cup. When it was full, Margarita reached stealthily down and caught a small fold of flesh of the back of Paul Klauss, just above his beltline and just over his right kidney, between a strong brown thumb and a strong brown finger. She gave a love tweak, a little pinch. But not only were her fingers, as a result of many years of the slapping and kneading of tortillas and other forms of manual labor, as effective as a pair of needle-nose pliers, she had also selected an unusually sensitive area for the caress.

Klauss's vision of the fair Barbara by candle light was gone in one small portion of a microsecond. His mouth opened in a soundless cry of anguish. When it was at its widest, Margarita whispered into his ear, *"Esta noche, querido."* She paddled away in her big red shoes, grinning back over her shoulder and swaying her hips a good three inches farther to each side than usual.

Hildabeth McCaffrey, on Paul's left, stared after the girl, then whooped and banged Paul solidly under the heart with her elbow and said, in a carrying voice, "I believe you've made a conquest, Mr. Klauss. I believe you have."

Paul looked around the table. Everybody was looking at him, most of them with amusement. He felt his face get hot. He wanted badly to explain, but there was nothing to say. His back where she had pinched it felt as if a red-hot wood rasp had been imbedded in it. He bent his head over his plate, a temporarily beaten man.

Chapter Eight

GAMBEL TORRIGAN stood beside the easel he had erected in the open patio and counted the house. On the second count he knew who was missing. Agnes Partridge Keeley, of course. And Park Barnum and the two girls from Texas. After lunch Barnum and the two girls had been yawning vastly and giving off telltale fumes of tequila.

He checked over his materials, faced the group, hooked his thumbs in his belt and glared at them. It was an act he had done many times. Torrigan's Demonstration.

"Try to paint the secret corridors of the heart," he bawled so loudly they all jumped, even Gloria who had heard it before. "Paint the climate of joy, or the articulation of the stars. Paint of the way something feels in the hand. An apple, a knife or a breast. Paint the smell of sickness, or the cold pride of a bird song, or the dead spell of winter, getting the stink of rotten snow into it. But for the sake of God, don't paint a barn or a tree or a horse."

He tilted the big piece of white board flat, yanked the top off a bottle and poured a puddle of dark blue oil ink onto the white surface. He picked up the board and tilted it this way and that so that the ink ran back and forth, making its own patterns.

"Where do you start? Start with color. Color is your language. Color is a form of light. The juxtaposition of color and form. Don't whine to me about communication. Communication is for newspapers. If you have to communicate, try to get in touch with yourself." He upended the board on the easel, snatched up a great hairy brush and edited the random droolings of the ink.

"Where do you start? Start with an accidental. What the hell does this blue mean? What does blue mean to you? What little creak do you hear in your soul when you look at blue, blue, blue?"

"My goodness!" Dotsy Winkler murmured.

And he began to press fat blobs of opaque water colors out of their tubes, applying them directly to the painting, mixing his colors directly on the surface as he worked, ranting at them, saying madnesses that, during the moment they were said, seemed to have meaning.

Miles Drummond was watching with his mouth half open. He looked up when there was a tap on his shoulder. Felipe Cedro was looking down at him with a certain amount of satisfaction. He said, "Señor, the men of the government are here."

"What?" Miles whispered. "What men?"

"To see you, señor."

As he headed for the lobby, Miles could hear the stentorian roars of Gambel Torrigan diminishing behind him. These were four men in Miles Drummond's office. They all carried shabby briefcases and wore shiny, dark-blue suits, frayed collars and neckties dingy at the knot. They were all uniformly short. Two of them were very round and sweaty and two of them were very lean and dusty looking. They introduced themselves. One of the round ones, a Mr. Lopez, performed the introductions in curious English. Felipe had brought two more chairs and they all sat down. Briefcases were opened and files taken out.

"Now, sir," Señor Lopez said, "it is to be seen that you are in operation of a hotel, sir. With not getting licenses." He ticked them off on short thick fingers. "License for handling foods. License for selling the bed. Special license for commerical bus operationing. License for employment of staff hotel workers. Special license to lease and operating hotel." Mr. Lopez paused and smiled broadly and lovingly at Miles. "Is very serious no licensing, sir. Very very serious. Big fine, big penalty, much trouble, sir."

Miles swallowed hard and smiled back and said, "There is some mistake. I am not operating a hotel. I am operating a school." He switched to Spanish. "It is a school here. It is a school of painting. It is not a hotel."

Lopez beamed even more widely. "Ah, sir. A school, sir. Then you do have the licensing for a school? Federal and also State of Morelos, sir."

"I did not know it was necessary, gentlemen."

Lopez kept smiling. "It is a school with students living here, sir, no?"

"Yes. That's right. They live here."

"Ah, sir. Then it is necessary the two big licenses for the school. And also the others, all the others as if it is a hotel operating also."

Miles stared at him and said dully, "What?"

"Oh, yes, sir. Big fines. Big penalties. You are citizen of Mexico, of course?"

"I am a *rentista* only," Miles said hopelessly.

They all smiled at him and Lopez said, "Ah, sir. Now it is of much more difficult. Maybe impossible."

"What will happen if it is impossible?"

"Just to close up everything only. Then fines and penalties, sir."

At that moment Gloria Garvey appeared in the doorway. She glared at the four visitors and said, "Just what the hell is going on here, Drummy?"

He flapped a hand at the four men. "These people are going to close me up. Nobody thought of the licenses."

Gloria stared harshly at Lopez until his smile faded away.

"Drummy," she said, "you scamper out of here and leave this to me. And close the damn door on your way out."

Just as he closed the door he heard the beginning of a torrent of Gloria's rough and ready Spanish. Miles paced up and down outside his office, hearing Gloria's voice frequently climb to shrillness, hearing the excited babbling of the men. Gradually the noise quieted down. The door opened. The four men filed out. They each shook Miles's hand, all of them smiling. They went out and climbed into an old Packard sedan and were driven away by a man in uniform.

"Come right back into your office, Drummy, and make out a check to Gloria Garvey for two thousand and forty pesos. Right away, dear. It so happened I had a big chunk of cash in my purse today. That made it a little cheaper, I think."

"What is this for? Are they going to close me up?"

"Of course not, dearie. The forty pesos is for a special, provisional, limited license that covers all the other licenses until the end of August." She clicked her big white teeth at him meaningfully. "And the two thousand is the bite, Drummy. The *mordida*. A little gift to hasten the arrival of the special license."

"Oh." He made out the check and gave it to her. She waved it dry and popped it into her purse.

"What would you do without me, dear?"

"Thank you, Gloria. Thanks so much."

"Lopez will bring the special license around in a week or so. And when he comes, you can be damn sure he'll try to gouge some more out of you. If you give him nothing, you'll hurt his pride and he may make trouble. If you give him too much, he'll be back again. Drummy, do you think you're capable of holding off just as long as you possibly can, and then give a hundred pesos?"

"I . . . I think so, Gloria."

"Tell him you're losing money. Tell him the school was a bad idea. Be *very* reluctant. Then you won't see him again, I hope."

"All right, Gloria."

"And for God's sake, stop looking like a rabbit with an ulcer. Everything is just fine, Drummy. The food stinks and this is a very creepy building, but most of your people are delighted. They're having a Big Adventure. Gam is currently confusing the hell out of them, but they'll learn to love it."

Gambel Torrigan finished his lecture and demonstration

97

painting at four-fifteen on that Saturday afternoon, the first day of July and the first day of the Cuernavaca Summer Workshop. Those of the students who had been thoroughly cowed by the experience came meekly up to get a closer look at the vivid, dramatic and confusing painting he had done. Hildabeth McCaffrey and Dotsy Winkler were convinced they would feel far happier with the more gentle devices of Agnes Partridge Keeley. Monica Killdeering and Harvey Ardos felt tremendously stimulated. They felt as if some dangerous and exciting new vista had been opened up to them. They didn't know just what it was, or what to do about it. But it certainly seemed exciting. For Gil and Jeanie Wahl, sitting side by side, thighs and shoulders touching, hands tightly locked, while the demonstration had taken place, it had been a most curious interlude. They had sat there in such a humid and hypnoid awareness of each other that it was as if they had been alone in a sunlit patio. Torrigan had been a minor annoyance, a noisy, gesticulating puppet seen infrequently through the wrong end of a telescope. They had sat in their awareness of each other, breathing shallowly. When it ended they stirred and looked around in gentle confusion, as people awakened from half sleep. They stood up and, with unspoken accord, hands still clasped, began to walk quite slowly back toward their room. The expression on Jeanie's round young health-poster face was almost stuporous, eyes heavy, mouth slack, throat too frail for the head's heaviness. And she wavered slightly from side to side as she walked. Colonel Thomas C. Hildebrandt, U. S. A., Ret., had sat through Torrigan's performance out of a soldier's sense of duty. He had sat there like a chained water bird being proffered spoiled frogs. When it had ended he had added a single grace note to the patter of applause, a parade-ground snort of such dimension and resonance that Barbara Kilmer, seated beside him, had jumped and turned and looked at him in a startled way. "No terrain," the colonel said, by way of apology. Paul Klauss, without seeming to do so, watched the lithe flex of Barbara's waist as she turned toward the colonel. He felt relieved to learn, from Torrigan's lecture, that he could perform quite adequately in Torrigan's group. It was not necessary apparently to draw anything. One attempt to sketch a fountain had been enough. John Kemp went up and looked critically at what Torrigan had done during the demonstration. He wanted to be quite fair. He sensed that much of what Torrigan had said had been not only shocking, but quite meaningless. The man did have some interesting color values and a reasonably balanced composition when he was through. John Kemp had no patience with that kind of intellectual insularity which says, "If I can't understand it, it's no good." He knew that nonrepresentational and abstract art had provided a creative and satisfying outlet for many painters who had become impatient with the restrictions of representational art. In his own work, though the source was always apparent, the treatment was abstract. He knew that public understanding of abstract art was seriously handicapped by the pretentious asininity of most art criticism. Yet something about Torrigan's work bothered him. There was a strange shallowness about it, a flatness. And suddenly he made what he felt was an apt guess. Perhaps the man couldn't draw. Perhaps he had never served the very necessary apprenticeship in pure draftsmanship that must precede any venture into nonrepresentational work if it is to have any validity, if it is ever to be much more than the smear and scrawl of a child obsessed by color.

He was aware that Barbara Kilmer was standing beside him. Torrigan was a dozen feet away, talking to Monica and Harvey.

"What do you think?" he asked Barbara.

She frowned. "I don't know what to think."

"We get a choice. Furious philosophy with Torrigan, or candybox tops with Keeley."

"Seems a little grim," she said.

"Maybe we could form a splinter group. Self-education."

"No. I think I'll stay with Miss Keeley for a little while anyway. I don't want to do the sort of thing she does, but I do want to get my hand and my eye working again. Then maybe I'll switch."

They could see, over the walls, high over the valley, the black afternoon clouds wreathing the peaks of Tres Cumbres. They could hear the thunder. Small quick breezes touched the patio, turning the leaves.

Gloria Garvey joined the two of them. It rather annoyed John Kemp that she should suddenly make Barbara Kilmer seem rather pallid and indistinct. "How did you people like the night-club act?" she asked.

"Quite impressive," Kemp said.

"Gam makes quite a pitch." She raised her voice. "Gam, you better get your junk under cover. It's going to rain in about four minutes." And then, smiling at John Kemp, she managed to turn and stand in such a way that Barbara Kilmer was dismissed, and Barbara walked quietly away.

"A little Saturday fiesta seems to be shaping up, John Kemp. I looked in on it. The Texas lassies and your buddy named Barnum had their siestas and now they're moving in on the tequila. In Park's room. We're invited. Interested?"

"Not very."

"Good! Neither am I. There's a much better idea. Friends of mine named Rick and Puss Daniels just finished a house at a sort of suburb called Las Delicias. A housewarming is going on. Nothing fancied up, but suitably gay and mad and sort of come as you are."

"I though I'd write some letters, thanks."

"My large friend, if you hang around here you're going to be hooked into local festivities, and we agree they sound dull. And this ought to arouse your professional interest. It's quite a house. It's one hell of a house, in fact. Indoor pool. Outdoor pool. A lot of glass and crazy roof angles and movable walls and all that sort of crap. Come on along. I'll show you some of the local characters."

Barbara Kilmer was in the lobby as the rain started. She saw Gloria Garvey and John Kemp hurry out to the blue Jaguar. Thunder obscured the roar of the car as it drove out through the gates. She went to her room and started a letter to her parents. After a shockingly close click of lightning and *bam* of thunder, the lights went out. She lighted two candles, and continued her letter.

Park Barnum's small room was crowded when the lights went out. He sat on his bed, leaning back against the wall, between Mary Jane and Bitsy, glass in hand, pleasantly glazed, wishing there was some Goddamn way he could stop thinking about Suzie and the twins. Torrigan, having made the mistake of demonstrating a feat of strength, was watching in awe and indignation as Monica Killdeering, in leotard, her legs perfect and unreal and like marble in the light of the naked bulb, did one-handed pushups in tireless tempo on the tile floor in the middle of the small room, while Harvey Ardos pridefully chanted the count.

The failure of the lights did not dismay the colonel. He had pumped up his gasoline lantern, adjusted the shade he had made for it, and sat reading *Lee's Lieutenants* for what could have been the seventh time.

Miles Drummond was in the owner's apartment, quarreling with Felipe Cedro over the cost of food. Felipe lighted a candle. He was intensely bored. Señor Drummond was very repetitive.

Hildabeth and Dotsy had been sitting in Dotsy's room, knitting and lying about their grandchildren. When the lights went out they put the knitting aside and continued the conversation while they waited for them to go back on.

Gil and Jeanie Wahl slept in each other's arms, a deep sweet sleep of utter content.

Agnes Partridge Keeley was tapping out business letters on the portable she had brought with her—the originals on her letterhead, the pink copy for her file, and the blue copy for her accountant. When the lights went out she said a word. And said it again. And sat in the dark wondering if Gambel Torrigan was a Communist, and, if so, what decisive thing could be done about it. She chained him in one of the damp dungeons in the bottom of her mind and began to do unspeakable things to him.

Esperanza Clueca, grimly determined not to be disturbed by the gabble of children in her parents' tiny hut on the barranca slope near the hotel, studied her lessons by candlelight until it would be time to return to work.

Alberto Buceada, totally undone by pulque and mescal, lay smiling and unconscious in the rain behind the servants' quarters.

Rosalinda Gomez, with the dubious help of Margarita and Pepe, was preparing dinner, resolutely boiling three great chunks of rubbery goat. When the lights went out, Pepe lighted the three old kerosene lanterns that hung from wall brackets in the big gloomy kitchen.

The new house, John Kemp had decided almost instantly, was a fraud. It had no artistic unity. It was part California modern, part half-ass Japanese and part Mexican exuberance. And he had met the people and they seemed equally fraudulent. There was a badly faded screen star with an arrogant manner, a surly poodle and a handsome and stupid young consort. There was a current film star, vast and blond, who had apparently practiced the rather nasty habit of being able to laugh one peach-basket breast out of its skimpy hammock of fabric. The length of the delay before she noticed the unveiling was apparently in direct ratio to the possible importance of the onlooker to her career. She was accompanied by a small, bald man with exceptionally hairy hands. Then there were three self-important and rather surly young men from the field staff of one of the picture magazines, accompanied by three glossy young women from Mexico City who had no English. And there were two novelists, one reasonably notorious, and one tall female poet who looked like an Australian tennis star, male, and dressed the part. And several staggered, bellowing drunks of both sexes, and a score of the usual expatriates with the usual diversity of mates, legal and extralegal, rather more than half of them heterosexual, rather more than half of them from the U. S. And two bars in operation, and two buffet tables, and more than an adequate number of little people in white coats to pass things. Rick and Puss Daniels were both small, gnarled, redheaded people who had inherited some sort of automotive concession in Mexico, and who busied themselves with making odd and rather ugly ornaments of enamel baked on copper. Concealed speakers played recorded music, flamenco, bullring and *mariachi*. Prism lights imbedded in the paneled ceiling made drama of casual groupings.

John Kemp stood alone in a corner and glowered at everyone. Whenever a tray was passed, he put an empty glass on it and took a full one without particular regard to content. He was feeling sourly philosophical. Life had been very orderly, very satisfying. And then Mary Jenningson had to go into an emotional tailspin and foul the whole thing up. He had thought this summer in Mexico would be something so different that he would be able to stop thinking of Kurt and Mary and the firm. But now he knew he had brought them all along with him.

All the problems were the same. Gloria Garvey was just a tired old problem with a new name. He had never taken any particular pleasure in promiscuity. It created too many problems. He liked best the casual and comfortable affair of long duration, preferably with a woman who had a career of her own and no intention of giving it up, a mature woman of taste and intelligence, so that the physical could be nicely leavened by companionship. There had been few such affairs, but he recalled them with pleasure, and remained a good friend of the women involved. Gloria Garvey was certainly not qualified by instinct or background to join that small group. He saw her standing with a couple by the lighted indoor pool, and saw her throw her head back and laugh largely and with gusto, white teeth gleaming.

Not qualified, but rather a splendid animal. It sounded so good mentally, so analytical and patronizing that he tried it aloud. "Splendid animal. Quite."

A man came over with a tray and a look of inquiry. John Kemp drained his glass and selected a new one. His mouth felt slightly numb. He realized he was getting tight. Possibly drunk. Hadn't been drunk, thoroughly drunk, in years.

And he thought of Barbara Kilmer. She came into his mind without warning. Vivid and complete.

"To dear old Barbara," he said solemnly. "Walked out on me. Left me with the splendid animal." He considered that sentiment very thoroughly, decided it did not make a hell of a lot of sense. One could not walk out on a nonexistent relationship. But in all honesty, ole John, leave us grant that there is a desire for such a relationship to begin. Physical? No. That would be fine, yes, but this is on a new and strange level. Want to be with her is all. Sit and listen to her talk. Watch her walk. Watch her comb her fine pale blond hair. Make her smile. Watch her laugh. Make her feel somebody is all the way on her side.

The face of Gloria Garvey appeared suddenly in front of his unfocused eyes. He focused on her. John Kemp had seen looks of invitation before. He had detected flirtatiousness. But the look Gloria gave him bore about the same relationship to flirtatiousness and coyness as a cap pistol does to a mass barrage by atomic cannon. She pierced him with a look and expression so prurient, so demanding, so entirely explicit that his heart leaped and withered within him. He wanted to turn and run like an alarmed adolescent. He was reminded of the fate of male spiders. Gloria, in one all-out projection, made the escaping-breast routine of the Hollywood blonde seem like the pigtail bit with a sand bucket on the beach. She looked as if she need merely shrug once, and her faded untidy clothing would fall to the floor at her feet. She slipped a hand out, hooked her finger tips around his belt, yanked him six inches toward her, banged a kiss onto his mouth that hurt and said, "Take me home now, Johnny Kemp. Quick like."

"But . . ."

"I don't want you drinking one drop more. I've said goodbye for both of us."

"Wait a minute, Gloria. I . . . uh . . . promised to give Mr. Daniels an opinion on his house."

"It stinks. Go tell him and then let's go."

John spotted Rick Daniels on the far side of the big room, standing near the end of the indoor pool, and started toward him. Gloria came right along with him, a special felinity now apparent in her stride. But John had the odd sensation of being a tame and rather toothless old lion accompanied by the female trainer, carrying whip, kitchen chair and pistol loaded with blanks, while the drums rolled ominously. He had the impulse to turn on her and stamp his foot and say, in a shrill and petulant voice, "I will *not*. I don't *want* to." It was a situation he had never faced in all his adult life. For the first time in his life he could appreciate the sticky dilemma of the frightened maiden who finds that inadvertently she has given a very dominant male some reason to believe that she is immediately accessible. Gloria had made her intent so clear that he felt as if he wore a placard reading, "Main Dish."

He wished desperately that he had not fogged his perceptions and ingenuity with a horrid mixture of too many drinks. He felt that if he got into the blue Jag with her, he was hopelessly lost. She seemed quite capable of clamping her big white teeth around the nape of his neck and bounding off into her lair with him. He knew that his alarm seemed out of proportion to the fate that awaited him, a fate that to many might seem eminently desirable; it was merely the quality and quantity of her aggression that upset him.

They came up to Rick Daniels. He was talking to a dark little woman of pronounced simian cast of countenance. As they approached, John Kemp had one desperate and implausible idea, and to his own consternation, he put it into effect the very moment it occurred to him. He faked a stumble and, while catching his balance, inflicted a most effective body block on Gloria. His hip met hers solidly. She went spinning away, made an effective arm tackle on one of the house servants walking along the apron of the pool with a loaded tray, and carried him with her into the shallow end of the pool. There was no moment of being poised in the air, no nonsense about slow motion. It seemed to John Kemp but a fraction of a second from the moment he conceived the idea to the moment when a sheet of water hit the simian woman squarely in the face and the blue water of the lighted pool closed over the faded stern of Gloria's Seminole skirt.

Gloria sprang, spluttering, to her feet. The water came to mid-thigh, and she stood in a jetsam of hors d'oeuvres, the sodden waiter scrambling to stand up beside her, looking at her with an expression of incredulous outrage. Her brisk mane was plastered flat, as were blouse and skirt, modeling the heroic limning of breasts and flanks so valid that they made the objects so frequently displayed by the cinema queen look like a confection too abundantly fashioned of pink junket.

All conversation had ended in shock, making the music seem much louder. Puss Daniels came at a fast hostess trot. Rick took one of Gloria's hands and John took the other and they hoisted her out of the pool.

As Puss was saying, in exclamation points, you poor dear, and you'll catch your death, and we'll get you some warm dry clothes, John said, "I'm sorry, Gloria. I tripped or something."

She palmed damp hair off her forehead and said, "I forgive you, you big clumsy son of a bitch. Puss, I've got dry clothes at home. John will drive me home right now."

"No, darling. I insist. Come on, now. Come with me, dear." A platoon of female guests and servants bundled Gloria off the field of play, toward the bedroom wing.

Just before she disappeared, she looked back and called, "I'll be right back, Johnny."

He realized that his single impulse would avail him nothing unless coupled with other tactical moves. He took the most direct. He began what he hoped was an inconspicuous and not too circuitous trek toward the handiest exit. His last glance at the party disclosed the cinema type standing on the pool apron, dangerously close to the edge, her back to the pool, awaiting her chance to be similarly victimized.

He went out the drive, oriented himself, and began walking briskly in what he suspected was the right direction. After a little while he began to hum to himself.

After Gloria had squeezed herself precariously into a blouse belonging to Puss Daniels, and an old pair of gray flannel Daks of Rick's, too big at the waist, too short in the cuff, and drum-tight across the rump, and after she had toweled her hair with great vigor and scrawled on more lipstick, it took her five full minutes to become convinced that John Kemp had actually walked out on her. It was an entirely new experience. Other men had walked out, some of them motivated by self-preservation, afterward. Never beforehand.

She felt betrayed, victimized, scorned, insulted . . . and furiously angry. His defection seemed to redouble her sexual ferment. She felt as if she could drop to her knees and bang her head on the floor. She stood squarely and indignantly and looked with hot fierce eyes at every man in the room in turn, tempted to make a savage and random selection. But they were as health bread to someone whose stomach is rumbling for steak. So she took another drink, a massive jolt, and she took her bag of damp clothing and her private torment and drove home to Las Rosas. By the time she had garaged the car and reached her suite, she was dangerously calm. Her jaw was clamped so tightly that little pale knots of muscle stood out at the corners. Her eyes were narrow. It is an index of her highly emotional state that she hung the borrowed clothes up neatly and tidied up the two rooms before she went, seething, to bed.

Barbara Kilmer wrote another letter, a letter to Rob's people, after dinner. When it was finished it was just late enough to go to bed, but she felt restless. She put on a sweater and went out onto the loggia, closing her room door behind her. The rain had stopped and the wind had stopped with the rain. A half-moon rode high and there was a gentle and elusive fragrance of the rain-wet flowers of the night.

She walked out into the patio and sat on a concrete bench and looked at the moon, but felt conspicuous there in the moonlight. After a time she went over and sat on the low wall of the loggia, under one of the stone arches, leaning her shoulder against a stone column.

The night is made for sharing, and a lovely night is especially made for sharing. Once in a while she could hear distant laughter. And the trucks droning and whining down the grades of the *autopisto*. And the night bray of a burro, starting with cynic laugh and ending on a fading note of despair. And, far away, the skirl and thud of a jukebox in a cantina far down on the other side of the barranca. She was conscious of a growing scission within her, an increasing concern with present and future which she resented as being an evidence of disloyalty to the precious past. The feeling was not yet strong, but its very existence troubled her. She did not want any change to take place. Just live the long days and, at night, go to sleep by going over every tender detail of one of the days with Rob. And, if very fortunate, meet him again in those dreams where he was alive and smiling.

But there, too, there were changes. The dreams did not come as often. And when they did, there was a random and disorganized quality about them. In the dreams Rob would be far off and acted strangely and he kept turning into other people.

And memory too. The vivid memories of the good days were becoming subtly blurred. Like paintings by an artist who has used materials which do not last. Colors fade and the bold lines become indefinite.

Yet, worst of all, the sour, nagging little suspicions that perhaps she had dwelt too long and too dramatically on her own grief and loss. It was a feeling that popped up into her conscious mind all too frequently, grinning and smirking at her. She had been able to suppress it very easily at first, and lately with more difficulty, by telling herself that it had been the best of all possible marriages, that it had been a love such as few people are so lucky to attain. But lately, before she could hammer it back down out of sight, it would stand there and say, "But, Barbie, are you quite certain you haven't come to really *enjoy* this role of tragedy and mystery? Aren't you really charmed with this chance to act such a touching part?"

She heard slow steps on the stone of the loggia. She turned and recognized Paul Klauss when he moved into the pale area of moonlight behind her.

"Hello there," he said quietly.

"Hello, Mr. Klauss."

"Make it Paul, please. And I'd like to call you Barbara if I may."

"Yes, you may, Paul."

"The party seems to be going strong in Barnum's room."

"Very."

"Mind if I help you watch the moon, Barbara?"

"Not at all, Paul."

He put one foot up on the low wall and stood half behind her in silence for rather a long time.

"Barbara, I don't want to sound rude or forward. I certainly don't want to be offensive. But I've had this . . . terribly strong feeling that we have more in common than the other people in this thing."

"You do?"

"I said that clumsily, I know. That's why you sound so cool and withdrawn now. This isn't a pass. I'm not a schoolboy, or a Park Barnum either. It's just this. I sense in you an area of . . . sadness and loneliness that strike a very responsive chord in me. You are saddened and lonely, aren't you?"

"Yes," she said in a barely audible whisper. Klauss began to feel more assurance. He congratulated himself on having the foresight to get access to the file of application blanks in Drummond's office by using a suitable excuse. And found the key word. Widow.

"I don't like to go around telling my troubles," he said. "Usually I don't. I don't want to cry on anyone's shoulder. But sometimes the burden of . . . just carrying the load by yourself is so great that you have this great urge to find someone to share it with. At a time like this. At night. When no one can look at your face. Would you listen to a very dreary and personal story, Barbara?"

"Of course."

"I was engaged to be married," he said. "She was lovely. She was the most wonderful thing that had ever happened to me. Her name was Ruth." He spoke slowly, feelingly. He made the story up as he went along. He added little vividnesses of detail, making it so real that he could almost believe it himself. When he came to the part where it was necessary to kill her off, he made it an automobile accident. He had been driving. He regained consciousness in the hospital two days later. They told him she was on another floor. By the time he was well enough to be told the truth, she had been buried for three days. By the time he came to that part, he did not have to try very hard to make his voice husky. He mourned for Ruth. In the silence, after he had finished, she groped for his hand in the darkness and found it and squeezed it hard. Her fingers were cold.

He waited with all the patience of an owl on a limb above a starlit meadow.

"I . . . I'm glad you told me, Paul. I hope it makes you feel better to tell someone. I've never really talked about . . . Rob. To anyone. Oh, I've said the normal things, but that isn't what I mean. Can . . . can I tell you . . . about him?"

She had released his hand. He moved a little closer to her, not quite touching her. "I knew I was right, Barbara. I knew my instinct was right. I'm sorry it was right. You were made for happiness."

"I had happiness. A lot of it. I don't know what to do without it. Let me tell you about Rob, the kind of man he was, the kind of person my husband was."

And it was a very long story. So long that Klauss began to feel irritable. But he listened carefully, remembering those parts that could conceivably be of use to him in this venture. At times she spoke in a broken, halting way. At other times there was a forlorn and husky eloquence about her. It was the lost heart speaking, on a night of moonlight.

When she was quite through, Klauss let the silence grow around them for a time, and then he said, "It isn't given to us to understand how such things can be, how

108

such things can be permitted to happen. It's so damnably cruel. I know how I feel. All the rest of my life stretches out ahead of me like a desert. I don't know what I'm going to do with all the time. I feel as if, for my own good, I ought to try to find some new emotional involvement. But I just . . . haven't been able to."

"I know. I miss him so."

He put his hand firmly on her sweatered shoulder and said, "What are we going to do with our lives, Barbara?"

"I don't know, Paul," she said. "Oh, I don't know," and he realized she had begun to cry, almost silently.

He put his hands on her shoulders and turned her gently. "Let me hold you for just a moment, Barbara. Just to make things seem a little less lonely for both of us."

She swung her legs over the wall and stood up into his arms, her temple against his cheek, her face in his shoulder, her body trembling with her grief. He held her very carefully, almost formally, and when he judged it time, he tilted her face up and kissed the salt wet patches under her eyes and whispered tenderly, "There, Barbara. There, Barbara, darling."

And in a little while he kissed her lips lightly and they had a taste of salt. And then kissed them with a most careful measure of insistence. His hands moved on her back, changing slowly from a gesture of comfort to the first muted measures of erotic play, with the anatomical precision of a master surgeon. He was quiveringly alert for the first subtle indications of physical response, and when they came he once again placed his mouth upon hers, adjusting his boldnesses to the increasing tempo of response, to her altered breathing and her arms suddenly around him, and the ripening and loosening of her mouth, feeling a great confidence as he knew he had taken her very gently and carefully beyond that point where she would respond as an individual, into the area where her responses were that of woman, primal, consecutive, instinctual and vulnerable.

Barbara, as a person, was dimly aware of the traitor responses of her body. She was kissing and being kissed, and holding this stranger close to her, dreamily aware of the pleasure of his hands. But there was a flutter of wrongness. This male she held was too slight, too small, without the bulk and weight of Rob. And his hands were too silky and sly and expert, his mouth too sensuously dainty. He was adept and . . . rather nasty.

Klauss stumbled back away from the very sturdy push against his chest. "Barbara, darling!" he said.

"Just exactly what the hell were you trying to do?"

"Barbara, don't be angry. Please. I wanted to hold you in my arms just for a moment because you were crying, and then I guess we both . . . I guess it turned into something else for both of us."

"Maybe for you. Not for me."

"But you were . . ."

"I was nothing, Mr. Klauss. I was fooled for a couple of moments by a very slick trick, and I have no intention of being fooled aagin."

"Please don't be angry. I felt so close to you. I felt you were a kindred spirit."

She sat on the wall, facing him. She sighed. "All right, Paul. I won't jump to conclusions. You got carried away or something. And I did too. We'll be friends. And kindred spirits, if you want. But please understand this, my friend. We are not going to comfort each other that way. We are not going to merge our broken hearts and have a big fat affair just because we both happen to be lonely. I'd feel cheap for the rest of my life. It's bad enough to feel the way I do without feeling cheap too. Good night, Paul." She walked by him.

"Good night, Barbara," he said thickly. He watched her down the loggia, moving alternately from moonlight to deep shadow and moonlight again, moving trimly, graceful and slim, and he could feel the sinuosities of her back against his palms with a taunting clarity.

Seldom had any venture gone so quickly and utterly wrong just at the moment when he had been most confident of a kill. He calmed himself. Other ventures had gone wrong. And had been ultimately made right again. Had he been less confident at the moment, he could have salvaged this one more quickly. When he felt the first stiffening of her body, the first indication of restraint, he should have stepped back quickly, and gone at once into the My-God-what-are-we-doing gambit, with references to the memory of Ruth and the memory of Rob before she could say the first angry word. Then she would have been disarmed and taken off the offensive so completely that the next step would have been made more easy, rather than more difficult. Certainly it was more difficult now, but certainly not impossible. And, after inevitable success, it would make a most interesting episode in the journal. At this rate, a rather lengthy one. He decided that when he wrote it up, he would not spare himself, but rather would call explicit attention to the

110

error in procedure and judgment he had just committed.

It did seem rather strange though that her rejection should be so violent. As he walked toward his own room he thought back over many in the journal category of widow. As a class they had provided little more than token opposition. His feeling of depression faded entirely away. He squared his shoulders. This was a temporary setback in what would be a most entertaining venture. She rated a full ten on the Klauss Scale. The more difficult she made it, the more lengthy and interesting the journal entry. Even if the hunt should take up so much of the two months that no time would be left for other episodes, the summer could be counted a success. And there would be no problems of competition. Kemp had been quite obviously gobbled up by the stupendous Garvey wench. Barnum would choose between the two young Texans.

He unlocked his door, shut it behind him and reached for the pull chain, certain that he had left the room light on when he left. He pulled the chain and it did not work.

He wondered if all the electricity had gone out again, and suddenly he remembered the details of the previous time when this had happened. He whirled and looked toward the shadowy wall where the bed was. He could see nothing, but his distended nostrils picked up the telltale effluvium of public-market perfume, with a counterpoint of chili. And he heard a dreadful clarion giggle.

He had the door partially open when she was upon him, the impetus of her charge banging the door shut again. As he tried to fend her off he learned that she was naked, as well as wiry, giggling and remarkably strong. She had gotten behind him and she had him around the waist and was laughing as she tried to tug him toward the bed. He grasped the doorknob and held onto it with all his strength.

"No!" he said, as loudly as he dared. "No! No!"

"Conejito mío," she crooned, panting with effort. "Mi rubio! Ándale, querido. Pobre hombrecito tiene miedo, no?"

Hands, sweaty with alarm, slipped from the round brass knob of the door and he stumbled backward and they fell together. Klauss turned as they fell. He landed on his shoulder and his head smacked the tiles with such a hearty thud that the room and the night dipped and spun, and his efforts at fighting her off became slow, ineffectual and dreamy. Many sad hours of his childhood had been spent with both larger and smaller boys beating him enthusiastically about the head on the red-brick playgrounds of Philadelphia. His mother would weep when he would come wailing home in his pretty, ruined clothing. The solid blow of his head against the tile floor took much of the spirit out of him. Margarita, talking constantly and soothingly, straddled his waist and unbuttoned his shirt. When he pushed her off and came blindly to his feet, she peeled the shirt back and down, imprisoning his arms, and propelled him onto the bed with a hearty push. And he thumped his head again on the wall beside the bed.

When he returned from half-consciousness, she had finished undressing him and, with yankings and tuggings and large hearty kissings, was working him down into the bed under the threadbare blankets. As before, in spite of all austere resolve, in spite of his outrage and his offended pride and his revulsion, in spite of the indignation he felt, he kept saying "No, no, no" until many moments after it had become humiliatingly obvious that her practiced and enthusiastic ministrations had been no less effective than before.

And, as before, her high, sweet, clear cry of "Geef me ten dollar" stirred him out of a stunned little half-death to find his trousers, fumble in the wallet and give her the money.

She dressed and he heard her go *clump-clop* to the door. "*Adiós, mi corazón,*" she said as though shouting to him across the barranca, and closed the door behind her and went *clump-clop-clump-clop* down the corridor.

Paul Klauss lay and bit his lip until it hurt. His eyes filled, and one tear went down the side of his face. His head hurt. He remembered how, when he had come home from school, she would put witch hazel on the places that hurt. And kiss them to make them well again. And bring his supper to bed, and sit and sing to him until he fell asleep to the sound of her voice. And he remembered his father, a great, hairy, vicious, unpredictable brute.

He thought of the smell of witch hazel, and the exact way the get-well kisses felt, and he thought of his mother and her funeral and how dreadfully he missed her, and in a little while he was crying in earnest, sobbing into the bunched pillow that still held the stale fragrance of Margarita's hair, a smell of ripe flowers and kitchen greases.

BOOK TWO

In which *the Disparate Personalities assembled establish Certain Routines, and make Practical Adjustments to Each Other and to the Group; a certain number of Anticipated Difficulties arise; two members of the group disappear for a Short Time; the circumstances of their return provide cause for an Impromptu Fiesta at which the Just and the Unjust are Rewarded and Punished by the Fates without regard to Justice or Merit.*

Chapter Nine

By THE LATE AFTERNOON of Thursday, the sixth day of July and the fifth full day of instruction, certain patterns of behavior had started to become apparent, and it was reasonable to expect that as the Cuernavaca Summer Workshop continued, these patterns would become more evident and inescapable.

It is a most fundamental part of the nature of the human animal that he responds to a new environment by establishing for himself those little routines which, however meaningless they may be in essence, serve the far greater purpose of giving him comfort and a sense of place and purpose whenever he conforms to them.

Place five men adrift in an open boat and in an astoundingly brief time they will establish a pecking order, will each have settled into some small area of the boat which he will think of as his place, will have established a schedule for doing things—and the more intricate the schedule the more satisfying, and, having cozied up their environment to the greatest extent possible, will await either rescue or death with that accretion of composure which can only come through the establishment of a complete social order, no matter how evanescent it may be.

With the possible exceptions of jail, school and military organizations, where one of the more important uses of authority is to prevent the group from composing its own group mores and structure, the weight of group desire is always more potent than the wishes of any self-constituted authority.

The communal dining table, which Miles Drummond felt was both pleasant and necessary, was the first social device to yield to group pressure. At dinner, on the first Monday, Gam Torrigan overheard Agnes Partridge Keeley say, in a voice that was meant to carry, "No one of taste or perception would ever hang in their home one of those horrid meaningless things that look like a dish of liver and spaghetti. The place for such paintings is in those shabby little pinko galleries in New York."

Gam had risen to his full hairy height and waited until all conversation had stopped. He stared down at Miles and said, with measured and almost Churchillian dignity, "I request permission to have my food served to me in some far corner of this baronial hall, Mr. Drummond. The asinine chatter of that fat embarrassment at the far end of the table upsets my sensibilities and sours my stomach. Anyone who shares my limited capacity to endure vicious nonsense is invited to join me." Thereupon be belched with the explosive finality of a spinnaker suddenly shredded in a gale, picked up his plate and silver, and stalked to a far dim corner of the room, to a small table in the shadows.

"Disgusting sort," Agnes said evenly in the awed silence.

Miles said nervously, "Really . . . I had hoped that we all . . . could get along well . . . and there certainly is room in the world for . . . many theories of art."

No one quite dared to join Torrigan immediately. But when the coffee was served, Harvey Ardos took his over to Torrigan's table, trying to look entirely casual. Monica Killdeering joined them. By Wednesday evening the splintering was complete. The long table was dissolved. And, as at a hotel, there was a tendency to eat at different times.

Miles thought that the maids and Rosalinda would have violent objections, but he found that the new arrangement suited them more than the old. The preparation and serving of thirteen simultaneous meals had severely taxed Rosalinda's organizational abilities. She far preferred extended periods of

114

amiable confusion to a twice daily climate of crisis.

One table for four became almost institutional in its rigidity. Agnes Partridge Keeley ruled over it with a manner more suitable to direction of the entire group. The table was composed of Agnes, Hildabeth McCaffrey, Dotsy Winkler and Colonel Hildebrandt. And they preferred to eat each meal as early as possible. And, each time, as soon as he had eaten, the colonel would ask to be excused, braying the token request at them, standing and making a half bow with iron gallantry, then striding from the room, setting his heels down hard.

It was also during this first week that Dotsy Winkler began to lose much of her hesitant shyness as she began to edge her way into the avocation which not only improved her own morale, but vastly benefited the group.

As Hildabeth McCaffrey put it, "Back in Elmira that Dotsy is known all over the county as a woman can take the apron off a butcher and serve it up so it turns out to be the best food you'd swear you ever put in your mouth."

Dotsy had wanted to see the kitchen ever since the first meal she had eaten at El Hutchinson. It took her until the following Tuesday to get up the courage to sidle furtively to the doorway while dinner was being prepared. She was appalled at the dinginess, the dirt, the primitive facilities. Had Rosalinda glowered at her, it is probable that the association which was to become very close before the summer session was over would never have begun. But Rosalinda's approach to the world was a wide grin and a meaningless though infectious giggle. And so Dotsy had smiled back and moved hesitantly through the doorway.

Dotsy spent a few days as observer, making Rosalinda Gomez quite uneasy, and another few days as a volunteer assistant, and a week as co-cook. From then on she was clearly in charge.

Rosalinda would complain wonderingly to Alberto Buceada, "That Señora Winkel, she is ridden by devils, truly. All must be scrubbed, endlessly. The white paint on the walls, purchased at her order, placed there by you, Alberto, it too must be scrubbed each day. Truly, she can cook better than I had known was possible. Never has food been more delicious. And I no longer have such great responsibilities, but one would think it was intended to eat from the floor, even way back under the stove."

The two women worked together with the aid of sign language, the fragments of Spanish which Dotsy learned, and the bits of English Rosalinda learned from her. The work went smoothly. They smiled at each other often and with a genuine affection. And Rosalinda, for the first time in her long career as a cook, began to take an interest in the preparation of food.

And Dotsy discovered the bewildering, noisy, filthy, labyrinthine public market. And, excited and enchanted by exotica unprocurable in Elmira's Soop-R-Market, she would instruct Felipe Cedro to buy strange things and carry them out to the red bus where Fidelio waited behind the wheel.

For the first time since the death of her husband, Dotsy began to feel like herself. She walked in confidence and a new air of authority, and she blushed and beamed when the others complimented her on the food.

Miles Drummond had felt very guilty about letting the situation develop. Dotsy had little time for instruction under Agnes Keeley. In effect, Dotsy Winkler had paid five hundred dollars and her transportation expenses to come to Cuernavaca to cook for her friend, eleven other students, the staff and such guests as might appear. He felt guilty indeed, but on the other hand, it had been years since he had eaten so well. As Dotsy had taken over, the intensely indignant complaints from the others had dwindled and ceased. And Dotsy herself was busy and happy, and had begun to expand her field of influence to include the housekeeping activities, to the extent that the insect life within the hotel was suffering a visible decline.

The only person with violent objections was Pepe, that soiled and lazy urchin, whose knowledge of evil was surpassed only by his talent for survival. He had not thought he would be persecuted by the little old American lady. But on one horrid and memorable afternoon, without warning, Alberto, the gardener, and Felipe Cedro pounced upon him. He thought they had lost their minds. He was taken out in back to where a large tub had been prepared for him, the water steaming ominously. He was stripped of his rags. The rags were thrown into the barranca. Though he writhed and wept and pleaded, Felipe held him strongly in the tub while Alberto, with strong yellow soap and a harsh brush, scrubbed him until he glowed red through his mellow brown hide, and the water that did not splash out of the tub during his struggles was the consistency of black bean soup. They rinsed him with a hose. They cropped the heavy matted thatch of black hair, and dispossessed the contented vermin with a substance that stung most evilly. Then, exhausted and weeping, he was forced to dress himself in new clothing, a pair of new blue jeans as rigid and unbending as sheet metal, and a blazingly white shirt. He was then told that this had been the order of the Señora Winkel, that henceforth he would keep himself spotlessly clean, that he would see to it that no stain or tear marred the new clothing.

That night Pepe left forever. Until he was found the next day by one of Felipe Cedro's friends and brought back to the hotel, filthy, torn, squalling with rage.

When Felipe Cedro had first reported Pepe's desertion to Señor Drummond, he had been told that Pepe was very probably incurably lazy and dirty and it might be best to employ another boy.

But Felipe felt it would be better to bring Pepe back. He had private reasons that he could not very well relate to Señor Drummond. When it had been Señor Drummond's desire to staff the hotel in preparation for the Workshop, Felipe had been instrumental in selecting Rosalinda Gomez (who had turned out to be disappointingly unco-operative regarding kickbacks from food purchases), Margarita Esponjar (who, as a source of income was proving to be less effective than he had hoped), Alberto Buceada (who unprotestingly kicked back fifty per cent of his pay to Felipe) and Pepe (who had turned out to be the best bet of all).

Only Fidelio, the driver, and Esperanza, the severe maid and waitress and potential schoolteacher, had not been added to the staff by Felipe.

Felipe had spent many patient hours with Pepe, training him. In much the way that a bridge master might deal random hands to a novice and ask him to bid the hand in order to instruct him, Felipe had repeatedly handed Pepe a battered old wallet containing random selections of both pesos and U. S. currency. After several long sessions Felipe was certain that he had taught Pepe how to decide upon the maximum amount of money which could be stolen without the victim being likely to note anything missing. If there were two five-peso notes in a billfold or lady's purse, only a fool would try to remove one. But if there were five, one could safely be removed. The objective was a steady return. If the students became suspicious, the venture might end abruptly.

Once Pepe had been trained, Felipe had given him a master key, a duplicate of the one he had at first loaned to Margarita, and later given to her after he had had copies made. And Pepe was also instructed to keep his eyes open and report on all readily portable items of value in the rooms, their location, description. Felipe did not have to take notes. He had the effective memory of the semi-illiterate. With the information furnished by Pepe he planned to quickly and efficiently clean out the hotel just before the Workshop ended.

And so Pepe was brought back, rescrubbed, reoutfitted. When this had been done, Felipe took him back of the servants' quarters and had a fatherly talk with the boy. He said that it would not be wise to run away again. He said that it would be excellent if Pepe kept himself spotless. To make his instructions more forceful, Felipe explained that should Pepe run to the furthest corner of Mexico, he would be brought back. Felipe took out his pocket knife and pressed the small thumb button which snapped the long slim blade open. He said that it might sadden him, but if Pepe did not co-operate, he would be forced to take out his digestive organs, one by one, and toast them over a little fire he would build in the barranca, and then throw them to the skinny savage dogs you always saw in such places.

Pepe remained clean. After Dotsy Winkler had solved the mysteries of the primitive oven, she began to bake rolls. A white coat was purchased for Pepe. He was given a basket of hot rolls, napkin-wrapped, to serve to the students at each meal. He decided he would much rather die than make such a fool of himself. But the memory of Felipe's knife was too vivid. And so, on the first occasion, he shuffled with black scowl into the dining room, went, in torment, from table to table. But, in a very short time, he became accustomed to it. And began to enjoy it. And began to take pride in the starched white coat. He beamed at the students, and bowed, and offered rolls more frequently than was necessary. And, in time, he even began to be a little sorry that he who served them such delicious rolls with such poise and grace should be the very same person who, in the dark hours of the night, moved like smoke into their rooms and lightened their pockets.

The other tables were not as unvarying as Agnes Keeley's table. Gil and Jeanie Wahl were always together, of course. They had no set schedule for eating, and they missed meals often. Sometimes Miles would eat with them when they arrived in the dining room at the same time. He felt that he should change from table to table.

There was no special pattern for the others. Paul Klauss would sit at the same table with Barbara Kilmer whenever he could arrange it, with Mary Jane and Bitsy when he

118

couldn't. The girls from Texas were not always at the same table, but Park Barnum was usually with Bitsy. Harvey and Monica were generally together. Quite often John Kemp would eat alone, an open book beside his meal.

By that first Thursday of the Cuernavaca Summer Workshop another change had occurred in the basic behavior of the group, but this change was due to the personal wishes of Agnes Partridge Keeley and Gambel Torrigan. Had either of them suspected that their wishes were identical in any respect, the change would not have come about. But Miles for once handled it exactly right. Gam Torrigan came to Miles in the owner's apartment of the hotel. He said, "I know the arrangement is to let the students split up, Miles, and pick their own instructor after this first week. Personally, I'd like to keep right on teaching in the afternoons, rather than having the group who will prefer me as their instructor all the whole day long. Hell, you can't teach all day. Maybe that woman can, but I wouldn't call that teaching. She might just as well be teaching them to knit. It doesn't drain her emotionally. And I can work on my own stuff in the mornings." Miles said he would think it over.

An hour later Agnes Partridge Keeley came to him with the same request. She wanted to teach in the mornings. She hoped to go back to California with dozens of paintings. It wasn't fair to try to do your own work and teach simultaneously. Miles said he would think it over.

He went to Gam and Agnes and said it was his wish that the students have as varied a program as possible. He spoke to them separately, saying that the other one had objected, but finally agreed to his proposal. Agnes would instruct in the mornings, Gam in the afternoons—and any student who so desired could attend both sessions, of course. He announced this change to the students.

And there were, of course, the individual habit patterns that were rapidly becoming solidified.

Colonel Thomas Catlin Hildebrandt, after two sketching sessions with Agnes, ceased attending classes. And, despite the heavy wheedling and coyness and pretense of hurt feelings by Agnes Keeley, despite the anxious queries by Miles, he made it quite plain that he would not attend any more classes. He had, with great ingenuity, and with equipment tested over the years, made his room exceptionally comfortable. He had brought with him weighty and obscure studies of Mexican campaigns, from Cortez to Zapata, and prior to his arrival he had made notations on a collection of detailed maps of the countryside.

On the first Tuesday of the Workshop he drove away and appeared some hours later, driving the old station wagon very slowly. Tethered to the tailgate, and moving with alarm tempered by resignation, was a white horse. Her name was Saltamontes. She was elderly and flabby. Her white hair seemed exceptionally skimpy. And under her hair, disturbingly visible, was hide the shade of bubble gum, or a cheap denture. Both the girls from Texas, more acquainted with horses than the other students, noted at once that Saltamontes had a habit they had never seen before. She yawned widely, silently, repeatedly. When she yawned she would shut her eyes, and expose a funereal collection of huge yellow teeth. Each gaping yawn ended in a gusty sigh. And she had in large measure that common affliction of malnourished beasts, chronic flatus. In the station wagon was the equipment furnished with the leased horse, one battered antique of a saddle with wooden stirrups.

Colonel Hildebrandt made arrangements with Alberto Buceada to care for the horse. This consisted mostly of hazing her over onto the grassy part of the barranca slope when she was not being used, and keeping an eye on her, and tethering her behind the servants' quarters inside the hotel wall at night.

Each morning, when occupied on a project which could not be reached by vehicle, the colonel would saddle Saltamontes deftly, lash his painting equipment aboard, swing competently up into the saddle and clop off toward the scene of some local skirmish or ambush. The colonel had a good seat and a practiced manner on a horse. But any possibility of good effect was lost not only through the obscene pinkness of the hide under the scanty hair, but also through the frequency of the vast yawns as they rode off, and, at the end of each yawn, before the windy sigh, the audible click of the big yellow teeth snapping down on the worn bit.

The colonel's collection of battlefield scenes grew rapidly. Each bore two dates, the date of the action and the date it was painted. And each bore a number corresponding with the reference sheet for that particular action. Though he was far more competent in his use of perspective, there was in his work the flavor of Grandma Moses. It was a sunny and colorful world of pure pigment. But unpeopled. Where blood had run dark into the grass of long ago, where men had shot and yelled and died, all was a stillness. The branches grew out only from the sides of the trees, and each leaf had turned to face the painter.

In the evenings when his research was done, he would sit in his room and write long letters to far places. Each day whoever brought the mail back from town would place it on the same small table in the lobby. The colonel received many letters, from Panama and the Philippines, from Washington and Tokyo.

In his reserve and his dedication, and his correspondence with old friends, he seemed apart from the rest of them. Some of them tried to make jokes about him. But such was his dignity the jokes never succeeded. He somehow managed to make them feel trivial in comparison to his diligence and his energy. And he seemed only remotely aware of their existence.

Miles Drummond quickly established a routine. He made it his custom to make a complete tour of the hotel and grounds once a day. He looked in on each class at least once. In the mornings he labored over his account books and the current inventory of supplies. He tried to make a point of speaking to each student in a friendly way at least once a day. When he received complaints, and there were many, and when he saw things that needed to be done, he would make a notation in a pocket notebook. And he would speak to Felipe. He directed the use of the bus and driver. And he tried to think up little social plans to make the evenings more enjoyable.

Most of all, he kept telling himself that he was doing everything possible to make the Cuernavaca Summer Workshop run perfectly. But he was in a constant state of despair. The accounts did not come out right, ever. The inventory never checked out. And the money he had set aside to cover total expenses was melting away at a sickening rate. On each tour he saw multiple evidences of sloth and neglect. The temporary permit had not arrived. He would take out his pocket notebook and tell Felipe what needed to be done, what the rest of the staff would be instructed to do. Felipe would look at him with surliness and boredom and say everything would be taken care of. But it never was. And when he tried to scold Felipe, his voice would tremble with frustration and helpless anger, and he would think he could see the amusement and contempt far back in Felipe's eyes. When he looked at the classes he was alarmed to see how poorly attended they were. And Mr. Torrigan's class sessions seemed to grow constantly shorter. Suppose they all requested the return of their money?

In addition, he never knew where the red bus was, or who had been taken away in it. And it broke down constantly. He thought up interesting ideas for social evenings, but there were never enough people who wanted to co-operate. In despair he would go back to his books and records. And find a notation which, even though it was in his own hand, he could not read. 12 cshaygn 48 pesos. Whatever they were, they were four pesos apiece. That, at least, was clear. What were they for? How many were there left? And how could you tell how many were left?

And Margarita would come in then, beaming wildly, and stand hipshot in her shapeless red dress, and say in her carnival voice, "Ah, señor, the *rápido* in the bathroom C, it is wounded. Felipe says it is the Señor Torrigan who fell while drunk. The flue is now on the floor in two pieces and Alberto cannot fix it."

"Go away and in a little while I look at it."

After she was gone he would feel like putting his head in his arms and weeping. He wanted his little house back. Strangers were using his dishes and reading his books. He did not know how long he could stand this. And he sensed that somehow, when it was all over, if indeed it ever ended, in some mysterious way the total expenditures would equal total income. To the final implacable centavo.

Mary Jane Elmore was not as quick to establish her own pattern. She felt at loose ends, restless and slightly irritable. Bitsy and that Parker Barnum were becoming constantly more inseparable, and so there were not as many laughs with Bitsy. She wondered if Bitsy might be going to have an affair with Park Barnum, with an older man. She did not think that was a smart thing to do, to get involved in . . . in such a cold-blooded way, sort of. If you didn't give a damn, it certainly would be no trick to get involved around this Weirdsville Hotel. Take that oily little Paul Klauss item, just for example. Just a harmless little stroll to look at the lightning in the mountains. He said sweet cute little things, and all of a sudden he had eight or ten hands, and you really had a time breaking it up. And somehow he'd managed to get you all bothered in a kind of sleazy way. But it wouldn't do to let him know that. Maybe he knew it anyway, without being told. Anyway, it would be terribly smart to be very sure you never had a little too much to drink before letting him cut you out of the string and take you off to his little old corral. Anyway, really, the easiest thing was to think of how that Paul Klauss would stack up against Chuck or Booker or B. J. Why if you were ever seen anywhere around home with that Paul Klauss they'd say you must have tossed the fish back in and kept the bait.

Torrigan had the usual ideas, all right, but he was a lot easier to handle. Hinting you could be a real hell of a painter if he'd let you learn all about Life from him. Always trying to load your drinks. And that tired game that goes I've-just-got-my-arm-around-you-because-I'm-just-a-big-friendly-guy. No trick in handling him. If Bitsy gets all mixed up with this Park Barnum, and it gets intense like, it doesn't leave much left over for ole Mary Jane. Now if that John Kemp could get notions, it might be different. It might be a whole lot different. But if he had any ideas at all, he was having them about Barbara Kilmer. And certainly getting no further than was Paul Klauss who also seemed aimed in that mournful direction.

And so, on the second Saturday, in the afternoon, she went into town alone. And sat alone at a table on the sidewalk in front of the Marik. And she was picked up by three crazy-wonderful boys from the University of New Mexico who were in Mexico on some sort of summer field trip in archaeology or something like that, and they had a four wheel drive jeep and curly beards. The three of them took her to Las Mañanitas for dinner and, the next day, when the one named Scotty was too hung-over to lift his head, she and Bitsy drove to Mexico City in the Mercedes with the other two, Hal and Jaimie, and went to the bullfights and didn't come back over the mountains until it was nearly dawn.

After that she had her pattern. She hadn't realized Mexico would be so full of wonderful kids on vacation. All you had to do was go look for them. Sometimes Bits would come along, and then it was the most fun. So the project was to pry Bits loose from Park all the time, not just some of the time. And go to a class once in a while.

For students and staff alike, with the possible exception of Barbara Kilmer, one aspect of all personal patterns was the same. They all had an intense interest in the mail table. And, on Tuesday, the eleventh day of July, there was more mail than could fit in the post-office box. No one was neglected. Miles brought it back at quarter of twelve just as Agnes was dismissing her class. Some took the letters to their rooms. Others sat in the lobby.

Jeanie Wahl was made to feel guilty by one portion of

the long newsy letter from her mother. "We do understand, dear, that you are on your honeymoon, and you are a married woman, but you can let yourself be just as thoughtless and inconsiderate as you were when you were a little girl, if you let yourself. I haven't talked this over with your father, but I can tell from the way he acts that he's worried about you. And so am I, dear. We have no way of knowing whether you actually got to that school. All I know is that since you and Gil left during the reception, we have had two post cards from you. Just two, mind you. And just a few words on each one. That isn't like you, dear. You sent one from New Orleans and one from Mexico City. At least two is all we have received. I certainly don't want to scold you at this time, but you must realize that your father and I put a great deal of time and thought and money into your marriage. You are in a foreign country and it seems to me, at least, that the very least you can do is sit down and write us a long letter about the school and how you are living and so on. You may be married but we are still your parents, remember, and we expect you to be thoughtful and considerate."

Right after lunch Jeanie started a long letter to her parents. She apologized and said the school kept them busy every single minute. She said she had never known anyone could be so happy. At that point Gil started reading over her shoulder. He said that any girl would be happy to be with him. She sprang up to do battle, and did not get back to her letter until late afternoon. She finished it at dinner time, and awakened Gil and read it to him. He said it was sure a long letter.

Harvey Ardos, who had expected no mail at all, received a letter signed, "Jimmy Waskawitz and all the gang in the third-floor stockroom." It told him who'd been drunk and who'd been fired, and who was on vacation where, and when and where the others were going. And at the end it said, "Harvey, old buddy, it doesn't seem like real that the guy who worked beside me is in Old Mexico in a fancy painting school. It's guys like you that save your money and do stuff that get someplace, and bums like me that is always broke by payday and get noplace. I wish you all the luck there is, old pal, and I hope you'll be famous sometime and I can say we worked in the same crummy place together. That Janie and I was talking about you just last week. I run into her by the time clock on the way out. I don't know her last name, but you know the one I mean she's got

124

blond hair and she's got a real good built and the only thing wrong with her is the way one of her eyes looks off the wrong way. She's the one that was in pocketbooks and now she's in kitchen wear the same one Morillo tried to take back into rug storage that time and she about kicked him loose of his teeth but didn't report it. Anyhow when you come back I think if you asked she'd give you a date because she was interested about Mexico and you could shoot some bull, but I can't be sure I'm right. Send me a present. Send me by airmail one of those cute little spic girls. Ha Ha Ha. Good luck."

That evening Harvey wrote Jimmy Waskawitz a long letter, thinking to write about Mexico, but when he read it over he saw that most of it was about Monica Killdeering. And so he tore it up. He knew Jimmy would show it around, and he knew what they'd say, all of them. Morillo and the rest of those wise guys. They wouldn't understand. They wouldn't get the right idea at all.

Parker Barnum had a chatty and amusing letter from an account executive named Trevor Helding. It related all the latest office dirt and confusions. He was grateful to Trev for taking the trouble, and was surprised that he should have. They had never gotten along too well.

He understood when he came to the knife. "By the way, both John and Herbie seem terribly set up about the way our Becky is gnawing on the bit. As an A.D., I think she makes a fine figger of a woman, and that's about all. She has come up with a few of those zany and startling ideas that impress hell out of everybody until somebody realizes that the stock isn't moving off the shelves. Anyhow, it doesn't look as if any of the stuff will be farmed out while our Becky is in high favor. I understand she has been given a raise. But, as old hands like you and I know, it can't last."

He balled the letter and threw it into a corner. A little later he got it and smoothed it open and read it again. There was a damp shifting in his middle, a visceral turning like the slow wringing of a wet warm towel. And he realized he had shut his jaws so tightly his teeth were hurting.

It took five drafts before he was really satisfied with his casual Dear Herbie letter. He had to achieve an unmistakable ring of honesty, optimism and complete mental health. He drew some quick and clever little Mexican cartoons in the margin. He added a postscript that said, "In my spare time I've been blocking out some new concepts in advertising art that seem valid and exciting to me. Most anxious to

125

check your reaction when I get back. I know how skeptical you are of anything too glib and flashy and startling."

He stretched out on the bed and waited for his headache to go away. That Goddamn Trev! Hell of a job trying to protect yourself at long range. Have to write some more. Schedule them out. One to John Sessions soon. One to Becky. Another to Herbie. Damn!

Agnes Partridge Keeley received a long business letter from her accountant. Much of it was concerned with tax matters. At the very end he became, she decided, impertinent.

"I strongly advise you to reconsider your decision on granting permission for your tenants at 55 Shore Terrace to sublet. Mr. Galt has been told by his doctors that he must get away from sea level. Your attorneys agree with me on this matter."

She wrote back immediately. She called his attention to the terms of the lease. She said that she was an artist, but she was also a businesswoman. She doubted that Galt was that sick. She said she would entertain an offer of half the remaining rental due under the lease, and an immediate transfer of the property to her so it could be rented again. And she asked him to employ at a sum not to exceed two hundred dollars, some investigative agency which could put together a complete report on the past history of one Gambel Torrigan. She wanted it as soon as possible. She gave him the facts the agency would need.

Colonel Hildebrandt received a letter from Brigadier General Thornton R. Pope, U. S. A. (Ret.) in Falls Church, commenting at length on the career and death of a long-term mutual friend and officer, and advising the colonel that the books he wanted should be airmailed within the week.

Miss Monica Killdeering received a long newsy letter from Eleanor Hipper in Kilo, catching her up to date on everything that had happened in the town since she had left. By a not very striking coincidence, Monica had a long letter to Eleanor partially completed. In it she said, "There is a very *intense* young man here from Philadelphia named Harvey Ardos. The quality of his mind is *excellent*, but he has practically *no* educational background. We have had very *long* talks about everything under the *sun*, and he is constantly amazed to learn that the greats of history have written down the thoughts he has arrived at independently. He is an *independent thinker*. I guess that we are the hardest workers in Mr. Gambel Torrigan's class. Mr. Torrigan assigns *problems* to us and we must come up with *solutions*. Mr. Torrigan never seems to like Harvey's solutions and it makes him *furious*."

Barbara Kilmer had a letter from her father, and she guessed that it had been typed by him on the office machine. "Your letters have been appreciated, my dear. You have a nice gift of expression, and it is almost as good as being there. I have noticed, however, that you make no reference at all to any social activity. I hesitate to write you in this way, but your mother and I have been alarmed to see how completely you retreated into yourself after Rob's death. I know what a sickening tragedy it was, but I also know that you are a young woman and your life is not by any means over. I debated a long time before taking the step of giving you the present of this summer course. I hoped that it would rekindle your interest in your art, and also make you more aware of the people around you. I thought this might happen if you were in some place where you had never been before, some place out of the country where there would be a minimum of things to remind you of your husband.

"But there is a flatness about your letters that indicates to me, though I have not discussed this with your mother, that you are still remote, standing to one side, a little apart from life. My dear, I can understand how you have a feeling of futility, of purposelessness. Perhaps you should realize that such feelings are not unique with you. I am 51 years of age and I have spent my productive years this far puttering around inside the mouths of friends and strangers. Perhaps I have relieved some pain. Possibly I have made some people happier by making them handsomer. And in many instances I have saved or prolonged lives by detecting the evidence of disease of which the dental patient was unaware. But, too often I suppose, I reflect that this was my one life given to me to live, and I seem to have spent it in a sort of haze, far removed from high adventure, great accomplishment or any particular degree of memorability. I have a comfortable home and a good marriage and a saddened daughter. Perhaps what I am trying to say is that for any introspective person there is an inescapable aroma of futility about life itself, regardless of how it is spent. Enough of this morbid nonsense, dear. I want you to live and laugh and love and be happy. I'd like to see all the stars back in your eyes."

The letter was in her mind all day. That night there was a sallow moon, and a wet and gusty wind. She walked beyond the wall and leaned against it and felt the sun-heat locked

127

in the stones. There was something chained loosely to the floor of her heart, some small creature that tugged at the rusty staples and fumbled with corroded locks. And when it gave sudden tugs to free itself, she could feel the reverberations in her whole being, rippling along her flanks and trembling upon her lips.

Bitsy Babcock received three letters from three young men, and all of them were so curiously similar, that she had to keep glancing ahead to the signature to keep clear in her mind who had written each one. Mary Jane had received one very like Bitsy's and one that was deliciously naughty. At least when they sat in the room trading letters, on first reading it seemed to Bitsy to be cleverly daring. But when she read it over again it seemed to her to be rather nasty and pointless. And all the rest of the letters were shallow and meaningless and boring. She knew she would answer her letters, and the three she would write would be almost identical.

Paul Klauss received a letter and financial report for June from his store manager. Business was slow. They were starting to tear the street up again. Some woman was driving him crazy phoning all the time, refusing to take his word that Mr. Klauss was in Mexico on vacation. She wouldn't give her name.

Hildabeth and Dotsy both had letters from friends in Elmira and from their married children. And the letters made them homesick.

Chapter Ten

IN THE UPLANDS OF MEXICO in the summer, during the hours of sunshine, the butterflies are busy among the flowers. There are an incredible number of blooms, most of them in the hot colors—reds and oranges and yellows. The butterflies are as vivid and seem as numerous as the petals. Here and there, on green slopes, are the bright little villages the beekeepers have constructed for their charges, cubical houses set aslant and in random pattern, each painted a different color, all pleasantly faded by the sun. There are great wild bees that come after the flowers too, angry, metallic, careless brutes that fly head-on into the garden walls, gorged with nectar and irritable with the frequent dizzying impact of stubborn iridescent head against stone. The large hummingbirds poise with precise hypodermic, and the throbbing of their wings is less sound than sensation. Grazing cattle move up off the barranca slopes, blandly furtive, to munch the gay blooms off garden walls until chased away into a lumbering, indignant trot.

But, in the dusk, when the bees and butterflies and hummingbirds and cattle are gone, there is the time of half light when the moths come to the blooms, gray and brown, soft and hungry, curiously sinister, coming with the first bawdy scent of jasmine on the evening air.

John Kemp sat at dusk on the stone bench in the enclosed patio, his pipe drawing well. It was a Friday evening, the fourteenth day of July. The thunder had mumbled and then moved off into the southwest. No rain had fallen at El Hutchinson, but the faint shift of breeze had the washed smell of rain. Though he did not consider himself to be a particularly thoughtful or introspective man, John knew that these quiet times were necessary to him. And enjoyable.

Classes were now limited to five days a week. The weekend was ahead of him, and he looked forward to it with anticipation in which was mingled a nice little tingling edge of excitement. From the moment he had seen her at the lunch counter in New Orleans his awareness of Barbara Kilmer had increased steadily, inevitably. He had been intrigued by the reason for her reserve, her air of grave remoteness, until he learned that she had been widowed less than a year ago.

She seemed always to be on the edge of his thoughts, so that there was a continual flavor of her about him, like music just beyond the edge of audibility. She had seemed determined to keep him at arm's length along with the others. But he had noticed that she was having difficulty with Paul Klauss. The pretty man was uncommonly persistent, never faltering in his attempts to ingratiate himself with her, apparently oblivious of the reasonably obvious fact of her distaste for him. John judged that something had happened between them very early in the session, that very probably Klauss had stepped out of line.

Though he felt slightly guilty when he realized that in his own way he was stalking her as determinedly as Klauss, and such conduct was perhaps equally reprehensible, he found in the matter of Klauss's pursuit, an opportunity to interpose himself. Though there was no word spoken about it, he knew that she quickly became aware of the way he would lengthen his stride in order to take the last remaining seat at a table where she was sitting so that Klauss would stand, obviously angry, and then turn away. And, at class, he would sit where Klauss obviously planned to sit. And once he had kept them apart on the red bus by arriving at the entrance door at the same time as Klauss and contriving to step on his foot before apologizing profusely and preceding him into the bus.

He sensed that in some unreadable area of her she was amused and grateful. She had turned toward him slightly in her emotional attitude, slightly but detectably, a flower making a quiet quarter turn toward the light. And, once she was assured that he was making no attempt to force conversation with her, she co-operated in the conspiracy, lagging behind until she could be certain they were both heading for the same table where two people already sat.

He told himself that this was summer intrigue, and certainly not on a very volatile level. Nothing more. Equivalent to one of those shipboard deals that never get beyond the stage of maneuver. He did not want it to be more important than that, and yet he had the uneasy suspicion that it might be. In attempting to analyze how she affected him, the easiest factor was the physical. She had a lovely body and moved with unconsciously provocative grace. He desired her. That was an uncomplicated drive. But there was more beyond that—or in another sense more that was perhaps more important. He felt a strong need to protect her. It was laughably close to those boyhood daydreams where he wanted so desperately to defeat a flock of scoundrels before the eyes of his eighth-grade beloved. He wanted to protect her, and more. He wanted to be able to watch her in homely things, brushing that white sheen of her hair with her strangely dark brows knitted in cosmetic concentration, brushing her teeth, putting on a robe, making coffee, washing plates, hanging out washing, pushing a supermarket cart. He wanted to see the shifting and untellable mysteries of her dissolved into the ordinary. More than anything, he wanted her to glow and laugh. At one lunch Park Barnum told John and Barbara and Bitsy about some of the trials and turmoils of a small advertising agency in Manhattan. He told it so amusingly and well that it was not spoiled by the consciousness that he had told it many times before, editing and exaggerating his material. One story was really very funny. And as John laughed he heard Barbara laugh beside him. It was the first time he had heard her laugh. And, he realized, it was not the sort of laugh he would have expected, not light and fragile at all. It was a hearty, husky, earthy burst of sound. He glanced at her and saw her face alight. A moment later she was composed again, smiling evenly and rather carefully at the rest of Park's monologue. And John Kemp felt a shaft of pain and loss so deep and sudden that for a few moments he was unable to identify it for what it was, pure jealousy and envy directed against the dead husband, and a sense of outraged indignation that one man should have been permitted to be given so much.

And after that he wished that he were the world's greatest clown, such a genius of comedy that he could make her laugh at any time.

Some days before, on the same day as a matter of fact that he had received, forwarded from New Orleans, the casual, proud, brave and deeply moving letter from Mary Jenningson in California, he had gone for an evening walk outside the wall and had seen Barbara standing in pallid moonlight against the wall, her shoulders held in a strange and rigid way, as though she faced execution.

He had gone over to her. She had kept her face turned away from him, but he had seen the glinting of moonlight on moisture below her eyes.

"Anything I can do?"

"Thank you. No. I do not want any kind of sympathy. It makes such a nice approach, doesn't it? Sympathy. Such a nifty gambit, John. Comfort the poor sad lady. Make her spill her woes. Tell her yours. And then you can comfort each other. I'm so damn tired of devices."

He stood silent in the moonlight, a few feet from her, looking at the way her profile was outlined against the wall. He sensed that this was a time of crisis in their relationship. The drawbridge, so tentatively lowered, had suddenly been snatched up with a great rattling of chains, and every battlement bristled with pikes, and all the bowstrings were drawn taut. There had to be some way of crying "Friend!" Some way to still her instinctive alarm. And she had spoken so bitterly.

Before he spoke he took a long time to think his words over very carefully. "Barbara, there is a very ugly fetish in our culture, a kind of erroneous folklore which says that divorcees and widows are uncommonly vulnerable to a male on the hunt. So that makes them fair game. So, from the way you talk, I'd say you've been a target. Certainly Klauss is as obvious as they come. To be entirely honest with you,

131

I suppose in one sense—in the sense that I respond in a perfectly ordinary way to a pretty woman—I'm a male on the hunt. But not devious, Barbara. I'm not that kind of guy. I haven't got any fancy program outlined which is supposed to end up with us in bed. I do like you. I'm attracted to you. I'd like to have you drop your guard a little. You can drop it without my changing my attitude or habits or approach to you one damn bit. I didn't follow you out here. I didn't know you were out here. This was an accident. You've been crying. So let's start over. Anything I can do?"

She was silent and motionless for so long that he began to think she would not speak again, that perhaps the least awkward thing to do would be to just turn and walk quietly away.

Her rigid shoulders slumped and she turned and looked at him. "I'm sorry, John. Gun-shy, or something. That Klauss person snuck under my guard right after I got here. For a few minutes. He makes me crawly. And our instructor isn't much better. He told me I was a lovely clockwork toy in a crystal case. The inference seemed to be he was ready and able to wind up my spring again. I suppose it's flattering. A long time ago it used to be sort of . . . reassuring to be pursued. A nice full datebook. But now it just makes me feel tired and depressed. I lost a husband I loved with all my heart. I'm not over it. Tonight I was, maybe for the first time, facing the idea—and it seems in a sense to be a terrible idea—that I will get over it. In time. In my own way. I don't want help. Not the kind of help that people, men, seem to be most eager to offer. It is such a horrid form of arrogance for them to feel themselves to be so utterly fascinating that they can easily make me . . . forget. Do you understand why I . . . keep my guard up?"

"Of course I do. But you can let it down a little for kindly ole John. I just want to be a friend."

She put her hand out suddenly and they shook hands solemnly in the moonlight. "Walk with me a little," she said. "Please."

And they had walked and talked about the school and the courses. She had begun to regain a large measure of forgotten skills, to the extent that the exercises imposed by Agnes Keeley had become unsatisfying. On the other hand, Torrigan's approach, so steamy and pseudo-philosophical and frantic, left her dissatisfied. They agreed that they would both enjoy spending the equivalent time on their own work, and were amused to learn that they both continued the classes because, due to the constantly increasing absenteeism, somebody had to attend to keep the classes from being embarrassingly tiny.

He talked to her about his own work, his hobby painting and its relation to architecture. He described some of the structures he had designed and she said she would very much like to see them some day.

Later, after he was in bed, he had the smug feeling that he had handled it well. She had begun to talk freely to him, and with animation. During the days that followed their relationship continued on the new level.

And yesterday, Thursday, he had dared to suggest to her the Saturday trip he had in mind. Park was going with Bitsy in the Mercedes up to Mexico City. So he would have no use for the station wagon, and was quite willing to lend it to John Kemp. He suggested to Barbara that they drive down to Taxco and see it, and on the way back cut over to Vista Hermosa for a swim and dinner.

She had looked as if she would make some excuse not to go, and when she said yes, he had the impression that her answer had surprised her almost as much as it had surprised him. The prospect of spending a whole day with her kept giving him recurrent prickles of excitement.

He sat in the dusky garden patio and knocked his pipe out on the edge of the stone bench. It had begun to look as though his Mexican plans would not work out the way he had thought. He had thought to paint a little and let all the emotional knots loosen and then, in a state of rest and calm, make the decision as to whether to take over Kurt Jenningson's share of the firm, or insist on being bought out by Kurt. He had not counted on any new factors in the equation. But it had begun to look as though Barbara might be a factor. He sensed that, if he was lucky enough, marriage might be the only possible answer to the whole thing. And, should he take over the whole shop, it would leave no time for either the careful and long-term courtship necessary, or the proper establishment of a life with a new bride.

He heard the clack of high heels on the stone path and felt his heart lift as he thought it was she. But is was that woman. Miles's friend. For a moment he could not remember her name. Gloria something. Gloria Garvey. She had not been near the school since that night they had left together and he had managed to attain a certain measure of sobriety during the long walk back to the hotel.

He stood up and said, "Hello, Gloria."

She planted herself carefully, facing him. "Hello there, John Sneaky Kemp." She was dressed brightly and untidily, and her coarse hair was unkempt. She swayed and caught herself, took two measured strides to the stone bench and sat down a little more violently than she had intended. She hiccuped once and patted the stone beside her. "Sit, Johnny my lad." He sat beside her.

"I am dronk," she said. "I am besotted. You know, ladies in their cups are horrible sights. Hate the sight of it myself. But you see, I got caught in a sort of a bind. Usually I can handle it just fine. But this time I had to take on a little more than I can handle. Know why?"

"I wouldn't have any idea."

"You hurt hell out of my pride, you basser, you big basser. Expected maybe you'd come apologize. 'F you didn't come, I wasn't ever going to come here, come near you. See?"

"Gloria, that was my time to get dronk. I don't know why the hell I did."

"Found out the next day, baby, that I didn't exactly go in that pool by any big fat accident. It was described to me. You took a little half step and swung it at me. Pow! Was all over town. All my friends. Great friends. Just deeeeelighted that Gloria got herself bunked into the pool and walked out on. What the hell, Johnny my lad?"

"Okay. I did do it on purpose. But I was drunk. That's my excuse. You were determined I was coming home with you and I was determined I wasn't. So I did a silly thing and I'm sorry. I thought of finding you and apologizing. But sometimes apologies just make things worse. You know."

"You are frank and honest, you basser, aren't you? Which leads us to the next step. Am I such a raddled old pig you got to bunk me into a pool to keep from sleeping with me? I talk real direct, don't I? I know it isn't because you're queer. Even when they look like a pro wrestler, I can spot a queer at a thousand yards. And li'l ole Drummy checked the records for me so I know it isn't one of those faithful-to-the-old-lady kicks. You're no prude, boy. You've been around. So, you see, I don't know what the hell it is. I got too much pride to come around here and try to find out. I know when I'm not wanted, all right. But I haven't been able to stop thinking about it. And so the only way to come here and find out, you basser, was to get real go to hell out of a bottle or two. I got a wrinkle here and a wrinkle there. Standard wear and tear. I'm thirty-seven. And I have kept

134

hell out of my shape, Johnny my lad. Just luck because I'm no exercise and diet bug. But it's there. And this face hasn't ever stopped clocks. So let's come clean with Gloria. Bad breath? Dandruff?"

There was an anxious sincerity behind her slurred chatter, and he sensed that she was not quite as drunk as she was appearing to be.

"I can't really give you a good answer, Gloria. I don't want to hurt your feelings, but you know, you were pretty damn aggressive. It made me a little jumpy. I haven't been scared of any female since I got used to playing kissing games a long time ago. I guess I was drunk enough to be filled with a kind of stuffy dignity. When I take too much I either get enormously dignified, or I get the girlish giggles."

"Aggression, huh?"

"I guess so."

She leaned forward, elbows on her knees. "Been about three weeks of self-evaluation. Never spent so much damn time staring in mirrors, front and back and sideways. You know something, Johnny dear? I'm no damn good. I gave three husbands a taste of hell on earth. I haven't got one real friend. Oh, I know a *hell* of a lot of people. No friends. I go my way. They go theirs. Lots of money. Oh, lots of it. And I know just where every penny is and how hard it's working for Gloria. No damn good, though." She straightened up and turned and stared at him, her face an oval of pallor on the edge of night. "I never in my whole life wanted to give anybody anything. Any part of me. All I want to do is take. I want things and people to make me feel pleasured and when I'm through I want them to go away quietly. That's what I came to, John Kemp. Three weeks to hit the answer. It wasn't you. It wasn't the Garvey physical assets. So it had to be that you were so smart you could see the nogoodnik part of me. And it's beginning to show more. Oh, I've got a mean eye. Never noticed before. Real mean. Cold as a toad."

"It isn't that involved. I just resented you, I guess, because there . . . wasn't any chase. No chance for pursuit. No business of the stone club and dragging her off to the cave by the hair."

"Hmmm. Hell, I'm pursued enough, but it's by spooks I wouldn't be seen dead with. When I see what I want, like when I came here and saw you, I get a billion butterflies and I can't take a deep breath. So maybe I get obvious. Aren't we supposed to be emancipated? Never had any trouble before. Just you. Damn you!"

135

"I guess I'm the old-fashioned type."

They sat in a rather strained silence for almost a minute until she finally said with exasperation, "So start pursuing, damn it!"

"What?"

"Here I am. Go get your stone club, friend. You certainly raise hell with my morale. You make me feel awkward and clumsy and guilty as all hell. And specially unattractive to men."

"Now listen, Gloria, I . . ."

"Here we go again. My car is outside. Aggress me or something. I went at it wrong the last time, so I'm trying to go at it right. Here's the keys. You drive."

He refused to take the keys. "Gloria, we just got off on the wrong foot in the beginning. It's something you can't go back and fix. I'm sorry. I don't want your morale to suffer."

"What have I done wrong now?" she cried.

"It isn't anything you've done. It's just the timing. I . . . I've gotten so interested in one of the women students that . . ."

"The slim blonde with the Jesus Saves expression?" she asked in a dull voice.

"I guess you have the right one in mind," he said.

"Having lots of fun and games?" she asked tauntingly.

"No. It's . . . more of a marriage bit, I think."

Gloria stood up slowly. "Some days, ducks, I'm older than God." He stood up and she turned and faced him. "Well, I have a file of testimonials that indicate you're missing out on a lot of natural talent and energy and the fruits of lots of practice, man. Don't suppose that gives you any regrets, does it?"

"Sorry, Lady Gloria."

There was just enough light left so that he could see her wry grin. She patted his cheek. "If some night you hear a dog howling outside your window, Kemp, it'll be me. Wish you'd been one of the tiresome three. I have the feeling I might have been able to stay married to you. Because if I'd stepped out of line you'd have beat hell out of me. Which any one of them should have done. God knows I gave 'em cause. Nighty-night, you basser."

She walked away quite briskly. He saw her silhouetted for a moment against the lights in the lobby as she went through the doorway.

Later, bystanders reported that Gloria Garvey came stalking through toward the front door, her face expressionless. When Gam Torrigan, who was sitting with Monica and Harvey, explaining to them the world of Picasso, spoke to Gloria, she gave no sign that she had heard him. But she paused with her hand on the door and stood there for long seconds before she wheeled around and marched straight to where Gam sat.

"Gloria, darling, have a chair. This might interest you. I was telling these young . . ."

"On your feet!"

"I . . . I beg your pardon."

"Up, boy!"

They say that Gam got up and was marched out the front door. He looked back with a certain plaintive look of apology, but they did not hear what he tried to say. They did hear the engine in the powder-blue Jag rev up to six thousand screaming rpm. It gave the auditory impression of rearing back and then plunging out through the gate.

They did not see the rest of it. They did not see her streak by the barracks, turn left, turn left again on the main road and drop down into Cuernavaca as if they were in free fall. In the stutter of street lights Torrigan looked with apprehension and the beginning of a primitive fear at the narrow eyes, clamped jaw and set lips of the Viking woman at the wheel. He looked at the road ahead. He clamped his big hands around his hard thighs. He shut his eyes. He opened them for a fraction of a second and saw a man in mid-air, leaping in terror toward the sidewalk. The next glimpse disclosed the gray furry rear end of a burro inches from the right front fender as she swerved. On the third glimpse he saw the big rackety bus starting across their bows, closing the gap between its front bumper and the rear end of a truck. He made a squeaky little sound as he squinched his eyes shut. There was a violent swerve, a tiny little ting of metal audible over the roar of wind and engine, and they were free again, dropping down into the city, with the shrill and angry *whee*ing of the policeman's whistle dying away behind them.

When they came to a screeching stop Torrigan opened his eyes and saw they were on a dark and quiet street, with the front bumper inches from the closed door of a small public garage. The garage door opened inward and a young Mexican came out and greeted Gloria. She got out of the car, gave the boy instructions in staccato Spanish and turned and started diagonally across the narrow street toward the high curb on the far side, her heels making a busy *clack-clock* sound in the stillness. She turned before she stepped up onto the curb and said, "Well?"

Torrigan pulled himself out of the car. His knees supported him. His shirt was pasted clammily to his ribs. He crossed over to her and walked beside her a short distance to the small tiled lobby of a hotel called Las Rosas. She went up the staircase on the right. He followed her, several stairs behind her, and down a corridor. She stopped in front of a door, got her key out and opened the door.

"Gloria," he said, "I . . ."

She turned on him, her eyes feral in the faint light in the hallway. He got the impression that she was half crouching, and that she could extend and retract her fingernails like a cat.

"Men!" she said. "My God, how I despise every one of you!"

"But, Gloria, I . . ."

"Men! I've heard you telling your tiresome little jokes and making your stupid brags. I've heard that weary saying you men have about the way you'd like to die. This, brother, is your chance."

"But I don't under—"

"I'd like to wipe the whole filthy tribe of you right off the face of the earth. And I'll start with you, Torrigan. If, indeed, there is any possibility at all of killing one of you in the way I have in mind, then say your prayers, because *I* am going to give it the old school try, boy."

And she edged around him and backed him through the door and slammed it behind her when they were inside. Even after pursuit had stopped, Torrigan kept backing, his hand half raised. He moistened his lips and swallowed hard, and there was a strange look in his eyes. It was something of the look of a glutton who, after years of classifying himself as a gourmet, is horridly confronted with a monstrous platter of broiled Eskimo.

Torrigan returned to El Hutchinson in a taxi on Monday, fifteen minutes after his class was scheduled to begin. Class met in the garden patio. Torrigan went to his room and appeared before the class ten minutes later. His class on that seventeenth day of July consisted of Barbara, Klauss, John Kemp, Monica, Harvey, Hildabeth and the Wahls. They had their easels set up and paint-boxes open, and were busily at work when Torrigan joined them. Nearly all of them hunched their shoulders slightly in instinctive preparation for his usual display of noise and energy, bounding from easel to easel, braying comment and criticism, chiding the timid, jeering at the confused. Every one of them knew he had been gone since before dinner on Friday evening. And they had heard reports on the odd circumstances of his leaving.

He stood there like a very old man, blinking placidly in the sunlight, dreaming the long memories of half-forgotten wars. The brave bristling of the big black beard had dwindled to a look of wilt. And the bold red brigand nose and the red lips nestling in the beard's blackness had paled to a pink tinged with gray. His once arrogant and demanding eyes, pale and with that Mongol tilt, had all the vitality of glazed glass marbles in the bottom of a fish bowl. John Kemp, barely able to conceal the amusement arising from his shrewd guess as to the cause as well as the nature of Torrigan's undoing, was nonetheless able to feel a twinge of very real sympathy for the man.

Hildabeth cackled loudly in the silence. "Mr. Teacher," she said, "you put me in mind of a fella my daddy used to tell me about when I was a little tyke. This fella fell off his horse into a wallow and a whole herd of buffalo stampeded right over him and didn't harm a hair on his head. But Daddy said he went around the rest of his life looking sort of far away, as if he lost something and couldn't remember what it was or what he done with it."

Torrigan looked at her blankly. "Eh? I . . . I guess I'm late. Please keep working." His voice was soft and hoarse. They kept working. He shuffled slowly around and looked at their work and made mild and almost inaudible comments which made little sense. Every few moments he would yawn so hugely, opening a tired red cavern in the middle of the beard, that Barbara was reminded of poor Saltamontes. Torrigan lasted about forty minutes. And during the last ten minutes he was tottering rather than shuffling. He excused himself and floated blindly away.

Barbara flashed John Kemp a quick and knowing and rather feline look of great amusement. On Saturday, after walking the streets of Taxco, they had climbed up to the terrace of the Hotel Victoria and sat near the railing and had a chilled beer as they looked out over the town. While they were there, realizing that now he knew her well enough and she might be amused, he told her of his clumsy escape

139

from the overeager grasp of Mrs. Garvey, and how her visit to the hotel tied in with the abduction of Torrigan. She was amused, as he had guessed she would be, and she was also touched by what he could recall of Gloria's grim self-analysis.

He enjoyed the day with her enormously. She was one of those rare people who use their eyes, who have a talent for pointing out special beauty and ludicrousness and ugliness and charm. She had been subdued when they left, and quiet again during the drive back to the hotel, but during the hours of the afternoon and evening she was very alive, and a delightful companion. She had been shy with a slight and touching awkwardness born of self-consciousness when, at Vista Hermosa, she had walked from the bathhouse in her blue-and-white swimsuit around the side of the huge pool to where he sat on the apron waiting for her. Her legs were long and slim and deft, smooth and pale, but lightly ivoried by the memory of the tans of other summers. In the lines of her body there was no trace of bloat or spread or softness. She swam well, with the smooth muscles of her arms and back moving sleekly under her skin.

He looked at her by candle light at dinner at Vista Hermosa. She was telling him about the art courses she had taken in college. He listened for a time, and then lost the meaning of the words as he watched her lips and her eyes. This was, he thought, a paragon. But paragons do not exist. We are all human. She is flawed, somehow, but I cannot detect it. I could bring her back here on a honeymoon.

And suddenly she had frowned prettily at him and said, "Pay attention, sir."

"I've heard every word you said, honestly."

"You were a million miles away!"

When they were back at the hotel she turned to him and held out her hand and said, "This was one of the better days, John. Actually. I'm grateful to you."

"We're tourist types. There'll be more trips if I can chisel a car again. All right?"

"Yes indeed."

"How about tomorrow?"

"No thanks. Not tomorrow. Things to wash out. Letters to write."

"How about a trip down to the center of town for the Sunday night band concert at least? Walk around and around with the rest of the people."

"Until the rain comes down in sheets. All right."

He walked slowly toward his room, wearing a half-smile of content. It was nearly midnight. Park and the girls from Texas would be the only ones still out probably.

As he approached the door to Paul Klauss's room he heard an odd scratching sound and saw a movement in the shadows. When he was close he saw that it was the maid, Margarita, and apparently she had been scratching at Paul's door.

"*Buenas noches,* Margarita," he said in a low voice as he passed her, heard her murmured reply. She had moved slightly and he caught a glimpse of her face in a patch of light, her usually merry expression completely gone. She looked sullen and angry, and he received the obscure impression that she was also afraid. He had sensed, as had a few of the others, that there was something between Klauss and this young girl in whose brazen mannerisms there was an odd flavor of innocence. Like Klauss, he thought, to take complete advantage of any passing opportunity. Seduction with such a man would be like a reflex. And he would drop her quickly in order to stalk more attractive game, such as Barbara. So Margarita could be left outside his door, scratching furtively, looking sullen and afraid.

He turned back and approached her again. "*Qué quiere, Margarita? Qué cosa?*"

"*Nada,*" she said flatly.

"Why do you make this sound on the door of the Señor Klauss in the middle of the night?"

"*Es nada.*"

"Come with me, please," he said, "where we can talk without making noise to disturb those who sleep."

She came with him sullenly but obediently, out through one of the stone arches on the opposite side of the corridor, out into the patio. At his request, she sat on the stone bench, her hands in her lap, her face quite still, not looking at him. He put one foot up on the stone bench wondering if his skimpy Spanish was equivalent to the situation.

"Did you wish to speak to the Señor Klauss?"

"Yes."

"Is he in the room?"

"I am sure he is there. But he will not open the door."

"Why won't he open the door?"

"I do not know."

"What is it that you wish to say to him?"

She suddenly erupted in a torrent of Spanish that he had no hope of following. He managed to stop her and tell her

141

to speak slowly and carefully, as he did not have much Spanish.

And, as the story began to unfold, as he stopped her from time to time to make certain that he understood, he began to feel the crazy laughter deep inside him which he wondered if he could hold. He kept his face sober and concerned.

It seemed that the Señor Ball was very shy. He had no Spanish. She had no English. On the first day he had looked at her in that way. But when she started to take off her dress in his room, he became frightened. It was very sad he was so frightened. He had cold blood. She told about the advice of Felipe, and the key that would open the door of the room of the Señor Ball, and how she had conquered his fear and warmed his blood. It was good to make love with the Señor Ball. He was such a very pretty man. But also a small rabbit. A most timid one. She told what Felipe had taught her to say to Señor Ball, and she wished the Señor Kemp to know that she was not a whore, not at all. It was a good thing she was doing for him, to turn him from a timid rabbit into a man. And it was clear that it had been a very important thing to him, to have Margarita, because even though he fought her as though he were the woman, a woman of virtue, and she a drunken soldier, afterward he would cry. It had happened three times. It was good for him, as anyone could see. But now he was making it impossible for it to happen again. The last time she had surprised him by hiding in the closet until after he was in his bed. She had love for Señor Ball. A great warm love for him. But she had not been given enough of a chance. Now he would not smile or speak. And he had purchased a small bright light to carry in his pocket, and each time he returned to the room at night, he would search for her and if she was hiding there he would run away and he would not come back. And when he was inside the room alone, he would fasten the chain to the inside of the door, a chain he had bought in the market, so that her key was no good. Felipe was very angry with her. He had beaten her several times because she could bring him no more money from Señor Ball. He would beat her again, and harder. Señor Ball knew it was his Margarita who scratched upon the door, but he was still afraid of love. His blood had not yet been made warm. And so he lay there in the darkness, trembling. Poor Señor Ball. She began to weep.

It was with a mighty effort that John managed to control

himself. And he suddenly had a monstrous idea. Klauss, with all his neat and fastidious little habits and mannerisms had doubtless been appalled, affronted and undone by the earthy directness of this sleazy and vital little moron. And for the almost professional lady's man, the necessity to pay Margarita must well have been the final blow at the heart. And his tears had been of helpless frustration.

"I can tell you how to get in," he said.

Her tears stopped at once and the broad smile glistened. *"Ay! Por favor!"*

"You must knock on the door. Do not scratch. Knock like this. Quickly, but not too loudly."

"Yes?"

"He will think it is someone else. He will come to the door. He will say something. You will not understand what he says. And then you must whisper, quite loudly, what I will teach you to whisper. When he hears that, he will open the door."

It took at least fifty repetitions before he was satisfied with the way she said it. The most difficult part was to get her to whisper "It's" instead of "Eet's."

He stood silently in the shadows ten feet from Klauss's door. She hesitated and then knocked briskly, as he had taught her. She waited and then knocked again. And then he heard Klauss say warily, "Who is it?"

She whispered loudly. An accent is much more readily disguised by whispering.

"It's me. Barbara."

He heard the sudden frantic jangling of the chain and thought how fevered was the energy Klauss was using to get his door open. The door swung wide. Margarita went swarming into the greater darkness, and her sudden clarion giggle was like a shower of silver needles in the night air. In counterpoint to her giggle, and just before the door slammed shut behind them, John heard a hoarse, dull cry of despair. There was a sound of scuffling, and a thump, and, muffled by the closed door, a clear, sweet cry of laughter from Margarita.

After John Kemp was in bed he could not stop chuckling. He felt thoroughly ashamed of himself. And just as he was sliding into sleep he heard, floating in between the bars of his window, a high, clear voice full of great joy, saying, "Geef me ten dollar!"

"Pay the girl, Señor Ball," he mumbled, and grinned and turned over into sleep.

Chapter Eleven

DURING THE FIRST FEW WEEKS of the Cuernavaca Summer Workshop, Parker Barnum had begun to feel as though all the little rips and abrasions on the underside of his soul were knitting and mending. He had begun to lose that odd sensation that, at any moment, he was capable of committing an act so luridly insane that the whole world would pause and stare at him with mouth agape.

And it had become increasingly easy for him to restrict Suzie to one fenced area in the side yard of his mind. During his waking hours her escapes were less frequent. But at night she roamed free, taunting, accusing, wearing—one by one—all of the things he had best liked to see her in.

Remembering the advices of Dr. Gottrell, Park sensed that he was in the delicate process of rebuilding his identity. Though he had the sophisticate's approach to mental illness and analysis, it still seemed shameful to him that he could have cracked wide open. You went to a head shrinker to let him unravel the knots in your psyche placed there as a result of childhood emotional trauma. And then, at cocktail parties, you could speak somberly and intimately with those others who were couchbound, or had completed the course. It was like a big club composed of the more sensitive types. With high dues to keep out the rabble. It seemed unfair and against the rules to suddenly have all your inner walls come tumbling down, leaving you quivering, naked as an egg.

He could sense the factors which were contributing to the new feeling of identity, the new shiny layers, like a tender new barnacle building its home, complete with lid. First there was the painting. He was aware that he was a one-eyed king in the realm of the blind, but nonetheless it was good to see the hand and brush create the desired stroke, good to sense the interest and envy of the other students. He and John and Barbara were the students with training and talent. And, to a lesser extent, the Wahls. But he felt that perhaps the Wahls would merit a higher rating were they not the obsessed victims of other interests at the moment.

Another reassuring factor was the smug knowledge that

Sessions and March thought well enough of his abilities to keep him on substantial pay during his rather indefinite leave of absence. This comfort was enhanced by the awareness that, for the first time in his working life, he was saving money. With the house and Suzie and the twins, he had often felt as if he was clawing his way along the wall of a bottomless canyon. But now, as he told himself, he was a young and talented man with a new car, clothes, manners, conversation and money in the bank. As he kept telling himself.

Also, Bitsy was important to his self-esteem. It had truly shocked him when he had learned not only what her allowance from the trust fund was at present, but what it would jump to when she reached twenty-one, a date a year and a month away. It made you feel somebody had put the decimal point in the wrong place. It awed him. So here was a rich and handsome young gal who seemed perfectly content to be with him, casually accepting their status as a twosome within the little Workshop world. She listened so well when he talked that he showed off for her, finding that special glibness and pyrotechnic turn of phrase which had also come easily with Suzie so long ago. And, as with Suzie, it was easy to be amusing. He enjoyed making her laugh. When they walked together, she had a sort of obedient puppy trick of slipping her hand in his. In the young contours of her body, in the way she handled herself, she often reminded him of Suzie.

In his relationship with her, Park had cast himself in the role of man of the world, with slight avuncular overtones. And Bitsy was the young and impressionable girl. The progress of the script seemed inevitable. He had been saddened and broken by the loss of a great love. She had recently shucked a meaningless young romance. And so, during this summer, they would have a bittersweet affair, intense and, knowing they must part, lingeringly tragic. Her young warmth would mend his broken heart. And from him she would learn something of Life, something she would need to know on her way toward becoming a Woman.

But Bitsy would not stay put in her role. She was an enigma. Across her considerable areas of naïveté were streaks of a sophisticated practicality that infuriated him. When he tried to edge, conversationally, toward that special rapport which would enhance their need for each other, she would be off and away, into Texas anecdote or local gossip, or even,

145

for God's sake, sports cars or popular music. It made him feel like a stubborn and overly optimistic old hound who has never ceased believing he can get a partridge all by himself, who after the quivering stalk and the shambling pounce, runs with fierce energy and comes to a panting, tongue-lolling halt as he sees the bird fly over the crest of the hill.

She was perfectly willing to be kissed. In fact, she upheld her share of the ceremony with such practiced and hearty co-operation that she tended to give him temporary emotional asthma. But it was disconcerting to have her give him one brief dreamy look, wriggle away and say, "I sure don't think that dress Mary Jane got yesterday is a good color for her, do you?" And such diversions left him feeling like the same old hound with one tail feather in his teeth and his heart heavy.

A certain amount of manual liberty seemed to be permitted under some unwritten covenant, but the moment he exceeded the limit, she had a knack of turning into a bundle of elbows, chins and shoulder blades. There was never any sigh of annoyance. She just blocked him into the boards and skated away.

Her background and education were curiously spotty. She knew the finest restaurants and hotels in the country the way most kids know the local drive-ins, and she had an equivalent attitude toward them. Mary Jane Elmore was the same. She had and used charge accounts in the most fabulous shops and department stores in Texas, but she would spend a half hour picking out a thirty-peso silver bracelet. She had hooked tuna off Bimini, traveling on a yacht out of Galveston, but she couldn't remember just what year that was or who owned the boat. She could speak superbly colloquial French, but she had no more idea of the history and geography of the world than any sparrow.

And she could so deftly avoid any serious conversation that he was in frequent despair, saying once, "Bitsy, my God, don't you even want to talk or think about life, or destiny or love? Do all the abstract words scare hell out of you? I don't even know what you're like inside. You don't give me a clue."

"I'm just little old Bitsy, Park. Nothing very complicated. I just go to and fro for laughs. Let's go dip up old Mary Jane for a gin session. It's your turn to be captain."

"You play too damn steep for me. You scare me. Bitsy, honestly now, are we ever going to talk seriously?"

"Well now, you just talk up a storm, and I'll listen. I

don't have all those deep thoughts. I just go to and fro."

"I know. For laughs."

But he retained his hope that he could get her back onto the right lines in the script that seemed so inevitable.

Until, alarmingly, the brand-new walls began to crumble. The letter from Trev Helding was the first tiny jar that started the flaking of the new plaster. Becky was doing well. It was too easy to remember all the evidences of her quickness, taste and intelligence. And, after all, Sessions and March was a business concern, not a charitable institution. They could damn well push Becky up into his job and send him a letter of regrets. Don't come back. They could get Becky cheaper. And it would make sense for them to do so.

It wasn't so bad if you were in an agency and sensed that you were under the ax. You developed a sixth sense about such things. So you started wheeling and dealing first. You could either mend your position by finding out who was holding the knife and either dealing with him, or striking first, if he was vulnerable. If neither would work, you could set up some lunches here and there while you still had a job, and say the right things about the stifling of your creative talents, and your need for a job with more challenge. And then when they were ready to drop all the hardware on you, you walked out smiling and fat.

But what the hell could you do from Mexico when you were on sick leave as the result of a well-known emotional disaster? Once they sent their regrets, you'd have to go back with your hat in your hand and hang around strange waiting rooms. You couldn't bargain from power. You were scared. And if they wanted you, they could buy you cheap. Then the big drop in income would show on the records. It was all a carnival ride, and if you slipped off, you never got back to where you were. So maybe Suzie had been his luck. All his luck.

He couldn't keep it from going around and around in his head, and when he tried to write the necessary friendly notes to Herbie and John and Becky, the jitters kept showing. In the end he finally sent them off, but each one had required more thought and rewriting than any national budget. The savings that seemed so pleasant were curiously shrunken, even though the figure remained the same. It was the variation in the basic question—not what you could buy with it, but how long could you live on it? And what the hell was the point in buying a car he didn't need just to come down

147

here? And the new casual clothes he couldn't use back on the Avenue.

When that wall began to crumble, it seemed to set off another one. The painting. For some time he had detected within himself a little nibbling of dissatisfaction with the work he was doing. And finally he detected the reason. He had become far too glib and tricky. He could create effects very readily, but the effects were achieved through the use of too many of the artifices of commercial illustration.. The work he had done long ago had been clumsier by far, but stronger and more honest. When he began to look at it that way he could see that even the work Ardos was doing was more valid than his own. It had strength. And his work had the careful illusion of strength, the sly imitation of honesty, the glib imitation of power. He had told himself for so long that one day he would paint again. Once security had been achieved he would find the privacy he wanted and paint. But he had worked too long with the superficial, with all the cloying indecencies of huckster art. And all its syrups had leaked down into his soul—so that now he spread them along with the pigments in every stroke of brush or palette knife. Once he was dismally aware of this skilled decadence, he seemed to see an expression in the eyes of John and Barbara and Gam that he had not noticed before. A mild and ironic pity. Poor little ad man, trying with such self-importance to make illustration look like art. He destroyed those few pieces he had set aside to take back.

And it was shortly after Gam's curiously humbling week-end in town, that the Bitsy arrangement began to crumble. When he had had her largely to himself, he could feel that somehow she would change and it would all be as planned. But Mary Jane, with constantly increasing efficiency, had begun to make a special talent of acquiring large, random young men who were summering in Mexico. These young men, stimulated by the proximity of the girls from Texas, could become uncommonly persuasive. And as Mary Jane's deliberate acquisitions began to use up more and more of the girls' time, they attended even fewer classes. It became most difficult for Park to keep track of Bitsy. He would be away from her for a half hour and return, only to find that the girls had left, accompanied by a pair of meaty, grinning young men who had come to El Hutchinson to pick them up.

In the long stillnesses of the insomniac night he would hear the giggling return, the traditional fragments of "The

Eyes of Texas Are upon You," the *chunk* of car doors, the donkey bray of some young tower of muscles. And he would know that if either of the girls made breakfast, she would be drab with hang-over, husky with song, talk and cigarettes, and almost indetectably musky with the last exudations of alcohol through young pores.

He found himself devoured in a jealousy of that special kind which has its roots in pride. And he wondered if he had gone about the whole thing wrong. Maybe his approach to her should have been to go about honking with laughter, making muscles, baking his hide brown in the sun and belaboring the obvious.

It was disappointing to be able to spend less and less time with her, and see his emotional plan become ever more improbable, but it was considerably more wearing to join her group. They had an unconscious talent for shutting him out. He was with the group, but not of it. His most reliable conversational performances, when he could wedge himself into the conversations, were met with a rather blank stare from all the sets of young eyes, a certain amount of courteous attention, and that small and polite riffle of laughter which is the usual accompaniment to all lead balloons. Age seemed an insurmountable barrier. He kept telling himself that thirty-one was far from ancient. When he tried to talk and comport himself in their fashion, he knew he struck all the wrong notes. Yet when he tried to be himself, that slight avuncular tendency he had shown toward Bitsy bloated itself into ridiculousness. He heard himself trying to make sage remarks, and could not stop. He began to feel like a philosophical filler on the bottom of a page of the *Reader's Digest*. "Yessirree, you find that the grass, hit grows a sight taller in the valleys."

He carried his apartness around with him as they went from bar to bar, like an albatross around his neck. He would look at them with his mouth spread in an aching grin, and he would hear their bright babble and look at their smooth young faces, and sometimes he would get the impression that he sat there in pathetic senility, with rheumy eyes and thread of drool and socially embarrassing incontinence. And wondered why they put up with him at all.

And so he drank heavily when he was with them. His training had eliminated the normal antics of the sometime drunk. He went from glazed to wooden to incomprehensible, without ever losing the ability to add up the check and leave the proper tip and walk out in a straight line. He did not pass out, and he surrendered with an old-timey courtliness when it was decided by the group that somebody else should drive the wagon instead of good old Park Barnum.

With a great deal more frequency, Suzie kept hopping over her fence and wading through his mind, picking up her skirts and stepping with a fastidious distaste for the goop underfoot.

He knew that something was happening to him, and he knew it was not good, and he was scared. Somewhere he had once read that when a person is in free fall, if he shuts his eyes, he cannot tell up from down. He was being carried in some indefinable direction, with constantly increasing speed. He wanted to be able to reach out and grasp something, but he did not know where to reach. And he had begun to be afflicted with nervous involuntary movements of his hands and facial muscles.

Something was going to happen and he could not imagine what it would be. It was just a terrible Something.

And it happened in Mexico City on Saturday night, the twenty-second of July. The activities of the day had begun in a most dissatisfying way. Bitsy slept late. Mary Jane approached Park in the lobby at about eleven o'clock.

"Park, honey, there's two boys staying down at Las Mañanitas, and a friend of theirs at the Marik and the friend has to get up to Mexico City today. So we thought we'd all go in a bunch, and we sure can't fit in my little bug, so we thought if you aren't using your wagon."

"Just during the day?"

"Well, no. We're all going to stay on and barge around here and there and come back real late. I don't know what time it would be."

"I've got a date with Bitsy tonight."

She looked uncertain and said, "I guess maybe there's some little mixup about that. Because we planned this whole thing last night and Bitsy didn't say anything, so I guess she thought it wasn't definite or something."

"Well, if I've been canceled out, there's no reason why I can't come too, I guess. What time do we want to leave?"

"I . . . I guess that would be all right," she said. And then she laughed. "I swear, Park, if you keep tagging along all the time, you're like to get wore down to a nub."

He stared at her coldly, and had the insane desire to kick her in the stomach. "Maybe if I grease the wheels on my wheel chair, doll, I'll be able to keep up."

"Now don't you go getting all scratchy, Park. I didn't mean anything like that."

"With your permission then, I'll tag along."

"Let's get out of here right after lunch then."

He could detect no reaction when Mary Jane told Bitsy he was joining the group. No pleasure and no displeasure. The girls dressed up for night life in the capital. Furs and gloves and fragile pumps. They drove down into town and picked up the boys. Their names—the ones they collected at Las Mañanitas—were Tab and Wally. Park knew he'd have difficulty telling them apart. They were the approximate size of the average telephone booth. They had big brown muscles and big white teeth. They had brown brush cuts, lazy eyes, and a tender honeychile drawl. As soon as they picked up the third one at the Marik, Park knew that he would never be able to tell the new one—Chris—from the other two.

He gathered that they were Texas Aggies, that the boys and the girls had twelve or thirteen thousand mutual friends, and that after a few weeks of muscular dissipation, they were heading back to Texas to harden themselves up for the football season with some exotic kind of manual labor that apparently had something to do with the oil fields. Park could not imagine why they had to be hardened. They looked as if they could snap chains with their biceps and dent oak with their massive fists.

So they went up and over the mountains. Bitsy was between Park and Chris or Tab or Wally. Mary Jane sat in back with the other two. Bitsy sat for about ten minutes. From then on she knelt, facing the rear. And the hulk beside her was swiveled around. They all talked at once.

" . . . and you remember that ole B. C., the way he strayed off and got jumped that time over in Piedras Negras. He was doing just fine he said, until somebody come up behind him and peeled his head with a hunk of pipe. They threw B. C. in the little ole jail they got there, and the next day they put him to scrubbing a street with a raggedy old broom and him with a tequila head like a bongo drum . . ."

" . . . bought that chute and had Dobie take him up and he jumped out. Scared the pure hell out of Dobie on account of Gus said it felt so good falling he waited long as he could before he opened . . ."

" . . . married her when she was just thirteen damn years old, believe me . . ."

" . . . after he got up about eleven times and got knocked down again, he stayed right down there and he looks up and says . . ."

" . . . not enough left of that Ferrari to make you a bushel basket load, man . . ."

Park sighed inwardly and drove the mountain road to the city. Once there it turned into the usual situation, a state of almost complete disorganization which, curiously, duplicated the pattern of other evenings so closely that the disorganization itself seemed to be planned with some subtle end in view. There was the usual routine of the old dear friend who was supposed to be in town. This involved many phone calls, some of them to Texas, several taxi rides, because it was simpler to leave the car parked near their base of operations, the Continental Hilton. Eventually it was discovered that good old so-and-so had left last week for Acapulco. The search was interspersed with pauses for refreshment. After that came an interval of serious drinking, and then another wide-ranging search for some special restaurant that nobody could quite remember the name of. And the inevitable decision, what the hell, let's have another drink and go eat at the Hilton. And finally came another vague hunt for that place that had that hell of a good floor show that Dutch told us about.

By that time Park was thoroughly blurred. But his orderly descent into wooden oblivion was marred by one little word that had somehow stuck itself to the inside of his skull. Silly. You, Parker Barnum, are a silly little man. You are silly to be traveling with this herd of muscles on the forlorn off chance of charming one lass with curly copper hair. Your painting is silly. Your job was silly and will be silly. And you made a silly mess of your marriage, old boy.

Perhaps it was in some effort to divert himself from this unpromising line of self-castigation that Park made the decision to at last enlighten these young people by explaining them to themselves. He began in one of the succession of small cabarets. When he had a chance to slip into the conversation he stared at them severely and said, "You all got a bitched-up sense of values, every one of you. All you want outta life is a lotta motion and no significance." His brain felt keen as scalpels.

They stared at him. "Easy off, professor," one of the hulks said.

"Conversationally, buster, you are all dead wood, buster. You couldn't entertain an original idea if it . . . bit on you. Just a lot of garbage about who did what to who when."

Mary Jane said, "What have they been putting in his liquor?"

He felt firm and fatherly. He would not be distracted from this important mission. He would awaken them to all the terror and mystery of existence. He selected his next phrasing most carefully. As he got well into it, he suddenly realized that he was out of the conversation again. Nobody was listening. He raised his voice but he could not get their attention. So he let it fade off into a mumble. He leaned over and said the next important things directly down into his glass. It gave the words a hollow and portentous ring. The world rocketed toward oblivion and its prophets went unheard. It was a sad thing. It made his eyes sting.

And suddenly, without transition, he was walking down a broad sidewalk. They were just ahead of him. Abreast, arms locked, singing. Boy, girl, boy, girl, boy. The girls looked tiny by comparison. Mary Jane lifted both feet free of the sidewalk and made running motions. Park trotted along behind them. He had to be heard. It was important. "Hey!" he said. "Hey!"

Suddenly the broad unconscious backs infuriated him. He paused to let them get ahead, and then went forward at a dead run and slammed his shoulder into the small of the back of the big one on the end. Chris or Tab or Wally.

It staggered the huge boy and he turned around and said softly, "Now you whoa!" They had all turned and they were looking at him.

"You won't listen!" Park yelled at them.

"Ole buddy, you got a package on, and you've run out of anything worth talking. You've got took by the wobbles. Now you settle way down."

Park had a sudden image of himself battered to bloody ruin by the big calm brown fists, lying broken in the gutter with Bitsy weeping over him. The vision made him want to try again.

So he swung with all his strength at a big square jaw. And missed completely and sprawled on his hands and knees. As he got up he heard one of them say, "This ole boy is getting right repulsive, men."

"We better should give him a place to rest up."

"Like with Mike that time?"

One of them grabbed him. "What are you going to do?" Mary Jane demanded.

"Now don't you fret yourself, doll baby. He's uglyin' up the party."

They hurried him along the sidewalk toward the entrance to an expensive-looking restaurant. "Hey!" Park yelled.

And suddenly one of them had him by the ankles and one by the wrists and he sagged between them, his pants a few inches off the sidewalk.

"A-one," they said and started to swing him. "A-two."

"Hey!" Park yelled.

"A-three!" And with an enormous heave he went flying up into the night, the street lights pinwheeling in a dizzy blur. He sensed himself reach the top of an arc and thought he would come crashing down onto the cement, but instead he fell painfully and abruptly and too suddenly onto something hard. He hit his nose when he landed, and banged one knee painfully. He lay there holding his nose.

"You hurt him!" Mary Jane said.

"Doll baby, he landed soft as a feather, didn't he, Chris?"

"Like in a bed. Come on, you gals."

"You know," one of them said, "ole B. C. could most always throw a man twice that high, all by his own self."

The voices began to dwindle. He lay and held his nose. He heard the song fading. " . . . all the livelong day. The eyes of Texas are upon yoooooou . . ."

He got up onto his knees. The sidewalk was below him. He realized they had thrown him up onto the marquee of the fashionable-looking restaurant. It was about ten by twenty, with a knee-high rail of ornamental grillwork around it. They were walking into the distance. Not one of them looked back. Both girls had pulled their knees up so that they swung free between the boys. The song was swallowed and lost in the traffic roar of Reforma. He heard an excited gabble of Spanish under the marquee. Park sat cross-legged. His nose bled. Tears ran down his face. The left knee was ripped out of his trousers.

In some inescapable way, this was the ultimate humiliation. No tragic battered figure in the gutter. No exchange of blows. Not even any anger. Anybody wants to ugly up the party, they get thrown up onto a shelf and abandoned. And there's nobody in the whole wide damn world that gives one damn whether you live or die. Nobody. This is the comic end. All the paths, all the chances, all the choices, all the decisions, and so you took the exact ones at every little crossroads, actually the only ones, which could place you at this terminal point, weeping, abandoned and drunk, a dreary Chaplin huckster perched on a marquee at midnight in Mexico City, propelled to this ludicrous perch by Texas beef. Where did I ever go? he thought with a puzzled expression. What ever happened to me?

154

And he became aware of a persistent voice saying, "Halloo, sir. Halloo, sir! Halloo, sir!"

He hunkered over to the edge and looked down. There was a gasp and stir of interest from the clot of people who stood down there, their faces upturned. He estimated that he was at least fifteen feet above the sidewalk level. The boys had indeed been both powerful and precise.

A man in the middle of the group smiled up at him with an air of nervous reassurance. He wore a white dinner jacket with a red flower in the lapel, and had the look of a head-waiter.

"Good evening, sir. You will come down now, sir."

Parker was weary of being pushed around. "You will go to hell, sir."

"But, sir, that is not for sitting. It is forbidden to climb to that place except perhaps for a parade."

"I did not climb up here."

The smile faded slightly. "But how else could . . ."

"I took a big run and jumped."

"Now, now, sir. It is impossible that . . ." Somebody tugged at his arm and there was a hurried conversation in Spanish. The man looked up again and ran the tip of his tongue along one half of a small black mustache. He swallowed and said, "I did not have complete information. It does not seem to be a thing easy to believe, sir. But my doorman explains that you were . . . hurled up onto that place." He swallowed again. "As a ball."

"Yes. It's a game. You know. A sport. It isn't widely known yet."

"There is blood at the nose, sir. I recommend you come down."

"I am not going to come down."

The man had another consultation with his doorman. "My doorman reports that you were hurled up onto that place by three enormous, angry men who went away singing, accompanied by two young women, also singing. It is a matter for the police, sir. You will come down and we will telephone them at once."

"I am not concerned about the police. And I do not wish to discuss this further. I want to stay exactly where I am." And he hunched himself away from the edge. For a long time he ignored the calls, with their note of pleading, and then he moved to the edge and looked down again.

"What do you want now?"

"Ah, sir, I appeal to you. This is a nice place. Many

155

Americans come here. The food is truly excellent, sir. We will welcome your patronage at some other time. But now it is not desired to have a disturbance. The police do not have ladders I am told. And there is no way to ask the firemen to come quietly. They enjoy the sirens, sir. Our guests will be alarmed. You will come down, sir."

"No."

"I shall send strong waiters and kitchen people up to bring you down, sir."

"The minute the first head shows over the edge of this thing, sir, it will get kicked in the chops."

"That is rude, sir!"

"That's the way it has to be, old buddy."

"Then it must be the firemen, sir. But I inform you it will also be the police. There will be much trouble for you, sir."

"On what charge?"

"Trespass, one would think, sir."

"When I was *thrown* up here? Nonsense!"

"If you were acquainted with the police here, sir, you would know that they will think of something. Perhaps inciting a riot. Or an indecency of exposure. Are you still bleeding, sir?"

"I think so. I haven't been paying attention."

"You are at least drunk."

"Correction. I *was* drunk. Now I am sober. Completely cold sober. And I shall stay here. You can throw food to me. I will become a landmark. Through cold of night and rain and frost and burn of sun. Indomitable. People will throng to look at me. Your restaurant will thrive."

"Impossible, sir. This is a very correct place. Your ambassador has dined here often. And we frequently serve titled people. Even once a king."

"Kings are just like everybody else. They enjoy something unique. I am going to spend the rest of my natural life right here on your flossy little shelf, buster."

"Oh, no sir!" the man said piteously.

"Park! Park! I'm over here."

The crowd had grown. He spotted her on the edge of it. And he did not see the others. She looked very concerned.

"Hello, Bitsy."

"Park, please come down. I want to talk to you."

He hesitated for just a moment. "Okay, Bits." He clambered carefully over the low railing and lowered himself until he hung by his fingers on the marquee edge. When he

156

was sure it was clear below he dropped and struck his chin sharply on his knee and stood up wearily and spat out a fragment of filling.

The head waiter was bowing and beaming. The doorman was dispersing the curious. Bitsy took his arm and walked him down the street. She stopped by a street light and gave him Kleenex and said, "You're an awful mess, honey."

"Where did everybody go?"

"It's a long story. They went. I'll tell you some time. They decided to go back. They took the car."

"That's just jimdandy and nifty," he said thickly. "What're we supposed to do, for God's sake?"

"Hush!" she said. "Come along, now."

They walked several blocks. His knee was beginning to stiffen up. The whole world was blurred and unconvincing. She backed him against a wall and pushed with gentle emphasis against his chest and said, "Now you stay right here. Don't you dare move. I won't be gone a minute. Promise?"

"All right. All right. All right."

He shut his eyes. And when the world began to tilt ominously he opened them. In a few moments she materialized in front of him. "Now you come with me and don't say one darn word, and you walk fast, hear? And try to keep your face sort of turned away from people."

He had a confusing impression of a small, almost deserted, lobby, and then they were in a birdcage elevator that tinkled and ground its way slowly upward. He looked down at her. She stood beside him, her face bland, biting her under lip.

They went down a long corridor, poorly lighted, until she found the number. She unlocked the door and found the lights. It was an old-fashioned-looking hotel room with very high ceilings, two brass beds, a worn flowered rug, ancient dark furniture, a private bath with a tub on claw feet and a prehistoric shower head.

He weaved back and forth and tried to smile at her, and said, "Bitsy, Bitsy, Bitsy."

"Now you hush. You get in there and you shower good. You just cold soak, hear?" She pushed him toward the bathroom.

As he was undressing she came to the door and asked him to pass out his worn trousers. When he did so, she passed him in a blanket to wrap up in when he'd finished showering.

When he came out of the bathroom the world had a

157

more substantial look about it. She was biting a thread. "You could be human almost," she said. "I wouldn't call this any invisible weaving, but it'll be better than having your bare knee hanging out in the wind."

She went over to the bureau and poured him a large steaming cup of black coffee. "I found somebody on the other end of that phone speaks English. No, you'll spill if you try to carry it. You're on the unsteady side, man. You sit over there and I'll bring it."

He sat in a big chair, all dark brocade and carving, and tucked his blanket around him. She brought him the coffee and lighted his cigarette and her own. She had taken off her shoes and stockings. She poured coffee for herself, kicked a small dusty hassock over closer to his chair and sat on it.

"Better now?" she asked.

"Lots."

"Are you too woozy to understand me if I tell you something?"

"No. I'm operating on the inside better than the outside."

"Well, you were getting to be real messy and tiresome, Park. And I swear, it sure was funny when you went a-flying up there, arms and legs going like mad. And I laughed. And I felt kind of ashamed and sorry at the same time. Do you understand?"

"Yes. It's not flattering. But I understand."

"So we went on, oh, maybe two blocks to a little place where it's two steps down. And they were bragging on how high you flew. It's one of those things that'll get told for years, here and there. They were betting on how much you weigh."

"A hundred and sixty-five, about," he said wearily.

"After a little time they started talking about something else, and then I said isn't it about time we go back and get him. I tell you, they looked at me like I lost my mind. And all of a sudden I realized that wasn't part of it at all. They weren't going back. Had no intention of it right from the beginning. And, for a little while, I tried to go along with that idea, but I didn't feel right at all. Maybe it was funny, but it was cruel too. And nobody stopped to find out what was up there. Too drunk to think about it. And I thought maybe iron spikes sticking up or something. So I said I thought we ought to go back. They saw I meant it, so they tried to laugh me out of it. I tell you, Park, I sat there and I looked at them a long time and then something inside me gave a little clunk and sort of turned over. Those wonderful boys and my best friend, all of a sudden they looked empty. I don't know how to say it. I've been noticing it a little bit on other dates and in letters and so on, but not enough to really rare back and take a look. They just looked empty, smiling like the face on the zoo lions. You remember I had the car key. I got it away from you. So I clunked it on the table and said I was going back. Mary Jane smiled nasty and told me to have fun and said she wanted to go on back to Cuernavaca, right away. So go, I told her. And I just walked out. When I saw all those people, I thought you were dead. I really did. And I really came running, man. And there you were setting up there like a toad on the roof, jawing at that poor man with the mustache. The thing I feel so bad about is, honey, that this wasn't the ordinary kind of fight with Mary Jane. This was a new kind. It will get patched some, but things won't be the same. All of a sudden like, I don't like her so much any more."

"I'm glad you came back, Bitsy. Damn glad."

"You better get some more of that coffee down you." She refilled his cup.

"What are you going to do?" he asked.

"I was thinking of staying right here, Park. Anyways, that's the way I signed us in. Had they got a look at you first, I never would have made it. There's two beds, and you're going to have to have somebody around in the morning to keep you from killing yourself."

"Big scandal at the Workshop."

"Pooh. I've been talked up lots of times. I still sleep fine. But don't you go around getting the idea there's more to this offer, Park. I can just as easy as not show you how much judo I know. And you're not in what anybody would want to call a healthy condition. You work on that coffee some more while I see if I can get some of the blood out of your clothes. Your nose looks pretty bulgy. How's it feel?"

"Not too bad, but I keep seeing it out of the corner of my eye. It makes me nervous."

She went into the bathroom. He heard the water running in the sink and the small energetic sounds of scrubbing. She came out and said, "They're drying on the shower rail. I didn't do all the good I wanted to. But I did some." She took his empty cup. "You better pile in, man. The more sleep you can get the less you'll feel like a dog's dinner tomorrow."

"Bitsy."

"Yes?"

159

"Bitsy, will you listen if I talk to you? I mean . . . I feel like I have to talk. Now. Or maybe I won't be able to say it later. Maybe you don't give a damn, but I want to tell you about me. I don't mean the crap I've told you. All those little inferences and hints designed to make me look so much better than I am. If I'm ever going to learn to live with myself, I've got to do an emotional strip tease. Strip all the way down to the silly little creature under all the pretense."

"You sure are one talker," she said.

"Will you listen, please?"

"I'll listen."

And he talked. Sometimes he walked up and down the room as he talked, the blanket clutched at his waist. He seldom glanced toward her, as though afraid of what he might see. It wasn't ornate. It was hard, bitter self-disgust and recrimination. The stale vomit from the soul. Waste and callousness and pretense. And fear. She sat on the bed and listened to him, and knew she had understood him from the first, and marveled that he had the courage to try to understand himself. At times his voice was dull and at times it was almost shrill. And finally, from the timbre of his voice she sensed that he was at last very close to some ultimate point of either fracture or release. So when he passed close she reached out and caught his hand, stopping him on midsentence.

She smiled up at him. "Talk, talk, talk," she said gently. And the fat tears stood on her under lids. She gave his hand a single tug, and that was all that was needed. There was a grotesque contortion of his face, and then he half fell to the bed beside her, and ground his face into the soft angle between her throat and shoulder, and let go the raking, convulsive, frightening sobbing of a man grown. She cradled his head and rocked him gently, making the murmur-sounds of comfort, feeling the small hot touches of his tears.

When he had quieted, she kissed him. As she kissed at him he groped at her clumsily but with a blind persistence born of needs deeper than those of the flesh. She felt a species of warm and ironic resignation, a special primitive knowledge. She whispered to him to get into bed. She turned off the room lights, and undressed slowly, her thoughts slow and sad and sweet. And she slid in beside him, into the trembling circle of his arms, and she pressed long against him and, with a sudden fierce and protective strength, she locked her hand on her wrist and hugged him around the waist.

Long after he was asleep she lay awake, her eyes wide, turned away from him. He was curled against her back, one arm heavy on her waist, his long exhalations stirring the hair at the nape of her neck.

She had not meant this to happen, she knew. From the beginning he had wanted it to happen. That was clear. And he had been so suavely confident of her. But it did not and it could not have happened his way. Not as a kind of game. There had been enough of games. It was time for the things that happen for real. And this, in its own way, had been a new kind of real. To be needed so blindly and helplessly and desperately by a man trying to cleanse himself of all illusion. And then, without any greediness of the body, to make of yourself, for him, a deep and warm and tender cradle, and feel exalted and purposeful and so necessary as you held there the bruised body and the torn spirit, and then to rock him in sweetness and gentleness and loving, rocking strongly to mend the hurts, to bring him down at last in warm collapse, with his racing heart and his long, long sigh of fulfillment.

Not like anything that had ever happened to her before. She knew in her native wisdom that this was not very much man. He was clever rather than wise, querulous instead of strong. He could never be cured of his self-doubts, his anxieties. He would always fuss at fate, and meet disaster only with indignation. But he would always need her. And there was a sweetness in him. With something that was almost amusement, she saw the exact dimensions of the trap into which she had willingly walked. Gone now the hope of that one-day, some-day man who would be larger than life.

This man was on smaller scale. A boy-man, who would resent deeply the slight loss of love when she had to spread it among their children, because he would have a greedy need of all of it. And when he wanted to strut, she would have to become a child, respectfully attentive to his instructions.

He sighed in his sleep and for a moment the muscles in his arms tightened. He was back inside himself somewhere, jabbing at his dragons with a paper knife.

She had no illusion that this was something just for a little while. His need was too great. And her response to that need was too strong. And there, in her heart, she became married. She had always wondered what sort of wife she would be. And now she knew she would be a very good one. And she would have to be a very good one. To keep him whole in the face of all his enemies, real and imaginary.

I found him on a roof thing, she thought. Got him down and cleaned him up and so that makes him mine.

No more to and fro, she thought. No more to and fro.

She nestled back to be more firmly against him; she sighed and yawned and then smiled in the dark and gave a little shake of her head in a sort of amused exasperation at herself, and then drifted peacefully into a dreamless sleep.

Chapter Twelve

WHEN MARY JANE AWOKE on Monday morning the twenty-fourth of July, too many hours since Bitsy had walked out of that cellar hole where the *mariachis* were too drunk to stay in tune, she noticed at once that Bitsy had not returned. She felt angry and worried. It was not at all like Bitsy to get so darn temperamental. And it was certainly a waste of sympathy and concern for her to be upset about Park. He was a desolate type.

After they had taken a cab back to where they had left the car, Mary Jane had decided that they would go look for Bitsy. They found the place where they had left Barnum. A restaurant man, who showed evidence of recent strain, informed them that the man had refused to come down until a girl had spoken to him. Then he had come down. And they had gone off that way. On foot.

They cruised until the boys got bored, and so they had one more drink and headed back across the mountains, singing everything they knew. But Mary Jane's heart wasn't in her singing. She was about as mad at Bitsy as she had ever been at anybody. She had been impatient and angry all day Sunday. And now she was still angry, but also apprehensive. Everybody was talking about it. That Klauss person had leered at her several times in a slimy and knowing way.

At breakfast she sat with John and Barbara and Miles Drummond and told them that she was really getting worried. And she gave them a more complete report on what had really happened.

"I keep feeling I should get in my car and go up there."

"There are how many people in that city? Four million?" John Kemp said. "You can't do any good that way. Park is considerably over twenty-one, and I haven't noticed anything incompetent about Miss Bitsy."

"But this isn't *like* her," Mary Jane said. "I suppose everybody has the classy idea they're holed up in a hotel room someplace. Bitsy isn't that kind of a girl. She isn't engaged to him or anything."

"I'd suggest you wait until tomorrow," John Kemp said. "If they aren't back by, say, tomorrow noon, I think we could notify the embassy. They must have some apparatus for tracking down wayward citizens."

"The child is under age," Miles said. "But I don't really think I could be held responsible for her. There's nothing in the prospectus . . ."

"Oh, stop sweating!" Mary Jane said angrily.

"Well, really, Miss Elmore!"

"I'm cross and you would be too. Drink your coffee and stop looking so hurt, Mr. Drummond. I'll wait until tomorrow. And then *I'll* do something. I don't know what it will be, but it will work up some kind of a storm."

Agnes Partridge Keeley paused by the table and said, "Class in five minutes, dears!" She wagged a playful chiding finger, and bracelets jingle-jangled on the fat-creased wrist. She billowed away, marshmallow haunches spreading the fabric of pale purple slacks, straw slippers slapping, and, under the flimsiness of the back of the peach-colored blouse, her bra straps cut deeply across the yielding flesh.

Mary Jane said reflectively, "Now just where would you go to buy a pair of slacks like that? What size would you ask for? My God!"

"Now, now," Miles said. "Don't be cruel, dear. She's really a very nice woman."

"Personally, I think she's as mean as a snake," Mary Jane said defiantly. "How about that poop sheet on Gam Torrigan she's been showing around, making out like it's a big secret? She showed me and I saw her whispering to Harvey Ardos, and I'll just bet she's showed it to every-damn-body. She show you, John?"

"Yes. Actually it doesn't say much. I guess if he was trying to get a job in the trust department of a bank it would queer him. But I don't think he's interested."

"She wanted me to . . . discharge him," Miles said uncomfortably. "But with the session nearly half over . . . and it would leave just one teacher . . ." He stood up suddenly and patted his mouth with his napkin. "I do so wish we wouldn't have these little intrigues."

After he walked away, Barbara said, "You know, I think he's really getting better. He's almost taking hold. You hardly ever see him looking as if he was going to cry any more."

"Time for instruction," John said. "You joining us, Mary Jane?"

"Oh, I guess so."

Agnes Keeley led her little group three hundred yards down the road, followed by the red bus. Fidelio unloaded the chairs, easels and paintboxes. Agnes busily supervised the placement of the chairs. The morning group consisted of John, Barbara, Mary Jane, Klauss, Hildabeth McCaffrey, Monica and Harvey. She set them up on a grassy area facing a wall forty feet away. The wall had once been painted bright blue and now it had faded. A lush flame vine, loaded with blooms, covered half the wall area. There was a stunted tree at the left.

"Now is everyone set up? Today we're going to see if we can't get more grace and delicacy into water color. As I've been telling you, you must work quickly, and you can't correct, not with transparent water colors. And please pay some attention to the shadows of the flowers and leaves against the wall. If you neglect the shadows, it will look as though your vine was pasted against the wall, or painted on it. Use your pencil very lightly to get the rough dimensions and perspective. I'm glad to see you with us today, Mary Jane. Monica, dear, I want you to try not to draw in each teensy detail. Just try to suggest the masses of color. And Harvey, please try to make your colors light and vibrant. Use more water and see if you can keep from making everything look so moody and gloomy. All right, everyone. Let's begin."

They worked under the increasing glare of the morning sun. Those who attended Miss Keeley's classes regularly soon acquired a high-altitude tan. Agnes merely became more pink, with a constantly peeling nose and forehead.

Agnes walked from person to person, with continual comment and criticism. When she looked over John's shoulder she said with a labored coyness that did not hide the edge of irritation, "You're not doing the assignment again, John. You're just doing the little tree and you're not even using transparent water colors."

"It has an interesting shape."

"That background looks terribly . . . smeary."

164

He did not bother to tell her that it was underpainting for the eventual abstraction he might do if he was satisfied with the composition.

"Hildabeth, you have a very good start. I'm very proud of you."

"Now I'm not so scared, I can just slash it right on there fast."

"Mr. Klauss, you're using too much water again, and your colors are all bleached out."

"Barbara! Oil inks? They're so dreadfully hard to control. I'm really afraid you're under John's influence. But at least you're tackling that wall, that lovely wall."

And so, in the hot morning silence, they worked, each with his own purpose and diligence. The bugs shrilled, and cattle bunched the barranca grass. In a house a hundred yards away someone had a radio on so loud that the speaker diaphragm blurred all the sounds into a metallic clashing. A big plane went over, very high. There was a far whine of trucks in low gear descending from Tres Cumbres.

And there were the inevitable spectators, content to stand and stare throughout the morning. Solemn ragged children. An old man who carried two live white pigeons, a horny finger hooked under the string that bound their ankles. The upside-down birds strained to keep their heads upright and, infrequently, they made soft hollow sounds as though they spoke to each other in sadness and wisdom of impending death. A pulque man paused to watch for a time, halting his burro which carried the goatskins full of the warm and sour brew. When they got too close, Agnes would run at them, taking several little steps, and say, "Shoo!" And they would back up slowly.

The man known as Monica's admirer arrived a little later than usual and, with the care and talent of a master strategist, selected a place that was as close as possible without risking being shooed back by Agnes, a place that was in the shade, and a place that provided an unimpeded view of Monica. On this day she wore short, short shorts of gray twill with the cuffs turned up, and a pale-blue seersucker halter which, with utmost valiance, was barely able to perform its function. The sun had browned her smoothly and deeply, and as she worked there was a glisten of perspiration on the brown roundness of thighs and calves, shoulders and waist.

The admirer was a loutish-looking fellow, a dark and broad-faced type, with a wide belly and loose jaw structure, and eyes like little damp blueberries set close on either side of a fleshy and flattened nose. The only sparkling thing about him was the crisp white straw sombrero which he wore pushed back from a low forehead, and held in place by a chin thong. He wore ragged, dun-colored shirt and trousers, and broken black boots. He could sit endlessly, tirelessly, on his heels, thick fists resting half clenched on his thighs. He looked out of proper time and place. He should have been back in the past, slitting gullets with Pancho Villa.

He sat and slowly chewed something unidentifiable. And the small eyes, quite expressionless and seeming never to blink, never moved from the figure of Monica. With each slow chew the lips gaped slightly to reveal the lower row of teeth, looking like little dusty brown pebbles. It was impossible to guess what slow thoughts moved through the brain behind the fixed eyes during the long mornings. John Kemp learned that it was easy to fall into the error of interpreting that blankness, of, in a sense, anthropomorphizing the man. If you thought you saw lust, you saw it. If you expected to see awe, you saw that. Kemp preferred to interpret it as a look of muted consternation, spiced with disbelief.

Monica Killdeering had become disconcerted by his stare the first morning he had appeared. Indeed, it was quite possible to imagine that were such a glance long leveled at the maiden in "September Morn," she would soon break and plunge into the water, immersing herself until only her head showed. After the first two days of it, Monica reported for Agnes' next sketching trip in a white turtleneck sweater and a full pleated skirt. Had it not been for her splendid constitution, she might have toppled off her stool by mid-morning. As it was she skipped Gam's afternoon class and napped that day. But the change of raiment did not affect the intensity of the observation of her admirer.

When Agnes chose the device of longer walks to more obscure places, she outwitted him once. From then on he hung about in the vicinity of the hotel and tagged after the group.

At approximately his sixth appearance, it was Jeanie Wahl who became sufficiently indignant to attempt to put an end to it. She marched over to the man and spoke to him firmly and at length, in perfectly grammatical Castilian Spanish, spoken rapidly and in the uncompromising nasality of the Midwest.

It was only when she had finished and stood waiting for an answer that the man suddenly seemed to notice her. He

166

unstuck his focused gaze and stared up at her blankly, stopping in the middle of his mastication with his mouth sagging half open. Jeanie spoke again. He kept staring at her. And then, with an almost imperceptible shrug, he continued with Monica where he had left off. Jeanie stamped her foot and marched back to her chair. John Kemp then went over to him. In his rough, make-shift Spanish he told the man it was not courteous to stare, to be on his way. The man looked up at him and for a few moments the tiny eyes were very ugly. He muttered something.

"What did he say?" Agnes asked.

"If I understood him, he was telling me this was now a free country, and his country, not mine."

Outside of dressing Monica in a Mother Hubbard, or building a well around her, it seemed that nothing could be done. For a few days they had made jokes about her admirer. And, gradually, his presence was taken for granted, even by Monica. She resumed her habitual briefness of attire. Only Harvey Ardos remained conscious of the man.

He felt a strange empathy with the rude and sloppy stranger. And a kind of envy. He wished he had the boldness to be able to sit and stare at her. But all he could risk were those fleeting glances which invariably made him feel giddy.

Harvey was deeply ashamed of the carnality which made him so constantly aware of the taut abundances of Monica. He felt as if he was dishonoring her. She was, as he said to himself, all lady. And she was an Older Woman—maybe four or five years older—and she had a College Education and she was a Teacher. And she was so damn patient with a stupid linthead. But oh dear Jesus God how she was stacked.

He wished she'd keep it covered up more. But it wasn't like she was waving it around, not like that Rose that would come into the stockroom when things were slow, swinging it as if she had a limp in both legs. No, Monica was just being comfortable. And practical, like. When they went down into town she always wore dresses and blouses and skirts and so on, on account of how it said in the guidebook the Mexicans didn't like it, women going around in shorts and so on. But around the hotel it was shorts and halters, or those leotard things. Maybe it was practical as all hell, but he wished she'd keep more covered up. It would make everything a lot easier all the way around.

He still wasn't real comfortable about calling her Monica. It seemed more proper if he called her Miss Killdeering. One thing sure, he was learning a lot from her. She got those books for him the time she went up to Mexico City, and she was all the time getting more from that little rental library down in the hotel court in town. And she'd made such a big long apology and turned so red in the face the time she asked him if it was all right if she corrected him when he used bad English. And he had to explain to her that he really did know better English than he was using, but when you didn't have hardly any education, then you made yourself talk worse. Defiance, like.

It was wonderful the way she was so patient. He'd never got such a boot out of anything as out of the long talks they had. He'd never talked about such stuff before. Thought about it, in a kind of fuzzy way, but never talked about it. Religion, philosophy, mankind. The real big things. And she never laughed at your crazy ideas. Not once. And she kept telling you what a good mind you had. Which is a lot of crap, but makes good listening.

But if she didn't have that built, it would be one hell of a lot easier keeping track of the conversation. After Gam's class they'd usually walk out to the main highway and take a bus down to the center of town, and get one of those sidewalk tables and sit there until it got to be dark and it was time to go back to dinner. They'd drink beer, and it was like in the movies, the people you see at sidewalk tables, really talking up a storm. But every once in a while he'd be talking along, trying to make the words fit the involved idea that was so clear in his head, and she'd do some damn thing like move without meaning to so their knees touched, or stretch a little, sort of arching her back, or twist in her chair to look back over her shoulder for the waiter, and that big idea he was talking about was just gone. Pow! There he'd be with his mouth half open and his whole head as empty as a brass drum. With a little help from her he could usually get back on the track, but sometimes it was gone for keeps.

And lots of times they had been walking and where it was uneven they'd accidentally bump hips. And that really scoured the mind clean. It made him want to drop and bang his head on the rocks and roar like a tiger.

One of the worst times was last week, when they had walked out after dinner to look at the moon and talk it up some more. She had been standing close beside him, wearing that white sweater of hers, and when she turned once, she accidentally brushed one of those things right across his

168

upper arm and dragged it back across again when she turned back. And it had been a damn good thing she'd been the one doing the talking at the time. It had curled his toes tight in his shoes. After they said good night, he tried staying in his room and knew he couldn't. If he'd stayed in there he would have banged his head on the wall. So he had dressed and gone out to the road and run as hard and fast as he could, all the way up to the barracks, and then turned and run all the way back down past the hotel, and turned and run to the hotel again. And just outside the gate that Texas redhead had said, "What in the blue-eyed world are you doing, Harvey?"

She'd startled hell out of him. "Me?" He had bounced up and down on his toes, swinging his arms. "Got to stay in condition. I do a little running every once in a while. Hi, Park. You ever do any running?"

"Not if it can be avoided."

He ran vigorously in one spot for a moment, bringing his knees as high as he could and then said, panting, "Good night, all," and went on in to his room.

The real big worry about the whole thing was he'd come so terrible close to turning around and grabbing her. And, brother, that would be the end. That would do it. She was an Older Woman, and a Teacher and she'd gone to College. She'd been wonderful to him, and she was the finest woman he had ever known. And it would certainly be one hell of a way to show gratitude, to grab aholt of her like some crazy animal. He guessed it was the beast in him. It made him ashamed of himself that he could think of Monica in that way. There'd been some girls. Sluts, if you want to use a better word for those pigs. Just a few times back in rug storage, and the couple of times he'd gone with some of the guys and they'd paid for it. He felt as if he was soiling Monica to even think about her at the same time he remembered those pigs. Not that there was a hell of a lot to remember.

He forced the evil thoughts out of his mind and concentrated on getting the shadow the little tree was making against the base of the faded blue wall. For a little while he made progress, and then he was aware of someone directly behind him. He thought it was Miss Keeley. But a hand was placed on his shoulder, and when he turned his head there, an inch and a half from the tip of his nose, was the distended pouch of pale-blue seersucker with its awesome burden. It was so close that Harvey's eyes crossed. Monica was bending over him, looking at the work he had done.

"It's very nice, Harvey," she said.

"Harf!" he said, and for one horrid moment he thought his eyes would not uncross. He turned his head away. "Uh. Thanks."

She went back to her chair. He bit the knuckle of his first finger until tears came to his eyes. He glowered darkly over at the squatting Mexican and wanted to race over and plant such a perfect punt that there would be a clicking shower of the little pebbly teeth. He looked at his painting again and had the mad desire to snap his head forward like a striking snake and bite a chunk right out of the middle of it.

For once the bus returned on schedule, just as Agnes was finishing her final critique of the work accomplished. Hildabeth received praise that made her beam and blush. In fact the second painting of the wall that she had done was, at a fair distance, almost indistinguishable from the works of Agnes Partridge Keeley, in both style and normal content and sweet color tones.

"You can certainly be proud of that, Hildabeth. I think you have a marvelous talent. You should take it home with you and have it framed. Anybody would be happy to hang such a lovely thing in their home."

They walked back. As was his habit, Monica's admirer walked about fifteen feet behind her until they had gone through the gate. And then he turned away, heading for the path that crossed the barranca.

Park and Bitsy arrived back at the hotel the next day, Tuesday, at lunchtime. They came sauntering into the big, sparsely inhabited dining room, smiling and at ease, halting all conversation and the random clink of silverware.

"Greetings," Park said.

"How you all?" said Bitsy.

They went to an unoccupied table. Park held her chair for her, kissed her on the temple when she was seated, and took the chair at her left, and they began to talk earnestly and inaudibly, their heads close together.

"A perfect picture of guilt," Agnes said to her table. "An attitude like that sickens me."

"Bet they had a time," Hildabeth said.

From the table where he sat with Miles, Harvey and Monica, Gam Torrigan looked over at the back of Park's head with a sad twinge of envy.

Jeanie said to Gil, "Look at them, dearest. I bet they'll get married."

"Everybody should be married, honey. It's all so damn efficient. No taxis. No tired little motels. No plotting and planning. No dark hallways. No sneaking around. Why, anytime you just happen to want . . ."

"You hush up, greedy boy."

John Kemp, sitting with Barbara, Klauss, and Mary Jane, thought Park looked much better. His color was better, and he did not have that look of springs wound too tightly.

"Hah!" Mary Jane said. She shoved her chair back, picked up her iced tea, and carried it over to their table and sat beside Bitsy.

"That's a new outfit," she said.

"Like it?" Bitsy asked.

"Very nice. Don't suppose you care much that I nearly went crazy worrying about you."

"She was in good hands, Mary Jane."

"That point is, like they say, debatable, chum."

"My outfit is new too. When your playmates got playful, it took the knee out of my pants."

"What a terrible, horrible, tragic shame!"

"Why are you being so nasty, Mary Jane?" Bitsy asked. "Feel guilty for not coming with me when I walked out of the party?"

"I wish to God I had. Then you wouldn't have made a fool of yourself."

Bitsy smiled blandly at her. "Of course, you're the one with all the good judgment, dear."

"What's wrong with you? You don't act like yourself."

"I'm not myself. I'm somebody else."

"If this is a game, I don't want to play. Who the hell are you?"

Bitsy, still smiling, said, "The second Mrs. Barnum."

Mary Jane stared at her, obviously shocked. She moistened her lips and said, "Now there's a spooky idea! Lose your mind, darling? Maggie will slash you to ribbons if you take home this kind of a meathead and you know it!"

Park bit his lip but remained silent. Bitsy kept her smile, but it was like something drawn on. "You're so sure of that, aren't you? We did a lot of phoning on Sunday. Maggie and the clan flew down yesterday. We were married late yesterday afternoon. A civil ceremony, but very well attended. Everybody missed you."

"I wasn't invited."

"Maybe you can figure out why."

Mary Jane's mouth trembled for a moment. She smiled, but wanly. "So I've said all the wrong things. Like I seem to always do lately somehow. Congratulations, or something. I want you to be happy, Bits."

"Thank you."

Mary Jane looked across the table at Park. "I guess you know I don't think this is the best idea she's ever had. It's done now, and I hope it works, and I want to be friends."

"Friends," Park said and took her hand.

"What are your plans, kids?"

Park said, "We thought we'd drive on down to Acapulco for a while. No plans beyond that."

"I've got myself some new plans all of a sudden," Mary Jane said. "With you gone, Bits, I'm not going to hang around here, certainly. I'm going up home."

"Why don't you wait until we come on back through, Mary Jane?" Bitsy said. "We won't be down there long. We can go on up in convoy."

"Fifth wheel?"

"Heck, no."

"All right. So you kids take my bug and leave me the wagon. It'll be a whee of a honeymoon chariot. Please. If you don't, I won't be here when you come back."

Bitsy looked questioningly at Park, and then nodded agreement.

Mary Jane stood up and hammered loudly on a glass with a spoon. "Big announcement, all you types. Big things going on. Introducing one bride and groom. A real sneaky pair. It happened yesterday. Gather 'round and kiss the bride. Gam, you go get some of those bottles of yours. Miles, you order up some ice. I here and now declare one official half holiday and we'll have ourselves a reception for the bride and groom. Let's have us a committee in charge of old shoes and rice. And music from someplace. I'm in an organizing mood. So let's party this thing up."

It became a party. Park and Bitsy had planned to leave early enough to drive on through to Acapulco. And then they decided it would be enough to get as far as Taxco. Eventually they got as far as the Marik down in the center of Cuernavaca.

Park had a chance to talk to John Kemp when he went to pack what he'd need at Acapulco and John came into his room, glass in hand, and sat on the bed.

"Pretty sudden, boy."

"I'm as surprised as anybody, John. God, I was a stinking

shambles on Saturday night. I was so close to the edge. I'd begun to feel like I was made of glass and pretty soon a violin was going to hit the right note and they were going to have to sweep me up. She picked me up and brushed me off. Sunday morning we walked miles in those parks. We sat on a bench and I looked at her and she smiled at me, and I knew I'd been thrashing around in a big, gray, empty ocean and by the damnedest luck in the world, I'd caught hold of the trimmest little lifeboat you ever saw. Part of this is the drinks talking, John, but it's all true. I knew I couldn't let her go, so I said I loved her and I needed her and let's get married. She said, 'I guess it's time for that,' and so we went back to the hotel and started running up the damnedest phone bill tracking down her folks. She got Maggie, that's her mother, on the phone and pretty soon they were both crying. And then I got on and Maggie cussed me out like I'd never heard before, and then said if I didn't make her happy she'd spread little chunks of me all over Texas. So a big batch of them flew down in a private plane. I don't know what it was, but it was big. They got in Monday noon. Maggie is a character. Her husband is a little Limey type who cracks the whip so you can really hear it. The little kids, her brother and sister, came too. And I couldn't get the big cousins and uncles and their wives straightened out. It was confusing, believe me. So . . . I'm married again."

"And to some heavy money, I would suspect."

Park straightened up from packing his suitcase, and frowned thoughtfully. "Yes. I know. But I'm not thinking about that. I mean it didn't have one single damn thing to do with my asking her. And she knows that too. She's a hell of a girl, John. I had some stupid ideas about her. I didn't have the faintest idea of what she's really like. I had the feeling she was immature. A fun kid. But her family deal has given her so many emotional knocks that she's grown up all the way. She doesn't go around advertising it. She's a thousand years older and wiser than I am. She's a hell of a girl."

"Will you go back to your job?"

"I don't know. I don't know what being back in that deal will do to me. Or if she'll be happy in the East. She hated hell out of it when she was in school there. But it might work. It's a decision for later. Put it this way, John. I'm going to work at my trade. I'm good at it. It wouldn't be a happy thing for either of us if I make a nice warm nest out of her dough."

"Don't ever rationalize yourself out of that position, Park."

"I don't think I will. All of a sudden I'm cured of Suzie. She's somebody I once knew, and loved very much. And now I know what it was about Suzie. She's so damn clever that there isn't enough room in her for warmth. I guess what I want now is a nice place to live and work to do. And I want to fix it somehow so my kids can come and visit. That little brother and sister of Bitsy's adore her. She'll be good with kids. And we want a great big batch of our own. Lots of them. And we want to give them the best kind of emotional security kids can have. Not the way she grew up, or I grew up. I'm talking too damn much."

"It's a good kind of talk to hear, boy."

"Good God, listen to them out there!"

"Torrigan is really ready."

"I'm through here. Let's join the group."

The best parties always seem to be the spontaneous ones. And the spontaneous ones can only occur when group tensions have reached a point where some kind of release is unavoidable.

A dining-room table was moved to a commanding location between the dining room and the lobby and converted into a bar, with Felipe Cedro as unexpectedly competent bartender. When a collection was taken up to replenish the liquor supply, Mary Jane drove with Gam to town in Park's station wagon and brought back not only liquor, but three wandering musicians from the *zócalo*, two guitars and a portable marimba. Gam spotted Gloria Garvey in front of the Bella Vista, the first time he had seen her since their weekend, and, with certain bravado, asked her to come join the party and bring her friends—a tall English girl named Margot, with a manner so completely languid that she seemed a victim of deep hypnosis, and a knotty pug-faced little man called Shane. And they arrived at the hotel a half hour later.

Had the party been planned in advance, it certainly would not have been anticipated that the hotel staff would join in. But when Miles Drummond looked over and happened to notice Fidelio, the driver, dancing violently and expertly with a barefoot Margarita, the two handsome jolts of Scotch he had consumed during the initial toasts to the bride reduced his potential objection to a slightly uneasy feeling soon forgotten. And not long afterward, when he saw Colonel Hildebrandt move across his line of vision, dancing in slow and stately ballroom fashion with that same Margarita, holding her at arm's length and maintaining a tempo that had little to do with the beat of the music, it seemed perfectly natural. It was only when he found himself dancing with Margarita, her face a perfect symbol of fiesta, that he again felt uncertain, and wondered about future difficulties in enforcing discipline.

Rosalinda Gomez quickly established her special niche, and from the delighted grinning of the *mariachis* and the general public approval, it was exactly where she belonged. She could sing with the eerie, spine-tingling whine of the true flamenca, or, snapping her fingers with exceptional loudness and precision, belt it out with the husky emphasis of a dusky Sophie Tucker. And she knew the lyrics of everything.

Esperanza Clueca had joined, very dubiously, in the toast to the bride. She despised the typical *borracho*, as exemplified by the sodden Alberto, the gardener. And she had never touched liquor. Yet, because she had been asked, it seemed a politeness to join them. And she did like the girl from Texas with the coppery hair. She had seemed genuinely friendly. The one with the yellow hair was different. There had been, in her, a kind of contempt, a roughness in her voice when she gave orders. It was said that in Texas all Mexicans were treated in such fashion, and Esperanza had been pleased to find that in the case of the Señorita Babcock, the information was wrong.

So she accepted the glass from Felipe, with the inch of raw tequila in the bottom. It did not seem very much. Surely such a little bit could not be harmful. She listened to the toast in English and Spanish, hesitated a moment and saw the way the others took it down in one gulp. She held her breath and did the same. White-hot lava abraded the lining of her throat. Her stomach gave a hard convulsive leap. She looked through tears and said, in a harsh and prolonged way, "Haaaaaaa..." And she felt a curious warmth that began at the pit of her stomach and spread out in every direction from that point. Within a few minutes the room had become more beautiful, all light and color. Her face lost its clinical severity when she smiled. Surely this could not be a thing of such horror, so long as one had only a little and did not become a *borracho*.

When Felipe came with the bottle again, she extended her glass shyly.

And later, it was so kind of the American Señor Wahl to teach her the American jeeterboog. It made the room whirl.

175

And she was certain that no one had ever danced more gracefully than she.

Of the staff, only Alberto Buceada did not join in. He had a bottle of mescal. He sat in the shade under the window with his back against the wall and quietly, without haste, killed the bottle, toppled over onto his side, and snored on into the dusk and the night.

Hildabeth, with cherry brandy ringing in her ears, was prevailed upon to demonstrate the hula she had learned in Hawaii. After considerable earnest instruction, the musicians were able to make a determined frontal attack on "Blue Hawaii," with ranchero overtones. Hildabeth was surprisingly graceful, and it was appreciated by everyone but Dotsy who stood by, crimson-faced, in an agony of sympathetic embarrassment.

Harvey Ardos could not dance. He had never tried. And his shame was compounded by the obvious fact that Monica Killdeering was a superb dancer. She had the physical requirements, the suppleness, the training and the perfect sense of timing of the professional.

Harvey stood by in jealous misery and watched her dance with Kemp, Barnum, Drummond, Torrigan, Klauss, Wahl, Shane and the colonel. Her popularity on the dance floor had become enhanced when it was discovered that she did not talk while dancing. For eight dancing men, nine if Fidelio was counted, there were eight women—the Texas girls, Jeanie Wahl, Barbara Kilmer, Monica, the languid Margot and the two maids. Harvey felt embittered and left out. By some kind of accident it had turned into one of those dancing parties. He wished they'd all drop of heat exhaustion.

Whenever she had a chance Monica would come over to him and say, "Please try, Harvey. It's very easy."

"Nah!"

"If you can walk, you can dance. I'll show you."

"Nah, thanks!"

"Come on, Harvey. It's wonderful exercise."

"Nah. I don't feel like learning."

And someone would come up and take her away. He drank and watched. He felt like going to his room and closing the door. Damn if he was going to go out and make a fool of himself. Just stand right here and get a little boiled.

He watched Monica dancing with that hard-looking little stranger who had arrived with Mrs. Garvey. Good clothes, but he looked like an ex-fighter, as if he'd spent a few years of having his face pounded. When they turned he could see

176

the thick hand pressed against Monica's smooth brown back, and it made him feel queer to see it. Quite suddenly he realized she was having some kind of trouble with Shane.

He had danced her over toward a far corner. He was talking to her and she was shaking her head. And he was holding her too tight, and they didn't seem to be doing much dancing. Harvey put his drink on a table and got over to them fast.

He tapped Shane on the shoulder and said, "Guess you can start giving me those lessons, Monica."

"On your way, bud," Shane said.

"I want to dance with Harvey!"

"You're dancing with me. Go away, Harvey."

As Monica struggled to free herself, Harvey moved in like a referee and pushed them apart.

Shane tugged at his belt, took several little dance steps, snuffled against his fist and said, "Get out from behind that glassware, bud. You and me are going around and around."

Harvey, slightly chilled by the professional gestures, tossed his glasses on a nearby table and squinted at the blurred figure. He took three hard left hooks to the stomach, followed by a right cross high on the jaw. As the wind was being driven out of him, Harvey led with one wild despairing right and hit Shane right in the middle of the forehead, a half second before the right cross dropped him onto his face. Shane did a couple of shuffling steps. Monica, her eyes narrow and dangerous, moved in from the side and suddenly snapped both hands down on Shane's left wrist. With one violent twist she spun him so that she had his wrist pinned high between his shoulder blades, and, as a result of pain and leverage, he was bent forward from the waist. She gave one hard shove to overcome inertia, and then, with three running steps, she ran him headlong into the stone wall. Shane dropped like a sack of spoiled potatoes.

As she turned toward Harvey he was just pushing himself up onto his feet. He tottered around in a small rubber-legged circle, his mouth slack, his eyes squinting at his myopic world. He drew his fist back to let fly at the vague image in front of him.

"It's me, Harvey! It's Monica!"

He stared around. "Where'd he go? I'll kill 'im."

She picked up his glasses and handed them to him. He slipped them on and stared at Shane. The scuffle had been over almost as soon as it began. Most of the others came running over. Harvey clenched his fist a few times and then sucked his knuckles. "Hey, now!" he said.

"What happened?" Miles demanded.

"That man got fresh and Harvey fought with him."

The languid blonde drifted over and looked down at Shane with what could have been satisfaction. "Welterweight champion of the Pacific Fleet," she said. "God only knows what that means."

"I'll be damned!" Klauss said softly. They all stared at Harvey.

He flushed and said, "Lucky punch, I guess."

"Will you take care of him, Margot?" Gloria asked.

Margot yawned and said, "Why the bloody Christ should I, darling? He joined the group in Vera Cruz and he's been going about striking people ever since. To use one of your Americanisms, he's all yours."

"Not mine," Gloria said.

They rolled Shane over and poured water on him. He stirred and suddenly came scrambling to his feet, dancing heavily, fists balled, peering around from under the thick scarred brows. The machine slowed down and stopped and he stared at them. "Who are all you people? Where the hell am I?"

Torrigan led him off toward the bar and the music started again. Harvey squared his shoulders. "Well . . . you might as well try to teach me, woman," he said gruffly.

"Yes, dear," she said humbly.

"Wha'd you call me!"

"I . . . I said yes, Harvey . . . uh . . . dear."

They stood staring at each other, their faces crimson, until they both looked away at once. And then she shyly told him how to place his hands, and got him to start walking in time to the music. Within a half hour he was, as Monica told him, doing splendidly. She wouldn't let anyone cut in. She told them it would spoil the lesson. And, as Harvey's nervous consciousness of his feet began to diminish as his confidence grew, and as the mental count of ONE, two, three, ONE, two, three, became more automatic, he became increasingly aware of the fact that he was holding Miss Killdeering within the half circle of the right arm that had knocked out the welterweight champ. Her back was smooth and vibrant under his hand. She sure had beautiful eyes.

And when the next slow number came, with Rosalinda singing of a girl named Maria Bonita, Harvey Ardos, with a masterfulness that appalled him, drew Miss Killdeering so close that she rested her head on his shoulder, her face turned slightly inward, her round forehead against the angle of his jaw. To be about two inches taller than the girl was exactly right, he decided. He had guided her away from the others, into a shadowy corner of the dining room, and they danced there in half time, in a lovely dream, their eyes half-closed. He was acutely and sweatily aware of the firm twin warmth of her breasts against him. He decided there was a lot to this dancing kick. A lot he hadn't understood. The music ended. In the moment he released her, just before she stepped back, she planted a very small, shy, nibbly kiss against the side of his throat, just under his ear. She stepped back with pink face and glowing eyes.

Harvey made one small strangled sound, and then he went up through the roof like a rocket. He sped up toward the sun and, as he lost velocity, he began to turn over and over. When he found he could use his arms like wings, he spiraled down until he could land directly in front of her.

"Holy Nelly!" he said in a voice that sounded as if somebody had him by the throat.

The party was a psychological necessity for Gambel Torrigan. He felt that through the episode with Gloria, he had lost caste. Before it had happened, he had been the volatile and expressive and somewhat alarming Mr. Torrigan, a person to be treated with respect, a person whose comments and instructions were of great value. But somehow he had become good old Gam. Somebody to chuckle about. He couldn't awe anybody any more, not even Harvey and Monica. It was as if he had become some sort of clown. He did not permit himself to dwell on the theory that this was not too different from his experience in all the other schools. He wanted to be a person of pride and dignity. And he felt he was, on the inside. But people were stupid. They see you a little bit drunk now and then, or they have knowledge of some of your other human weaknesses, and they get that damn jocular attitude toward you.

This party was the opportunity for proof, the chance to reestablish the original relationship. By God, once they'd all let their hair all the way down, they would see that they weren't any more righteous and proper than Gam Torrigan. So he resolved to drink an adequate amount, but not too much. He would have the party spirit, but he would be proper. And as the others went off into the stumbling staggers, he would be there to record, to remember, to be politely amused. Dignity would be regained.

To make certain of the success of this program, he quietly

179

bribed Felipe to make the drinks as massive as possible. And he vowed he would nurse his own drinks. This would be the new Gambel Torrigan, now and forever more.

For Paul Klauss the party was an opportunity to improve the dismal performance of the first part of the summer. And, more importantly, a chance to bolster his sagging morale. That damnable Margarita had managed to outwit him and humiliate him four times. The final episode had been the most disheartening. She could not have accomplished it without coaching. Every time he thought of how his heart rode high in his throat as he had scrabbled at the night chain to admit the lovely Barbara, only to be overwhelmed by the joyous fervency of Margarita again, he felt sick. Progress on all other fronts had been equally distressing. Before there had been even a slight chance to launch an effective campaign against the Babcock girl, that fool Barnum had married her. He did not doubt but what Barnum had cheated him of success. In the case of the Kilmer woman, circumstances had conspired to defeat him. True, the initial approach had not been handled too well, but such a thing could have been corrected had not that large, dull Kemp person become so friendly with her.

As for Mary Jane Elmore, there was apparently something unnatural about her. So he could not really be blamed for failure, not under those circumstances. Hers had been a very strange response. He had strolled with her out beyond the main gate one evening a week ago, talking, he had thought, quite pleasantly to her about horses and Texas and the cattle business. She had seemed attentive and responsive, and just a promising bit drunk. So he had told her how lovely she looked in the starlight, and had put his hands on her pliant waist and, smiling fondly at her, had drawn her toward him. She had even been smiling back. But just as their lips were about to touch, her elbow had chopped him sharply under the chin and she had stomped him on the instep with a sharp high heel. When the pain had subsided somewhat he was willing to accept her apology that she really didn't know why she'd done it. It was a sort of a reflex. And so he had recreated the original setting and atmosphere. The second time he had caught the elbow high on the cheek, and a small hard fist in the pit of the stomach and a ringing crack of a kick on the shin. When he could breathe in again without making a gagging sound, and when he could stand relatively upright, she had helped him hobble over to the bench Fidelio had improvised for himself near the gate. As he sat and rubbed his tender shin, she apologized more profusely than before. She said that if he wanted to try again, she would try to control her reflexes, but she couldn't promise anything. After thinking it over he told her that his only intention anyway had been a friendly kiss, and under the circumstances it didn't seem worth it. It was a pity there was something so unnatural about her. Really a pretty child. It seemed a problem for a psychiatrist. The next day he was aware that Mary Jane and her friend Bitsy were doing a lot of giggling, but he decided that it must be some private joke. They certainly could never see anything humorous in Mary Jane's curious affliction.

The party was, to his way of thinking, an interesting variation on standard procedure. It was like the difference between the stalk of a game animal and the use of beaters. In the stalk the hunter used his guile and experience and knowledge of the habits of the game to get within range for the kill. And he knew which specific animal he was after. But when beaters were used, the hunter had merely to station himself at some strategic spot and keep his wits about him as the game was being driven toward him. He did not know which animal would burst out of the brush, or where it would first appear. The noise of the beaters made the animals lose much of their natural caution. The hunter had to be ready to move like lightning to take advantage of the unexpected opportunity.

Eliminating Mary Jane and Bitsy, there remained Barbara, Jeanie Wahl—a rather remote chance but one to bear in mind—Monica, definitely of low priority but much more acceptable after one had danced with her, Margot, and Gloria Garvey. He rather hoped that Margot would be the one to create a situation of opportunity. She had high round hips and small high breasts, and a manner that was at once remote, dreamy and evil. Gloria Garvey would make a truly handsome trophy, but there was something overwhelming about her which disturbed him. Part of that impression was due to her size. He had never been partial to big women. It had been his experience that no matter how perfectly they were constructed, his tactile memories of them were of a ponderous fleshiness which offended him. Also, she had a raw, bold eye, an earthy laugh, and a look of untidiness. His most valuable journal entries concerned those who had been dainty, shy, slim, small-boned and fastidious. The ones who had wept. Of all the women, Barbara was closest to his ideal target. Mother had been small and shy and sweet. He remembered

181

how she hugged him, and her tears against his face when that hairy beast had been ugly to both of them. "Just the two of us, my pretty darling," she would say. "Just you and me, Paul."

While dancing was so popular there was little he could do. He danced several times with the Englishwoman. She moved rather stiffly, but did not object to being held closely. Back when Paul had learned that the ballroom is one of the fertile areas for the hunt, and learned that he had little natural talent for dancing, he had taken an extended series of lessons and had acquired a pleasant competence.

Margot peered at him as they danced and said, "You are really a very pretty man, darling."

"Thank you. You're an exciting woman."

"Ah, such a perfect reading of such a tired line, darling. And you dance so well."

"I'd say we dance well together, wouldn't you?"

And she had laughed in his face and said, "Oh, dear God, I really do think that I am about to hear one of those little things I haven't heard for years. I thought it had all died out of this brazen world, ducks. The next thing I hear from you is a terrible subtle hint that perhaps if we dance so well together, maybe we could do other things well together. Said with a naughty gleam in the eye. Do say it, darling, because maybe I can get all confused and girlish. I haven't been confused and girlish since Rommel was chased out of the desert. You know, I might even hold my breath and see if I can get a little pink into these withered old cheeks."

"I was just trying to be complimentary, Margot."

"Oh, dear. Now you've gone all stanch and honorable. And I am really getting quite winded, darling. Couldn't you launch us toward that nice bar and then haul me to a shuddering and exhausted stop and give me a transfusion? Just Scotch, darling. A great coarse dollop of it, with a dash of water and no ice."

Agnes Partridge Keeley sat with Dotsy and Hildabeth, drinking a sweet rum drink and talking about the sound of the music, telling them about her life in Pasadena, her home, her classes, the paintings she had sold, her investment properties. And quite suddenly she found herself sitting, in consternation, back inside herself, listening to her own voice going on and on. ". . . always wanted to take advantage of a single woman in a business way, trying to cheat me on leases and things, but I've got a head for figures and I can tell you that I don't let them get away with a thing." She hauled herself to a stop with an effort. "My goodness!" she said. "Do you know, I think I'm tight! I never never get tight!"

"Well, you've got an inch left there of your third one," Dotsy said, "and this is a full half of my first one, and we're drinking the same thing, some kind of a punch he said, a Planter's Punch, and if they made yours the same as mine I don't wonder a bit you feel funny, because I feel pretty darn funny myself on a half a one."

"I have the feeling I should go outdoors," Agnes said.

"When you feel that way it's a real good thing to do," Hildabeth advised her.

Agnes stood up. The floor seemed a long way away. When she took a step her foot came down too hard. She waited for balance. Then, with her pink face screwed up into a look of great determination, looking like the face of a fat, vicious child trying to get even by burning down the house, she plodded, implacable and monolithic, through the dancers, out through the lobby, and out through the main gate. The sun was nearly down. She felt she should walk. She did not want to walk up and down the hot road. She turned onto the path that led down into the barranca. It was not a steep path, but she could not seem to adjust to the angle of descent. She would slow to a stop with one foot poised out in front of her, or she would find herself trotting heavily forward and have to fight for balance. And suddenly, to her horror and alarm, she found the trotting was out of control. It had become a waddling lope, and then a joggling, flapping, suety gallop that could have but one horrid termination when her churning legs could no longer keep up with the upper half of her. She tried her utmost, squeaking with fear. It is to her credit that she very nearly reached the bottom before she pitched forward. Through some miracle of primitive instinct, she tucked her chin down and rolled her right shoulder under, so that she took it almost professionally. After the roll she was clear of the ground for a moment and then came down in a sitting position with a thunderous shocking thump of the seat of yellow linen slacks against the earth. There was still enough forward momentum to roll her back up onto her feet and pitch her over onto her hands and knees.

She could easily have been seriously injured. She had not struck any rocks. She was merely shaken up. She remained upon her hands and knees for several moments, weeping with anger, fright and relief, trembling with the excess of adrenalin in her blood, that adrenalin that had burned up the liquor in moments. She was on a grassy spot. When her breathing was easier and she was not shaking so badly, she rolled slowly over into a sitting position. Under normal circumstances Agnes Keeley had difficulty in arising from a sitting position. She puffed her way up out of chairs. But on that occasion she had barely touched the ground when she found herself on her feet. The only thing, she thought, which could have duplicated such a sensation would be to sit on a carpet of hornets and have each one bite simultaneously and with enthusiasm. She clapped her hands to her seat and received such a hot renewal of sensation in those fractional areas where her hands touched that she yelped involuntarily.

It did not take much search to learn the cause. Through some malignancy of fate, as though to even the score for an escape without serious injury, she had been permitted to thump the broadest part of her anatomy solidly on a squatty species of broad-leaf cactus plant. In luxuriant life it had been about eight inches high and about one yard across its roughly circular dimension. It lay flattened, compressed and ruined, the dark luxuriant green of the broad thick leaves split to expose the pale pithy centers. But in its moment of demise, it had accomplished, at last, the age-old ambition of all cacti, instantaneously to lose all available needles to maximum depth in an all-inclusive target of opportunity.

Agnes reached back with caution to touch herself with one finger. It was like backing into a live wire. The dusk shadows were gathering in the bottom of the barranca. She looked around the area until she saw a sister plant of the smashed one. She bent over and peered at it. The slender needles on the broad leaves were almost as thick as fur. She touched the needles with her fingers, very lightly, and three of them, almost as fine as glass fibers, stuck into her finger and came free of the plant. She pulled them out carefully.

The problem had monstrous aspects. Self-treatment presented incalculable difficulties. Dr. Dorothy Stepp was in Pasadena. It was unthinkable to ask the assistance of one of the female students. She was aware that her condition had very probably been noted when she had left. And she had enough objectivity to know that it was just the sort of disaster that too many of them would find hilarious.

She climbed slowly back up the path, still snuffling from time to time. Climbing was uncomfortable. Each flex and ripple of the great buttocks seemed to send streaks of fire from side to side, as though she was being followed by a careless person with a blow torch. Once she reached the top she found that walking was hardly more comfortable. She soon adjusted to a gait which provided a minimum of discomfort. She walked carefully and rather stiff-legged, planting her feet wide and setting them down easily. The straps of her straw sandals had chafed her feet during her run, so when she reached the corridor, she kicked them off and picked them up. She padded silently down to the door of her room. Even such a minor matter as reaching into the pocket of her slacks to get her room key created shocking discomfort by tautening the seat of the slacks across the billion needles.

When Pepe heard the unmistakable sound of the key being inserted into Agnes' door, he was standing at her bureau, her red leather wallet in his hand, the top drawer open. After the first instant of panic, he reacted swiftly. There was no time to wriggle out between the narrow bars on the window. He dropped the wallet into the drawer, closed it, and disappeared under the bed like Richie Ashburn sliding into second base. The overhang of the spread left a gap of about five inches between the edge of the spread and the tile floor. He pressed himself back against the wall, out of sight. He could only hope that it was a short visit to the room. The boy was very angry at Felipe Cedro. Felipe had told him that this would be a very good time to sneak into the rooms, while they were drinking. Pepe had not thought so. He had objected. Felipe had answered his objections by rapping him on the head with hard knuckles.

He heard the door close, saw her bare feet go by close to the bed, and heard the jangle and clatter as the heavy faded draperies were pulled shut across the window, the sound of metal rings sliding on the wrought-iron bar. The feeble light was turned on. He heard her sigh, very deeply and heavily, with an odd little squeak at the end. Then there came rather frequent little grunts of effort, and swishings of fabric. The fabric sounds stopped, but the gruntings continued. From time to time she spoke fervently. Pepe could not understand her words, but it was clear that she spoke in bitter anger and frustration.

Inevitably his curiosity became stronger than his caution. He determined that her bare heels were aimed toward the bed, and wriggled cautiously forward until he could look out at her, and see all of her. Agnes Partridge Keeley was five

185

foot five and weighed one hundred and seventy-eight pounds. She was pink and white.

Even had Pepe been blind and deaf, he could hardly have survived those years of his childhood spent in a two-room hovel with parents and older brothers and sisters without acquiring basic knowledge of the ways of the world. With his acute senses and his active curiosity, he had long since passed the point where any peculiarities of anatomy could be expected to startle him. Yet nothing had prepared him for the vision of Agnes Partridge Keeley in the buff. It was a stupendous vision, particularly from his low angle of sight. She was engaged in some incomprehensible effort, armed with hand mirror and tweezers. Each violent effort set up a veritable cascade of ripples which, much like tidal movements in a constricted pass, met at random angles to form visible wave patterns.

Even as a Balboa, catching his first glimpse of the broad and shining expanse of the Pacific, might be expected to stand long in awe and reverent reflection, Pepe forgot all caution, until suddenly he realized she had ceased her efforts and her tilted face, purple with effort, was staring at him from around one Jello hip, staring with a frozen consternation which matched his own.

As she straightened up, screaming like all the sirens of the Cruz Rojo and ran toward her closet, Pepe scrambled out from under the bed and raced for the door in a wild panic. Apparently his flight changed her immediate objective, because she caught him at the door and, as he wrested it open, she inflicted a series of surprisingly heavy blows on his head and shoulders.

When the door burst open, Dotsy Winkler was directly opposite it. It was a violent tableau which would never completely fade from her memory. Pepe fled. Agnes stood for a moment just inside the door, her expression maniacal, and then was abruptly, helplessly hysterical. Dotsy went in and pulled the door shut and found a robe and put it around the shuddering, whooping woman's shoulders, and smacked her face with precision and energy. As the hysterics changed into a milder sobbing, Dotsy urged Agnes back and had her sit on the bed. This, it turned out, was a mistake. Agnes leaped high with a strange wild cry and from her incoherencies, Dotsy at last pieced together what had happened.

Dotsy Winkler was a kindly and practical woman. It did not take long for her to organize things to her satisfaction. The patient lay face-down on her bed, with the robe up

186

around her waist. Dotsy had borrowed the colonel's Coleman lantern. It hissed busily and cast a white and pitiless light on the broad areas of injury. Dotsy used her own broadnose tweezers and Hildabeth's rectangular magnifying glass that she used to read newspapers.

She pulled a chair close to the bed, placed the lantern in the most advantageous position and surveyed the field of operation.

"Land sakes!" she said. "You look all over like the top side of a caterpillar, Agnes. I just don't see how anybody could have done it so . . . complete."

"Are you sure the door is locked?" Agnes asked weakly.

"It's locked tight. Now don't you worry. This may take some time, but it's got to be done. And it shouldn't hurt any, pulling them out."

She began to work deftly and logically, starting from the edge and clearing each area completely, rapping the spines off into a dish beside her.

"Dotsy," Agnes said after a long time had passed.

"Yes?"

"I'm so grateful to you. But . . . you won't tell anyone, will you?"

"Now it would be real easy for me to say no, wouldn't it?"

" But . . ."

"If Hildabeth knew about this she'd just about bust. It would be kind of a sin to keep it from her. I mean, begging your pardon, it seems right laughable to me, and she's got a lot more sense of humor than I have. I can't promise not to tell her, but you know, she can't keep a thing to herself, so I'll promise I won't tell her until this thing is over and we're in the car going home. I'll tell her on the trip. But I better not tell her while she's driving. That's a promise, Agnes."

"It's kind of you."

"Am I hurting you at all?"

"It's just sort of a tingle."

Dotsy hummed to herself as she worked. When she was about half through she said, "You know, I'm not one to go back on a promise, Agnes. I like to keep my word."

"What do you mean?"

"You've been carrying on about Mr. Torrigan. I'd say you've been real nasty about him, showing around that report. I'm not one to defend sinners, but everybody has to live their own life and go to the reward they've asked for. Mr. Torrigan certainly does a lot of drinking and a lot of talking. I don't know what to say about his pictures. I just don't understand them. But maybe that's my fault."

"There's nothing in them to . . ."

"Now you just lay quiet and don't raise your voice, Agnes. The way I look at it there's room in the world for almost anything a body can think of. If an Aye-rab feels he's got to have nine wives, that's his way of doing, and if I don't think much of it, that doesn't mean I have to try to make him give them up. A long time ago I stopped giving money for the missions. They were after me when I stopped, and I said that instead of spreading the word of Christ in those foreign places, they should start spreading it a little more heavy around home. Right there in Elmira, Ohio, we've got some terrible things going on.

"The way I see it, it's like this fuss you're making about Mr. Torrigan. I do think that he's a kindly man in spite of his habits. I don't think he's mean. So if you think you've got the best way of doing a picture, you should keep on trying to do your pictures better and better, and teach people how to do them your way instead of going around plotting and scheming, trying to do some kind of hurt to Mr. Torrigan just because his ideas are different."

"But he . . ."

"I know just how you feel about him. Land, you've said it often enough. But I just wanted to tell you that I like to keep a promise. And I can keep promises pretty good, except when I get a little mad and then I forget myself. I'm afraid if you don't hide that report away someplace and stop fussing at him, I might get upset and tell how you got a little tiddly and fell onto a cactus."

Long seconds passed before Agnes said, "All right, Dotsy."

"I want to tell you I do admire what you're doing for Hildabeth. I've known her all my life, and when she goes into something, she goes all the way. The way you've got her painting, I can tell you she's going to have a painting on every wall in Elmira before she's through. And she's enjoying every minute of it. It's more practical for her than knowing how to hula."

"I wish you'd attend more classes, Dotsy."

"Oh, I just haven't got the knack. I'd rather see that everybody eats good."

It was long after dark before the task was finished. Dotsy finished off by painting the entire area with iodine after a final inspection. Agnes stood up and belted her robe. And then, as Dotsy watched anxiously, Agnes lowered herself to the bed. She winced slightly as she sat down, and then winced a little more as she rocked from side to side.

"There's a few left, here and there," she said. "But nothing I can't stand."

"There was some drove in too deep, I guess. You've had a real bad evening, Agnes. I'll just go get you some nice hot tea and toast and you go right to bed."

"What are we going to do about that horrible child?"

"Oh. I just guess he was in here stealing. Must have a key, like you said. Don't expect it will do much good to get him fired. Next one might steal more. I just guess I'll hint around and take up a little collection, and next time I go to the market, I'll pick up some good hasps and padlocks."

"That child should be beaten!"

"Agnes, you got a streak of mean in you, and if I were you I'd pray for the strength to control it. It looked to me like you were giving him all the beating he needed. That last belt across the side of the head crossed his eyes for him, and when he went down the hall he was yelping and running crookedy."

Chapter Thirteen

SHORTLY AFTER AGNES had left the dining room, the character of the party had begun to change. As the first few began to lose their taste for dancing, there began a slow and inevitable disintegration of the group, caused by the alcoholic effects on the individuals.

Park and Bitsy Barnum left after dark, trying to sneak away in the Mercedes, but, once detected by Torrigan, submitted protestingly to the shower of rice, and went off with the cans tethered to the back bumper clanging and bouncing. Shane was roundly denounced by everyone for using cooked rice from the tepid and glutinous pot he had found in the kitchen. They explained that it was contrary to custom. Gloria Garvey was particularly indignant. Shane had thrown with great power and poor aim. The Barnums had escaped unscathed. But Gloria, standing off to the right and waving goodbye, had been struck squarely on the chest just above the yoke of her rather ratty peasant blouse by one compacted wad which, after landing with a stinging splat that drove her back a half step, clung clammily and then slid down inside the front of the blouse. Shane, confronted with such a concert of disapproval, became filled with black remorse. He went about apologizing to everyone, telling them that he had never been any damn good anyway, how, after he got out of the Navy he had fallen in with evil companions and now owned two vending-machine companies in California and small pieces of three joints in Las Vegas. He took out a platinum bill clip stuffed fat with coarse money and showed it to everybody and explained that it was dirty money, that he had always been a bum and always would be a bum, and shouldn't be permitted to associate with such wonderful people.

The look of the money made a faint stirring of greed in the hearts of several, but it electrified Felipe. Shane's next drink, lovingly constructed by Felipe, was a tall tumbler containing a curious concoction, half Scotch and half tequila, with a little ice and a dash of lime juice. Felipe watched Shane narrowly as he took his first large swallow of it. Shane shuddered slightly, but made no protest.

Felipe quickly improvised a plan of action. He found an opportunity to tell Margarita to be more than pleasant to Shane. Margarita, who had been hovering close to Klauss, to his evident displeasure and nervousness, made a face and told Felipe that Shane obviously belonged in a tree, nibbling fruit and scratching his hairy ribs. She would have nothing to do with him. Felipe informed her that unless she responded to this simple request he would be pleased to turn her into an object so distasteful that strong men would faint at the sight of her and small children would lose their minds.

Margarita focused on Shane. She danced with him. She stood with him. And, wearing a wide frozen grin, she listened as he spoke endlessly to her in a heavy and dolorous voice. In the meantime Felipe had enlisted the aid of Fidelio after discovering that Alberto had rendered himself unavailable. When the time was ripe, Felipe motioned Margarita to come over to him. He told her to disappear, to leave the party and not come back. Immediately. When she was gone he took a fresh drink to Shane, and said confidentially, "The girl in the red dress likes you, señor. She has not much English. She ask me to say she waits out back for you, señor. In the building in back of hotel."

"Huh?" Shane said, and Felipe took a clinical satisfaction in the glazed look in the stocky man's eyes. He repeated what he had said. "Oh, sure," Shane said thickly. "Cute kid."

Felipe absented himself from his bartending. He went

with Fidelio, whose greed was only slightly greater than his trepidation, and they stationed themselves just inside the open doorway to the small room assigned to Alberto.

"I will strike," Felipe said, holding the short piece of pipe he had wrapped in a rag. "You have not done this sort of thing. Out of fear, you may strike too hard. You will catch him as he falls. Then we will carry him around through the shadows and put him into the vehicle of the Señora Garvey. It will be thought that he wandered out very drunk and went to sleep in the vehicle."

Felipe looked toward the hotel. Soon Shane came around the corner of the hotel, walking unsteadily in the light from the kitchen windows, peering toward the servants' quarters.

When he was close enough, Felipe went, "Pssst!"

Shane altered course and came to the open doorway. "Hey, cutie!" he said, and came through the doorway.

Felipe struck with force and precision. The padded pipe made a dull sound against Shane's skull. Shane wavered and said, "Hey!"

Felipe gritted his teeth and struck much harder than before. Shane turned toward him and said, "Cut it out!"

As Felipe raised the pipe high in superstitious panic, a great force smashed against the side of his face, and he danced sidelong and fell into a corner. He shook the spinning lights out of his head and was aware of a curious and busy sound just inside the door. There was a shuffling sound, a rhythmic snorting, a heavy and somewhat moist thudding, and a muffled squealing that went eerily up and down the scale. The squealing stopped and there was the sound of a fall and then a silence. Felipe had gotten his feet under him. He tried to plunge out through the door. A blow drove him back. And he was blocked back into a corner. He flapped helplessly against a hard shoulder and a bullet head that kept him wedged in place while slow bombs went off in his stomach, destroying him, and the animal thing snorted and grunted as it carefully ruined him. And then lightning blazed through his skull from side to side, and he tumbled backward off the black edge of the world.

Shane stood in the middle of the little dark room, breathing hard. He worked his hands to check for broken bones. He fingered the top of his skull. It was tender. From long habit he checked to see that he retained wrist watch, money clip and wallet. He took out his lighter and held it high. Just the two of them. No gal. Messy little room. He squatted by each of them in turn and stuck blunt fingers against their throats to find the pulse. When he was certain they were both alive, he took what they had. The older one had a small tight roll of American money tied with a string, and a big wad of pesos. The young one had a small wad of pesos.

Shane went back to the hotel. He made himself a drink. The party was thinning out. He found Gloria arguing with the little guy who ran the school and he beckoned to her and she came over to him, and looked down at him.

"Bend your knees or something," he said. "How can I talk to you, you hanging over me like a house?"

"Get up on a chair."

"Look, the party is dying. Let's roll."

"A splendid suggestion, sport."

"Where's Margot?"

"She disappeared a while back. I think she went off with the pretty man, the creep with the curly hair. Want to try to find her?"

"Hell with her. Le's go."

As they drove through the main gate, Shane said, "Where are we going, big doll?"

"I know where there's a big party that ought to be jumping by now."

"Okay. Good deal. Jeez, I don't know what the hell is wrong with me tonight. I got this headache. I never have headaches."

"Something you ate, no doubt."

"No. Maybe it's getting hit. But I never got a headache from being hit before. You see, two of those servants there, that bartender and a pal, they suckered me out back and got cute. They busted me on the head a couple times and they made me mad. So I knocked them around."

Gloria was laughing. And she was on the long hill down into town, picking up speed. And suddenly Shane moved closer to her and she gave a yell of pain as he reached over with his foot and stomped hard on the brake. The car slewed and she brought it back under control and, under the pressure of his foot, came to a stop.

"What the hell!" she exclaimed.

"I don't like the way you drive, big doll. I didn't like it on the way up here and I don't like it any better now. I didn't come down here on vacation to get spread all over the road by some crazy dame."

"So get out!"

"The hell I will. You drive and you drive nice or I'll stop

it again, and the next time I stop it, big doll, I'm going to yank you out and rough you up. I won't mark you none, because I think it's a pretty low type guy marks up a pretty woman. But when we get through going around and around, you're going to be hurting here and there."

"You're a filthy little animal, and you wouldn't dare lay a hand on me."

"You mean like chivalry, doll? Or because you're important? You don't get the message. I'm Shane. I'm on vacation. I was with that Limey dish since Vera Cruz, and she's Lady something or other, and she's got that house here and one in the south end of France, she says, and dough up to here. Am I impressed? Every time she acted like a pig, we went around and around. So now I'm not with Margot any more, big doll. I'm with you. Or say it the other way and it's better. You're with Shane. I want careful driving, understand. Slow and nice. We'll go to the party and then we'll go to the hotel and pick up my stuff because I'm moving into your place."

"That's . . . absurd. I won't permit it!"

"You don't seem to get the message. I can't seem to clue you nice. I'm trying to be a nice guy. I don't want to bust you around unless you can't get the message some other way. So get out of the car, big doll. Go on, get out. It'll be over quick and then I'll drive because you won't feel like it for a while."

She stared at the blunt hard face. He hadn't spoken in anger. More in weary resignation, facing an unpleasant task that had to be done.

"Why, you really would!"

"That's what I keep telling you. Get out."

"I could go to the police."

"That's what Margot did. She caught on slow too. So I gave them my doll-beating permit. It's got that picture of General Grant on it. Those Vera Cruz cops catch on fast. So why don't you relax? I'm a nice enough guy. I got money to spend. Hell, I'll get you some clothes. I like big dolls, but not dressed so sloppy. And you can get something done to that hair. You'd look a hell of a lot better if you'd take care of yourself. You're not built bad."

"Are you crazy?"

"Now that's no thing to say to anybody who's fought both pro and am. I've had fifty-six bouts, doll, and one thing I get sensitive about is anybody thinking I'm punchy because I'm not. I'm just Shane. I got a lot of friends. I'm not afraid to spend a buck. I like things nice. If I don't like the looks of your place, we'll move back into the hotel. But I like home-cooked food. And a woman around to keep things picked up. Somebody to talk to. And a little loving now and then. I know you've got a place of your own and no husband and no steady boy-friend so it isn't like I was moving somebody out so I can move in. And it don't matter to me one damn that you don't think much of me right now. You'll get to like me. I'm a pretty nice guy. I've got a lot of friends. And that Margot was getting on my nerves something terrible. So let's go to the party, on account of it's a waste of good liquor the way mine is wearing off so fast."

"I have the crazy feeling I'm dreaming all this, Shane."

"Take a clue. You're not. Jesus Christ, woman, what do you expect when you go churning around by yourself? A ticket to Bible class? You just made a new friend. So either get out now and get convinced—because I got the feeling it's going to have to happen sooner or later anyhow—or drive on slow to the party."

"How . . . how long is your vacation?"

"Until a certain guy gets tired of waiting and figures he better withdraw a certain warrant. And then I can get back and keep those clowns working for me from stealing me blind."

"I'll drive slowly," she said.

"That's using the old head, big doll. What's your name again?"

"Gloria, Shane. Gloria Garvey."

"That's right. I forget names. Nice name, Gloria. Kind of fits a real big woman like you." They drove slowly toward town. "Now we're getting straightened away, Gloria, just you don't get tricky. There's no way you can wheel and deal me out without giving yourself some big miseries."

"All right, Shane."

A few minutes later she began to laugh, and she could detect an edge of wild hysteria in the sound.

"What's so funny?"

"It would be . . . hard to explain. I was thinking of how I was accused of being aggressive not long ago."

"You? That's what they used to write about me in the ring. Even when I was getting my ears slapped off. Shane was aggressive. Always boring in. Hell, it was the only style I knew. Like Armstrong. Keep that leather flying."

When they got to the house it was easy to see that it was a big noisy party. As she started toward the door Shane

194

grasped her arm strongly and hauled her back. "One more thing, Gloria."

"Yes?"

"No being a pig. No getting drunk. No loud talk. No cootch dancing. Don't tell dirty jokes. No going off with anybody, like that Margot pig. You're with Shane now, and when you're with Shane, you're a lady, and you better not forget it. I'll have an eye on you. And when I'm ready to go, I don't want no argumentation." He gave her a small but powerful shake, his blunt fingers painful on her arm. "This is getting to you? You're reading me loud and clear?"

"Yes, Shane," she said humbly. And they walked together to the door, and she suddenly discovered, to her dismay, that she was walking with her knees slightly bent so as to minimize the discrepancy in their height.

Colonel Hildebrandt left the party early. He had danced with the bride and some of the other females, and had left by mid-afternoon to complete his current painting project. Upon his return it took but a casual inspection to convince him that it was unlikely that he would be fed. So, in his room, he opened tins of rations and cooked on his two-burner gasoline stove. Mrs. Winkler arrived just as he was finishing, and he loaned her one of the two gasoline lanterns, lighting it for her and assuring her that it was not in the least dangerous.

He kept his hearing aid on as he read until the lantern was returned. And then he removed the hearing aid and sat and read a little longer in the utter silence which he had learned to appreciate. He was in bed by ten, with tomorrow's project all planned. He would have to use Saltamontes again to get to the canyon he wished to paint.

Hildabeth was also a rather early casualty. She found enough in the kitchen to satisfy her hunger, and as she was preparing it, Miles Drummond appeared on the same errand. She increased the portions, and when it was ready they carried it on trays to the owner's apartment.

Miles, she noticed, was in a most precarious state. He was glassy, unco-ordinated, largely incomprehensible, and solemn as a little white-headed owl. He ate very little of the food. When she finished he decided he would teach her how to play chess. He was deaf to her spirited protests. He wobbled over and got his board and men. As he was setting them up, his eyes suddenly rolled. He hiccuped once and leaned gently forward and came to rest with his head in the middle of the board. A few moments later he began to snore.

Hildabeth went around and straightened him up, pulled his chair out, picked him up bodily, staggered to his bed with him and dropped him on top of it. She removed his glasses and shoes and loosened his belt. She put the chessboard and men away, stacked the two trays and the dishes, began to turn out the lights. The final light was the one near his bed. She turned out the light, leaned over heavily and kissed him on the forehead and murmured, "Poor little chicken."

She took the trays to the kitchen and then went to bed. She worried about Dotsy until she got up and dressed again and went looking for her. But she could not find her. A few minutes after she had gone back to bed, Dotsy came in, and shut the door quietly.

"You can turn the light on. I'm awake. Where *have* you been?"

Dotsy turned the light on, and began to unbutton her blouse. She yawned. "Quite a party, wasn't it?"

"You mean isn't it. You didn't answer my question."

"Well . . . I've been here and there."

"Nonsense. I looked all over for you. Where have you been and what have you been doing?"

Dotsy suddenly grinned at her, and Hildabeth thought it a very evil and malicious grin. "I won't tell you."

"What!"

"I made a promise. I can't tell you. Not yet. When we're on our way home I can tell you."

"I'd like to get right out of this bed and shake the tar out of you!"

"You do that, and I'll never tell you. You know I won't. You know how stubborn I can get."

"I certainly do. Suit yourself. Don't ever tell me. Good night." She turned her face to the wall.

After the light went out, Hildabeth heard Dotsy get into bed. In a little while she began to chuckle.

"What's so funny?" Hildabeth demanded.

"I'll tell you on the trip home."

"I could learn to hate you, Dorothy Winkler! I really could! You know how I feel about secrets."

"Certainly do. You love 'em. You love 'em so much you got to share them with everybody you know. Good night, dear."

Gil and Jeanie Wahl were trying, with all the ingenuity

at their command, to break each other's hearts. Gil had drunk too much. He had become very festive. He had been a dancing, singing fool, in love with the whole world. And he had thought the whole world loved him. He and Mary Jane had been improvising a burlesque of the Mexican Hat Dance when he had looked around and hadn't spotted Jeanie. He felt vaguely troubled, but he kept dancing.

Finally he said, "Better quit."

"Hey! Not now. You know, you're a fun guy, Gil. Haven't hardly had a chance to say a word to you. You too busy being a bride."

"Don't see Jeanie," he said.

"She's around someplace. Come on!"

"Nope. Gotta find my li'l Jeanie."

So he had looked everywhere, and finally had gone to the room and unlocked the door. She was in bed, reading.

He went grinning over and plumped down on the edge of the bed and said, "Hi, Jeanie! Wassa matter? You don't feel good or something?"

"I feel perfectly all right, thank you."

"Looked all over. You were gone. Looked everyplace."

"I'm astonished that you missed me, Gilbert. I really am. You were having such a terrific time when I left."

"You sore or something?"

"Why should I be sore or something? I'd say I just got bored. It was so boring watching you blundering all over that dance floor too drunk to even know who you were clinging to."

"Now wait a minute," he said, scowling. "Put that damn book down and let's get a couple things straight around here."

She sighed and closed the book and put it aside. "All right. We will get a couple of things straight around here."

"This was a party. Right?"

"I guess so. I had a delirious time. I should have danced all night."

"Dint I dance with you, dint I?"

"Twice, I think. I am so terribly grateful to you, really I am."

"Katy Hepburn yet. So I danced with the others too. Everybody was dancing with everybody. So what the hell does that mean?"

"Oh, I don't know. Just the spectacle you were making of yourself. It just seemed boring. I got tired of watching it."

"You danced with all those guys!"

She smiled. "I really didn't have any other choice, did I? If I wanted to dance, darling. You were otherwise engaged. Yes, I danced with them. And I was fondled by them, of course."

He jumped up. "Who did that? Who's the wise guy? I'll kill 'im!"

"Oh, sit down, hero! I was merely being subjected to the sort of attentions you were giving the others."

"I was not!"

"Every minute you were dancing with the Garvey woman, you had your hand on her big nasty rump. Everybody saw it."

"I had my hand on her waist!"

"Really, dear. What kind of a fool do you think I am?"

"Well . . . if I was I didn't know it. She's pretty tall, you know."

"And that lovely dreamy number with Mary Jane. You two made such a pretty picture together. If you'd gotten any closer to her, you'd have been standing behind her. All that romantic dipping and swooping, and you with an expression on your face like some kind of sweaty animal. I could have died of shame. Everybody was looking at you two."

"You listen, Jeanie!"

"I really don't think there's anything you can say that I would very much care to listen to. I guess you've given me the word, Gilbert. The honeymoon is over. You've made it so terribly clear." Her mouth began to tremble. "And I thought we were different. I guess I was a fool."

"Now hold on!" he said angrily.

"But now I find out it's really a very ordinary marriage. There's nothing special about it. You can go around being the big party boy, and when I'm bored I'll just leave, dear. I won't cramp your style. But the least we can do, in all honesty, is to stop pretending that this relationship of ours is unique. We don't want to kid ourselves."

"Okay, okay, okay," he yelled. "So if it's going to be ordinary it'll be ordinary."

"Obviously!"

"If you want to take a sour-puss attitude toward a party, go ahead. Spoil the fun."

"Fun!"

"You don't understand innocent fun, do you? You don't understand how a person can have an innocent good time."

"Not old sour-puss me, darling."

"So read your book."

She picked it up. "Thank you. I will." She held it close to her face. He stamped around noisily, getting undressed. She stared at the blurred meaningless words, the silent tears running down her face.

He snatched the light off and got into his bed. "Night," he grunted.

"Good night, Gilbert. Sleep well."

She put the book on the floor and stuck her face into the pillow and tried to cry without making a sound.

"Jeanie?"

"Yes?"

"I got a little tight."

"That's news?"

"A person tries to explain something and all they get is that nasty, bitter, sarcastic stuff. So why try? Good night."

She did not answer him. After a long time she said, "Are you awake?"

"Yes."

"What I mean is, Gilbert, that maybe it's time we made an adult adjustment to this marriage. I have sometimes worried a little about the strength of the . . . physical part of it."

"You haven't acted a damn bit worried."

"You don't understand. I think it's time we started to use a little more restraint."

"Like now?"

"Precisely."

"Big deal. How about in the book on marital relations? Remember, it said that when the woman starts to use her sex on a reward and punishment cycle, then it's an emotionally unhealthy situation. Okay! You think I goofed. I don't think I did. So comes the punishment."

"You *know* I didn't mean anything like that. You're being just as ugly as you can possibly be. I think you're drunk and horrible and cruel."

"Thanks, honey."

Again there was a long silence in the dark room. The sound of the music was far away.

"What gets me," he said moodily, "is all of a sudden this restraint kick. Sort of a puritan idea. Anything that's fun is sinful. That old lady of yours is a prize example. She can't even smile without looking as if her mouth hurts."

"My mother has nothing to do with this discussion!"

"How can you be so sure, honey? She brought you up. And I'll bet the way she had it organized, if your old man spent a poker night with the boys, he couldn't get within forty yards of her for a month."

"Oh, shut up!"

"You're the one started this adult adjustment routine. I don't figure I'm a pagan or anything. And I don't think I've got any obsessive or compulsive approach to sex. Let's put the cards right on the table. We're starting out in life, like they say. And we're doing the kind of work we want to do. We both like kids and we know how to handle them well, and there'll be a lot of satisfaction in that. Not much money, God knows, but what I guess you could call emotional fringe benefits. All right. Since we've been married, and every chance we had before we got married, we've spent a lot of time in bed. If it's more than average, I don't know and I don't care. A lot of marriages never get straightened away in that department. I enjoy it. Unless you're one hell of an actress, you do too. And it's something we get better at, I think. I even think you could call it some kind of an art form. If there wasn't any deep emotional or even . . . spiritual aspects to it, then it would just be a lot of hunger and sensuousness and nothing else. You follow me? But because it's what it is, I don't think you can logically start talking about restraint unless you're trying to hurt me because you got jealous."

"I was *not* jealous! I was bored!"

"Those drinks hit me hard. I didn't have too many of them. Maybe I became too much of the big old party boy. But I didn't make any passes at anybody, and I didn't even think of making any passes at anybody. I danced. It's a social custom or something. So I get the word that this is a very ordinary marriage. I guess if people go around thinking a thing like that, it comes true."

"Oh, Gil!"

"All right. You're over there crying. There's tears on my face too. This is what they call the first quarrel, I guess. But I don't like this ripping and tearing at each other, this trying to find the soft spots so you can really hurt."

"Oh, I don't like it either. I hate it, darling!"

"I don't think it's so ordinary."

"I think it's . . . terribly special."

And when he went over and slid in beside her, she turned into his arms with a little shuddering sob, and he kissed her salty eyes and both sides of the small nose, and the tip of the nose, and her lips, and the sides and hollow of her throat, and they mended all their wounds with a special lingering sweetness.

For Gam Torrigan, the departure from the original plan of dignified restraint was so gradual that he was not aware of when it happened nor, in retrospect, could he remember which specific act was out of keeping with his intended design. Surely, when they had played a fast number, his demonstration of the Cossack dance, staying well down on his heels, kicking his legs out strongly, had been a display of skill, not a drunken exhibition. Nor, when he had improvised the bongo drums from kitchen utensils, had he been offensive. Though the musicians had not seemed appreciative of his efforts, it had been for a time a popular diversion, with others taking his place. Perhaps the edge had been reached when he had sat out in the patio court on the stone bench with Mary Jane. Mary Jane kept saying she had lost her best friend in all the world and then she had wept. The tears of this lovely child had touched him deeply and so he had wept too, gulping and snuffling, the tears trickling down into his beard. He had held her gently and tenderly, without any motive but to comfort her. She had clung to him and they had rocked and mourned, and he had kissed her as a father might.

But the next incident had been unquestionably questionable. He had looked at the starry sky and had seen a section of the terminal N and a top slice of the O in EL HUTCHINSON, dark against the sky. And his eye had wandered to a possible route to the roof. A low wall, and a higher wall, a low roof and a cornice and the high roof.

Mary Jane, sniveling against his chest said, "Everything I ever do turns out miz'ble."

"Hey!"

"What you want, Gambel?"

"Bet if you got up there you could sit on those big letters and look all over hell."

She stared up. "Lovely idea! Get the good old ice ax and the crampons. We got to climb it because it's there."

"My feeling exactly."

The climb was easy. After he helped her over the cornice, they stood up and looked around. They could see the car lights on the main highway, all the lights of the city, and the little beads of lights winding down the mountain.

"Wow!" she said.

"A perfectly adequate comment, my dear. It has the proper semantic ring about it. Say it again."

"Wow!"

They walked to the front of the roof and looked down.

"Cars look like beetle bugs," she said. "Shiny old beetle bugs. Gives me an icky feeling I want to jump."

"Inconsiderate. Messy."

They investigated the huge concrete letters. They were eight feet tall, square cut, festooned with the frayed wire and the broken and burned-out bulbs from the brave days when the sign had been lighted. The big letters made for lovely games. They played like children. He would think of a word beginning with each letter, and she would drape herself on, in or against the letter in a pose to illustrate that word. She was particularly successful with *horror* and *lazy,* and he banged his big fists together in applause. Then they sent code to each other. This was accomplished by trotting back and forth and pausing in front of the desired letter, and slapping your hands once to indicate the end of a word. But they ran out of words. And it was tiring. He sat in the curve of the U and she sat in the curve of the O.

"One thing wrong up here, Gambelino."

"What's that?"

"Terrible room service."

"We could let down a rope. Some lovely co-operative gentleman might tie a bottle on the end."

"No rope."

"You have a practical mind. Practicality upsets me."

"Maybe we can unravel something. Make a rope. You wearing anything unravelly? Can't use anything I got on, Gambelino. Be left up here bare as a wood nymph."

"That vision would be artistically sound but socially undesirable. And I am wearing khakis. They don't unravel."

"Maybe we could weave something out of that beard. What the hell is under that beard, Torrigan? I'll just bet you've got one of those chipmunk mouths and no chin at all."

"Young woman, I have a powerful face. I haven't seen it in years, but I bear a distinct resemblance to Burt Lancaster."

"So why goop it up with hair?"

"Your questions are impertinent and personal. But as you are too young to know better, I shall answer you. It is a reverse play, my pet. Artistic gamesmanship. Because it is obviously trite for me to wear a beard, a rather evident cliché, it would be reasonable for me to go about clean-shaven. So I take it one step further, back to the beard. In addition, it leaves me in a constant state of readiness for any historical pageant that may pop up. The hundredth anniversary of the

American Garden Club or something. In addition, I find a sensuous pleasure in combing and brushing it. I am not a slave to the razor. It cushions any blow at the jaw. It gives me freedom of action because it advertises the fact that I am a practicing eccentric. It gives my most trivial comment an emphasis of portentousness. And it attracts women."

"Hah! Like Gloria?"

"You are making sport of me, my child. I knew the lady long ago and far away. I will break, for once, my inflexible rule against speaking of old affairs, particularly to a minor. She was married then. And full of an antic, reckless joy. It was in Maine, and we could hear the sea from my windows. But, to my disappointment, child, she has aged very poorly. Not in appearance. But in the texture of her spirit. There is no more tenderness, no flair for the romantic nuance. She brings to the gentle arts of love all the implacable purpose of a riveting machine. She is a truly alarming organism. What, I ask you, is dalliance without the flash of wit, the clever turn of phrase, the lazy heart-to-heart conversations? But I bore you."

"Gambelino, you are a hairy fraud."

"Of course."

"I am not attracted by a beard. I want to run through there barefoot, pushing a mowing machine."

"The mental picture sickens me."

"So leave us go get a drink to settle your stomach, Torrigan."

"I think of you as my lovely daughter."

They went to the edge of the roof. Mary Jane started down first. She stood on the cornice and turned to put her foot down to the ledge and lost her balance. She teetered for a moment, her back to the drop, arms waving madly. And just as she started to go, Gam grabbed a flailing arm and yanked her back. She huddled against his chest, breathing hard, and he held her tightly.

"Lovely daughter nearly becomes small smear on stone," she said weakly.

"If you knew how sensitive I am, you wouldn't do things like that."

"I am sober. I am humbled. I'm sorry I bad-mouthed your beard."

He released her. "Perhaps you will have to be lowered on a rope."

"When they crack up the aircraft, you send them right on up again into the wild blue stuff, man. Don't think I haven't got eyes for this fine solid roof, but the bar service is nowhere."

She moved with great care. He followed her down. After they jumped down from the final wall they bowed and shook hands. "The Big Top will miss you, Madame Scaloppini," he said.

"I have make zee farewell pair-formance. Giff me my severance pay."

"But first we shall become dronk."

She took his arm and they marched inside.

It was at about that time that the little blackouts began. When they had first begun, years before, they had terrified him. He was afraid that while the conscious mind was blacked out, he might do some unspeakable act of violence. And he was afraid that they signified the beginning of serious alcoholism. But, through canny questioning of his friends, he had learned that there seemed to be no detectable difference between his actions while still functioning and when blacked out. And, as the affliction did not seem to become worse as time went by, he had gradually come to accept it as a standard phase of his drinking times, a personal idiosyncrasy. But when he looked back over an evening of periodic blackouts, it was as though he looked at a movie where the projection bulb burned out at intervals. When it burned out, however, the projector kept functioning. So when the light would come on again, the thread of the plot was lost.

The light came on once and he found himself having an involved argument with John Kemp and Barbara Kilmer about communication in art and the responsibilities of the artist to his culture. At another bright interval, he was standing in the lobby and Mary Jane was vividly angry at him. She was shouting into his face, backing him up step by step as he protested feebly. She was explaining forcibly that it would be a waste of rope to hang him and a waste of lead to gut-shoot him. He gathered that he had offended her by making certain disparaging remarks about Texas and Texans.

In one most curious sequence which seemed to bear no relation to the rest of the evening, he was in a room he did not recognize, and he was sitting on a bed with a glass in his hand. The drooping, indifferent Margot sat in a weary wicker armchair, talking endlessly in her flat British monotone. Her pale slender legs were drawn up into the chair and her only garment was a towel with wide blue-and-white stripes knotted around her waist. She had a glass in her hand and as she talked she ran it up and down her forearm and occasionally touched it to her cheek. He sat there nodding agreement to talk he found almost impossible to follow. It seemed to be a long story about some American officer in London a long time ago and what it had done to her marriage. She seemed to have a special talent for being able to recall every dull and insignificant detail, the date and time of day of all telephone calls, and precisely what she was wearing at the time, and when the kippers at breakfast had been too salty, and the exact roads and mileages and villages they had passed through when they had driven together to someplace or other.

He looked at her, and saw how nicely made she was, how slimly delicate, how smooth and flawless her skin texture. He looked at her with no more desire than if he had been staring at a figurine that held up a lamp. His jaw creaked as he kept stifling yawns. And he began to feel an enormous sympathy for that young major so-and-so if he had had to long endure this total recall of statistical, gastronomical and geographical trivia. There was a crushed-petal look about her long slim face, a bruised look that seemed to promise a dissertation on evil when she opened her mouth. But the flat dreary voice went on and on and on.

"It's been so good to talk with someone mature, Mr. Torrigan. Someone with wisdom and sympathy. Everyone seems so hurried." She uncurled her long legs and stood up slowly. She put her empty glass on the bureau and drifted over to the other bed, in slow ivoried slimness. She unknotted the towel and took it off, stretched out on the bed and placed the towel across her middle.

She yawned and said from the shadows, "I'm really teddibly widdy. D'you mind too awfully much, darling?"

"Mind? No, I don't mind. Not at all."

"It's act-ly despicable to encourage you, darling, and then disappoint you, but really I'm emotionally exhausted from pouring my heart out to you. Catch the light like a dear."

Gam turned out the light and heard her sigh as he quietly closed the door behind him. As he turned, a figure sprang at him in the darkness of the hall, and before he could protect himself a hard fist crashed against his jaw. He recognized Paul Klauss. The smaller man stood in front of him, fists clenched, face distorted.

"What's the matter?" Gam asked.

"You know damn well what's the matter. I hope you're

satisfied. I hate every damn one of you. I'll get even with all of you somehow. You're a dirty stinker, Torrigan!" And Paul Klauss began to cry. He struck again, and hit Gam solidly in the same place as before.

"You keep doing that and I'm going to . . ."

But Klauss had turned on his heel and he went scurrying up the corridor, his shoulders hunched, sobbing audibly.

The final flash of memory was the most distasteful. Kemp and Ardos were walking him to his room, his arms across their shoulders. They held onto his wrists. He was trying to make his legs work, and it was a strange sensation. Like riding a rubber bicycle.

And he was saying, braying, "Rumors are flying. And I'm not deny-innng la da da da dut da dada dado . . ."

"Easy, old horse," John Kemp said.

And the world faded away again as they got him through the doorway of his room.

After Torrigan had been bedded down, John went back out to the lobby. Barbara was waiting for him. "Get the key?" She nodded and handed him the key to the station wagon. "And how was *she* doing?"

"Pretty good, considering."

Rosalinda had disappeared. The bar was empty. The marimba player lay under his marimba. One guitar player was curled up nearby. The other sat on the floor in a corner, plucking slow . sad chords, his nose almost against the strings.

After surveying the situation, Harvey, Monica, John and Barbara had a policy discussion. If they could be restored to partial life, it would be best to take them down into town in the wagon. If not, they might as well be left right there. Every bottle on the bar was completely empty.

The marimba player responded. He was even able to help fold up his marimba. The sleeping guitarist took longer. John selected what he hoped was the proper fee, divided it in thirds, and gave it to them. The small group walked out to the station wagon, Harvey carrying the marimba.

"No need of any of the rest of you coming," John said. "This one here says it's all right to let them off in front of the palace. And that's right on the *zócalo*."

"I'll come along for company," Barbara said.

"Good. Thanks, Harvey. And Monica."

"The clean-up boys," Harvey said. "The old reliables, hey, John? Monica and me, we'll get some of the crud out of the way. Some party, hey?"

"We can say it was long," John said.

He drove the musicians into town. They mumbled their thanks and trudged sleepily away. The *zócalo* was empty. The city slept.

"This may sound insane, John, but I'd like to walk around a little."

"I'd like that too." He parked the car. They walked around the three contiguous public squares and sat on an iron bench under the tree shadows in the *zócalo* nearest the post office. A taxi deposited somebody at the Marik and drove away.

"How good a time did you have?" he asked her.

"I had . . . an interesting time, John. I guess I'm a people-watcher. Adore airports and railroad stations. I've never been a participant in group stuff. When I was young I was horribly shy. I have a lot more confidence in myself now, but I guess I'm the introvert type. So I watch. And I wonder why people do what they do, and what makes them act the way they do. So I guess I had a good time. But—and I guess this sounds odd—I wouldn't have had a good time if you weren't there."

"It's nice to hear, but I didn't contribute any sparkling observations."

"Did I? I can't remember any. No, I had a feeling of stability with you there. I knew that if anybody got drunk enough to be difficult, Klauss or Gam or anybody, you wouldn't let it get messy. So it was like having a . . . ledge to watch from."

"Makes me sound stodgy and reliable. And I guess I am."

"Not stodgy. A woman alone has special problems when a party goes that far off the rails. I've no objection to drinking. But I don't like to see people . . . wallowing around."

"I've wallowed a time or two."

"So did Rob. The poor darling always wanted to sing. And he had no more voice than . . . one of those horns on boats. He sure was loud. That's odd!"

"What?"

"I've tried to learn to be so terribly casual about bringing up his name. But it has been imitation casual. Like sticking a knife in my heart, and sometimes bringing up his name so I could feel the hurt. But that time . . . it really was casual. That isn't the right word. Casual sounds like indifferent."

"Natural."

"Yes, that's much better! To be able to do that makes me feel . . . sad and faithless and disloyal. But it also makes me feel fatuous about myself. Proud that now I can begin to believe I've got the emotional guts to get over it. Not ever completely over it, John. But enough so it won't count in this . . . business of living."

"Obligation to live."

"Yes. To myself first."

"And Rob secondly."

"That's what my father tried to tell me. I couldn't believe it. It seemed horrible. But I'm beginning to understand what he meant. He was more of a person than I am. Maybe this affair of . . . mourning my life away is something he wouldn't want. But I've felt that any other choice is a . . . violation of privacies. I have a kind of fastidious dread of . . . dirtying up sacred memories with substitutions. That horrible little Klauss person caught me off guard and somehow hypnotized me into kissing him. Into responding for a moment. It was vulgar and exceedingly nasty. I wept with shame. And I scrubbed my mouth with a brush until my lips were sore."

"I can understand that."

"Rob was very smart about people. He would have seen through that Klauss person in a minute. I was always the gullible one. So I've always been a little uncertain of my own judgment about people. That's why it took me so long to be able to relax with you, John. You know, you are quite a different sort of human being than Rob was. But in so many ways you are alike. Mostly, I guess, it's that flavor of strength. When Rob felt that he had used his own best judgment to reach a decision, he did not give one damn what anybody in the world might think of him or his decision. I think you're like that too."

"A flattering description of a stubborn man. Yes."

"I've always been too impressed with what other people might think of me. Too concerned. Sometimes it would irritate Rob. You know, you two would have liked each other."

"I hope so, Barbara."

"Lately you've let me go on and on about myself. I guess you've got the complete personal history of one Barbara Kilmer, bit by bit. But aside from your work, you haven't said much about yourself. I'm not really quite sure why you're here, John. It seems strange that you could just take off, when your firm is doing so well."

"It messed up quite a few contracts. There's a good reason, Barbara. I'd like you to know about it. I've wanted to tell you. And I want your advice. I think that women have a sounder approach to this sort of . . . fiasco."

He started way back. He told her of the young marriage and why it didn't work and why it couldn't have been made to work. And then he covered the years that followed, the good exciting years of struggle and growth. He told her about Kurt and Mary, the kind of people they were. Their goodness. And Mary's determined attempts at matchmaking. And how it ended for the three of them. How she had not been able to hide her love, and how the interwoven relationships between the three of them had been hopelessly destroyed. He told her of the decision he had to make, to buy Kurt out or be bought out by him. He explained to her what it would mean in terms of effort were he to buy Kurt out.

"How perfectly terrible for all three of you, John! And especially for Mary. She must be a fine person. You can't just turn love off and on like a switch."

"So there it is. Any ideas?"

"I really don't know. Could you sell it to outside people and just . . . split what you get?"

"It would mean a big loss. The relationship with clients is personal. Our contacts and our personal professional reputations are solid assets of the firm. If neither of us is left, there isn't a hell of a lot left to sell. If he buys, he has to locate a good design man and bring him in. I would have to locate somebody as good as Kurt is on structure. We've got fine kids working for us, but nobody who can be boosted that fast in either department."

"I can tell you what you should do and why, John."

"So positively?"

"Don't make fun. You are whole. It's hurt you, but not the way they've been hurt. Kurt is a fractured man. I imagine it's a very drab thing for him now. Where is his motivation? I guess that running any business is creative in a way. And particularly with that sort of business. And he's right there where everything will keep reminding him of . . . how his world blew up all of a sudden. You say he is very good on the real technical side. I suppose that is stresses and all that sort of thing."

"Yes."

"And he could get a job at any time, couldn't he?"

"Oh, yes."

"Then you owe it to him to take over, John. Maybe it seems a little tasteless to you now, but nowhere near as tasteless as it must be to him. You are a whole man and you can make it run, and you can take pride and pleasure in it. If you sell out to him, I don't think it will last very long. I just don't think an . . . unmotivated man can run anything very well. A heartbroken man."

He thought it over for long minutes. "You are completely right, Barbara. Absolutely right. I was too damn close to it. Just a few careless decisions on big jobs and he would be done."

"You'd save him from drowning, wouldn't you?"

"Of course. That's an odd thing to say."

"Is it? John, I think I'm going to make you very angry at me. But I don't care. I suppose it was really quite flattering to the male ego to have such a woman fall in love with you. Dramatic pathos. And you thought how terribly difficult it was for you. So you've been down here, sucking your pipe, considering yourself sad and mysterious or something, while that poor partner of yours is up there trying to keep the store when he has no special reason to give a damn about it. If anybody should have gone away, he should have. So I guess it's time you stopped being a romantic figure and went back where you belong."

"Good Lord!" he said softly.

"Do you think that at this point he can get very concerned about protecting his own interests, much less yours?"

"All right, all right."

"You could have . . ."

"Barbara, will you please give me a little time to get adjusted to this unfortunately accurate picture of myself as a pretentious ass? Just a few minutes, that's all."

He got up and walked slowly back and forth, his heels tocking in the silence. He stopped in front of her and smiled down at her. "Mary was utterly honest. So was Kurt. So I had to play a part written for Charles Boyer. I have done them a disservice."

"You're not angry?"

"At you? No. A little bit at myself for being dense." He sat beside her again. "In all conscience, damn it, the only thing I can do is go back right away. But I don't want to leave you."

"I . . . I don't know what the response to that should be."

"I wanted all the time I could have with you. And more,

when this part of it is over. Not pushing you, Barbara. Not rushing you. Just watching you come alive, a little at a time."

"You sound like . . ."

"Let me finish. You are it. What I want. For keeps. And you're not emotionally ready to listen to that kind of a pitch yet. So don't try to make any answers or objections or anything else. I love you."

"You love me, and you will go back there right away because you can see, from what I've said, that it's the right thing to do?"

"Yes."

"I keep wondering what I would feel like right now, what I'd feel toward you if you'd said you couldn't go back now because you love me. I have the strangest feeling about that, John. I don't love you."

"I know."

"But . . . because you're doing it this way, I think I can love you some day. I don't know when. Some day."

"It's more than I thought you could say."

"More than I thought I'd ever say. Would you kiss me, please?"

He turned toward her and put his arm around her, tilted her chin up and pressed his mouth against those level lips, felt there the tender stirring of her life, felt her finger tips so light against his cheek. She pulled away slightly and he looked down into eyes that seemed enormous, that reflected in their dampness the highlights from the distant street lights.

"I can't afford to be hurt," she whispered, her breath warm on his mouth. "I have no reserve against hurt. None."

"You won't be," he said. He kissed her again, and it was a little longer, a little more meaningful.

"That was a goodbye," she said.

"For how long?"

"I don't know."

"We can write?"

"Of course."

"Will you stay here?"

"Maybe not until the end. For a little while, I think. It was a present, you know. It was supposed to do me good."

"And it has."

"Yes, it has. Oh, yes, it has, John."

"If Mary Jane will lend Park's wagon, could you find your way back alone from Mexico City if you ride with me to the airport? I ought to be able to get a flight out to-morrow."

"I can manage that."

"And drive carefully. That's an order."

They walked back to the car and drove back to the hotel. There was a false dawn in the east, and nearby roosters crowed. She tilted her mouth for a good-night kiss, and smiled, and closed her door without another word. He went to his room, filled with a great joy that threatened to burst his heart.

Monica Killdeering and Harvey Ardos did not sleep that night. They had talked before, but never in this way. After her shy but unmistakable kiss, he had read all of the bright miracle in her eyes. There was no need for another drink, no desire for more dancing. They had gone out into the night. No structure on earth was huge enough to contain this miracle. And even the sky seemed low. They had kissed as soon as they reached the first patch of shadow, kissed with all the damp-eyed hunger and intensity of all the lonely people in the world. They kissed and used the first broken words that tried to tell of this miracle. And the words became more assured with each retelling. They talked and walked and stopped to kiss until they'd bruised their mouths and dizzied themselves, until they staggered in close embrace and caught their balance and laughed with each other and walked on, finding new ways to say it, finding better ways to explain it all to each other. They stopped to look at each other searchingly in the starlight. She was breath-takingly beautiful and he was handsome.

His, he knew, was the greater miracle. He was the humble soldier who had gone to do homage to his queen, only to have her take his hand and bid him rise, and take him in her arms. The implausibly remote had, in a wondrous moment, come within his reach. And, as a bonus to miracle, there was her response. This was no austere queen, with prim and chilly lips, shrinking from boldness, drawing back in sterile alarm. This was woman, round and firm, meeting him foursquare, matching the gallop of his heart, duplicating the husky race of breath, hungry of mouth, creaking his ribs in her strength and need, turning her hip against him, crushing her breasts against his thumping chest. He walked forty feet tall, and could have howled until the stars heard him, and thumped fists against his chest until great stones tumbled down the flanks of distant mountains.

They talked dreams and nonsense, sobrieties and purposes, and were little aware of where they wandered. They were both aware of their yearning for complete possession. But they were equally aware of its inevitability. There were a thousand smaller things to be savored first on this magical memorable night and during the days and nights to follow. They had that curious patience which can only come from instinctive and utter trust. The greater need was merely to be together. They had spent their lives with the dreary awareness that nobody in all the world really deeply cared whether they lived or died. Nobody really on their side. And suddenly, for each of them, here was another individual who clearly and unmistakably cared for you more than you cared for yourself, who would gladly and willingly die for you, thinking of it as a small favor.

When they wandered back to the hotel many hours later just in time to help John Kemp and Barbara with Gam and the musicians, they both felt that they had both been marked in some obvious and indelible way. But John and Barbara did not act as though they could see any change.

When they had cleared away the empty bottles and picked up all the glasses they could find, they wandered out into the night again, and they picked their way down the barranca path and over to the far side to a grassy place where there was a crumbling length of gray stone wall to lean against.

He leaned his back against the wall, and she lay on her back, the nape of her neck fitting his thigh with significant perfection.

They were both slightly hoarse from all the words that had had to be said.

"Who should worry about three years?" he said. "Nothing. When I'm eighty-six, you'll be eighty-nine. More important is the education, Monica. I'm a stupe."

"You're brilliant! I won't permit anyone to talk about Harvey Ardos that way."

"There's so damn much I don't know."

"There's a lot I don't know. We'll learn together."

"I don't even talk right."

"You've said beautiful things to me, darling. I'll remember them my whole life long. I'll remember them forever." She caught his hand and pressed it to her lips.

"There's one thing. This Kilo. What's it like?"

"It's just an ordinary little place, Harvey. Good people and bad people."

"There's no sweat about making a living. I mean I can get along any place. I've done every kind of low-type labor. Pick and shovel. Dishwashing. Stock clerk. Truck driving. Pin setting. Sweeper. You name it—I've done it. But I've been in those little places, and I never liked them much. People look at you like you were a bug. In a big city nobody cares. Drop dead and they step over you. But those little places, they got to know all about you. Makes me itchy."

"But I've explained, darling. I've got a good position. And we can find a place to live. You could paint all the time."

"None of that jazz, Monica. Painting is my real work, but I pay my freight on the other stuff. If anybody starts to buy the paintings, that's something else. But I'm not going to be that little nogoodnik Monica Killdeering brought home and married and supports, see? I'm a man. I got pride."

"All right, darling. I'm sorry. I just thought . . ."

"How the hell am I going to get used to you calling me darling? Something goes *boing* every time. I want to look around behind me and see who you're talking to."

"Only you. My darling. I knew I was going to find you down here. I knew it on the plane. Such a feeling of expectation and tension and excitement. I knew, somehow, you'd be here."

"You think this Kilo will work out?"

"We'll make it work. We'll be happy there."

"Okay. I'll give it a good whirl. You know, I can't get it through my thick head this is *happening*."

"Has happened, honey."

"Who would fall for me? Somebody like you? Crazy, man."

"But I did."

"You've got lousy taste. I got all the taste in this family. I'm getting the big break. You're getting a dog."

She rolled her head slightly, turning her face away. In a small and humble voice she said, "I wish you were getting . . . just a little bit better break, darling. I wish it with all my heart. If I could only have been sure you were going to happen to me. If I'd had any faith. But when it happens, Harvey, you won't be . . . the first. I didn't want it to happen with somebody else but . . ."

"Shut up!" he said harshly. "Stop the moaning. So it isn't the first for me. Should I expect an egg in my beer? A wonderful girl like you. Who blames you? Look at me a minute. Get this straight. We don't run any confession hour. I don't want any details. You don't get any details. Then nobody has anything to brood about. You know. Factual stuff that kind of sticks in your mind."

"All right, dear," she said meekly.

"Just one thing. Does this joker live in Kilo?"

"No. And it didn't happen there."

"Okay. That's all I got to know. Now we change the subject. Pick a new subject."

"Russia? Bird watching? Tennis? Love?"

"Let's kick that love deal around. I hear it's going around this year. Lots of people catching it."

They talked a long time, until Monica said, "Don't look now, but isn't everything getting that pearly-gray dawn look?"

"It sure is. Old sun on the way."

She smiled up at him in the gray light. "I can see you better."

"I got more to look at."

"I want you to like what you look at," she said, and she took his hand and cupped it on her breast and held it there firmly. He shivered slightly. Looking questioningly up at him, she said, "Do you mind my acting . . . this way? I mean . . . brazen. Darling, I love you so."

He said thickly, "No. No, I like you to act this way. It's . . . just fine. But we made a kind of deal, didn't we? Not to go jump into bed the first minute? I like this just fine. Things are crawling up and down my spine. But, honey, if you keep doing this kind of thing I'm . . . just not going to last, believe me. Something is going to give."

She took his hand away. "Better?"

"That isn't the word I'd pick. Easier. Hell, it would be a lot easier, Monica, if you were one of those little, old, withered-up-type schoolteachers. I've seen a lot of calendars. I've never seen anything like you yet. Any place. It makes a hell of a pressure."

"And it's all for you, Harvey. All yours."

"Cut it out!" he said in an anguished voice. She sprang up lithely and took his hand and yanked him to his feet. They walked to the road and up the slope and watched the sun come up. And then they went slowly, hand in hand, back to the hotel.

BOOK THREE

In which *the Grisly Effects of varied forms of Overindulgence are inflicted upon the more Reckless Members of the Group; for Various Reasons the Group begins to Dwindle; the Institution is at last Closed; a Brief Look is taken at Various Instances of Aftermath; a Plan for the Future is explained.*

Chapter Fourteen

On Wednesday morning, the twenty-sixth of July, the morning following the prolonged and spontaneous marriage fiesta, Esperanza Clueca arose at dawn. She inspected her reddened eyes in a fragment of mirror, dressed carefully, and walked three miles to church. She had gone without sleep most of the night, fingering the beads of her rosary, kissing the little gilt cross. She hoped to arrange a special confession as she did not care to contemplate living with her great burden of guilt any longer than absolutely necessary.

Ai, what a strumpet she had become. It could not all have been the fault of the tequila. No, there was an evil inside her, a depth of blackness and sin that she had heretofore been unaware of. She remembered the abandon with which she had danced. Most unsuitable in one who hoped to teach the young. And then she had permitted that oafish Fidelio to entice her out into the whirling night, her head full of giddiness and her mouth full of laughter. He had taken her into a corner of darkness, and there she had strained upward to meet the hard male pressure of his heavy young mouth on hers. And writhed and whined at the strokings of his hands. And rubbed against him in lechery and wanton invitation. It was only when he had forced her down and she realized that his heavy knee was forcing her legs apart, that fright came to her. And then she had fought desperately in the darkness like an animal, thwarting him, tearing away from his grasp, running, running through the night, hearing his angry shout behind her.

She had coldly condemned all the bawdy girls only to learn that in her heart she was no different than Margarita, she of the two bastard children and the red slut dress. As she walked to church she cringed inside herself to think of how she must have looked and sounded there in the dark corner with that lazy, loutish driver. This could not be any portion of the true Esperanza Clueca. But it had happened. She lengthened her steps, hastening toward the church and the candles, the images and the priest.

Dotsy Winkler was up early. She worked alone in the kitchen. There was no sign of Rosalinda, Pepe, Felipe, Alberto, Fidelio or the two maids. Dotsy made a great quantity of strong coffee. Monica and Harvey were up. She had seen them out in the patio, holding hands and talking. Soon the colonel and Hildabeth put in an appearance. Contrary to their habits, neither Agnes nor Miles appeared.

The colonel finished breakfast, caught Saltamontes and saddled her without help, and clopped out of the hotel grounds, heading north. John Kemp appeared with Barbara and they smiled good morning and sat with Monica and Harvey. Monica and Barbara voluntarily took over the serving duties of Esperanza and Margarita. There was general talk about the festivities.

John Kemp announced that he was going to have to drop from the school and return to the states.

"We're dwindling away to nothing at all," Hildabeth said. "Not too darn many to start with. Place is going to pot and it isn't even half over yet."

Agnes Partridge Keeley appeared at nine-thirty. She smiled most pleasantly as she came in, but she was darting quick little glances around, venomously suspicious. She handled herself as though her muscles had stiffened up, and Dotsy noted that she sat down with caution.

"I seem to have overslept," she said. "Too much party. Class will be late."

"Might as well skip it," Hildabeth told her. "You won't get much business. John Kemp is dropping out and Barbara is driving him up to Mexico City a little later. Torrigan skipped his class yesterday. You won't get much business today. Just me, maybe."

"I'll see if anyone else is interested."

Esperanza showed up. She seemed much more severe and gloomy than usual. When Miles came to breakfast, his face pouched and sallow and his tread heavy, Esperanza went over to him. "Señor, Rosalinda is too ill to work this day. She has an agony of the stomach. I do not know where Margarita is, or Pepe. Felipe and Fidelio are very sick and tired. They were badly beaten by someone last night, I think. But they will not speak of it. Alberto cannot be awakened again."

Miles stared up at her. "You are the entire staff, then."

"It is evident. Señor, last night I was permitted to drink and to dance at your fiesta. I assure you it will never happen again." She whirled and stalked toward the kitchen.

Miles went out and checked on Felipe and Fidelio. They lay on the pallets, with large areas of dark discoloration under their coppery skin. They were uncommunicative, their voices weak, their dark eyes dull. When they moved it was with a vast and painful effort that contorted their faces and made them wheeze with hurt. Evidently they had been fighting, and evidently that was all he would ever learn. He spoke of his disappointment in both of them, and trudged wearily back to breakfast. He discarded the idea of looking in on Rosalinda. She would merely giggle.

After John Kemp came back from the Hotel Mandel where he had phoned the ticket office, he finished his packing and carried his belongings into the lobby. "What's the matter?" Barbara asked.

"I'm trying to think who I've missed. Klauss, Torrigan, the Wahls, the colonel and Mary Jane. Say goodbye for me. Please don't skip Paul Klauss."

"How could I! Seriously, John, I think Mary Jane would like a personal farewell. I'll have to ask her about the car."

They went to her room. John stood a little way down the corridor while Barbara tapped on the door. As she started the third sequence of tappings, the door opened a crack and then was opened wide enough for Barbara to enter.

Mary Jane, her eyes sleep-puffed, her cropped blond hair frowzy, her lips pale without lipstick, held her robe closed around her and said, "What's the scoop, Barbie? Gawd, I feel horrible!" She padded over to the bureau, took a cigarette, lit it and made a face. "You look so darn alert."

"Three hours' sleep," Barbara said. She suddenly noticed in the other bed, in the shadowy room, a clump of tangled blond hair on the pillow, a mound of hip under the blanket. "Who is that!"

"Oh. Lady Margot. Left over from the party. I don't know the details, but she was sacked out when I came lurching in."

"I'm sorry to bother you, Mary Jane, but John Kemp has to leave today. I'd like to use the station wagon. We'll drive up to the airport and I'll bring it back."

"Leaving? Darn! Sure, you can take the wagon."

"He has to leave soon. He's out in the hall to say goodbye."

"Let me dust off the merchandise." She went to the bureau and yanked a brush through her hair. She leaned close to the mirror and made up her mouth. Then she began to button the small, round red buttons that ran from the collar of the robe to the hem.

"A nice guy, Barbie."

"Yes."

Mary Jane looked at her obliquely, with wisdom far older than twenty. "Not letting him get away, are you?"

Barbara felt heat in her face. "No."

"Good deal. Something good ought to come of this operation. Okay. The eyes look like smoked clams, but there's nothing to be done. You know, I had a wild dream about nearly falling off the roof of this place. And Torrigan saved me. You think that's significant?"

They went out into the hall. Mary kissed John goodbye. Then John and Barbara drove up into the mountains, and from the high curves they could look down into the lovely morning bowl of Cuernavaca, and they saw El Hutchinson, like a slightly soiled, little cardboard toy in the sunlight.

Torrigan got up at noon. Hang-over blanged in his head like an endless succession of oil drums rolling down concrete stairs, and like trunks being moved in the attic. He looked upon the world with that bleak and weary pessimism of the person who, after an unsuccessful suicide attempt, has been released from the hospital with the kindly admonition to try to look upon the bright side of things. In his slow accomplishment of his morning routines he attempted to arm himself against a hostile world, but he had the feeling there was artillery just over the hill, zeroed in on the base of his brain. He put on fresh khaki shorts, slipped his

220

bare feet into sandals from the public market, and pulled a white T-shirt on over his head.

He went tentatively out into the corridor. As he shut his room door a woman turned and looked at him and walked slowly toward him. She wore a white robe with small red buttons from throat to hem. It was a little too short for her and a little too full for her at shoulders, bust and hips.

"Theah you are, dearie. I'm in a bit of a flap."

He yanked open the squeaky drawer of a mental file, fumbled for a soiled card. Something about this item in a strange room, talking and talking, wearing a blue towel. Margot. And it was connected with the dull ache on the left side of his jaw.

"Good morning, Margot."

She peered at him. "You really look undone, ducks. This is a problem of clothing. I borrowed this thing. Simply crawling with all these ghastly little buttons."

"Where are your clothes?"

"I should say one could expect them to be in the room of that dreary little mannequin with the curly yellow hair. And my purse too. But which room?"

"Oh, that's up around the corner and down about three doors."

"Would you please come with me, dearie? You were so wonderfully efficient when he became so sticky."

"Margot, I was pretty well loaded. I'm not too clear about some of the details."

She sighed. "It was ineffably dreary. I was so terribly anxious to get away from that squatty little Shane person, that I let the blond one entice me to his quarters. I sometimes feel I entice too readily, you know. After we had disrobed, it turned out he was of no use whatsoever. And he had some madly hysterical story about it being the fault of some hotel maid person who apparently had been pursuing him. The entire tale made no sense, and he was horribly upset, weeping and carrying on. I had no intention of remaining there with him, but he wouldn't let me leave. He seemed to become violent, and you can take my word, Gambel dear, I've had quite my share of violent little men of late. I panicked and screamed out, and the scream startled him enough so that I was able to pull free of him and canter to the door and get it open. One seldom sees nude women scampering down hotel corridors with howling, blubbering little men in hot pursuit, but you, you perfect

221

darling, were on hand and you rose to the occasion splendidly."

"I did?"

"You tripped him sprawling and found a nearby door unlocked and bundled the lady in distress into the room and locked the door. We had great fits of laughter while he pounded his poor little fists on the door, bawling threats and obscenities. When he finally trundled away, you crept out and brought back a pair of great walloping drinks for us."

"You sat in that wicker chair wearing a blue towel and you told me about the American major who ruined your life."

"Yes, ducks! You do remember. You were terribly sweet, you know. And all my brave plans to reward you came to absolutely nothing when suddenly I was so exhausted I couldn't hold my head up. Apparently some woman lives in that room. I found this little robe. Now I would like my clothing, Gambel dear."

He went with her to Klauss's room. He knocked loudly.
"Who is it?"

"Torrigan."

"What do you want?"

"There's some clothes and a purse in there, Klauss. Let's have them. The lady wants them."

"Just a minute."

They waited. Margot smiled her thanks at Gam. Suddenly the door was yanked open. A wad of fabric was hurled out. It disintegrated in the air and fell gently in a shower of tiny, wispy fragments. A purse struck the opposite wall with considerable force, bursting its clattering contents onto the tiles. Two shoes followed, with equal force. The door was slammed shut.

Margot dropped to one knee and picked up a handful of the fragments of fabric. She stared up at Gam with awe and tears of anger. "Absolute scraps!" she said. "My lovely dress and slip and bra and panties and hose. It must have taken him hours and hours. The man is absolutely mad!" She reached and picked up a shoe, threw it aside. "He even slashed the shoes to ribbons."

"I guess you hurt his feelings."

They gathered the contents of the purse and put those articles not damaged beyond repair into it.

"He's a monster," she said. "He's sick. He needs help. What shall I do for clothing? I could send someone to my home, of course, to bring clothing back here. I have closets and closets of things. But it would look queer, don't you think? Make a very poor impression on my staff."

222

"What room did you sleep in?"

"That one."

"Oh, Mary Jane's room. Must be her robe. You go back in there and I'll find her. She must have some stuff she can lend you."

"You're sweet," she said. "I must say you Americans have exciting parties."

Gam found Mary Jane in the dining room, sitting alone and drinking coffee. When he sat down with her, she gave him an opaque glare. "Did you happen to save my life last night?"

"Let me think. Yes. Yes, I did."

"Today I wonder why you bothered. But thanks."

"Quite all right."

"I'm depressed. Bits is gone. Park is gone. Now John has left for good." She explained the circumstances. Then Gam gave a slightly edited version of Margot's plight. Mary Jane got up wearily and went off to help her. Gam poured himself some coffee. There was a somnolent air about the hotel, a brooding silence. Mary Jane came back with Margot in fifteen minutes. The coffee had made Gam feel minutely better. Margot had been outfitted in a pale-blue denim wraparound skirt, a white short-sleeved cardigan, straw sandals.

She did not feel up to breakfast either. She had coffee with them from a fresh pot brought by a grim-eyed Esperanza.

"I'm so grateful, dear," she said to Mary Jane. "I'll see that these things are returned veddy quickly."

"No rush," Mary Jane said morosely.

"I must go now," she said. "Could some sort of transportation be arranged?"

"We're kind of running out of automobiles around here," Mary Jane said.

"I don't want to be any more bother, really."

"I'll see if I can line up the red bus," Gam said. He went and found Miles who found Fidelio and told him that if he was incapable of driving the bus, he was fired. With a great and heroic effort, like the hero of a Western movie dragging himself through the badlands, Fidelio made it to the bus and sat slumped over the wheel, breathing audibly.

Gam went in and told Margot her transportation was ready. She smiled at him and said, "I have a great high wall around my place to keep out the infidels. And quite a lovely little pool. And a crowd of little people who scuttle about bringing cold drinks. I should like you to come home with me, ducks." She turned to Mary Jane and with much less enthusiasm said, "You too, of course, dear, if you'd care to."

"No, thanks," Gam said.

"No, thanks," Mary Jane said.

Margot pouted at Gam. "I really must have made myself terribly unattractive last night."

"You were just nifty."

"But I will see you some time, lover? Soon?"

"I suppose it's possible," he said. Margot stood up and looked down at him with eyes and mouth of stone, turned and left. After they heard the bus clatter out, Gam sighed.

"Well, well, well," Mary Jane said acidly.

"What's your trouble?"

"Just intrigued. You intrigue little old me."

"Maybe I'm complicated."

"You go around beating all the bushes in a very heavy-handed way, trying to find some gal to be your real close buddy buddy, and then when a languid, sexy, rich, titled dish like that falls into your lap, you brush her off."

"Kindly get off my back, child."

"You didn't even make the usual pass at me last night."

"I apologize."

"Class this afternoon, Teach?"

"Oh dear God," he moaned. She got up, gave his beard a small affectionate tug, chuckled at him and walked away, leaving him alone with his coffee and the silence and the dusty patterns of sunlight on the floor of the empty room.

The four officials in their old Packard and their shiny blue suits arrived at three o'clock that afternoon, arousing Miles from his siesta. He scowled at them. The spokesman, Mr. Lopez, said, "It is here the temporary permit, dear sir, but there can be more difficulties, I am sorry. The regulations are of the utmost complication." He smiled his broad, loving smile. "There is administrative expenses. Many pesos, dear sir. Or the school must be boarded closed."

It would have been difficult for them to have approached Miles Drummond at a less opportune time.

"It is almost impossible to continue?" he asked.

"It is most difficult, dear sir."

Miles matched his smile. "Then let us say it is impossible."

The officials glanced at each other. This did not seem to be the same man they had talked to last time.

"I am not clearly understanding," Señor Lopez said.

224

"It's easy. It is impossible to continue. So I will not continue. I cannot pay the fines. I will go to jail. Let me pack a bag and I will go right now."

Lopez smiled nervously, "But dear sir, it is only a matter of pesos. From a place of such profit."

"Hah!"

"Only perhaps . . . five hundred pesos only for administrative expensiveness."

Miles stood up. "I will pack."

"Dear sir, perhaps it could be done with more cheapness, because you are a friend of Mexico."

Miles took out his wallet. He took two fifty-peso notes and placed them in front of Lopez. Lopez stared at them with the troubled smile of a man who does not quite catch the point of a joke. His shoulders lifted slowly and fell. He reached out and took the notes. "The expensiveness will be handled at a loss to the administrators," he said.

They shook hands all around and walked out, arguing softly among themselves, leaving the large florid permit, a-blaze with stamps, on Miles's desk. Miles tottered back to bed.

At the same time the four men were leaving Miles's apartment, John Kemp was taking his leave of Barbara. His flight had been announced. They had talked long and honestly. They would write to each other. When she was finished at Cuernavaca, she would fly home. When he had the firm functioning with sufficient smoothness, and if it was agreeable to her at that time, he would come and meet her parents. By then they would know if she would return with him. She did not know if it would ever be possible. But she would be honest with him in any event.

He walked out with her and kissed her at the gate and went on alone. He waved from the top of the steps. She watched until the plane was a tiny silver glint in the north, high above brown hills. She dried her eyes and blew her nose and drove with great caution back to El Hutchinson.

At last that interminable Wednesday ended. Park and Bitsy reached Acapulco in the torrid, sticky dusk. Dinner at El Hutchinson was a small and nearly silent conclave of the survivors of fiesta. The staff began again, with great reluctance, to shoulder their lightened duties. The hard rain came down at nine and lasted until nearly midnight. The thunder clanged off the hills and the lights went out. And lightning danced blue on the dead faces of the sleepers.

Chapter Fifteen

THE NUPTIAL FIESTA of the Cuernavaca Summer Workshop at El Hutchinson had certain short-range traumatic effects of a certain predictability. Of more interest were the long-range effects.

There was, for example, the transformation of Fidelio Melocotonero. It was Mary Jane's theory, as expressed to Torrigan, that Fidelio ever since birth had been handicapped by the non-functioning of some small and essential gear and pinion assembly in his head. Something had failed to mesh, and the inoperative parts had rusted in place. The beating had effected repairs, and she cited as an example the common knowledge that when a piece of apparatus refuses to function, it can often be repaired quickly by a brisk kick.

Torrigan, in rebuttal, pointed out that Fidelio had begun to show unmistakable signs of an emotional involvement, and it was well known that love could work miracles.

At any rate, during the few days of his painful convalescence it gradually became apparent to all that Fidelio had changed. His heavy expression of sullen apathy and indifference was gradually replaced by a look of polite attention, almost of alertness. He held his head high and walked with a detectable briskness. He kept himself and the red bus cleaned, brushed and well-maintained. He took over from Alberto the task of keeping the other vehicles glossy. He developed the knack of appearing when he was needed, eliminating the previous necessity of an average twenty-minute search to find out where he was dozing. His driving improved. At some implausible place in town he purchased himself a used yachting cap, restored it to black, gold and white brilliance, and wore it behind the wheel with an uncompromising jauntiness.

When the true owner of the red bus tried to cancel the rental arrangement with the school, Miles Drummond, in the process of dissuading him, learned the reason for the attempted cancellation. Fidelio had suddenly ceased to be the sweetheart of the owner's daughter, a rather squatty and torpid young girl with a large red mouth whose name was Anita. It was observed that Fidelio made himself smilingly

226

available for any kind of kitchen duty and janitor service.

Also noted was his dogged progress in an unexpected direction. After completely ignoring the changed Fidelio at first, Esperanza Clueca began to permit herself to speak to him when necessary, though with a grimness and a cold reserve. And, in time, after walking a dozen yards behind her when she left work, he was able gradually to decrease the distance until he was permitted to walk with her to her family hut. It was not long before Esperanza began to permit herself to smile at him.

As Fidelio enhanced his standing and reputation in the small world of the Workshop, Felipe Cedro suffered a more than equivalent loss of standing in the larger social complex of Cuernavaca. Fidelio, sitting on his heels beside the red bus when it was parked near the public market, contributed to Felipe's decline by telling the interested loafers of Felipe's fiasco. "I would have little to do, Felipe said. Merely to stand and catch the small man when he fell. And I would be rich. It was a vast success. When I awakened, sick and bleeding, I was forty-one pesos poorer. Ai, Felipe is a clever man."

In his forays into town to check on his various business enterprises, Felipe detected the new lack of respect, the derision, the dwindling of fear. It became very difficult for him to enforce his orders. Everyone knew of his grotesque failure. In the bull ring he had been a figure of fun. The laughter had made him want to kill himself. Now the world was laughing again. The little man with the stone fists had removed an alarming percentage of Felipe's working capital. And his plan to recoup hastily was frustrated by the unexpected appearance of the bright brass hasps and sturdy padlocks on the doors of all the occupied rooms at El Hutchinson.

One night in a small cantina near Los Canarios he attempted to regain through an act of violence the fearful respect he had lost through gossip. They took his knife away from him and snapped the blade, hurled him in a high, punishing trajectory onto the cobblestones, and then jammed the doorway, hooting and whistling at him while he picked himself up and walked slowly away into the night. The empire of Felipe Cedro was crumbling before it had begun to achieve its expected dimensions. Fading in the remote distances of his mind was the golden vision of the land and vehicles and silken actress companions of the powerful Don Felipe.

While Felipe was becoming a subject of gossip in one stratum of the local culture, Gloria Garvey had become the subject of much wonderment in other areas. She was no longer a morning fixture at her sidewalk table outside the Marik, with the Dos Equis and the Mexico City *News*. She was sometimes seen there in the late afternoons, accompanied by the short, wide and powerful-looking little man named Shane. He wore a look of sleepy indifference, and seemed almost unaware of her presence. Gloria seemed full of tensions and an alert nervousness. She had lost weight. There was a drawn look about the handsome face. Her hair was beautifully cared for, her clothing smart, fresh, crisp and immaculate. As she sat there with Shane, drinking little, there was a look about her that was reminiscent of a racing greyhound which waits in quick-eyed, chop-lapping tension on the weighing platform with its handler, waiting for the prolonged clang of the bell which signals the beginning of the race.

It was noticed that when Shane was ready to go, he got up without warning and left. Gloria would hasten after him and catch up with him. It was common knowledge that the little man had moved in with her, and so invitations were extended to include both of them. At parties Gloria was unexpectedly subdued. She hovered close to Shane, and spoke very little. The neat and tailored Gloria had lost that air of casual magnificence, and had become merely another pretty woman. When it was discovered that Shane was quick to take offense at imaginary slights, and that when he took offense he knocked people down with brutal efficiency, the invitations were fewer.

As it was known that Shane was an acquaintance of Margot Tazely-Jones, attempts were made to pump her for additional facts. But aside from saying that his real name was, she believed, Shanelli, she would say, "Just a veddy horrid little type, dears. Terribly selfish and domineering. Not really nice at all. He joined our party one day in Vera Cruz because he took a fancy to me and I really couldn't discourage him the slightest bit. Do let's talk about something more pleasant."

One American resident, more enterprising than the others, remembered that her cook was related to Amparo, the maid at Las Rosas. She requested a report from the cook. She thus learned that when the small American señor had become the guest of the Señora Garvey, there had been several beatings, and it had been possible in the upper hall to hear the whimperings of the señora. But now there were no more

228

beatings. The señora kept the apartment very clean indeed, and much care had to be taken over the food of her guest.

When this report was circulated, a man managed, at a party, to have a few moments of private conversation with Gloria.

"We're all worried about you, dear," he said. "We wonder if that little spook is blackmailing you or something. We old hands down here should stick together. All you have to do is say the word and . . ."

"Oh, no! Please! Shane is . . . a very good friend. Really! I'm not in any kind of trouble, honestly! I'm perfectly happy."

The friend reported that she had turned slightly gray around the mouth and had looked quite haunted.

On a few occasions, residents driving up to Mexico City had passed Gloria and Shane in the blue Jag, with Gloria at the wheel. Such conservatism was worthy of comment. There were few who had not experienced the shaky sensation of having Gloria ram noisily past them like a big blue bomb.

Paul Klauss was another whose habits were altered by that portion of the fiesta which affected him alone. He ceased attending classes immediately. Though he retained his room at El Hutchinson, he occupied it no oftener than one night out of three. When he ate at the hotel he took a table by himself. Miles ate with him once and, after enduring Klauss's silent rudeness, did not attempt it again. He arrived and departed by taxi, a remote and silent man with a look of busy preoccupation, a climate of belligerent haste.

Gil and Jeanie Wahl reported seeing him one evening on the terrace porch of the Bella Vista, sitting at a table for two by the railing with a small, pale, rather pretty but rather worn-looking woman in a pink suit. Jeanie reported that they were looking into each other's eyes with great intensity, Klauss smiling fondly and the woman responding with a sort of jittery, nervous delight, like a sparrow at a feeding station.

Monica, Harvey, Mary Jane and Gam saw him not long afterward at Sanborne's in the lower level of the Del Prado when the four of them had gone up for the *novillero* bullfights. Klauss was at a table for two against the wall, with a dark-haired, tiny, rather sallow and quite pretty woman in a rust-colored suit. Klauss was looking into her eyes and smiling in a sad, wise way. He held both her hands in his across the table. She was looking back at him and trying to smile. Her mouth was trembling and tears were running down her cheeks.

The defection of Klauss saddened Margarita. Instead of the gay clumsy trot, the oversized red shoes clopped slowly. There were minor-key dissonances in the bright, piercing voice. While serving she began to sigh heavily and audibly from time to time, and the rollicking swing of her hips as she walked was muted to a motion and involved not more than three inches of weary sway. And, as though there was some subparagraph of the law of conservation of energy which required that there be a certain minimum of excess motion required, as Margarita's walk and carriage became more subdued, Esperanza's prim and undeviating stride began to take on a supple flexion that seemed more pronounced when Fidelio was within visual range.

Agnes Partridge Keeley suffered a barely detectable but desirable personality change as a result of the fiesta. She became warily civil to Gam Torrigan. She was willing to admit, when thoroughly cornered, that she was not completely infallible. She had less to say about her sales record, her investment properties and her hundreds of loyal, successful ex-students. Gam was bemused by the sudden wilting of the opposition. He guessed that such an alteration could have come only from a chastening experience, and he wondered what it possibly could have been.

Gil and Jeanie Wahl were not as they had been before the party. They were less frequently absent from meals and classes. Jeanie expanded her volume of outgoing mail. Also, when they were with the group, they were more involved with and responsive to the group. There was considerably less of that humid and hypnoid and heavy-eyed awareness of each other which had closed out all the rest of the world. And, to the unspoken relief of many, they ceased entirely to feed each other small choice morsels while at table. They were pulling themselves free of the swampy lubricity of the present, and beginning to think of the future, of home and work and kids.

Gam Torrigan felt the uncomfortable ferment of change within himself, accompanied by an irritating and unwelcome objectivity. He began to work, almost with diligence, on his own painting in an effort to forget that, when this session ended, for the first time in his life he had not even the slightest clue as to where he would go and what he would do. His helpful contacts had given up trying to aid him, having tired of his abuse of their efforts. He had sent out a lot of letters all over the country, but had received alarmingly few answers, and those so noncommittal that he had begun to feel a little white, hot patch of alarm on the lining of his stomach.

He had set himself up to use the last of daylight one day and was annoyed at the way the painting was going, and scared of the future. Mary Jane stopped to watch him and when he quit and began to clean his brushes she said, "Where will you go from here, Gam?"

He turned on her and yelled, "How the hell do I know!" He heard his own shrillness and knew he had told her more than he intended to.

"Blow me down!" she said softly. "Like that, huh?"

"Like what?" he said sullenly.

"You know like what, old Torrigan. Worn out all your welcome mats, I bet."

"Shut up, child."

"You are the child, my hairy friend. Your painting, Gam. How about it? Do you really think you're any good at it?"

He did not look at her for a long time. He turned slowly and said with unanticipated honesty and humility, "I don't really know, Mary Jane. I used to think I knew. Now I don't know."

"I'm not picking on you."

"I know that, too."

"And you haven't a soli-damn-tary place to go when this hassle folds."

"Something will turn up."

"How much cash money will you have left?"

"I haven't tried to figure it out. A hundred dollars." He pulled himself together. "The way of an artist, my child, is a hard road in our mechanistic, opportunistic culture, and I can only say . . ."

"Come down off it, Gam. Stay human another couple of minutes."

"How will that help?"

"When Bitsy and Park come back through, I'm leaving too. You know that."

"So?"

"I'd just like to find out if that stuff you do is worth a damn. All that functional symmetry and functional balance and dynamic whosis. So I'll make a deal. If you don't find any place to light, you come to Fort Worth. Check in at Daddy's office. Rixon Elmore. You'll find him in the book. I'll set up a deal for you, if you want to try some straight painting for a change."

"I don't adjust comfortably to charity, Miss Elmore."

"Stop bristling your beard at me. Daddy's got some scrubby land down in San Saba County. I know there's a range cabin on it that you can get to by jeep. It isn't in use. There's good water and no electric. Out of my allowance I'll set it up so if you stop at the office you'll be taken down there and staked to a used jeep, and a line of credit for supplies over in Brady. You'll have to take in all the painting supplies you'll need, because it won't be so easy to go out and get them once you get in there and settled."

"I don't want . . ."

"*Will* you hush up, Torrigan? The offer is good only if you agree to stick it out one full year. Just you and the painting. No house guests. At the end of the year somehow, I don't know how yet, I'll set you up for a one-man show, in some New York gallery. And I've got friends who can make sure the critics at least take a fast look. If nothing sells, you've found out something and I've found out something. If they sell, Torrigan, I get back my expenses. Maybe I only get a part. But if I get them all back, and more money comes in, we split that right down the middle. Is that charity?"

"Uh . . . no."

"Could you stand a year of yourself?"

"I don't know. God, the idea of a show is terrifying!"

"You don't have to tell me a thing. If you want to do it, get yourself up to Fort Worth and go to the office and you'll find that everything will be set for you."

"Why are you doing this?"

"I guess maybe I want to be a patron of the arts or something. And you saved my life, didn't you?" She slid off the wall and dusted the seat of her shorts. "When you get cleaned up there, I'll buy you a drink." She walked off. His mouth felt dry and his hands trembled. So far it had all been a big poker game and he had been running a bluff. He hadn't ever looked at his hole card. They had been sweetening the pot for him. But now all the cards had been dealt, and through the offices of a surprisingly tough-minded blond kid, the world was about to call him. If something else turned up, he could fold his hand without ever looking at the hole card, and save the expense of that last big bet. But if something else did turn up and he took it, he had the feeling that he would be forever lost.

Of all the staff and students, Monica and Harvey had

been most changed by the fiesta. Had not Torrigan bribed Felipe to load the drinks, it was entirely possible that Monica would never have acquired the courage to acquaint Harvey so vividly with her state of mind. And he was too much in awe of her to have made any advance. Love would have hidden behind the awkward shyness and restraint of two chronically lonely people. He would have gone back to Philadelphia, miserable at the thought of never seeing her again, but grateful that such an unattainable goddess had been nice to him. And she would have gone sadly back to Kilo to the energetic treadmill of her days, and perhaps gone on to other summers where her special shame awaited her.

They had spent more of their free time together before the party, but after the party they were inseparable. They talked incessantly. For each of them it was a delicious experience to have someone to talk to who would really listen, who did not get that glazed look of polite agony, who actually followed every word with avid interest. They decided they would be married in Kilo. They talked seriously about whether an artist as dedicated as Harvey should accede to the dull formats of their social order by going through a marriage ceremony. But, in spite of their rebellious talk, they were deeply conservative at heart. They said that because of the danger of risking Monica's position through unorthodox behavior, they would go through the legal motions of marriage, meaningless as such motions were compared with the unshakable texture of their love.

They discussed announcing their intentions to the others, but felt that it was something too personal and precious to be shared. In calm discussion, while sitting a cautious distance from each other in daylight, they accepted the fact that it would be but a minor exercise in guile to consummate their love here at the hotel before the session ended. He certainly could enter and leave her room unobserved. They talked this over with a spurious calmness of voice and expression grossly at odds with the racings of their hearts.

But, they decided, such a sneaky venture, though exciting to contemplate, would cheapen the relationship. Even though no test was needed, certainly, an exercise in restraint was another way of proving their love for each other—even though no proof was needed. Also, aside from the exercise of character, restaint made more sweet their anticipations. Finally, though the physical aspects of their union were doubtless of importance, the more valid closeness was in the matters of the mind and the spirit.

On Monica's part, though she had a truly savage and overwhelming desire for him, her apprehensiveness about her own response made restraint easier to sustain. The sickening memories of her weakness during other summers made her believe that when at last they were joined, her frenzies might easily repel a man of Harvey's sensitivity. So she was willing to delay that turbulent revelation.

Harvey, on the other hand, though subjected to inner pressures to a degree which made his eyes bulge, felt obscure alarm at the impending responsibility of bedding down a lady. His prior experiences had been both hasty and limited. He was certain that there must be some important ground rules, some delicacies of social behavior of which he was unaware. It was like dreading a formal dinner invitation because of not knowing which fork to use. So his desires were blunted by his shyness.

But day by day and evening by evening, in closeness and talking and kissing, and in the constantly expanding area of the physical liberties permitted, they were inadvertently creating a degree of sexual tension which, like the accidental accumulation of gas under a city's streets, needed but one spark to blow every manhole cover in town a hundred feet into the air.

On one particularly tortured moonlight night he stood outside her window and she sat just inside the window, talking in low tones until the stars faded in the gray of dawn, kissing between the bars so hungrily that he had red vertical welts on his cheekbones the next day.

On Saturday, the fifth of August, having arranged to borrow Colonel Hildebrandt's old Dodge station wagon while he was off on a project requiring the services of Saltamontes —and bearing with them a Thermos jug and basket lunch prepared by Dotsy and Rosalinda, Harvey and Monica drove up into the mountains on the old free highway, found the turn that had been described to them, and drove a little way on an old dirt road that ended in a place of exceptional charm. The old forest was as dark and still as the illustrations for fairyland. Grass was soft and thick in sunlit glades and hummocks. The small clear lakes were nine thousand feet above the sea.

They swam in ice water and came out gasping, their lips blue, to toast in the high hot sun. They ate in a private shady place. There was a special stillness about the whole world, a gothic hush at the edge of the dark forest. There was an end to talk. And then, solemnly at first, and then with all restraints lost in furnace breath and bongo hearts, they made their first love, and made love again throughout the cathedral afternoon, the sun, through high leaves, making small coins of brightness on their bodies.

After dark they drove slowly down the mountains through the rains. She sat close beside him, and her heart was full. There was a perfect communion in their silence which made talk a clumsy contact. It had been so perfect a reaffirmation of all they had said to each other that they felt an almost superstitious awe. The little doubts and fears and hesitations had endured for the first few moments, and been swept away forever.

They moved slowly down toward the bowl of Cuernavaca, the round of her hip and the length of her thigh warm against him. The fringe of rain rebounding from the road was silver in the headlights. He wore golden armor from head to toe, and there was a silken riband in her colors fixed to his lance. Her midnight hair, when braided, would reach from tower window to the edge of the castle moat. On either side the road were strewn the stiffening bodies of dragons bravely slain, and the gentle knight dwelt upon the sweet memories of his perfumed rewards.

Bitsy and Park arrived the next day, Sunday, at three in the afternoon, both a deep and startling bronze tan, smiling, happy, comfortably in love, slightly weary from the drive up from Acapulco, bearing small gifts. They told of Acapulco, of the sun and sand of the afternoon beach, the strolling girls selling hot boiled shrimp and icy beer, the vendors who would paddle up to you while you were swimming, pushing ahead of them small floating trays, the marlin and sail they had caught, the boys who dived from reckless heights for money, the moonlight on the Pacific, the prominent actress they had seen—hopelessly, helplessly drunk, the tourists aflame with sunburn and prickly heat, the night club and floor shows and the showoff boys and girls of the beaches.

While Mary Jane packed everything, and Bitsy packed the things she had left behind, Mary Jane brought her up to date on the local scene.

Then Mary Jane turned and looked squarely at her and said, "Are you really happy, Bits?" Bitsy's yes was obviously heartfelt.

"I'm glad."

Bitsy sat on her bed and lighted her cigarette and frowned

at the huff of smoke she exhaled. "I know what you think of him. And what I thought of him. I'm not blind, Mary Jane."

"I didn't say you were."

"He's sweet. And he's fun. He needed somebody. He's still not sure way down deep that I'm really here, that I won't step aside when he leans a little bit. I've never been responsible for a thing in my whole life, Mary Jane. Not the little brother and sister. Nobody. I had only myself to take care of, and I didn't do much of a job of that."

"Now, Bits . . ."

"It's true. I'm no great strong pillar or something. But now I've got to be. If I'm strong right now, I won't have to be quite so strong later. And that will be good. And you know, I find that I like it. I want to be of use to him. I feel smug about being strong, learning how to be strong without his guessing that I'm going to slowly, carefully set him back on his own two feet. He'll be a man again."

"Noble," Mary Jane said. "Real noble, doll. Wipe his wittle nose and pat his wittle head. So he needs you. And you need to be needed. But aren't you missing out on something marriage should be?"

"What is that?"

"Isn't it a little dull, making love with a wittle helpless boy?"

Bitsy gave her a startled look, and suddenly her mouth widened into a broad and bawdy grin that turned her back into the Bitsy of the good old days. "Darling," she said, drawling the word, "his only troubles have been emotional and psychological. You happen to be looking at a very contented woman. I'm the kitty that lives in the creamery." She yawned, curling a pink tongue.

"I asked for that, didn't I? Should I get married, Bits?"

"Without delay. You'll love it."

The two-car convoy left at nine-thirty on Monday morning, the seventh of August, Bitsy and Mary Jane in the Mercedes, followed by Park in the Ford wagon. When they turned the corner beyond the barracks, Gam and Barbara walked slowly back to the main gate.

"And so we bid farewell to the happy couple," Gam said sourly.

"I think they'll make it," Barbara said. "I didn't think so at first, but now they seem so . . . integrated. It's almost a visible thing. I think if you met them in a large group, you'd sense they belonged together."

As they walked into the lobby, Gam said, "Attrition. Nine little Indians left. Eight, actually, with Klauss off on private adventures. This world isn't going to end with a bang. This is the whimper department. I shall miss Miss Mary Jane. She is a top quality urchin, a long and leggy gamin with superior defenses. Well, it looks like Miss Agnes is hustling up an eager group. Go join it, Barbara. I am going to go sit in a shady corner and eat worms."

On the Thursday after Park and the girls from Texas had departed, Colonel Hildebrandt rode Saltamontes over into some small and shaggy hills, not far off the Tepoztlán road to make sketches of a small sloping plateau where Zapata had ambushed a company of *rurales*, deploying his forces in such a manner that he had inflicted heavy punishment with the loss of but three men. It was a still and sullen day, more sultry than usual. Saltamontes cropped sparse grasses in the shade while the colonel worked. At noon the colonel ate the lunch he had brought. He worked through the hot glare of the afternoon and at four o'clock he packed up, swung up onto Saltamontes and started back toward the highway. He sat slouched in the saddle, his old campaign hat tilted forward, eyes squinted against the sun glare on the loose brown rocks. He was weary, and slightly dazed by the heat, and he let the old horse pick her own way at her own speed, reins slack in his brown hand.

She stumbled and went down so suddenly he did not have time to leap clear. He was dazed by the impact. She gave a single scream of pain. She lifted her head, jabbing at the stony ground with one front hoof, and struggled violently for a time to get up, then rested her long head on the ground and began to sigh.

When the colonel's head cleared, he braced himself on a bruised elbow and inspected the situation. Saltamontes had fallen on her left side into a shallow cleft in the rock about three feet wide, two feet deep and a dozen feet long. She was firmly wedged there, her head down the gradual slope. His left leg, from the knee down, was pinned between her and the harsh edge of the cleft. He reached and caught the edge of the saddle and pulled himself up into a semi-sitting position. From that position he could see the horse's front left leg, sickeningly smashed, the hoof twisted, a pink shard of bone projecting through the hide.

He lay back again to think. They were in a shallow bowl. In no direction was his horizon more than a hundred yards away. His leg was beginning to hurt, quite badly. After a little while he sat up again, braced his hands out behind him, planted his right foot against her back and pushed with all his might, hoping to shift her enough so that he could work his left leg out. But she was immovable. She began to struggle again, making a thin whimpering sound as she did so, but it seemed to the colonel that she only wedged herself more firmly. He lay back again, shading his eyes with his hand.

Damned old fool, he thought. Got yourself into it this time. Nobody will ever come by here by accident. Birds will pick you clean, and the rains will wash the bones down the gully. Horse bones and soldier bones. Both of you too damn old to be worth a damn. They tried hard to kill you in the two big wars and couldn't do it, and now you have to go ahead and kill yourself in what looks like it could be on the unpleasant side.

Class of '15. Damn near everybody who stayed in and didn't get killed made general officer. You got as far as chicken colonel. Your ideas were too strong. Kept talking instead of listening.

He shaded his eyes and thought of the long years, of a dead wife and a dead son. And he felt there was a meaningless futility about his continued existence. The big project was without meaning. It was just busy-work, the meaningless details you assign your men in garrison to keep them occupied.

So if it ended right here, best to make sure it was as comfortable as possible. Too damned undignified to die of heat and thirst, raving and gibbering like a maniac.

He parted his fingers and squinted up at the blue glare of the sky and saw the slow circling of the buzzards. He was the focal point of the circle, and he wondered how they had gathered so fast. A dozen of them. By tomorrow noon they'd be standing just out of reach, watching him. He worked his pocket knife out and opened the large blade. So do you cut your throat now or later?

He looked at the birds again and suddenly had a feeling of outrage, of vast indignation. He sat up again and set his jaw hard and looked around him. He picked up the open knife and inched to his left until, with a long straining reach, he could catch the cheek strap in his left hand. He planned the motions in advance, then hauled back on the cheek strap, pulling the horse's head up and back into position for the quick, deep, strong and merciful slash of the blade across the soft throat. Blood rushed thick down the funnel of rock, soaking quickly into the sand and the cracks. The horse died with a prolonged and gentle spasm. Immediately he felt more alone. Saltamontes had been a living entity, a thing that shared pain and fright.

He sawed through the girths and pushed the saddle aside. And then, with the little four-inch blade, he began to cut the body of the horse away from his imprisoned leg. It was dusk before he had freed his leg. His hands were cramped with exhaustion. He had paused many times to sharpen the blade on the stones. It had been a sickening task. He backed away a half dozen feet and rested. He examined his leg in the fading light. The edges of stone had deeply gouged the tough old shank. The ankle was badly puffed. Bracing himself against pain, he rotated the ankle and prodded the puffed tissues until he was reasonably certain there was no break. He doubted his ability to crawl back to the highway. He could not put his weight on that leg. He hesitated a moment before he cut the partially completed canvas out of the stretcher. He cut the tough fabric into strips, bound his foot and ankle as tightly as he could, and worked his foot back into the blood-sodden shoe. When he tried again, he found that he could endure putting his weight on the foot. He put his painting equipment and the saddle at the base of a scrubby tree, settled his campaign hat in place, and began to walk northwest. A hundred yards from the scene of the fall, he cut a stout walking stick from a dead tree. After dark it was difficult to walk on the rough terrain. He fell heavily several times. Each time he would curse, gather his strength and get up again. He reached the Tepoztlán road and turned left. In a few moments he heard a vehicle behind him and turned and saw it was a lighted bus coming from Tepoztlán. He stepped into the middle of the highway and stood waving his stick. He did not move. The bus came to a shuddering halt a few feet from him. He hobbled to the door and told the driver in his clumsy forceful Spanish where he wanted to be taken. He climbed aboard the bus. Two dozen pair of dark awed eyes stared at the charnel specter as he paused in the aisle. They saw the scuffs and bruises and tears from his falls. They saw the spattering of blood, the caking of blood to the elbows. They looked at the tough old face and the uncompromising eyes.

"*Buenas tardes!*" he brayed at them in his great hollow voice.

"*Buenas tardes, señor,*" they said in their soft voices.

239

They made room for him to sit. The bus deviated from its normal route to let him off at the main gate of El Hutchinson. The driver made no attempt to collect a fare. The bus had been silent ever since he had boarded it. The moment they drove away from the hotel, everyone began to talk at once.

By Monday, the fourteenth of August, the colonel pronounced himself perfectly capable of driving his car back to the States. He did not look at all well. All attempts to dissuade him failed. He would leave the next morning.

On Monday evening Barbara went to Colonel Hildebrandt's room before dinner. He had just finished his packing.

"Colonel," she said, "would you do me a big favor?"

"Of course, of course."

"I'd like to ride with you. You have room and . . . I could share the expenses and the driving. It would be a big help to me. I understand you're going to Washington."

"Get this leg looked at. Doesn't feel right to me."

"Could you take me along?"

He frowned at her. "Long trip in an old car, my dear."

"I know. But it would be a great favor to me. Please."

"Won't look right, you know. Not very proper."

"When we get rooms at a motel, you could register me as your daughter, I suppose, if you think it would look better. Please, Colonel."

"Well . . . if you want to come along, you're welcome. Be a little easier having somebody do some of the driving, I guess. Understand, I don't want to fadiddle around here until noon, young woman. You be packed and ready to leave by eight sharp."

"Thanks a lot, Colonel. I'll go pack."

She went and reported her success to the others. "I certainly will feel a hundred per cent better," Hildabeth said. "I was sure he wouldn't take you. Stubborn old fool. Now you keep him from getting overtired, and if he doesn't act right, you stop wherever you are and make sure he sees a doctor."

Barbara and the colonel left at eight on Tuesday morning.

The survivors continued. Gil and Jeanie. Hildabeth and Dotsy. Monica and Harvey. Agnes and Gam. Paul Klauss was seldom seen. Miles Drummond rented a room down in town to move into when school ended, a room that would suffice until he could move back into his own little house.

Miles had imagined that the Workshop, even in its shrunken form, would continue right up until the last day of August, but it did not work out that way. Gil and Jeanie decided that they wanted to see San Miguel de Allende, and so they left on Friday, the twenty-fifth. On Monday, the twenty-eighth, after a lot of confused scheduling, Agnes Partridge Keeley left, taking Monica and Harvey as far as Mexico City where they had obtained reservations on the same flight. Hildabeth and Dotsy left the next day in the pink-and-blue Buick, having made an arrangement with Gam to take him as far as Texas. Miles Drummond, Fidelio, Rosalinda and Margarita waved until they were out of sight and then went back through the main gate into the compound in front of the hotel where the red bus stood lonely in the morning sun.

Rosalinda snuffled and said, "The very last, señor. Now they have all departed. This is a sad time."

"The Señor Ball, he is the very last," Margarita said loyally.

There was a dreary echoing emptiness about the hotel. On that day Miles made the final arrangements to close the Cuernavaca Summer Workshop. He arranged for disposition of the small amount of excess supplies. He paid off the small staff, giving each one a little bit more than was due, even Alberto.

After consideration of all factors, he told Felipe Cedro that he would not need him any longer. Felipe had been sullen and insubordinate of late. Miles realized he had always been a little bit afraid of the man. But Felipe's black scowl did not alarm him at all now. He felt relief at being at last free of him. And Fidelio was delighted to be employed as Señor Drummond's personal servant. In the late afternoon Fidelio loaded Miles's belongings into the red bus and moved them down to the room Miles had rented.

It troubled Miles that Paul Klauss's possessions were still in the hotel, in his padlocked room. It offended his sense of order. He wanted the school to be terminated cleanly and completely. He had arranged that on the first day of September he would meet with the representative of the owners of the hotel and, after an inspection of the premises, turn over the keys. Also, on that day, he would return the red bus to its owner. He was annoyed that such efficiency should be compromised by the carelessness of Paul Klauss.

On the morning of the last day of August, Margarita Esponjar slipped away from the household tasks assigned her by her mother, and wandered over to the hotel in the hope that she might see Señor Ball once more. Such a shy and pretty man. Such a strange and timid man, who wept easily.

When she walked through the main gate she saw that the big front door was ajar, and a taxi waiting. She ceased strolling and trotted toward the front door. When she was ten feet away, Felipe came out. He was carrying a suitcase which she recognized at once as belonging to Señor Ball. He was moving quickly and furtively.

"You are stealing from Señor Ball!" she cried. She tried to wrest the suitcase from him but he cursed her and gave her such a mighty push that she trotted backward and sat down suddenly in the dust. As she scrambled to her feet, the taxi turned out through the main gate. She watched it go, and then she went into the hotel and went to the room of Señor Ball. The things Felipe had thought not worth stealing were scattered on the floor. All the beautiful clothing was gone. Señor Ball was on the floor, on his side, sleeping. There was a great ugly lump on his pretty forehead, right at the hair line, and a trickle of blood that ran down into his delicate, blond eyebrow. With a great, clear cry of concern and love and pity, Margarita dropped to her knees beside him, picked up his limp hand and kissed it, pressed it tenderly to her cheek and looked down at him with brimming eyes.

When Miles arrived at the hotel the next day he was very pleased to see that Paul Klauss's room was empty and the door open.

Chapter Sixteen

ON A THURSDAY in early December, Gregory Hayes, a tall and rather elegant young man, left his desk in the U.S. Embassy in Mexico City and went next door to Sanborne's for a milkshake at the counter. It was a crisp and beautiful morning and he felt very much at home in his world. He had been in Mexico City for over a year and did not like to think of the eventual inevitable transfer. He was a very junior vice-consul. The intensive courses in Berlitz method had given him a good working grasp of Spanish. He had a knack for languages. A current affair with a young Mexican dancer, being conducted with utmost discretion, was improving his fluency. He liked the Mexican people, their warmth and courtesy and pride.

On his way back to his tiny office he looked in on the area where Mexican nationals, employees of the embassy, were interviewing Mexicans who had come to the embassy, screening them so that they could be either routed to the proper officials or told that they had come to the wrong agency with their requests.

He looked at the line of chairs where they were awaiting their turn to be interviewed. Most of them sat with the empty bored faces that are used to hide anxiety. He could make a reasonable guess as to what most of them wanted. It was his habit sometimes to short-circuit normal procedures by selecting at random someone waiting to be interviewed and handling it himself. As the interviewers did not resent this form of intrusion, particularly by Greg Hayes, and because it improved his Spanish, and because he had a sound grasp of procedures, and because there was a possibility that such personal attentions were good public relations, his superiors were tolerant of this practice, though they did consider it rather eccentric.

Gregory stood inside the doorway and looked along the line until he spotted a young woman. She wore a dingy red dress and over it she wore a short, green wool coat obviously new and of a shade so poisonously virulent that it almost hurt to look at it. In contrast to the glum faces of all the others, she wore a wide, interested, friendly smile. Her face was quite pretty. There was an Indio look about it. And there was the stamp of the slattern, a bland, amiable and automatic sensuousness. He guessed that she was from outside the city. There was a string bag at her feet, bulky and faded. He guessed that she was of low intelligence, one of the ones who had suddenly decided they would go to the United States and, with no knowledge of the difficulties involved, would show up and ask blandly for permission.

Gregory went to Raoul's desk and said, "Got any idea of what the girl in the green coat wants?"

"Not the slightest. But I know that ranchero one is with her. The one sitting beyond her."

Gregory had not noticed him before. He sat stolidly, bare brown feet planted on the floor, a ratty sombrero with a broad frayed brim pulled well down over his forehead. He wore one of those white pajama suits all field workers used to wear, which are now being supplanted by the ubiquitous blue jeans and work shirts. He wore a drab brown-and-gray serape of rough heavy wool.

"Okay if I take them, Raoul?"

"Go right ahead, Greg."

The girl's smile widened as he approached. He said in a low tone, "Will you and your companion come to my office, señorita, and I will see if I can be of service."

"*Cómo no?*" she called in a voice so loud and clear that those waiting nearby jumped and gave her a look of annoyance. She got up and took the arm of her companion and, with small cooing, urging sounds, got him to his feet. They followed Greg to his small office. He sat behind his desk. The girl tugged the man over to a chair and pushed gently against his chest until he sat down. She took the other chair, directly in front of Greg's desk, and put the heavy string bag on the corner of the desk. He decided her smile was so happy and infectious as to be disconcerting.

"How may we help you, señorita?"

"This is the second time in my entire life that I have come to Mexico City, señor. It is more enormous than I remembered. So many people in one noisy place. Such danger from the vehicles. They seemed to try to kill us, señor."

"It is a beautiful city. May I have your name?"

"Margarita Esponjar y Roca. I have twenty years, señor. Very soon, in the next month, I am to be betrothed to Señor Roberto Prisma y Martinez. He is the complete owner of a blue truck. He works on the caminos. When one has a truck, it is possible to be employed in an important task and receive much pay. Roberto is a very kindly man. His wife died of fevers of the stomach many months ago. There are small children. He is lonely, señor. His house is large. Three rooms and a shed and a place for the blue truck close beside the shed where it is safer from rain and bandits. There is room in the house for the five children, the three which are his and the two which are mine."

Greg stared at her rather blankly. "Uh . . . congratulations."

"I have never been married. My Roberto is very kindly and understanding about my two little ones. He knows that it is because I have a loving heart. He will take my children as his own, and feed and clothe them. He is a good man."

"I . . . I am certain that he must be. I am certain you will be very happy. You have my sincere best wishes, Señorita Esponjar. But I do not understand what it is that you wish us to do for you."

"Roberto is a kindly man, but there is one thing he has

244

become most angry about. It is Señor Ball. I am not permitted to keep him. When I move to Roberto's house, *mi madre* will not keep Señor Ball. She says I have been wrong to care for him. Roberto will agree that room could be made for him in such a big house, but he says that it is an indecency. A man is not a pet. And with such a one, whose head is not right, there could be great trouble one day. I have at last agreed. And so, señor, I have brought him to you. He is yours."

"What? What?"

"He is now yours." She opened the throat of the string purse and dug into it and took out a wallet and handed it to Gregory Hayes. Greg opened it. It contained no money. He took out the identification cards and the tourist card. Margarita had turned toward her companion and reached and took off his sombrero and placed it in his lap. The companion looked placidly at the wall beyond Greg's left shoulder with pale, empty eyes. His face was darkened by exposure. He had long blond hair, tangled, matted and dirty, and beard stubble darker than his hair.

"If you will excue me for a moment, señorita."

"Of course!"

He came back in five minutes with a file folder. He had been right when he had thought he remembered seeing the name Paul Klauss on the Inquiry List. Year after year, American citizens disappeared in Mexico, some by design and some by accident. Of both groups most of them were eventually located, but there were, each year, a very few who were never seen again.

"This is a matter of great seriousness, señorita," he said gravely. "According to our records, Mr. Klauss was supposed to have been back in Philadelphia over three months ago. He attended some sort of little art colony affair in Cuernavaca. After he was reported missing, a Mr. Drummond was contacted. Mr. Drummond stated that as far as he knew, Mr. Klauss had left when the school ended, to return to the States. I do not understand this at all. Mr. Klauss. Mr. Klauss!"

"He does not listen, señor. It accomplishes nothing to shout at him."

"What is wrong with him?"

"He was given a great *golpe* on the head, señor, by an evil person who took away his suitcase and clothing and many valuable things. He has been this way ever since that moment."

"How do you know this?"

"I was employed by the Señor Drummond. I worked at the school as a maid. I became a most close friend of *el* Señor Ball. The hotel was empty when I found him, and the *golpe* on the head had made him sleep upon the floor. I awakened him and in a little while I was able to lead him to my home. It is a small place and crowded. My mother was most angry and she said it was a matter for the police. I was afraid the police would remove him, and I wished to care for him. Does not one wish to care for a dear friend who has been injured by an evil person?"

"Uh . . . I guess it would be a good and generous thing. But what about a doctor? Did a doctor see him?"

"Oh, yes. My cousin. He is not a *certificado* doctor, but he heals with injections. He works on the railway. He examined Señor Ball most carefully and determined that his head bone had not been shattered. He said that it had been such a great *golpe*, the Señor Ball had been hurled back into his childhood, and nothing could be done."

"But has it not been very difficult?"

"Oh, no, señor. He is not difficult in any way. Sometimes in his sleep he makes a great shout, but not often. He slept in my bed until it was decided I would become betrothed to Roberto, and since that time he has slept upon a pallet in our small shed where lived the two goats. We made a new place for the goats and made the shed very clean for Señor Ball."

"Does he ever speak?"

"Never, señor. Except for the shouting of words I cannot understand in the night. When food is placed before him he will eat. He can be given any simple task to do and he will work until it is completed. He has worked very hard with my brother who is a cutter of wood. Behold." She took Klauss's slack hand and turned it over to reveal the thick crust of callus. "It is a strange thing," she said, frowning. "He will do all things a man will do. He will eat and sleep and work and make the act of love. But to all these things he must be led as if he were a small child, and while he is performing these things, he seems far away. He is so little trouble I am distressed at my mother for not being willing to keep him."

"And so you just . . . brought him back?" Greg said, repressing an impulse to beat his head on his desk top.

"He is now yours because I cannot keep him and my mother will not. I shall worry about him, señor. I hope there will be those who love him who will care for him. But, señor, even in this condition, I have though that he is better than before the great *golpe*."

"What?"

"Before it happened, señor, he had very cold blood. He was a timid and unloving man who was terrified of women, and who wept as easily as a woman. I tried to make of him a man, but he was alarmed by me for some reason. He was much more pretty then, of course." She sighed heavily. "I have brought with him his things, everything not taken by the thief. It is all here in this bundle. Some big books and some tools of painting. And the clothing he was wearing. And, of course, his shoes. But I believe they are too small. He has walked long miles barefoot carrying heavy loads of wood, and his feet are now more wide and strong."

Gregory looked at the sensuous, dazzling smile. He suspected that he should gather information for a much more detailed report. Perhaps he should have the Mexican police hold the girl for further investigation. He believed every word she said. There was a dazzling, transparent honesty about her. He obtained her address and wrote it neatly under her name, and told her that it was possible someone might have to come to see her and ask more questions, but he hoped it would not be necessary.

She opened the string bag and dumped the contents on his desk, folded the bag and put it in a pocket of the green coat. Gregory pulled one of the notebooks over. It was a loose-leaf notebook with an expensive leather binding. He opened it at random. The loose-leaf sheets were of heavy, creamy stock, covered with green single-spaced typing.

He read a few words and then suddenly bent closer to the sheet. His eyes widened and his jaw sagged. "Son of a gun!" he said.

"*Que dice, señor?*"

"Nothing of importance, señorita. On behalf of my government, I wish to thank you for bringing Mr. Klauss to us."

"Now I may go? I have here the return ticket for me alone on the bus, and twenty pesos given to me by my Roberto to buy for myself a present, but I have decided I will buy some small thing for him."

"Yes, you may go now, señorita."

She stood up and her smile faded. "I must be certain of one thing, señor. You will forgive me if I say that governments are often cruel and indifferent. I must have your word of honor that he will be cared for. I do not want to leave this place thinking that it is possible that when I am gone, you will push him out onto the street and forget him. He could not care for himself. It would be a cruel act."

"I give you my word of honor that he will be taken care of, señorita."

"I cannot ask for this, but I hope it is a loving care. For those who are hurt . . . and, señor, for everyone, loving care is a good thing. And a rare thing in a world of governments."

She went over to Paul Klauss and put her hand lightly on his shoulder and bent over and kissed him on his unresponsive lips. *"Adiós, mi probrecito.* I have done what I can. I leave you in sadness. *Adiós.*"

She smiled at Gregory and thanked him and left, closing the door softly behind her. Klauss turned slowly in his chair and looked toward the closed door. He made a low sound, a wordless sound of pain and question.

"We'll take care of you from now on, fellow," Greg said. He set an order of precedence in his mind. First arrange hospitalization and complete examination, with approval of the expenditure from embassy funds earmarked for such purposes. Contact the person or persons who had made the inquiry and advise them that Klauss had been found, and advise them of his condition. Inventory Klauss's possessions, have them packaged for locked storage. As he reached for his phone, he decided the final step could be delayed until he had made a more careful examination of the notebooks.

On that same Thursday in December, Mrs. Harvey Ardos remained at the George D. Insley High School after class to meet with the Decoration Committee in regard to planning the decoration of the gym for the Christmas Dance. She was, she was certain, the happiest bride in Kansas. Last week they had picked out a hilly, beautiful acre of land on the old Hadden Road. The disadvantage was that it was so far out of town, but they wanted privacy and a little room, and the eight hundred dollars they thought they could spare would buy a lot less land closer in.

This winter they would plan their house, plan it in such a way that, except for foundation work, they could build it with their own hands. There would be a big studio for Harvey, with north light. And a wonderful view. By spring they would have enough money for the foundation work and the first batch of construction materials. During the winter evenings they would plan a perfect house, and read the do-it-yourself manuals.

Harvey had a pretty good job driving a bread truck. He had to leave early in the morning and cover a lot of miles each day, but the pay was good.

It had been such a lovely wedding . . .

"I guess we're all here, Mrs. Ardos."

"Oh. All here? Splendid! Now at our last meeting I think we decided on a tropical motif. Christmas in the Tropical Islands. Richard, will you please give your report on the sand situation, and then we'll discuss the lovely palm tree Martha has made."

On that same Thursday Parker Barnum completed his third week as partner and art director in the Dallas firm of Hilldane, Durling and Barnum. It had been Hilldane and Durling, a young firm with aggressive ideas and limited capital. Before he had settled on them, before he had made his intensive survey of the advertising agencies in the Dallas-Fort Worth area, Parker had long talks with Bitsy, and several long business conferences with Maggie and her husband. Maggie had been most generous in giving them the little gem of a house out near Richland Hill as a wedding present, and she was prepared to be equally generous with what he thought he would need to buy into an agency. But he insisted on its being handled in a businesslike way, with interest-bearing notes with due dates extending over a period of years. If the income he hoped for did not materialize, the loans could be paid back out of Bitsy's inheritance, but he hoped it would not be that way.

Marty Hilldane and Jack Durling had been skeptical about it. He had taken them to lunch separately, and then together. They felt that his New York background, good as it sounded, would not be of much help in the Dallas-Fort Worth area. But in the end they agreed, the papers were drawn up, and Park purchased a one-third interest at a figure higher than he had planned.

On that Thursday in December, Park and Jack Durling said goodbye at the elevators to the executives from Janet Anne Shops, Inc., and walked from the conference room back to Park's office. Jack came in with him and dropped into the chair beside the new blond desk.

"One hell of a workout, Park," he said. "What's your guess?"

"I don't know. Except for Goldman, I'd say yes. The rest

reacted. He didn't give me a clue. And he's the boss man. You did a hell of a good job of presentation, Jack."

"Because I had something to present for once. The copy is sound. And that art work is really terrific. Did you hear them grunt when I unveiled those sketches for the series of big boards?" He stood up. "So we sweat it out until tomorrow noon. I think they'll go for it."

"I'll be in your office waiting for the call to come in."

Jack turned in the doorway. "I guess it's a little late to be saying this, Park. But I had a drink with Marty last night. We found we've both got over wondering whether we did the right thing. We just wish now you'd showed up a year ago."

"Thanks, Jack. Thanks for telling me."

A few minutes after Jack left, Bitsy phoned him. "I thought you were supposed to be taking a nap, woman."

"Well, I was taking a nap, darling, but . . ."

"What's the use of paying a doctor for advice?"

"Don't be such a growly bear. Mary Jane phoned me. She got back from Hawaii last night. And she wants to stop by about six for a drink, so I wanted to be sure you wouldn't work until all hours of the night again at that stinking place."

"I can shake myself loose tonight. I was planning on coming home early. But I thought we weren't going to do any entertaining until . . ."

"It's just Mary Jane, and it's important to her. She's bringing along some fabulous sort of dreamboat she met out there for us to look over. She sounds sort of serious. I'm glad you'll be home early. How did it go with Mr. Goldman?"

"I couldn't tell. We'll find out tomorrow."

"I don't see what the good is in owning part of a business when you work like some old spooky slave."

"I am a spooky slave. Go take some more nap."

"I don't feel like it."

"How do you feel, darling?"

"I keep telling you that all day long I feel fabulously good. It's just that going woops in the morning gets tiresome. All the time I have a beautiful old lazy kind of feeling."

"Four months to go. There ought to be a faster way."

She giggled. "Like that joke about the Martian."

"Love you," he said.

She made a small kissing sound in the mouthpiece. "Love you extremely much. Hurry on home, hear? Bye."

After he hung up Park sat wearing a fatuous smile for a

few moments, and then began to look over the sketches one of the kids had turned out, sketches of a little man for possible television animation in the local area to advertise a local chain of appliance stores.

At five-thirty on that December Thursday when Barbara Kilmer came home from her factory job, her mother said, "Hello, dear. My, it's getting dark so early. There's another letter from him, Barbie. I put it in your room."

She hurried upstairs after she had taken off her coat, and snatched up the letter, turned on her bed lamp, lay across her bed to read it. She read it slowly and carefully, half smiling as she did so. She sang softly to herself as she took her shower. When she was in her robe, she stretched out on the bed again and read it through.

". . . a client who looks like he could be an older brother of Gloria Garvey. Quite a majestic type, who finds it necessary to keep informing me of how busy he is, how many other earth-shaking projects he has on the fire. Yet he does find time to pester me constantly about when he can see preliminary sketches. The curious shape of the available piece of land had me stymied for quite some time, but now I have a solution which pleases me, but will quite probably enrage him. Once I have finished this letter to you, I will go back to my sketches. When my work is going well it is like a disease with me. It becomes too enjoyable to set aside.

"Please write often, as you have been doing. I feel that I am coming to know you a little bit better with each letter, my darling. Your letters were so stiff at first. Now they are a delight, and more necessary to me than I can tell you.

"Things here are coming along far better than I dared hope. Strickland is working out very well. He is no Jenningson, of course, but he has the capacity to be. I had a good letter from Kurt yesterday. He is now working for a firm in Los Angeles, and living in a small apartment hotel. He says that he is in at nine and out at five, and that it is refreshing not to have to worry about whether or not the business as a whole is making a profit. He said that he has taken Mary out to dinner several times and, the last time, they both were willing to admit the possibility of eventually being together again. I hope so. He is half a man without her. And that sorry state of affairs is something I am now better able to understand, Barbara.

"I had thought of making a strong plea in this letter, asking you to permit me to fly up there over Christmas to see you. But that would be a violation of our solemn pact. I can safely say that by Christmas, and from then on, I will be able to get away from here with very little advance warning. And so all I can do is tell you once again that I love you, and that I am waiting for you to set a date for me to come to you."

And quite suddenly she knew when it would be. It would be in April, if she could wait that long.

On that Thursday in December, at noon, Gam Torrigan decided that the painting on which he had worked with sustained creative energy for the past fifteen days was finished. He had worked with polymer tempera and casein on a huge rectangle of quarter-inch untempered Masonite.

He leaned it against the front of the range cabin, in the cold watery sunlight. As he cleaned his equipment he would stop from time to time and go and glower at it from varying distances and angles. After he cleaned most of the stains from his hands, he stripped off his rough clothing and turned on the outside shower he had improvised. When he stepped under the icy gout of water, he pranced wildly and roared like a bear before he began scrubbing himself with yellow soap. His hair had grown long and his beard was untrimmed. In the middle of toweling himself, he went back to the picture and stood twenty feet from it, glaring at it, unmindful of the fifty-degree temperature and the chilly wind.

A sudden big grin split the beard and he yelled, "You can paint, you son of a bitch! You can really paint!"

The stentorian roar awakened the fat brown dog who had adopted him, and who had been sleeping in the sun on that side of the cabin that was out of the wind. She came apprehensively around the corner of the cabin, knees bent, and stopped to stare at him, her tail tucked under and moving tentatively.

"Come here, old gal," he said, and she came to him joyously to lean against his leg and be scratched. "See that painting, Mrs. Garvey? Look at it, gal. It jumps out at you and sings, doesn't it?"

She wagged her tail with more energy at the sound of her name, looking up at him with love.

He suddenly realized how cold he was getting. He went in and dressed, fed himself and Mrs. Garvey, and then drove to town in the jeep for supplies and a haircut, Mrs. Garvey on the seat beside him. After he got back he put the painting up to dry in the racks he had built and took down another big square of Masonite.

In Pasadena that Thursday afternoon, the South City Garden Club put on a reception and tea to open a one-man show of the Mexican paintings of Agnes Partridge Keeley. According to Agnes' carefully kept records of her professional career, it was her twenty-seventh one-man show and, based on previous averages, out of the thirty-two paintings she could reasonably expect to sell from seven to ten during the week the show would be open. Agnes, in a pale lavender suit, white gloves, shoes and picture hat, had stationed herself near the tea table where she was the center of a constantly changing and shifting circle of admiring ladies. Her thanks were effusive when she was told how perfectly beautiful the paintings were, how they captured the real flavor of Mexico, all the charm and quaintness of the place.

She consented, graciously, to lead a small group around the gallery and explain each picture. The women thought she had been terribly clever in the way she had captured those darling fuzzy little burros carrying those perfectly huge loads.

On the first circuit only two paintings bore, on the frame, the little red star to indicate it had been sold. On the second circuit she was pleased to see that two more had been sold. One of the women, upon leaving, remarked to her friends, "I was in Mexico, you know, five years ago. And something seems strange to me. I just happened to notice it. There isn't a single cactus in any one of her paintings. Not one. And Mexico is positively teeming with all kinds of cactus. Perhaps it's very difficult to paint. Hundreds of flowers in her paintings, but no cactus at all."

During the evening of that same Thursday, Gil and Jeanie Wahl entertained the student and faculty members of the Spanish Club in the small frame house assigned to them on Faculty Row. Jeanie served cider and cookies. Each member who forgot and lapsed into English had to put a penny in the milk bottle in the middle of the table. And in Elmira, Ohio, Hildabeth McCaffrey gave the tenth public showing of the colored slides she had taken in Mexico to the Household Club at their December meeting in the basement of the Methodist church. Dotsy Winkler assisted with the refreshments and the slides. Hildabeth always needed help with the slides. When she did it herself she always managed, somehow, to get more than half of them into the projector sideways or upside down. After the slides, one of

Hildabeth's new paintings was auctioned off for the benefit of the club treasury. It brought in thirteen dollars and twenty-five cents. And that same night Colonel Hildebrandt stayed up until midnight doing research on the battles between the U.S. Army and the Plains Indians. He was not particularly enjoying this portion of his project. They had seemed to conduct too many of their battles on some damned dull terrain. Hardly enough contour to hide a gopher.

On that Thursday morning at ten-thirty, Gloria Garvey had been sitting alone at a table in front of the Marik, with her Mexico City *News* and her Dos Equis, cold and dark in the bottle. It was a coolish morning and she wore one of the suits she had acquired during the Shane era. The color was a soft blue-gray. But there were spots on the left lapel, a split shoulder seam, a missing button. The skirt was thoroughly rump-sprung, and her white moccasins were run-over and grubby. She scratched her scalp through the wild mane of hair and shooed flies away from her glass.

When Miles Drummond came and took one of the empty chairs she gave him an indifferent glance, mumbled a greeting, and kept on reading. Miles ordered coffee. He took off his rimless glasses and cleaned them on a spotless handkerchief.

"When you're through with the paper, I'd like to talk to you, Gloria."

"Talk away. I can read and listen."

"Well . . . I guess I told you before, the Cuernavaca Summer Workshop didn't come out anywhere near as well as we hoped. According to my final figures, I made just nine hundred dollars. A little over eleven thousand pesos."

"Um."

"Expenses ran much, much higher than our estimates, Gloria. Of course it was your idea in the beginning, and I'm very grateful to you, but it didn't . . . accomplish its objective."

"Um."

"I have been very, very busy lately, Gloria. And I would like to get your opinion on what I am doing."

She sighed and put the paper down. "All right, Drummy. All right. What *are* you doing?"

He smiled proudly at her. "I was very green in the beginning. I actually dreaded it, you know. But as time went by last summer, I began to take hold. I do believe I have a certain . . . administrative ability."

"That's nice."

"I've written to the students and the faculty. Except for Hildabeth McCaffrey and Dotsy Winkler, no one seems to be able to return."

"Return for what?"

"Of the nine hundred dollars, Gloria, I have decided to use two hundred to help meet my living expenses this winter. And I shall invest the other seven hundred in supplies and promotion."

"Supplies and promotion for what, for God's sake?"

He straightened his small shoulders. "For the Second Cuernavaca Summer Workshop. Aren't you astonished? It really makes a great deal of sense, Gloria. Last time we didn't begin early enough. We didn't even secure the proper permits. And the hotel staff was selected very, very carelessly, you must admit."

"Oh, my God!"

"If I start earlier, I am certain I can get an enrollment of forty people instead of just thirteen. And I feel that the program should be expanded. We should have handicrafts. Pottery, perhaps." He leaned toward her and said confidentially, "I've already entered into certain tentative negotiations for a faculty. And I might say I have gotten into contact with some people who look *very* promising. For example, there is a very competent woman named Wilmetta Longman. She has a little school of her own at St. Augustine, Florida. If I decide to include creative writing, a very talented instructor named Stanfield Henderson Dorn might be available. His poetry has been widely published. And, in painting, I can get Thorna Francine O'Day and possibly Jon August Anderson, both of them enormous talents, really."

"Have you flipped, Drummy? Have you lost your keys?"

He laughed fondly and shook his finger at her. "You can't discourage me, Gloria. I've been over this carefully. Very carefully. In black and white. I've been so terribly busy lately. You have no idea. I must get along to the post office. I'm expecting some important mail."

"Then you just trundle right along, Drummy."

He stood up. "I have big plans, Gloria. I'll make a success of next summer. After it becomes a success, I think I may take a long-term lease on the building, a lease-purchase agreement, really."

"Buy that old horror?"

"It is perfectly adequate. Doesn't it make you feel a little bit glad that you are really the one who started all this?"

She looked up at him and smiled. "All right, Drummy. I'll feel a little bit glad."

He looked around in a conspiratorial way and then bent over, close to her. "If you promise not to tell, I'll let you in on a secret. It came to me just the other afternoon. Out of the blue. While I was playing chess, as a matter of fact. It's an idea so simple and so . . . dramatic that you will wonder why you didn't think of it first. It's for the future, of course. But not the very remote future, believe me. And, combined with your idea, it will put me on the threshold of great things, Gloria. I feel like a young man again. You'll never guess what I'm planning."

"I have the feeling that I'd better not try."

He leaned a few inches closer and whispered, "The Cuernavaca *Winter* Workshop." He screwed half his face into a tremendous wink, and turned and walked rapidly away toward the post office.

Gloria stared after him. She shook her leonine head and shrugged her big handsome shoulders. To all students, past and future, she said to herself, to you a message. Forgive me, please.